PENGUIN BOOKS

The Paris Affair

Fiona Schneider lives in Cambridgeshire with her German husband and three children. She graduated from Cambridge University with a degree in English, and in 2000 moved to Ireland to complete a M.Phil. in Creative Writing at Trinity College, Dublin. She now works for a multi-academy trust as a marketing and communications officer, writing novels in her spare time. *The Paris Affair* is her English language debut.

T0332871

The Paris Affair

The Paris Affair

FIONA SCHNEIDER

PENGUIN BOOKS

PENGUIN BOOKS

UK | USA | Canada | Ireland | Australia
India | New Zealand | South Africa

Penguin Books is part of the Penguin Random House group of companies
whose addresses can be found at global.penguinrandomhouse.com.

First published 2024
001

Copyright © Fiona Schneider, 2024

The moral right of the author has been asserted

Set in 12.5/14.75pt Garamond MT Std
Typeset by Jouve (UK), Milton Keynes
Printed and bound in Great Britain by Clays Ltd, Elcograf S.p.A.

The authorized representative in the EEA is Penguin Random House Ireland,
Morrison Chambers, 32 Nassau Street, Dublin DO2 YH68

A CIP catalogue record for this book is available from the British Library

PAPERBACK ISBN: 978–1–405–95821–9
EXCLUSIVE EDITION ISBN: 978–0–241–71142–2

www.greenpenguin.co.uk

MIX
Paper | Supporting
responsible forestry
FSC® C018179

Penguin Random House is committed to a
sustainable future for our business, our readers
and our planet. This book is made from Forest
Stewardship Council® certified paper.

For Michael,
Max, Karla and Lukas

'. . . the smell and taste of things remain poised a long time, like souls, ready to remind us, waiting and hoping for their moment, amid the ruins of all the rest; and bear unfaltering, in the tiny and almost impalpable drop of their essence, the vast structure of recollection.'

– Marcel Proust, *Remembrance of Things Past*

Prologue

Lisette

August, 1942 – Paris

Lisette closed the door and pressed her forehead against the wood. The narrow hallway of the apartment was dark. The scent of Christoph's cologne – woodsmoke and bergamot – still cloaked her skin. The taste of that last kiss lingered in her mouth, warm and urgent . . . but now he had gone.

The crack of a bomb cut through her reverie. She had to think fast. He'd be back before morning. That's what he'd promised. She picked up the bag and the pot of Eintopf mit Bohnen und Kartoffeln and walked through the apartment, averting her eyes from the bedroom door. But her body remembered: the heat of his skin, his lips moving downwards.

Lisette exhaled. Remembering wouldn't help anyone. Her breathing slowed. She'd trained for moments like this. Emotions had no place here. It was her feelings that had got her into this mess in the first place.

In the living room, she grasped the blackout curtain and pulled it aside. Her fingers trembled. The rooftops were pearlescent in the moonlight. A formation of planes flew low in the sky. She followed the hum of the engines. The planes were heading west, in the direction of

Boulogne-Billancourt. Another bomb exploded, louder this time. She winced, heart stammering. The sky flashed unnaturally bright. There wasn't much time.

The kitchen door opened. The creak startled her. A young man with a thick shock of hair stood in the doorway. She let out her breath. Of course, Jacques. She'd forgotten he was here. He was older than she remembered from the brief glimpse she'd had the other day, in his early twenties, she guessed. He came to the window, limping slightly.

'What are we going to do?' he whispered in French.

His voice was deep, but she detected a tremor. Lisette remembered the receipt. The reference to 'Jacques M.' Christoph had helped keep him safe. She couldn't abandon him here.

'Are you strong enough to travel?' she asked.

Jacques straightened up. 'Of course.'

'Then I think we should leave,' she said. '*Maintenant.*' Saying the words out loud made them real.

Swiftly, she calculated. There was enough food in the cupboards for a few days. Paris would be quiet tonight on account of the bombing. Lisette knew the secret ways, the doors it was safe to knock on. She could get them out.

'What about Christoph?' Jacques jerked his head towards the door.

Lisette's heart contracted. It wasn't safe to write a note. She must leave no trace of herself or Jacques. Christoph would only complicate things. Now was the perfect time to go. She bit her lip. It would break Christoph's heart, but what choice did she have?

Another bomb detonated. Closer this time. They both

flinched. The girders of the Eiffel Tower glowed briefly from the explosion.

Jacques turned to Lisette. 'Are you sure you want to go out in this?'

Lisette shrugged. 'I don't think we have a choice. Would you rather stay here?'

Jacques looked around the apartment, rubbing the stubble on his chin, and gave a brief smile. 'No, I'd rather take my chance with you.'

Lisette nodded. She drew the curtains closed and glanced at the bag. Inside, Christoph had packed her recipe book and a change of clothes. That was all. Plenty of room for tins and the Eintopf mit Bohnen und Kartoffeln. Her insides weakened at the thought of the journey ahead. *My love, I hope you understand why I had to go.*

I

Julia

May, 2002 – London

The auditorium of Wigmore Hall was empty. Julia gripped the arms of the red velvet chair, hoping the silence would soothe her mind. She closed her eyes and tried to hear Beethoven's 'Polonaise in C major' in her head, but nothing came.

Below the balcony where she was sitting, a vacuum cleaner whirred, breaking the silence. Her mother's voice came back to her: 'There's no time to sit about. You need to prepare for the concert.'

She *had* prepared. The usual ritual had been gone through – going over the score, arriving early, trying out the piano, sitting in the auditorium – she'd done everything to the letter. But today, something was different. It fluttered in her veins like a bird trapped behind glass.

She'd played here many times, jumping the hurdles of national piano competitions year after year. Now she was here as part of a tour that Sebastian had arranged. Nerves twisted her stomach. Julia opened her eyes and stood up. The spring-loaded seat flipped upright with a thud. The audience would be arriving soon.

Julia's bag was where she'd left it in the green room, the score ready to peruse one last time. Her breathing slowed. She avoided looking at the other performers and the photos of pianists who'd played here: Daniel Barenboim, Edwin Fischer, Angela Hewitt. They made her nervous.

'How are you doing?' Sebastian said. He crossed the green room. He wore a pinstripe suit and a white shirt. Thank goodness: he was here. She felt her nerves settle slightly. 'Are you ready?'

'Almost.' Julia fiddled with the satin folds of her dress. 'This is far too long.'

'Heels could have cured that,' Sebastian said with a smile.

He sat down. She felt comfort in their closeness, helped by the fact they were almost the same age. She'd been his first signing six years ago, when she was just twenty-one. He'd flown over to Bonn to hear her play at a recital. The whole thing had nearly been a disaster, but thankfully Sebastian had heard enough to know he wanted to represent her. He was one of the youngest managers at the agency.

'It doesn't matter about the dress,' he said, gazing at her. 'You look breathtaking.'

'Sebastian . . .'

He straightened his cuffs. 'There's no rule against telling you the truth, is there? It's a good night to look amazing. Another step on the way to the Queen Elisabeth.'

'I know, don't remind me.' Everyone agreed that Julia's star was on the rise. The Queen Elisabeth competition in Brussels was one of the most prestigious international piano competitions in the world. But as she climbed higher, the air got thinner and colder, and sometimes Julia felt dizzy at the thought of it all.

Sebastian nudged her and laughed. 'Come on, don't tell me you're nervous. Not a seasoned performer like you.'

Julia forced a smile. 'Of course not. I can't wait to play.'

Sebastian held out his hand. 'Come on, I'll take you to the stage.'

He led her through the green room, towards the stage door. His hand against the small of her back and the black curtains at the side of the stage concentrated her thoughts. In a few seconds, she'd be out there.

'Remember to dazzle them,' Sebastian said. He drew her hand to his lips and kissed it softly before she could protest. The door opened and she walked on to the stage into the glaring lights.

She faced the audience and bowed. Applause rippled towards her. Her stomach clenched like a fist. She sat down on the piano stool. The Steinway gleamed. *This* she knew.

The applause died away. Dazzle them, Sebastian had said. That's what she'd been doing most of her life: eliciting gasps of delight at her dexterity. It was addictive *and* terrifying. Tonight was no exception.

She began to play. The opening bars of Beethoven's 'Polonaise' spilled out from her fingers. Perhaps it was going to be all right.

Nothing compared to this feeling. She was alone on a sea of music. Her body swayed, buoyed by the melody. The notes appeared in front of her and, like magic, her hands knew where to go.

But suddenly, without warning, Julia's fingers stiffened. It was barely perceptible at first. She played on, stretching across the octaves, dancing up and down the sequences. The notes flashed in her head, but her fingers couldn't keep up.

Blood rushed in her ears. Fragments of melody shattered and fell. No matter how hard she tried, the music was breaking apart, right here in front of everyone. She wrenched her hands away.

Julia's heart thumped against her ribcage. She couldn't face the audience; she couldn't face anyone.

Stumbling on the hem of her dress, she darted off the stage. She had to get away. She heaved the fire-escape door open and fled outside.

'Julia.' Sebastian had followed her into the courtyard. 'My God, are you all right?'

'I don't know. I'm sorry. I can't . . .' Her chest heaved. Rain fell and made her shiver.

'What happened?' he asked.

She didn't dare tell him that her hands had failed once before, during a practice session two weeks ago. She'd pushed it to the back of her mind, hoping it wouldn't happen again, but now . . . Panic rose in her chest. 'I can't go back in there.'

He touched her arm. 'All right, calm down,' he said. 'You're allowed one mistake, I guess, it's just so out of character.'

Julia held the tears back. No way was she going to let this night ruin everything. 'I promise it won't happen again.' But even as she said the words, she knew it was out of her control.

Sebastian squeezed her hand. 'I'll get your bag and call a taxi.'

The rain kept falling and soaked through her dress. Far off, she could hear the next performer playing. It was Chopin: the notes perfect and flawless. The beauty of the music made her heart ache.

Fischkotelett

1 large haddock
1 egg, beaten
4 tablespoons breadcrumbs
1 teaspoon each of salt and pepper
1 tablespoon cooking fat
3 tablespoons mustard

1. Fillet the haddock.
2. Beat the egg and coat both sides of the fish.
3. Cover the fish in breadcrumbs.
4. Season with salt and pepper.
5. Pan-fry in the fat until golden on both sides.
6. Serve with mustard.

2

Julia

May, 2002 – London

The meal was a disaster. Julia tried to wipe the sauce off the hob where the beans had boiled over. She'd been checking the Beethoven score for the umpteenth time, trying to work out why it had all gone wrong, instead of concentrating on the cooking. Even the fishfingers she'd bought at the supermarket were burnt to a crisp.

The front door clicked open. She flung the cloth in the sink. They were back already.

'What's all this?' Anna put her bag down on the table. Her daughter, Daisy, stared at the mess. 'You're supposed to be resting, love.'

'I wanted to make tea for my niece and my wonderful big sister,' Julia said. 'I'm afraid it didn't go to plan.'

Daisy glanced at her mum. 'I don't have to eat it, do I?' she asked.

'You go and watch CBeebies,' Anna said. 'I'll bring you a snack.'

A lump formed in Julia's throat. After everything her sister had done since Julia had fled Wigmore Hall three days ago, and she couldn't even cobble a meal together. Tears filled her eyes.

'Oh, love, it's all right.' Anna's arms encircled her, the

chunky-knit cardigan comforting against Julia's cheek. 'You've had a tough time lately with your hands.'

'I'm just so afraid of it happening again.'

'I know.' Anna smoothed Julia's hair back and sighed. 'You always did push yourself. When Dad left, you got so intense about the piano. You were only seven, just a bit older than Daisy.'

'I suppose it was a way of keeping Mum distracted,' Julia said. 'Just think, Anna, she'd be so disappointed if she could see me now.'

Anna sighed. 'I don't think anything made her happy. She couldn't let go of her bitterness about Dad leaving.'

'Maybe if he'd at least had a relationship with us,' Julia said, 'she might have softened.'

Anna gave Julia's hand an anxious squeeze. 'I just don't know.'

Julia wiped her eyes and tried to pull herself together. She didn't want Anna to worry.

'I'll be fine,' she said. 'There's the concert in Prague in a couple of weeks, then Salzburg. Sebastian thinks I can put that concert at Wigmore Hall behind me.'

She glanced at her long fingers and square palms. Outwardly, there seemed to be nothing wrong. She still hadn't mentioned the recurring problem to Sebastian, only to Anna.

'Why not give your hands a rest from the piano and do something else? You could take up painting or gardening. Heavens, you could even learn to cook.' Anna chuckled.

'I haven't got time to learn how to cook,' Julia said with a smile. Cooking had never been her strong point. 'This is the year, remember. The big piano competition.'

'But you need a break, little sis,' Anna said, frowning. 'Jake made me take some time off after Mum's funeral last year. It's done me the world of good.'

Another reason for Julia to feel guilty. She should've been around. Instead, she'd been on tour, not even in the country the night her mum died. Her mum had insisted she go. Julia remembered her pale face, still lopsided from the stroke, words slurring as she spoke. 'You might not get a chance like this again,' Mum had said.

Julia squeezed Anna's arm. 'That's why I wanted to make you both tea. To do something to help, after all you've done for me. Maybe I should postpone going to see Christoph. Stick around a bit longer . . .'

Anna shook her head. 'Absolutely not. If anyone can sort you out, it'll be Christoph.'

Julia hadn't seen Christoph since last year. He'd turned eighty recently. She was looking forward to sitting in his music room in Bonn, discussing the merits of the Italian pianist and composer Ludovico Einaudi and the Beethovenhalle's acoustics. Hopefully he'd know what would help her hands.

'It'll be good to see him,' she admitted.

'Do you remember how nervous you were when you went to stay with him in Bonn? You couldn't quite believe that the famous pianist Christoph Baumann had come out of retirement to mentor one last student.' Anna shook her head. 'You must have really made an impression that first time you met.'

It had been a life-changing moment. She'd taken part in a recital in Frankfurt. Afterwards, there was a reception, and she'd been astonished when a sprightly old man – who she knew instantly was *the* Christoph Baumann – approached her. She had all his recordings in her LP collection and had read every article he'd written about the piano. Her mouth had gone dry, her mind blank, but then the first words he'd spoken had put her at ease.

She smiled now at Anna. 'He said, "Julia, your playing was extraordinary, and I know we've never met before, but I have the strangest feeling that, somehow, we have. Tell me all about yourself." We didn't stop talking that day.'

'Well, I'm glad you're going to see him,' Anna said. 'His kindness and insight is just what you need.' She paused. 'But I hope Daniel's still working abroad. He's the last person you'd want to see with all this going on.'

Daniel. Christoph's son. He must be thirty-two by now: a late and longed-for child to older parents. Christoph used to joke that he was old enough to be Daniel's grandfather. Every now and then, Daniel appeared in her dreams, startling her awake at three in the morning, a surge of warmth across her skin. Even now, the thought of him made her blush.

'No, he won't be there, he's never there when I am,' she said.

Julia hadn't seen Daniel for six years, not since 1996. She rubbed her temples. If there'd been even the slightest chance of Daniel being in Bonn, then she wouldn't be going.

3

Lisette

May, 1942 – Normandy

The Lysander bounced over air currents above the English Channel, flying south towards the coast of France. In the breast pocket of Lisette's jumpsuit was the obligatory silver compact case, a tiny shield across her heart, and, in her suitcase, the 'L tablet', a cyanide pill sewn into the hem of her skirt, just in case. Lisette hoped she would never need to use it.

Lisette wasn't her real name – that had been buried months ago – Lisette was the name used by her handlers and other agents.

That evening's dinner churned in her stomach. If *she'd* been cooking, she would have made her grandmother's favourite supper: soufflé and green salad. As her grandmother was French, the art of making a soufflé was in her blood, and she'd not rested until Lisette had mastered the recipe. Instead, Lisette had been served tough beef and carrots boiled to mush in the airbase canteen.

She took a deep breath as the plane turned eastward.

'We're over France,' the dispatcher shouted, a short, stocky man who'd introduced himself as Harry on the airstrip at RAF Tempsford. He poured Lisette a hot toddy from a flask. 'Ten minutes until the drop.'

She smiled her thanks and swiftly downed the drink.

The plane started to descend. Lisette swallowed to ease the pressure in her ears. She'd trained for jumping at RAF Ringway, but this time she'd be landing behind enemy lines in occupied France.

Harry hitched the static line of Lisette's parachute on to the hook. 'Are you ready?'

Lisette nodded. This was it. No going back. Harry opened the hatch in the fuselage. Air rushed in. The earth looked nearer than she'd expected. She sat, legs dangling over the empty space. Down below, a tiny light flickered.

'There they are. We'll send your bag down after,' Harry shouted. 'On the count of three. One, two . . . three.'

The engines cut out for a second and suddenly Lisette was falling into darkness. Wind rushed up her nostrils. The line went taut and then the parachute opened. Lisette's armpits burned with the pull of the harness. She spun round, trying to find the lights and steer the chute towards them.

Without warning, the ground rushed up. She tumbled on the rough earth, the parachute tangled around her legs. She heard the thud of her suitcase a few metres away. Gradually, the plane's engine grew faint.

A flashlight bobbed towards Lisette and shone in her eyes.

'*Bonjour. Un bon vent pour une chasse au sanglier,*' a man's voice said.

'The last time we hunted we caught two,' Lisette replied in French. This was the answer she'd been taught. She wriggled out of the parachute strings.

The man dropped the torchlight towards the floor,

casting a soft light. Without the glare, Lisette saw a tall man with a pair of piercing blue eyes gazing down at her.

'I'm Seraphin,' he said, handing over her suitcase. 'Welcome to France.'

The instructions from London had been clear. No personal effects could be brought on the mission; it was too dangerous. Lisette's suitcase had been checked twice while she waited in the anonymous, bare room in Baker Street.

But she couldn't leave England without her notebook full of recipes. At the last minute, she had extracted it from the waistband of her trousers and slipped it into the suitcase between her dress and nylon underwear.

Now, in the attic of the farmhouse where Seraphin had brought her last night, Lisette opened the suitcase and took out the recipe book. She'd given up so much to come here, including her identity, but she couldn't bear to give up the one thing she treasured most: her grandmother's recipes. Lisette had written them in the book while sitting in her grandparents' kitchen at the scrubbed wooden table in their house in Normandy.

She leafed through the pages. Her grandmother had grown up in the Alsace, speaking French and German, before moving to Gerberoy when she got married. Mathilde, Lisette's mother, spoke German and French too, a gift she'd passed on to Lisette. Lisette's father, Albert, a British soldier who she'd met during the Great War and settled with back in England didn't approve, instructing his wife to speak only English.

On cold nights, Mathilde had slept in Lisette's bed, the covers pulled up over their heads to keep in the warmth, whispering stories from the past in the forbidden languages. The happiest moments of Lisette's life were visits back to her grandparents' house in Gerberoy.

No, she could never have left the recipe book behind. Besides, it fitted with her cover identity. While she was called Lisette by the agents and handlers, she was to be known as Sylvie, an aspiring cook, to the outside world. These were the two sides to her new persona. The recipe book, Lisette had reasoned, was an integral part of who Sylvie was. By day, she'd weed the vegetable patch and cook. By night, she'd help the local resistance against the Germans.

She clenched the book tightly. German bombs had killed her grandparents and sunk her fiancé's ship at Lazaire. A fire rose in her throat as she recalled Johnny's words the last time they'd said goodbye. 'I'll be back,' he'd promised her. But now he was gone.

Lisette tucked the recipe book back into her suitcase. That's why she was here in France. To avenge them all.

The farmer's wife tossed shallots into a deep-bottomed pan. The oil fizzed. A brace of rabbits lay in a metal tray on the table.

'*Puis-je vous aider?*' Lisette asked, coming down the stairs.

'*Non merci,*' the woman said.

'I know how to prepare rabbit,' Lisette said. The woman ignored her. 'I'd recommend roasting it with rosemary. I can skin it for you if you have a knife.'

This time the woman looked up. '*D'accord. Très bien,*' she said.

Lisette deftly sliced the skin and pulled it free of the carcass. Next she made a neat cut along the rabbit's belly and scooped out the innards, then she rubbed butter and herbs into the pink flesh and placed it on the tray with a sprig of rosemary from the bunch that hung above the stove.

'*Merci*,' the woman said with a quick smile.

Outside, under the pump, Lisette cleaned her hands. The blood from the rabbit washed away, soaking into the mud.

'I hear you've been helping in the kitchen.' Seraphin came outside, a camera case slung over his shoulder. He leaned against the stone wall and smiled. 'She's impressed with your culinary skills.'

They'd told Lisette in London that her handler in France was experienced. Glancing at Seraphin now, his eyes astonishingly blue in the sunshine, his gaze friendly and open, Lisette knew instinctively she could trust him.

She shook her hands dry. 'Well, I have my grandmother, catering college and an apprenticeship at the Savoy to thank for that.'

Seraphin smiled. 'I hear that's how the Special Operations Executive found you. Talking French and German like a native to a table of Swiss diplomats.'

Lisette had been explaining the complexities of quail consommé to the diners. She hadn't realized anyone else was listening. A man had approached her after her shift with the offer of translation work. During the interview in Baker Street a week later, she'd found out that the role involved much more than that.

'I was eager to come,' Lisette said.

'And we're glad to have you,' Seraphin replied. He took out his camera. 'Now, stand just there, by the whitewashed wall. I need to take your picture.'

Lisette did as she was told.

'All done,' he said. 'I'll get these developed for your identity papers.'

'Are you a photographer?' Lisette asked. The camera looked very professional.

'I was before the war,' he said, putting the lens cap back on. 'Now it's my cover. Weddings, christenings: one click, and I record the memories.'

'I don't really like being photographed,' Lisette said.

Seraphin smiled. 'Neither does my daughter. She wriggles off her mother's knee every time I try to take a picture.' He glanced over his shoulder. 'Listen, I'm afraid there's been a change of plan.'

'What do you mean?' Lisette frowned. In the barn, she could hear pigs rootling in their trough.

'You're going to Paris. We need an agent to make deliveries and listen out for information.'

'Paris?' Lisette said. 'I thought they wanted me to blow up train lines.'

'An opening has come up in a restaurant. The head chef is sympathetic to our cause. He's agreed that we can place someone qualified in the role,' he said, gesturing towards Lisette. 'Only the Germans and collaborators dine out in Paris now. It's the perfect opportunity for you to be our eyes and ears.'

Paris. The very centre of the German occupation of France.

'Which restaurant?' she asked.

'Maxim's. Have you heard of it? The Germans can't get enough of the food there, and when the wine flows, they talk.'

Of course she'd heard of it. Maxim's was one of the best restaurants in Paris. In normal times, working at Maxim's would have been an opportunity for her. But this was war. She wouldn't be there to learn from some of the best chefs in the world, she'd be there to cook for the Germans.

'I thought Horcher was in charge of Maxim's now,' Lisette said.

It'd been the talk of the Savoy kitchen: how the Nazis had ousted the owners, the Vaudables, and appointed the acclaimed German restaurateur, Otto Horcher, in their place.

'Indeed,' Seraphin said, 'and that's what makes Maxim's so interesting to us. It has protected status.'

Lisette swallowed. It wasn't the kind of war work she'd imagined, but it was exactly what she wanted: to be at the very heart of things and make a difference.

4

Christoph

May, 1942 – Paris

'*Entschuldigen Sie mich, bitte*. Will you take a photo of me?' A German soldier approached Christoph. 'I want to send it to my mother.'

Christoph nodded gruffly and put down his briefcase. He'd seen his colleagues doing the same thing when he'd arrived here six months ago but the notion of taking holiday snaps while in Paris was abhorrent to him.

The soldier posed with his finger pointing at the Eiffel Tower. The shutter opened and closed, immortalizing the moment.

'Isn't it marvellous?' the soldier said. 'Paris is our pleasure ground now.' He took a guidebook out of his pocket and opened the pull-out map. 'Do you know the best place to get a woman?'

'*Nein*,' Christoph said, nauseated by the soldier's words. He wished Paris wasn't their pleasure ground but still the city he'd dreamed of visiting, a place to explore and learn from, not a place of destruction and fear. He handed the camera back. 'You're asking the wrong man.'

He walked off, startling a flock of pigeons. The soldier's ignorance reminded him of his fiancée.

'You won't forget me, will you, *Liebling*?' she'd said. 'All that fun you're going to have in Paris. How I wish I could visit too.'

Hilde was the prettiest girl in the village and he'd been flattered by her attentions. The night before he was forced to join the army, Hilde and Christoph had stolen out into the barn. Cows snuffled in the stalls, and Hilde, determined not to lose him, had pulled him down into the hay. He'd made love to her willingly, grateful for a moment's respite from what was to come.

Only afterwards, in the awkward silence, had he thought what it signified. It seemed only right to propose to her, to ask the question she'd been longing to hear. When she said yes, a cold, flat feeling settled in Christoph's heart. Marching to Paris had been a way to escape. But the feeling had followed him here. He'd never pictured his life like this. Trapped.

Christoph crossed the road and turned left, heading towards the Hôtel Le Meurice on the rue de Rivoli. The briefcase was heavy. Christoph had to deliver some papers to Kommandant von Gross-Paris Schaumberg by noon.

Christoph nodded at the guards outside Le Meurice. He'd never been here before. He was stationed at the Majestic. He hadn't wanted to serve, but when the recruiting officer came to the farm, threatening to take his sister, Lotte, away because of her mental disabilities if he didn't, he had had no choice. Hilde's father had connections in the Nazi Party, and, at her insistence, had secured Christoph a role as a junior administrator in the Department of Agriculture and Food Supply. Despite his reluctance at being forced into the war, he was at least grateful for this small mercy.

Apparently, the Kommandant had asked for him

especially. Christoph hurried up the steps, hoping to get this over and done with as quickly as possible.

The atrium had swirling marble floors and sparkling chandeliers. The brightness made him blink. It was beautiful, but also rather inhuman. The scale dwarfed the young soldier on reception. Christoph showed his identity papers and was directed up to the Kommandant's personal apartments.

'Ah, Herr Leutnant Baumann,' the Kommandant said. He stood behind a vast mahogany desk. 'Heil Hitler.'

'Heil Hitler,' Christoph replied, raising his right hand and clicking his heels together.

The Kommandant was a handsome man with dark brown hair swept over to one side and a thick moustache that gleamed above his upper lip.

'Thank you for bringing these over.' He took the papers from Christoph.

'You're welcome, Herr Kommandant.' He waited to be dismissed, but the Kommandant pointed to the chair.

'Christoph, isn't it?' he said. 'Do sit down. It's not just the papers I want, it's your other skills too.'

This didn't bode well. From the room next door came the crash of piano chords and a voice wailing. The Kommandant raised his eyebrows.

'My son, Otto,' he said. 'My wife does her best, but she struggles to teach him.'

Christoph stiffened. Where was this leading?

'Perhaps he's homesick,' he said.

'Perhaps, but it's important for him to see our victory over Paris. That's why I've brought my family here. I want them to witness the subjugation of the French for themselves, and experience my proudest hour as I enjoy the conqueror's spoils. Hitler himself approved it.'

Christoph flinched inwardly. To him, the very essence of Paris was freedom.

'I insist on Otto continuing lessons while he's here, including the piano, but the poor child needs better instruction. Hence . . .' The Kommandant waved his hand towards Christoph. 'I want you to teach the boy. I understand from your superior that you're a talented pianist and have been entertaining the troops.'

'I wouldn't go so far as to say that, Herr Kommandant,' Christoph said, thinking of the occasional sing-song in the boarding house. 'I was accepted into the Bonn Conservatory, but then I was conscripted.'

He hadn't wanted to sign up. He hadn't wanted this war. A career as a concert pianist was his dream. Christoph's parents were encouraging. His father, a prosperous landowner and farmer, was proud of his son, who took French lessons with a tutor and could play Beethoven by the time he was eleven.

After his father died, Christoph went to agricultural college, dutifully learning enough to be able to manage the farm and looking after his mother and sister. Once the farm was secure, however, and they'd hired a good manager on the recommendation of Hilde's father, Christoph's mother suggested that he should finally audition for a place in the Bonn Music Conservatory. But not long after that, conscription had been introduced, and Christoph had been forced to sign up.

'Far better to serve the Führer, I'd say.' The Kommandant saluted the portrait of Hitler again.

'Indeed,' Christoph murmured. He followed suit, clicking his heels and raising his hand, but without the vigour of the Kommandant's flamboyant salute.

The Hitler Youth had seemed like fun back when he was younger. He'd enjoyed camping, hiking and map reading. When he got older, though, and the military training started, he'd hated it. Christoph's father had been a member of the Zentrum Party until it was abolished in 1933, and had been opposed to Nazi ideology right up to his death. Hilde's father talked of Hitler restoring German pride, but the reality of learning how to shoot a gun and, later, being in Paris, made Christoph question this.

Discordant notes reverberated through the walls. The Kommandant winced.

'Well, word has got out about your talents. I don't want a Frenchman teaching my son the piano. I want him to learn the greats, like Beethoven and Bach, from one of our own. So I'd like you to have a go at teaching Otto while he's here.'

There was nothing Christoph could do but agree.

'Place your thumb on E,' Christoph said. 'Here, I've got a pencil. I'll mark the score with the fingering.'

Otto frowned and tried to stretch his fingers. His small hands couldn't quite reach.

'Nearly,' Christoph encouraged. The boy was doing his best. 'Try adding the D major chord with the left hand.'

Christoph thought of his little sister, Lotte, who had preferred to listen rather than play. A childhood illness had left part of her brain damaged. She hadn't developed like other girls in the village. Christoph often had to play Beethoven to coax her out from her hiding place under the table. He wondered what she was doing now. Weaving those straw dolls she loved, perhaps, or running barefoot in the fields with the calves. Hopefully, she didn't realize the danger she was in. A sixteen-year-old girl with mental disabilities was deemed 'useless' by the Nazi regime. Hilde's father had sought assurances from local officials that she'd be overlooked in the round-ups, provided Christoph did his duty in Paris. But every day he was terrified something would happen to her.

'How are you getting on?' The Kommandant stood at the doorway with his wife.

Frau Schaumberg had a fragile prettiness which might have blossomed into beauty, but for the worried look around her eyes. Rumour had it the Kommandant was unfaithful to her.

'Listen to this.' Otto played the first few bars.

'Well done,' Frau Schaumberg said. 'You're lucky Leutnant Baumann was here to show you.'

'Can he come again?' Otto said.

Christoph tensed. He'd hoped to stay invisible, to get through the war unnoticed and return to his mother and Lotte, his dignity and soul intact. He didn't believe in the Nazi cause, and certainly didn't want to lose his life on account of it. Working for the Kommandant would bring him closer to the heart of Nazi command. It was the very last place he wanted to be.

'Indeed, he can,' the Kommandant replied. 'Herr Leutnant, I've arranged for you to be billeted here. Those papers you brought need someone with an eye for detail. You speak fluent French, I understand?'

'Yes, Herr Kommandant.'

'Then you're just the man, and you'll be on hand to teach Otto as well.'

Christoph tried desperately to think of an excuse to decline. But this wasn't an offer. It was a command.

'*Danke*, Herr Kommandant,' he said.

Christoph walked back to his lodgings through the Tuileries Gardens. The scent of blossom reminded him of the orchard at home.

For the first few weeks of being here, he'd strolled around Paris with his colleagues, visiting the Moulin de la Galette, the Trocadéro, the Sacré-Cœur, the Champs Élysées. Places he'd only heard about from his French tutor. He'd been told the army was doing something worthy, that the Reich would restore Paris's glory days.

But then he'd noticed the look in people's eyes. Defiance. Fear. Hatred. His comrades ignored it. But Christoph couldn't. Every footstep was a trespass. One morning, on the way to work, he'd witnessed a horrific sight: a mother and her baby, dead in a doorway. They must have been living rough, deprived of food. Soldiers were ushering people away, but he'd caught sight of the lifeless child clutched in the woman's bony arms. He'd walked on, embarrassed by the hostile stares of the Parisians. The shame had lodged deep within his heart. What the hell were they doing here? The whole enterprise was madness. Yet Christoph knew he had no choice but to remain in Paris and that desertion would put his mother and sister at risk of reprisals.

Christoph sighed, passing through the iron gate and on to the street. Perhaps this move to Le Meurice made no difference. Wherever he stayed in Paris, he didn't belong.

5

Lisette

May, 1942 – Paris

Lisette sat in her room on the rue de Vézelay and watched the morning light seep through the curtains. During her SOE training in Scotland at Arisaig House, she'd been taught how to endure periods of waiting. Huddled behind lichen-covered boulders on the hillside, rain pouring down, she'd learned to keep her mind alert. But somehow, in Paris, it was harder to bear the quiet.

At least she had work to keep her occupied. Her shift at Maxim's started at noon every day. Until then, it was simply a matter of passing the time, trying not to think about her fiancé, Johnny.

That was easier said than done. She had nightmares about Johnny flailing in the icy Atlantic waters, sinking out of sight. She woke unable to breathe, struggling to accept that he'd really gone.

She'd known Johnny her whole life. He was the only child on the street who didn't tease her for having a foreign mother and a funny English accent. They'd spent hours playing at the playground, building dens in the hedges and climbing trees. Best friends, that's what she told herself. Until one day not long after her sixteenth birthday the playfighting had turned into something else, infused with a physicality that was both exciting and frightening. It was a journey they'd taken together, allowing friendship to blossom into something more. A journey that the war, and the Germans, had ended for ever.

Lisette went to the window, wiping away her tears. Use the anger, and let go of the grief, she told herself. She took a deep breath, glancing outside. There was no sign of the famous sights from here. Just the grimy windows of other apartments and the iron fire escape leading to the courtyard.

A rapid tapping at the door made her jump. She wasn't expecting anyone.

'*Oui, qui est là?*' she said.

'It's me,' came the voice from the other side, 'and I'm hungry.'

Seraphin. Lisette hadn't seen him since they'd parted at the Gare du Nord. It was a relief to hear his voice.

She opened the door. He came in and handed her a parcel. 'Smoked haddock,' he said with a wink. 'Don't ask me where I got it. I'm hoping you can turn it into something edible.'

Lisette smiled. 'I'll make you a fish cutlet.'

She placed a dollop of cooking fat, purloined from Maxim's, into a frying pan. Reaching into her bag, she rummaged for a box of matches, pulling out a packet of cigarettes, a compact mirror, her papers, a needle and thread, and a ball of string before she found the matches at the bottom.

Seraphin smiled. 'You're just like my wife,' he said. 'She doesn't travel light, either.'

'You never know when these things might come in handy,' Lisette said.

'I didn't know you smoked.'

'I don't, but Baker Street insisted on the French cigarettes for authenticity. Help yourself, if you want one.'

She lit the gas and placed the pan on the hob. Then she sliced a stale roll to make breadcrumbs as best she could. Seraphin watched her, his cigarette smoke curling up towards the ceiling. She covered the haddock in rough breadcrumbs, wishing she had an egg to make them stick properly, and fried it. Seraphin stubbed his cigarette out on the windowsill, and then they sat down to eat at the wooden table.

'This isn't too bad,' Seraphin said.

'*Merci*. It should be served with mustard, but I don't have any,' Lisette said, sitting opposite him. 'I used to make this for my father when he had a hangover. Sometimes he ate it, sometimes he threw it at the wall.'

Seraphin glanced at her. 'That doesn't sound very appreciative. My daughter, Estelle, once made me some eclairs. The pastry was undercooked, the cream overwhipped and the chocolate overheated. I ate the lot.'

'Estelle is lucky,' Lisette smiled.

Seraphin put his fork down. 'I have a task for you. Look out for consignments of flour in the coming weeks. The head chef will give you instructions.'

'What's in the flour?'

Seraphin leaned closer. 'Radio crystals. They need to be delivered to radio operators near here.'

Lisette folded her arms. 'I'm capable of more than just deliveries, you know.'

Seraphin smiled. 'I'm sure you are. You come very highly recommended. But in France, where an agent can expect to last a few months, I want to make sure you're one of the survivors.'

Lisette clenched her hands. 'I want to do more. One of my colleagues at the Savoy had escaped from Poland. He told me about the ghettos, surrounded by walls and barbed wire. Thousands are dying. I want to be involved in helping them.'

'It's worse than that. There's a death camp too,' Seraphin said with a tired look on his face. 'Last week, the underground Polish Socialist newspaper *Liberty Brigade* reported that tens of thousands of Jews are being gassed at Chelmno.'

'My God.' Lisette's blood ran cold. 'We have to stop this.'

'I know,' Seraphin said quietly. 'I look at my daughter and wonder how any man or woman could treat another human being like that. But we can only do what we can.' He sighed heavily and stood up. 'I must go. Keep making those splendid desserts at Maxim's. The head chef says he's impressed with you.'

Lisette shook her head. 'After what you've just told me, making desserts seems a poor way of fighting the Germans.'

'Don't worry, you'll get your chance. You must stay strong. We can't let the horror of what the Nazis are doing paralyse our resolve.'

Lisette opened the door for him. 'Where can I find you if I ever need to?'

'Café Lille, on the Left Bank. I'm there most days.'

After he'd gone, Lisette wrenched open the window, sick at what Seraphin had told her about the camp, desperate to do more. The lack of action was frustrating.

All those months training with the SOE, only to be doing the same job she'd done at the Savoy.

Unfortunately, the Special Operations Executive manual was unequivocal: *It is essential to security as well as to efficiency that an agent should obey his chief's orders exactly and without dispute.* For now, Lisette would have to do as she was told.

Lisette arrived for her daily shift at Maxim's. It had been a few days since Seraphin's visit and the news of what was allegedly happening at Chelmno was still etched on her mind. The head chef came over as Lisette was hanging up her coat.

'There's a café on rue des Ursins,' he said, placing a packet on the table. 'They're short of flour. Go now, before you start cooking. Tell him you've brought the ingredients for the cake.'

With trembling hands, Lisette placed the packet of flour in her bag. It was going to be heavy, with all her other bits and bobs in there, including the recipe book, which she didn't want to risk leaving at the flat. This was it. Her first delivery.

The street was busy. A group of grey-clad soldiers whistled as she crossed the road. Lisette kept her eyes on the pavement: attention was the last thing she needed.

A man at the street corner gazed intently when she walked past. Could he see inside her bag? Her clammy hand gripped the strap. The Special Operations Executive manual warned: *Some agents are inclined to relax their precautions. That is the moment to beware of.* She nodded at the man, determined to stay focused, and walked briskly past.

Eventually, Lisette reached rue Clémentine and rang the bell. Two soldiers strolled by on the other side of the road. She stiffened, certain that her duplicity must be written all over her face. But they didn't stop. The heat in her cheeks subsided. At last, the door opened, and an old man appeared.

'I've brought the ingredients for the cake,' Lisette said, using the phrase she'd been told.

'*Merci*,' the man said. 'Come in.'

He led her down a narrow corridor and out into a small garden.

'Any trouble on the way?' he asked.

'None at all.' She handed him the bag of flour.

'This will come in useful,' he said.

'Pray God that it does,' Lisette replied.

Minutes later, she stepped back on to the street. Her heart was racing. She'd done it. Her first delivery. She lifted her chin and set off back to Maxim's. Hopefully, in time, Seraphin would be able to give her more than just deliveries to undertake.

6

Julia

June, 2002 – Bonn

'How are you feeling?' Sebastian said. He'd offered to drive Julia to the airport, so they were on the M25, motoring towards Gatwick.

Julia glanced at her hands. She'd finally confessed to Sebastian that the stiffness in her hands had happened before. He'd been very sympathetic and insisted she see a specialist in movement disorders, but checks had found no physical reason why her hands had failed her.

'I'm okay, thanks,' she said. 'Trying not to dwell on it.'

Just the thought of that moment on stage made Julia want to retch. She turned towards the open window. The fresh air cooled her face.

'I wish you weren't going to Bonn,' Sebastian said. 'It feels like you're running away.' His fingers tightened around the steering wheel. 'If you stayed, maybe I could help to sort the problem out.'

'You've been amazing already.' She turned towards him, an anxious smile on her face.

'I could be more amazing, you know,' he said.

He took his eyes off the road briefly and met her gaze. There was no denying how handsome he was. But

Sebastian was one of the best managers around. She wasn't going to risk losing him.

'We've talked about this,' she said. She thought they'd resolved things, but his words suggested otherwise. 'I don't know what happened in Madrid last year. You were so wonderful when Mum died, supporting me during that tour. But that kiss was a mistake. I thought you agreed?'

'Not exactly, but I respected *your* wishes to keep it strictly business.' He gave her a sidelong glance and raised his eyebrows. 'However, it's good to see you're still focused on your career.'

'If I still have a career after what happened,' Julia said, hoping the subject of Madrid was closed. She needed Sebastian as a friend and manager right now.

Sebastian laughed. 'Winner of the BBC Young Musician of the Year 1999, protégée of Christoph Baumann. Of course you have a career.'

Julia looked up at the shiny tiled roof and wooden shutters of Christoph's house. The flight to Bonn had passed smoothly and now, at last, she was here. They'd organized the visit months ago, before Julia had gone off on tour. When she'd phoned Christoph a few days ago to confirm the arrangements, he'd sounded tired but pleased she was coming. He'd offered to pick her up from the airport, but Julia had told him it was no problem to get a taxi. She knew that he hated driving on the Autobahn nowadays.

She breathed in the scent of the roses growing in the front garden. It was a relief to put the last few weeks behind her. Seeing Christoph always calmed her.

He lived on the outskirts of the city, in the former diplomatic quarter, with its impressive villas and tranquil, leafy gardens. Peace. That's what Julia needed. If peace was to be found anywhere, it would be here with Christoph.

She unlatched the gate and dragged her suitcase up the path. Sunlight dappled the ground. Just like it had in 1996.

Back then, she'd arrived flustered and anxious from the train station, over two hours late. She'd been looking after a little girl on the platform who had lost her mum, and a handsome stranger had stepped in to help them both. They'd taken care of the girl together, playing Hangman to ward off her tears until, eventually, her mum was found. The handsome stranger's eyes and easy smile were still giving her butterflies when she'd appeared on Christoph's doorstep. They were still giving her butterflies as she remembered it now.

That evening, back in 1996, Christoph's wife, Hilde, had been stony-faced, but Christoph had made Julia feel welcome: showing her to the spare room, warming up some food in the microwave. She was just starting to settle in when the doorbell rang. 'Ah,' Christoph had said, 'My son. He'll have lost his keys again. Don't worry, Hilde will get it.'

Now, her chest tightened. Nothing compared to the shock of seeing Daniel that day. *He* had been the handsome stranger from the train station, except all his friendliness was gone once he realized that Julia was his father's latest piano protégée.

Julia gave the suitcase a sharp yank and pulled it on to the front step. Well, Daniel wasn't here now, thank goodness.

37

Julia caught sight of Christoph through the bay window. He was sitting at the piano staring at her. He looked confused, as if he couldn't place her. She leaned over and tapped on the glass. 'It's me,' she mouthed. He got up and shuffled towards the door.

It didn't make sense. Last year, he'd been the judge at a piano competition in Köln. They'd gone for dinner afterwards. He'd seemed his usual self. There was hardly any hint to his age, but somehow this felt different. Had he forgotten she was coming?

Christoph opened the front door. He wore slippers, tracksuit bottoms and a shirt that hadn't been ironed. This was not the Christoph she knew.

'Is everything all right? You look like you've seen a ghost,' Julia said.

At the sound of her voice, his gaze cleared and he smiled.

'Oh, *Entschuldigung*. Julia, what a pleasure to see you. My eyesight's not what it used to be. Just now, seeing you come up the path, I thought it was someone I knew from long ago. You always did remind me of someone.' He waved the thought away. 'Come in.'

The music room was unrecognizable. A bed had been made up on the sofa. The air smelled musty. Books and newspapers lay strewn across the floor. Even the Schimmel piano was covered in dust and piles of papers.

Christoph lowered himself into a chair and propped his stick against the bookshelf.

'It's wonderful to see you,' he said.

'I'm so glad to be here,' Julia said. 'Thank you so much for having me to stay.'

Christoph smiled with a sigh and nodded.

Something wasn't right. Julia glanced at the disarray. How long had he been like this?

'Are you sure everything's all right?' she said, sitting next to him. 'You look very weak. I thought you sounded weary on the phone the other day.'

'Oh, it's just old age,' he said.

Come to think of it, he looked thinner than she remembered. As if he hadn't been taking care of himself properly. 'When was the last time you ate?' she asked.

'I don't know.'

He needed to get his strength up. 'Let me find you something.'

The kitchen was at the back of the house. Dishes lay piled in the sink. The fridge contained only a wrinkled red pepper and curdled milk.

This was bad. After Hilde died, he'd managed the house and cooking by himself. But now it seemed to be too much for him. He must have lived like this for several weeks. What was going on?

'Christoph, I'm popping to the supermarket.'

But he was no longer in the chair. He lay sprawled on the floor, legs askew and arms flailing. Julia's throat constricted. Christoph moaned. She grabbed a cushion and placed it under his head. A bruise bloomed on his temple.

'Don't move.' Her mind went into overdrive. 112. That was the number over here. 'I'll call an ambulance.'

'No . . .' he said, faintly. 'Ring Daniel.'

Julia stiffened. 'There's no time. You need a doctor.' Not Daniel. Anyone but Daniel.

'Please,' Christoph gasped. 'His number . . . it's by the phone.'

His hand clutched her wrist; his eyes implored her. She couldn't refuse him.

'I'll be back in a minute,' she said.

'*Danke*,' Christoph said, his eyes closing.

Julia flicked through the address book, her fingers fumbling the pages. There were countless addresses under Daniel's name. Australia, America, India, Italy. Each country had a line struck through it. Where did he live now? Hoping it was as far away as possible, Julia turned the page. Her heart sank. Germany. Frankfurt. Only a hundred miles from Bonn.

She grabbed the handset and punched in the number. Thankfully, it went straight to messages. She cleared her throat and waited for the beep.

'I'm with your father. He's had a fall. I'm about to ring an ambulance. Anyway, he wanted you to know, so that's why I'm calling. It's Julia, by the way. Right . . . bye.'

Crikey, she'd made a right hash of that, but hopefully he'd get the gist. Well, she'd done what Christoph had asked. It was time to ring an ambulance.

The hospital room was quiet. Christoph's chest rose and fell. It had taken hours in A&E. Julia still wasn't sure what was wrong with him. The doctor wanted to wait for the test results and Daniel before saying more.

A drip hung by the bed, a tube extending to the cannula in his arm. Christoph had been old when Julia met him, but not like this: fading away in the flimsy hospital gown and white sheets.

While the nurse checked the monitors, Julia went to get a cup of coffee. Visitors milled around the vending machine.

She carried the cup back to Christoph's room and tried to open the door. It jammed and sent the coffee spilling over Julia.

'Oh,' she cried out.

The door opened. It was Daniel. The sight of him took her breath away. He had the same dark green eyes, like a forest wet with rain.

'*Entschuldigung*, Julia.' He glanced round, then grabbed some paper towels from above the sink. 'Here . . .' He passed them over. 'Sorry.'

Julia took the towels, careful not to touch his fingers. He was staring at her. Noticing how tired she looked, probably. She dabbed at her shirt. Any excuse not to look at him. The last word he'd said to her six years ago had been 'sorry', and now here he was, standing right in front of her, saying it again.

'It's fine, don't worry.' Her heart did a reverse dive. 'So . . . you got my message.'

'Yes. I came as soon as I could.' He glanced over at Christoph, who lay with his eyes closed, seemingly asleep.

Julia's mind went blank. She put the towels in the bin and wished the ground would swallow her up.

'Have you spoken to the doctors?' she said.

'Not yet.' Daniel's forehead creased with worry. 'What happened?'

'I arrived today. When he opened the door, he didn't recognize me at first. He was very weak; the music room was a mess. I went to the kitchen to get him some food and, when I came back, he'd collapsed on the floor.'

Her voice wavered. It'd been quite a day, and now, Daniel turning up like this. 'It was awful, Daniel, I didn't know what to do. He's normally so strong, but he just lay there, helpless.'

Daniel shook his head, concern in his eyes. 'I'm so sorry you had to deal with all of this. I didn't realize things had got so bad.'

'You haven't seen him lately then?' she asked.

A twist of annoyance sharpened Daniel's gaze. She should've remembered that his relationship with Christoph was a sore point.

'I mean . . .' Julia said.

'I know what you mean.' He ran his hand through his hair. He did that when his defences were up. 'I try and come back to Bonn every weekend, but things have been crazy at work recently, so it's been difficult.'

Christoph's eyes opened, confused for a moment, then he saw Daniel. 'What's happening?' he said.

The door opened and the doctor came in, a tall woman in her fifties.

'Good afternoon. You must be Herr Baumann's son. As you're his next of kin, I'd just like to explain to you where we are, if that's okay?'

'Yes, of course,' Daniel said, folding his arms.

'When can I go home?' Christoph asked.

The doctor patted his arm. 'As soon as you're strong enough.' She glanced at her notes. 'You see, the short-term problem is malnutrition and dehydration. We suspect you haven't been looking after yourself for a few weeks. The lack of food and water would account for the confusion.' She glanced at Daniel. 'He might be like that for a while, until he recovers properly.'

Daniel listened intently. 'And the long-term problem?' he asked.

'Given his age, we need to explore the possibility that this could be the early signs of dementia.'

Daniel took a deep breath. 'Occasionally, he has spells of not being certain about things – dates, events, appointments. But I put it down to him getting older.' Julia sensed the fear in his voice. 'Surely it could just be that?'

'Of course it is,' Christoph said weakly. 'Don't worry, Daniel.'

The doctor smiled compassionately. 'It could be. But when you're feeling better, Herr Baumann, it would be good to discuss the option of doing some more tests.'

The doctor departed, leaving them to digest the news.

'Are you okay?' Julia asked Christoph. He nodded and closed his eyes, like he couldn't take any of it in properly. 'I don't think that's what any of us wanted to hear.'

'It's not dementia,' Daniel said firmly. 'I'm sure of it. He'll be fine.'

He was putting on a brave face. Now wasn't the time to probe further. They had to sort out care for Christoph. She ushered Daniel away from the bed.

'What's the best way to organize everything?' Julia asked in hushed tones, not wanting to disturb Christoph. 'The house is in a complete state. It's too much for him. He's going to need someone there.'

'The thing is,' Daniel said, rubbing his temples, 'this has come at a really bad time.'

'What do you mean?' Her eyes widened. She'd thought

43

he'd drop everything to help his father. Despite the fractious relationship they'd always had, Christoph was still his father.

He hesitated. 'I'm in the middle of something really important at work,' he said. 'I just need a few days. I'm sorry, it's the worst timing.'

'What could be more important than looking after your father?'

It came out more harshly than she'd meant it to. But seriously, how could he prioritize work over his father?

Daniel clenched his jaw, then he seemed to think twice, his stern expression softening a little.

'I know, you're right. Nothing's more important, but I can't get out of this. I promise I'll be back in Bonn soon,' he said. 'It's not ideal, I feel guilty as hell, but if you could hang on until then . . .'

Julia glanced up at him. 'You want *me* to stay and look after him?'

'Christoph thinks the world of you,' he said. 'He never misses an opportunity to mention it. He'd much rather be cared for by you than by me.'

His eyes were liquid green, staring right into hers. She smelled the woody scent of cedar. The outdoors. *Him*. Julia sucked in her breath. How had she spent six years trying to forget him, only to be disarmed in five minutes?

Julia looked out of the window. 'He's your father,' she said firmly. 'You can't just leave him. Besides, I've got a concert in Prague next week.'

Daniel gazed at her. 'Could you just manage a few days? Please, Julia. It'd really help if you didn't go yet.'

Christoph stirred. 'What are you talking about?' he murmured. He glanced at Daniel, then reached out his hand to Julia. 'You're not going, are you?'

'No, of course not. Not yet.' She took his hand and squeezed it tight.

'You too, Daniel? I'd like to spend some time with you both,' Christoph said, his voice faint.

Daniel sat down on the chair beside the bed. He reached over and touched Christoph's arm, clearly torn by his responsibilities.

'I wish I could stay, but I can't, I'm sorry. I'll get this thing at work sorted out and come back as soon as I can, I promise. I'm hoping Julia will be here until I get back . . .' His eyes implored her. 'If that's okay with you, Julia?'

What could she say? She'd never leave Christoph alone; Daniel knew that. Whatever he had to do, it must be important. 'I guess it'll have to be okay.'

Christoph smiled and patted her hand. '*Danke*.' His eyes closed again.

'I really am sorry,' Daniel said to Julia. 'I appreciate you staying.' He sounded weary, the edge gone from his voice.

'It's fine,' Julia said. 'I can stay until Thursday, but then I need to fly out to Prague.'

Daniel nodded. 'I'll be back as soon as I can. I'll sort out a cleaner. I don't want you doing that, it isn't fair.'

'Thanks, that'll give me time to rehearse.'

'And meals. I'll organize for them to be delivered. That way you won't have to do any cooking. I think we both know it's not your strong point.'

A smile lit up his eyes. It was impossible not to smile back. She knew exactly what he was referring to: the sticky chocolate thickening to a sludge in the fondue set, the fruit getting stuck in the gloop and coming off the skewers. Heat prickled her cheeks, remembering what had come next. Quickly, she tried to push the memory away.

'Yes, well, that's definitely true,' she said.

He held her gaze for a moment. Was he thinking of that night too?

'Anyway, thanks for doing all this,' he said. 'I'll be back as soon as I can.'

He bent down and kissed Christoph's forehead. The gesture was brief but full of tenderness.

The door clicked shut, and he was gone. Julia took a deep breath. All this time, she'd dreaded running into him again, wondering how she'd react and what she'd do. Thank God it was over. She sat down on the chair and watched the blue lines going up and down on the monitor. She couldn't think of Daniel. The priority now was Christoph.

Crème Brûlée

250ml double cream
6 egg yolks
2 tablespoons of granulated sugar
4 tablespoons of brown sugar

1. Preheat the oven to 190°C.
2. Heat the cream.
3. Beat the yolks with the sugar and add the cream.
4. Pour the mixture into ramekins.
5. Pour some warm water into a roasting tin and place the ramekins in it. (The water should not be higher than the top of the ramekins.)
6. Bake in the oven for 30 minutes or until set.
7. Remove from the oven and leave to cool.
8. Sprinkle on a layer of brown sugar.
9. Brown the top with a blowtorch, or place under the grill.

7

Julia

June, 2002 – Bonn

Christoph had been home for two days. His condition had improved, but he was still weak and had little appetite. Julia had tried everything to get him to eat the meals that were delivered. In desperation, she'd rung the doctor and asked her what to do. 'Maybe you can think of a dish that will tempt him,' she'd said. 'The main thing is that he eats something, or we might have to readmit him.'

Julia sat with Christoph in his bedroom. He pushed aside the plate of chicken that had been dropped off that day.

'I can't eat it,' he said wearily.

'But you have to eat something,' Julia said.

Christoph turned towards the window. He was slipping away. She couldn't bear it. He was the closest thing she had to a father figure. His weakened state reminded Julia of her mum. Julia had felt such a sense of helplessness. Surely it didn't have to be like that with Christoph too.

'Would you like pancakes?' Julia said desperately. 'Or something else? I can go to the shops if you don't like these meals on wheels.'

'Sorry,' Christoph said, his shoulders slumped. 'I don't know what I want, but I'm not hungry for this.'

Julia bit her thumbnail. It was hard to know how much he remembered from the hospital. When he was discharged, the doctor had explained to him again that the memory lapses could be the result of dementia and that he should consider having further tests. Christoph had waved her words away, apparently too tired to take them in.

Julia settled him down with a sigh. Perhaps she could try and talk to him another time. She closed the bedroom door. Maybe he just needed a few more days to rest.

She paused on the landing, glancing at the narrow staircase to the attic. Daniel's room. No one would know if she popped up there. Just one quick look. Seeing his room might answer the many questions burning in her head. Was he still going out with Kat? What was keeping him in Frankfurt?

The stairs creaked under her feet. Heart pounding, Julia opened the door. The wall above the bed was still covered in photos. She inhaled the scent of patchouli. Just like that night.

She was about to go in, but something stopped her. What was she doing? She didn't need to see his room to know that nothing had changed. The bean bags and coffee table. Candles on every surface. Too many memories. She closed the door and went back downstairs. She was here because of Christoph. No one else.

She went downstairs, determined to sort out the music room. While Christoph slept, she yanked the window open. A breeze rippled over the grand piano, fluttering the papers strewn across it. It was on this piano that she'd written her own ending to Mozart's 'Fantasia'. She'd fired off the notes with a pent-up energy she'd never possessed before. Julia sighed. It was also the last time she'd ever tried composing.

The whole place would need tidying before she could do any practising on the piano. She went to fetch the vacuum cleaner from the cupboard under the stairs.

The narrow space was full of clutter. As she pulled the vacuum cleaner out, it knocked a box off the shelf and sent the contents tumbling on to the floor.

Damn it. She ducked down to pick up the debris that had fallen, hoping there were no spiders. Among the seed packets and catalogues, she found a hardback notebook with a tatty leather cover.

Intrigued, she opened it, holding the flyleaf towards the light. There was a dedication written in cursive handwriting: *À Christoph, nos recettes. J'espère qu'ils te ramèneront à moi. Tout mon amour, Sylvie.*

Julia translated it. *To Christoph, our recipes. I hope one day they lead you back to me. All my love, Sylvie.*

What was a book of recipes doing shoved away in here? And why had this woman dedicated the book to Christoph? Julia backed out of the cupboard, bringing the book with her. Sylvie. She'd never heard him mention that name, but then the main focus of their conversations had always been music.

Julia wandered into the kitchen, the vacuum cleaner forgotten, and sat down at the table. She turned the pages carefully. They were dry to the touch and had aged to yellow. A long-ago scent rose from the paper. Each page contained a recipe, some written in French, others in German. The pages were covered with instructions and scribblings. The ink had faded to brown, and Julia could see blots and scratches from the nib of a fountain pen. Even more intriguing were the stains – a splatter of sauce or a smudge of cooking oil – that revealed the cooking process itself. The pages were well thumbed, as if the recipes had been used often, revisited and loved.

Up on the kitchen shelf, there was a row of Hilde's recipe books, all by well-known chefs. But this book was more personal; it was handwritten and curated.

The first recipe was a scribbled note for Fischkotelett. It looked quite plain: just haddock and breadcrumbs. The next recipe was for crème brûlée. Across the top, Sylvie had written: *Do you remember? It was the first time we met.* Julia read on, fascinated by the detailed instructions: *Heat the cream. Beat the yolks with the sugar and add the cream. Pour the mixture into ramekins . . .*' Sylvie sounded like she had known what she was doing.

Julia thought of Christoph, thin under the bedspread, his eyes weary. He was disintegrating in front of her eyes, and she was powerless to stop it. Julia's breathing quickened. She glanced at the old recipe book. The food from the meal-delivery service meant nothing. But these recipes might mean something to Christoph.

There was one huge flaw in this plan, however. Julia couldn't cook for toffee.

Why *was* she so useless at cooking? True, she'd been too busy with the piano and had seen cooking as a chore, but there was more to it than that. Her mum's angry voice came back to her. The day she'd tried to make a birthday cake for Anna: 'Clean this mess up. You should have been at the piano, not making a cake.'

Julia straightened her shoulders. Well, she was a grown

woman of twenty-seven now, not a girl of ten. Surely she could have a go at making one simple meal from the recipe book for Christoph.

Hours later, after tidying the music room and making a trip to the supermarket, Julia began to wish she'd never attempted the crème brûlée. Her initial burst of confidence had ebbed rapidly. The kitchen table was strewn with eggshells and ramekins.

Julia took the final batch of crème brûlée out from under the grill. It was her fourth attempt, and it had to work because there weren't any eggs left. The same quest for perfection she experienced while playing the piano had taken hold. Unfortunately, despite her best efforts, the crème brûlée fell far short of perfection.

She placed the ramekins on the cooling rack. Five of the crème brûlées were charred black. The sixth looked all right though. Julia wasn't sure if the custard underneath had set properly, but it would have to do. She only hoped Christoph would eat it.

8

Lisette

May, 1942 – Paris

Seraphin visited Lisette's apartment again a week later. His face looked haggard, as if he'd been up most of the night, grey smudges under his eyes.

He hadn't brought any food this time. Instead, he handed her a matchbox and a tiny key. 'You've seen one of these before?'

'Of course,' Lisette replied. Weapons training had been standard at Arisaig. It was a mini incendiary device hidden inside a fake box of matches. The key was used to wind up the clockwork mechanism that ticked down and then, after a few minutes, activated a striker to ignite the box.

'I need you to deliver it to an agent at the le parc des Buttes-Chaumont. She'll be waiting on a bench with her baby in a pram.'

'I could operate it myself, you know,' Lisette said. She twisted the silver key in her hand. 'Imagine if I offered to light Otto Horcher's cigar with this.'

'A compelling thought,' Seraphin said with a rueful smile, 'but I won't let you jeopardize your position at Maxim's. It may yet prove useful.'

'It hasn't so far.' Lisette rarely got the chance to venture out into the pleasure-soaked dining room where Nazi officers ordered bottles of champagne by the dozen and girls danced around the tables.

'Be patient,' Seraphin countered. 'An opportunity will present itself.'

'I'll follow your instructions, don't worry,' Lisette said. 'I know how important it is.' She slipped the fake match-box into her bag.

'Can you ride a bicycle?' Seraphin asked.

'Of course.'

Johnny had taught her. He'd lent her the bike he used for paper rounds and taken her to a quiet lane where no one would see her wobbly efforts. He'd been so patient, so encouraging, cheering her on when she finally managed it herself.

'A bike will be waiting outside Maxim's tomorrow when the head chef sends you to buy apples,' Seraphin said, interrupting her thoughts of Johnny. 'Get to the park and back as quickly as you can.'

Lisette nodded. Every small task was a chance to prove her worth.

The next day, Lisette felt a nervous twinge every time she thought about the incendiary device in her bag.

Her task at work today was to make tartes tatin. She took the puff pastry she'd made the day before from the refrigerator and went to look for apples. As planned, there were none.

She approached the head chef. He was a small, wiry man who never gave the slightest hint that they were working together against the Germans.

'*Excusez-moi*,' Lisette said.

He looked up from filleting salmon and frowned. 'What is it?'

'There are no apples for the tartes tatin,' she said.

'Then you'd better go and get some,' he replied curtly, 'and be quick about it.'

Lisette went to get her bag. Her heart thudded as she approached the back door. Seconds later, she was out in the delivery yard, and there was the bicycle, leaning against the wall. She arranged the bag over her shoulder and across her body and set off.

She pedalled unsteadily on to the rue Royale and headed down the rue de Rivoli alongside the Tuileries. The street was almost deserted. The porticoes along the Hôtel Le Meurice were spiked with flagpoles, thrusting out over the pavement, red-and-black Nazi flags wafting in the breeze. Lisette tried to avert her eyes, but it was hard not to stare. It was disturbing to see the buildings branded by the enemy.

As she turned eastwards, and along the rue des Petits Champs, Lisette passed a line of women queuing for meat, despite there being none in the window. Children sat waiting on the kerbside, drawing on the pavement with chalk, their clothes threadbare. She'd only been here a few weeks, and already the city felt oppressive. What must it be like for Parisians, who'd spent months enduring the subjugation of their once proud city?

By the time she crossed the canal St Martin, Lisette's legs were growing tired. Thank goodness it wasn't much further. She sped up, readying herself for the final push, when suddenly, the pedals began to spin out of control. The chain had come off.

This was the last thing she needed. Luckily, Johnny had taught her what to do.

Lisette wheeled the bike on to the pavement and turned it upside down so it rested on the saddle. She glanced at her watch. If she was quick, she could still make it to the park on time. She tried to wiggle the chain from between the chainwheel.

'Can I help you?'

Lisette took a deep breath and turned around. A German soldier stood watching her. He must have been only seventeen, judging by the soft hair above his upper lip and gawking expression. His colleagues stood by the corner, watching him, smirks on their faces.

The soldier came over.

'Where is your tag?' he said, speaking French with a German accent. He glanced at the rear mudguard.

Damn. The yellow tag, that showed the bike was registered, was missing. Julia smiled nervously.

'*Pardon*,' she said, 'it must have come off. This bike is practically falling apart.'

The soldier hesitated, then shrugged. 'Put it on as soon as you get home.'

He wrestled with the chain, spinning the chainwheel until it slotted back into place.

'*Merci*,' Lisette said, smiling deferentially.

She bent down to turn the bike over. The soldier helped her.

As they twisted the bike the right way up, a matchbox slipped out of Lisette's bag. Before she had time to see which matchbox had fallen out, the soldier grabbed it in his hand. Her heart froze. Which one was it? The one containing matches or the incendiary device?

'*Darf ich?*' he said. With his other hand, he took a cigarette from his jacket pocket.

Lisette watched in horror as he put a cigarette between his lips and slid open the matchbox. Lisette still couldn't see which box he had. She should run, but her legs were rooted to the spot and a strange calm settled over her, a willingness to accept her fate.

But to her relief, the soldier took out a match and struck it against the box. Thank God. The matchbox with the incendiary device was still in her bag.

He offered the cigarette to Lisette, but she shook her head, her mind spinning at how near the precipice she'd been. She had to get away.

'*Merci*,' she said again, gesturing to the bike. She gripped the handlebars to hide her shaking hands and climbed on the saddle.

'*Au revoir*,' the soldier said with a wave. Then, as she cycled off, he called out. '*Fräulein*. You've forgotten your matches.'

'Oh,' Lisette called, 'you can keep them.'

She kept cycling, willing her legs to bear up, not daring to look back, half terrified, half elated, at this lucky escape.

Thankfully, the woman was still at the parc des Buttes Chaumont when she got there, sitting on a bench, a pram at her side. Lisette glanced into the pram, seeming to admire the baby, then slipped the incendiary device under its blankets.

'Your baby is charming,' Lisette said with a smile, before casually walking on.

She got on the bike and cycled back to Maxim's, stopping off for apples on the way. Her heart was still pounding but, somehow, the near-escape had given her courage. She hadn't buckled or panicked. Instead, she felt invincible.

Seraphin shook his head when she told him what had happened. 'Christ, Lisette, you must be more careful.'

They were sitting outside a café not far from the Moulin Rouge. The street was busy, people hurried about doing their errands in the last hour before the curfew's black pall fell on Paris.

'The strange thing was, I was ready for whatever came.'

Seraphin took a sip of red wine. 'Just because your fiancé is dead, that doesn't mean you have to be *sans cœur*,' he said firmly.

'I do have a heart,' Lisette protested, trying not to show how the harshness of his words had affected her. 'The fact that I'd be willing to die for France proves that. Anyway, how do you know about my fiancé?'

Seraphin sighed. 'I always ask the SOE what an agent's weakness is. It's more important than knowing their strengths. In your case, do you know what they told me?'

Lisette shook her head, curious to know.

Seraphin leaned forward; his gaze fixed on her. 'They said your weakness is how much you hate the Germans for what they've done to your family.'

Lisette frowned. 'But you hate the Germans too. Isn't that the point?'

Seraphin leaned back. The wicker chair creaked and

settled. 'No,' he said, 'because hate blinds you to the cracks that every heart contains, even German ones. It's those cracks that we must find and exploit. Remember that.'

Later that night, her cheek against the rough pillowcase, listening to a baby wailing on the floor above, Lisette thought about what he'd said. *German hearts.* The phrase was a contradiction in terms. Johnny and her grandparents' deaths, the starving faces of the Parisians, the Jews who'd been sent away, the hundreds of buildings bombed, and all the people killed in the Blitz: they all proved this. She clenched the sheet, fire rising in her chest. If she was *sans cœur*, then so be it. Being heartless was the only way to fight an enemy that appeared to lack all humanity.

9

Christoph

May, 1942 – Paris

The Kommandant bit into a piece of rare steak. A speck of blood settled on his chin. The sight of it made Christoph's stomach heave. He hated coming to Maxim's, but it was the Kommandant's favourite place to eat.

The woman sitting next to the Kommandant giggled and wiped the blood away with her napkin. Christoph didn't know her name; he didn't want to. On the short journey to Maxim's the car had stopped and the woman had got in. It wasn't for Christoph to outwardly express judgement.

Now, she snuggled next to the Kommandant on the red banquette. Candles glowed at each table. Swirling mirrors hung on the ceiling. Lotte, with her love of shadows and light, would have been fascinated by this place. He wished he could have shown it to her in other circumstances. She'd have loved to draw the patterns. He could picture her, hair tucked behind her ears, concentrating as she held her pencil.

'Doesn't your bodyguard want to eat?' The woman glanced at Christoph. Her red lipstick glistened.

'He's not my bodyguard, he's my administrative assistant,' the Kommandant said, 'and he's already eaten, haven't you, Herr Leutnant Baumann?'

Christoph nodded. Dinner had been a plate of boiled ham and swede at his desk in Le Meurice. He'd been dragged here to deliver agricultural statistics to the Kommandant's colleagues, not to eat. The meeting had finished before dessert. Christoph longed to be dismissed.

He picked up the menu. All this food – where did it come from? Could the dishes here be worth such inflated prices? A crème brûlée cost four hundred francs. It was outrageous.

Suddenly he heard a crash of glasses and a brief scream from behind the kitchen door. For a moment, the conversations and laughter ceased, then they rushed back like the tide.

'Go and check what's happened,' the Kommandant said.

'Yes, Herr Kommandant.'

The kitchen doors swung open. No one noticed Christoph at first in all the steam and activity. A man in whites, who Christophe presumed was the head chef, looked up. At the sight of Christoph's uniform, a hush descended.

'*Qui a crié?*' Christoph asked.

The chef jerked his head towards the back of the kitchen. 'It was Mlle Sylvie.'

A woman was kneeling down, surrounded by fragments of glass. Christoph glimpsed the slant of her nose, her cheekbones jutting out, the pucker of her lips.

'*Je vais bien*, it's just the shock, that's all,' she said, turning round. 'Too much haste, less speed.'

Her accent – French-Belgian perhaps – and voice was richer and fuller than most women's. A gash on her thumb oozed blood. She was trying to tie a makeshift bandage over the cut.

'*Puis-je aider?*' Christoph said.

'*Non, merci.* I can do it myself.' She gave him a brief smile, dismissing his help, but he couldn't bring himself to go. 'I shouldn't have tried to pick the pieces up.'

She twisted the bandage around her hand, tied a knot and held one end between her teeth to pull it tight. He watched, captivated by her determination.

'Done,' she said with a nod. 'May I go back to work?'

'Of course,' he said.

She fetched a blowtorch from the cupboard and disappeared to the other end of the kitchen. He gazed at the space she'd left.

'*Tout trié,*' the head chef said. 'Sylvie is one of my best cooks. Tell the Kommandant, he will soon taste the finest crème brûlée in all of Paris.'

Christoph returned to the shadows and glitter of the dining room.

'Well?' the Kommandant said.

'One of the cooks dropped some glasses and she cut her hand on the shards when she was trying to clear it up,' Christoph explained. He pictured her red lips against the white fabric, the glimpse of her tongue.

'A fuss about nothing, then. Ah, look, *Liebling,*' the Kommandant said to his companion. 'Here comes our dessert.'

The waiter placed two ramekin dishes in front of the Kommandant and his companion. The top of the crème brûlée was like a pane of glass, perfectly browned yet translucent. The Kommandant's spoon cracked the surface, and he ladled the golden substance into his mouth.

'*Wunderbar,*' he said.

The woman pushed hers away. 'I'm sure it's delicious, but I have my waistline to consider.'

The Kommandant laughed. 'Here, try some,' he said, passing the ramekin to Christoph.

Christoph was about to decline, but he was curious. So, this is what that woman in the kitchen – Sylvie – had needed the blowtorch for. He plunged the spoon into the mixture. The shard of toffee was sweet, the vanilla smooth and sublime. The textures and flavours soaked his tongue. He'd never tasted anything so delicious.

The Kommandant pulled the waiter aside. 'I'd like to meet the chef who made this.'

Hastily, Christoph put the dish down. The thought of seeing her again made him nervous. After a few minutes, Sylvie came out of the kitchen, trailing reluctantly behind the head chef, her eyes downcast.

'This is Mlle Sylvie. She made the dessert, Kommandant,' the head chef said. 'I insist on my sous-chefs taking the credit, even if they are women.'

'*Bon soir*,' the Kommandant said to Sylvie. His unctuous tone made Christoph's skin crawl. 'May I congratulate you on the best crème brûlée I've ever eaten. Isn't that right, Herr Leutnant?'

'It's the only crème brûlée I've ever eaten, Herr Kommandant,' Christoph said. His words seemed inadequate, clumsy even. Sylvie glanced at him but didn't smile. He could feel her disapproval radiating like heat from a fire.

The Kommandant didn't seem to notice.

'What a novelty – a female chef in an establishment such as this. I suppose the absence of men has allowed the women to rise.' His eyes roamed over her body and settled on the bandage around her hand.

'So, it was you we heard scream. Gave us all a fright. Be more careful next time.' He waved her away.

Sylvie followed the head chef back to the kitchen. She didn't look back at Christoph, not once, but then why should she? He was just another soldier in German uniform. Perhaps beneath her brittle exterior she was as soft and sweet as the custard of the crème brûlée. Christoph sighed. He'd never know.

On his days off, Christoph liked to walk through the city. The day after meeting Sylvie at Maxim's, he wandered south, towards the vast cemetery of Montparnasse. The woman from Maxim's, Sylvie, lingered in his mind, just as the taste of the crème brûlée lingered on his tongue. He couldn't put his finger on how or why, but the very thought of her sharpened his senses.

On these walks, Christoph hoped to find the Paris that his French tutor had told him about: vibrant and bustling, the cafés full of philosophers, artists and poets. No doubt they still existed, in a narrowed form, furtive and wary, perhaps on the Left Bank, but they could never exist for Christoph. The hard clack of his boots as he crossed the Seine by the Gare d'Orsay caused the civilians he passed to harden their faces.

Halfway down boulevard Raspail, a crowd had gathered. A truck stood outside one of the buildings, and Christoph saw the distinctive round caps of the French police.

'Hey, you there,' one of the policemen called out to Christoph. 'Want to help us do your dirty work?' He laughed.

'I'm an administrator,' Christoph said. 'I'm not really . . .'

'*Bien sûr*, we know how it is,' the policeman said. He turned back to his fellow officers. 'Let's get these ones loaded in.'

A subdued group of men and women stood encircled by the police. Each wore a yellow star sewn tightly on to their jacket. Since May, more and more Jews had been singled out in this way. Christoph found it abhorrent. It made him ashamed of his uniform.

One of the women was crying and pleading with the police. 'Please, don't take me, my child is only young. I beg you.'

The policemen ignored her and pushed her into the back of the truck along with the others.

'Please,' the woman shouted to those watching, 'help my child!'

Christoph followed where she pointed. The tear-stained face of a boy, no more than eight years old, peered out of the window on the second floor of the building. Before anyone could respond, the truck's engine started, a cloud of diesel fumes choked the air, and it drove away. The crowd tutted, moaning about the disruption, but gradually, they dispersed, continuing with their day.

Christoph looked up at the window again. The child had gone. Was no one heeding the woman's plea? He went towards the door of the building, but it was locked. Surely one of the neighbours will help the child, he thought. More police arrived on the street. A lorry pulled up. He couldn't risk getting involved. Soon the apartment would be emptied and sealed off. The furniture would be sent to Germany. He prayed to God the child was safe.

The cemetery at Montparnasse was almost deserted. Christoph's stomach churned from the desolation in the woman's voice. He was ashamed that he'd heard her pain, yet done nothing.

Wandering among the graves, he found Baudelaire's cenotaph. *Les Fleurs du Mal* had been his French tutor's favourite text. A line came to Christoph now, as he stood in front of the great poet's memorial: *How little remains of the man I once was, save the memory of him! But remembering is only a new form of suffering.*

The first time he heard this, Christoph had imagined the lines were spoken by an old man looking back on his life and his youth. But now, the round-up of Jewish people fresh in his mind, Christoph realized that even a young man could suffer that way. He didn't know how to recover the man he once had been.

10

Lisette

June, 1942 – Paris

Lisette climbed the stairs in the apartment block, her bag heavy on her shoulder. It had been two weeks since she'd cut her hand. The wound had healed, leaving a red line on her skin. Every time she caught sight of it, she thought of the soldier at Maxim's. It had been foolish to treat him so brusquely; he could have severely reprimanded her. She'd heard of others being punished for less. But the sight of him watching while she fumbled with the bandage had inflamed her. She needed to be more careful in future.

Two flights up, she reached the flat she had been told to visit. She knocked on the door.

'What do you want?' a voice said.

'Cloves to make a dish fit for a king,' Lisette replied, using the line the head chef had given her. The door swung open.

A woman stood in the half-gloom of the narrow hallway. 'I may have a few,' she said.

Lisette closed the door behind her and followed the woman in. The flat was like Lisette's: empty and impersonal. The cloves were a pretence. Lisette had come to deliver a bag of flour. She took it out and put it on the table.

'Would you like a drink?' the woman asked. Lisette nodded. The woman handed her a cup. 'Ground acorns, I'm afraid. There's no coffee anywhere.'

Lisette sipped the brown liquid and screwed up her face.

'There's no food either, except in the restaurants,' she said. 'How are you managing?'

The woman's face was thin.

'I get by,' she said. 'The loneliness is the worst. But now you've brought me this gift' – she gestured to the flour on the table – 'I'll take a trip to see my aunt . . .'

There was no aunt; they both knew that. An agent was waiting for the radio crystals in the flour.

'Well, I'd better call it a day,' Lisette said.

'Be careful as you go.'

Lisette passed a child on the stairs on her way out. She was playing with a tin of buttons, putting them in order. She smiled at Lisette, content in her own little world.

Out on the street, Lisette breathed a sigh of relief. She'd accomplished yet another delivery, without a hitch this time. She was about to cross the road, taking care to look left first, when a voice stopped her.

'*Halt und stehen bleiben!*'

She turned round. A German soldier was staring at her.

'Who are you?' he barked.

'Sylvie Dubois,' she said, trying to keep calm. These were just routine questions.

'Where do you come from?'

'Saint-Quay-Portrieux. I'm in Paris to work.'

'Show me your papers.' She handed him the counterfeit papers, hoping they were as good as Seraphin claimed. 'Hmm, they seem to be in order,' he said.

He gave her the papers back. Lisette began to breathe more easily. Nearly done.

'And what are you doing here?' he asked.

'*Je fais des courses.*' Her hands shook as she lifted her bag.

'Empty it, please.'

'It's just vegetables . . .'

The soldier grabbed the bag and tipped it upside down. The contents scattered over the cobbles. Make-up, compact mirror, the cigarette box, followed by the recipe book. Julia's composure faltered. She shouldn't have brought it with her today but she never liked to leave it in her room.

The soldier's eyes narrowed. '*Was ist das?*' He reached down and picked the book up, frowning at the French and German writing. '*Bist du eine Spionin?*'

'No, I'm not a spy. *Je suis un chef.* Maxim's,' Lisette said.

The soldier frowned. 'What's this then?' He pointed at the German writing.

'My grandmother was from Alsace-Lorraine. She spoke French and German,' Lisette said desperately.

The soldier didn't believe her. He grabbed her arm. 'You'd better come with me.'

'No, please, it's the truth . . .' She didn't feel calm this time. The grip of his hand was tight. She'd been caught.

People were staring, pity in their faces. They knew what was going to happen to her, but they averted their eyes and hurried on. She didn't blame them. No one wanted to be hauled down to Avenue Foch.

The cell was cold and damp. The hard bench made it impossible to sleep. Moans and screams from the other cells interspersed the night. Lisette lay awake, filled with terror.

She went over her SOE training. *Have a simple, straight-forward story and stick to it. And above all go on denying at any price.* She needed to be Sylvie with every fibre of her being: an innocent French girl who aspired to be a chef.

Hours later, she was hauled into a bare room with dark stains on the floor. She shivered in the chilly air. The interrogator was a short, bald man. There were no introductions. He slapped the recipe book down in front of her.

'*Vous êtes une espionne, n'est-ce pas?*' he said. He spoke French with a heavy German accent. 'We know everything. You've been taking notes in this book.'

'It's my grandmother's old recipe book,' Lisette said. 'Nothing more.'

'You were seen coming out of a building on rue des Renaudes,' the man said.

In the long hours of waiting in the cell, Lisette had prepared for this.

'The head chef at Maxim's often asks me to go on errands. I source ingredients. Today he wanted cloves.'

'Cloves?'

'I heard a man in rue des Renaudes could get us some.' The man curled his lip. 'Black-market ingredients.'

This was a crime, but a lesser one than being a spy.

'*Bien sûr,*' she said, risking a smile. 'We need to ensure we're only sourcing the best for our clientele.'

'Hmm.' He glanced at the scar on her hand. 'What happened?'

'I cut myself when I was sweeping up some broken glass a few weeks ago,' she said. 'Please, I'm just a chef – we're always covered in injuries from the kitchen. It's the mark of our trade. I'm supposed to make soup today. *Pommes de terre et oignon.*'

He sniffed. 'I prefer German food.'

'I know German recipes too. Sauerkraut. Page twenty-three. Simple, and so delicious.'

The man flicked to the page and perused the recipe. His face gave nothing away. 'You speak German?'

Lisette pursed her lips. Should she tell him? The SOE manual said: *If you speak German, provided such knowledge agrees with your cover, it is probably best to admit you understand a little.* Lisette decided to risk it.

'My grandmother taught me a little, just enough to read the recipes.'

'Hmm,' the man said. 'I'll cross-check what you've told me. Until then, you'll remain here.'

'And my book?' Lisette asked.

'Confiscated as evidence.' He clasped the recipe book in his hand. 'We searched the building you visited on rue des Renaudes. A woman was arrested. They found wireless crystals in her flour jar. Her name's Hélène. Do you know her?'

He slid a photo across the desk. It was her. The woman from the flat.

The sight of the photo sent a jolt through Lisette's body. She tried not to let the mask slip.

'I've never seen this woman before. It's just a coincidence,' she said, wringing her hands. 'I was looking for cloves. I told you, I'm a cook.'

The man folded his arms. 'And this man who sold cloves, did you find him? There was no mention of any cloves found in your bag.'

Lisette moistened her lips. At Beaulieu, SOE agents had been trained how to cope under questioning. She'd already thought this one through.

'No, I didn't find him. The address must have been wrong. It's like that on the black market. Rumours of where ingredients can be obtained often turn out to be false.' Lisette's stomach clenched. Hearing the words she'd prepared out loud, they sounded unconvincing.

The interrogator frowned. 'Indeed. Well, let's see. Perhaps when we interview Hélène, she'll be able to shed more light on things.'

Back in the cell, Lisette's strength faltered. The walls were black, the air thick with fear. What if Hélène told the interrogator that Lisette had brought the crystals? She stuffed her fist against her mouth to stop from crying out. Terror gripped every part of her being. She felt along the hem of her skirt. There it was, the tiny bulge of the L tablet. One bite on the capsule and she'd be dead in two minutes. She prayed she wouldn't need it. She wouldn't let them break her.

Lisette closed her eyes, visualizing each recipe in her mind, her grandmother's steady voice as she dictated them, in the hopes that it would calm her.

She took a deep breath and thought of the soldier, standing obediently behind the Kommandant at Maxim's. It wasn't right that men like him were still alive. Not when Johnny and her grandparents had died. Tomorrow, she'd give nothing away and would stick to her story, no matter what they did.

Sauerbraten

750ml vinegar
Bay leaves
Cloves
Peppercorns
500g beef joint
1 onion, finely chopped
Breadcrumbs from 1 crust of bread
4 tablespoons flour

1. Boil the vinegar with the bay leaves, cloves and peppercorns.
2. Pour the infused vinegar broth over the beef until half covered.
3. Leave to marinade for a few days, turning regularly.
4. Remove the beef from the broth and pan-fry on a low heat for 30 minutes.
5. Add the onion and breadcrumbs to the vinegar broth and mix well.
6. Heat the broth at a simmer and stir in the flour to thicken, then pour the broth over the beef.
7. Serve with salted potatoes.

11

Julia

June, 2002 – Bonn

Julia stood at the door of the music room and gazed at the piano. The black and white keys beckoned. She turned away, intending to clear up the kitchen after last night's cooking, but with Prague only five days away, it was time to start practising again.

She sat down on the stool. Nothing too hard, something simple and familiar. She played the opening bars of 'Für Elise', holding her breath.

Halfway through, her fingers stiffened. She carried on, but the feeling was inescapable. Her hands turned to wood. The notes crashed, discordant and out of time.

'*Meine Liebe*,' Christoph was leaning against the doorway in his dressing gown. 'So, that's why you're here.'

'Did I wake you?' she said. 'I'm sorry. Here, let me help.' She took his arm and helped him over to the sofa. His eyes were a little brighter. The sleep had done him good.

'The sunlight woke me, and I came down to watch you play. The music was beautiful, and then . . .' He glanced at her. 'What's going on?'

'Oh.' She closed the piano lid. 'It doesn't matter. You've got enough to worry about.'

'You can't fool me. Music flows from the heart to the

head and through the body on to the keyboard. I can tell something isn't right with your hands.'

Christoph's gaze was unwavering. There was no use pretending.

'I messed up the concert in London. This was supposed to be my big year, the year of the Queen Elisabeth competition. I have to play well or else . . .'

'Or else what?'

'It's all I know. If I'm not playing the piano and moving forward in my career, then I don't know what will become of me.'

She shouldn't burden him with all this, but it was a relief to talk.

'That stiffness in your hands is a warning sign,' Christoph said. 'It's telling you to stop.'

'That's what Anna said, but I can't just stop. There's nothing physically wrong, I had it all checked out. I just need to keep practising.'

'Don't stop altogether,' he said. 'Just divert your energies into something different for a while, like you did last night. That crème brûlée was delicious.'

Julia went and sat down next to him. 'Honestly?'

'Yes,' he said. 'What made you cook it?'

'I found a recipe book under your stairs when I was looking for the vacuum cleaner. It's dedicated to you.'

She fetched the book from the kitchen and showed him the flyleaf.

'Goodness.' He held the book, rubbing his thumb over the cover. 'I've no idea where this came from.' He pressed his forehead. 'My mind's been in a fog since Hilde died. Nothing fits together.'

'What do you mean?'

'Last night, when I ate the crème brûlée, I thought about Paris, and the restaurant, Maxim's. I could picture a kitchen, steel countertops and white tiles, and a woman who'd cut her hand. She made the most delicious crème brûlée.' His face darkened. 'I've no idea what it meant or who the woman was.'

Julia turned to face him. The subject couldn't be avoided for ever.

'Have you thought any more about what the doctor said about having further tests?' she said.

Christoph kept his eye fixed on the recipe book.

Julia took a deep breath, determined to carry on. 'The fog you mentioned could be the sign of something more . . .' She tailed off, hoping he understood what she meant.

Christoph glanced at her. 'Dementia, you mean?' he said.

'Possibly. It might be worth having the tests so it could be ruled out.'

Christoph shook his head. 'It's not that, I'm sure of it, but even if it was, I'd rather not know.'

Julia sighed. She could understand his fear. 'Then what do you think causes the confusion?' she said.

'I don't know. But your crème brûlée conjured a memory in my mind.' He frowned. 'I tried to stay good in the war, I tried my best, but I can't remember if I succeeded or not.'

Julia took his hands. 'I'm sure you did.'

Christoph sighed. 'Why don't you stay longer? You could cook some more of these recipes for me, help me remember. It might be a good diversion for your hands.'

'I wish I could, but everything's arranged. Sebastian's expecting me in Prague in a few days.' She took his arm, feeling guilty she couldn't extend her stay. 'Come on, let's get you back upstairs.'

At the top of the stairs Christoph stopped, his brow furrowed anxiously. 'This recipe book. Don't mention it to Daniel, will you?'

'Why not?' Julia asked.

'I have a feeling he won't like it. He was always so protective of Hilde. If he saw the dedication, he might be angry. Our relationship is complicated at the moment; in fact, it always has been. Can we just keep it between us, until I get things straightened out in my mind?'

Julia nodded. 'Of course. Don't worry, I'll keep it out of sight.'

While Christoph slept, Julia tidied the papers on his bedside table. There were bills and letters, and one, handwritten, caught her eye. It was from Daniel. She hesitated, glancing at Christoph to make sure he was still asleep, then began to read.

The letter was short. He wrote about his job doing research for a food-production company in Frankfurt. Nothing personal. She was about to put it down, but then she reached the last paragraph:

. . . I've got a venture of my own to work on, so, if possible, I need my share of the money that's tied up in the house. It's what Mama wanted, and it's such a big house for one person. I hope you'll consider it, and respect her wishes at last.

Julia shoved the letter to the bottom of the pile. No

wonder Christoph was anxious about Daniel finding out about the recipe book. There was enough going on between them if this letter was anything to go by. Surely Daniel wouldn't bring this up again, not while Christoph was so weak. It was yet another worry to lodge in her mind.

Julia practised all day, hoping to banish from her mind Christoph's advice about taking a break. The stiffness in her fingers came and went. The unpredictability was the most frightening part.

It was a relief to break off and ring Sebastian. She sat in the hallway on the bottom step of the stairs. At last, he answered.

'How's Christoph doing?' he immediately asked.

It was good to hear his voice. He'd be at his desk, no doubt, in Tavistock Square, a cup of black coffee by his computer.

'He's out of hospital but very weak.' Julia stretched her legs out over the tiles.

'And you're looking after him?'

'Yes, until I leave for Prague . . .'

'That's cutting it a bit fine, isn't it? I thought you were coming back here first.' His voice was edged with tension. The tour meant a lot to him too.

Julia's chest constricted. 'It'll be fine. I'll meet you there.'

'How's the practice going?'

Julia bit her lip. The stiffness was still happening. If she kept practising between now and Thursday, she might be able to iron it out before Prague. 'The problem with my hands comes and goes.'

'But it's improving?'

The screws tightened in her chest. She didn't dare disappoint him. 'A little, I think.'

'Good. Then keep at it. Look, I was thinking, would you like to stay a few extra days in Prague after the concert?' Sebastian said. 'I've got some time free and I thought we could spend it together.'

'Oh, Sebastian . . .' This was dangerous territory.

'I can't stop thinking about what happened in Madrid,' he said. 'I know it's been a year, but we kissed, Julia, that has to mean something.'

Julia closed her eyes and sighed. It had all been a mistake. After the concert at the Auditorio Nacional de Música, she'd got the call from Anna to say their mum had died. Sebastian had been there, gathering her in his arms, staying with her as she digested the news, trying to assuage her guilt about not being there. He'd held her close, comforting her, and when he leaned down to kiss her, just for that moment, Julia had wanted it as much as he did.

'Sebastian, I think the world of you. My career would be nothing without you. But we have to put that night behind us for the sake of our professional relationship.'

He sighed. 'I know. Forget I asked.' He cleared his throat. 'Is Daniel in Bonn? I don't want him messing things up for you again.'

'He won't. I'll be on that plane on Thursday, I promise.'

She put the phone down and stared at the receiver. Why was everything so complicated? Her fingers ached. Her head was spinning. One thing was clear, though. Christoph *had* to regain his strength before Daniel came back. Perhaps she should try another recipe from Sylvie's book; it was what Christoph wanted. He'd enjoyed eating the crème brûlée and, what's more, it had seemed to clear a little of the fog in his mind.

Julia lugged the shopping bags into the kitchen. She'd bought a beef joint, vinegar, bay leaves, cloves, peppercorns, onions and flour. Sylvie's recipes were straightforward to follow. Julia imagined a woman who knew what she wanted and how to accomplish it.

Julia found a frying pan and a chopping board in the cupboard. The next recipe from Sylvie's book was for Sauerbraten. Sylvie had added a note in the margin. *June 1942. Le Meurice. Serve with potatoes and add white wine and beef stock if you have only a few hours to marinade the beef. Cook this meal as if your life depended on it.* The page was soiled with blotches of sauce.

That year, 1942, Paris would have been under German occupation. What had she meant: *cook this meal as if your life depended on it*?

The front doorbell rang. Julia glanced down the hallway. A familiar silhouette stood behind the coloured glass. What the hell? Daniel wasn't expected for another two days. Julia tucked the recipe book into a drawer, remembering what Christoph had said about keeping it a secret.

She headed down the hallway, took a deep breath and opened the door. Daniel stood on the doorstep looking unusually smart in a black suit and white shirt. In one hand he carried a suitcase. A man loitered behind him with a clipboard, examining the front garden and scribbling notes.

'Hi, Julia. I have a key, but I didn't want to startle you,' Daniel said. His eyes darted across her face as if reading her reaction.

'I wasn't expecting you today,' she said. He looked tired, his tanned skin faded, smudges under his eyes, his hair dishevelled. 'Are you okay?'

'Yes, it's just been a hard week.'

She stood back to let him in. He didn't look okay. A long-buried impulse to reach out to him stirred, but she suppressed it.

'How's Papa?' he asked. 'I've been worried sick about him.'

'He's still very weak,' Julia said. 'He doesn't have much of an appetite, so I'm trying to cook food he likes.'

Daniel raised his eyebrows. 'But I ordered those meals so you wouldn't have to cook.'

'I know, that was kind of you, but so far Christoph's barely touched them.'

The man with the clipboard came into the hallway. He glanced at the ceiling and wrote something down.

'As you can see, it's a bit dated' – Daniel turned his attention to the man – 'but there are still some original features. I'll show you the rest of the house.'

Julia frowned. 'Christoph's sleeping. What's going on?' The man looked at Daniel. 'Have I come at a bad time?'

'No,' Daniel said. 'Of course not. You head down to the kitchen; I'll be along in a minute.'

Daniel turned to Julia, a pained expression on his face.

'I'm sorry. I should have rung and warned you. He's just doing a valuation.'

'I don't understand. Christoph's ill, and you're trying to sell the house.'

Daniel frowned. 'I didn't say that.'

It was here, six years ago, that she'd seen Daniel

walking out of the music room, a wad of Christoph's cash in his hand. Now here he was, talking about valuations. How could he think about money at a time like this?

'I saw the letter you wrote to him when I was tidying up his room,' Julia said. 'Christoph doesn't need that kind of upheaval now.'

Daniel's cheeks reddened. 'You read my letter?'

'I'm sorry. I didn't mean to; it was just there.'

Daniel sighed. 'I don't mean him any harm, Julia. I'm just checking out his options.' He raked his hand through his hair. 'You don't always have to think the worst, you know.'

Julia's mind flew back to 1996. 'Can you blame me?' she said.

Daniel's eyes dropped. 'No, I guess not, but I promise, my intentions are good. Please, Julia. You'll see.'

Julia let out her breath. It was hard to trust him after everything that had happened, but his face looked so pale and drawn she decided not to argue.

'Fine, just don't wake Christoph.'

He strode off to the kitchen. The slope of his shoulders and the way his hand gripped the suitcase made her want to follow him. To ask him . . . what? She exhaled. *Just leave it alone.*

Cook this meal as if your life depended on it, Sylvie had written. With all this talk of valuing the house, it seemed more important than ever to cook something that Christoph would eat and help him regain his strength. Hopefully it would take her mind off Daniel too and settle the flutter of nerves in her chest.

12

Christoph

June, 1942 – Paris

After what he'd witnessed on boulevard Raspail, Christoph couldn't get used to the luxury of Le Meurice: the marble floors and chandeliers, the mahogany bar lined with spirit bottles. He felt more dislocated than ever, as if the young man who'd fed scraps to the pigs, practised endless scales and swum with his sister in the stream had never existed.

He spent his days working in an office assigned to him by the Kommandant. His job was to plot the location of farms in occupied France, starting with Normandy. The department was preparing for inspections and Christoph was to take part in them. The Kommandant believed that farms were selling their produce to the black market rather than handing them over for the 'greater good' and could do more to boost production.

'It's their own people they're starving,' the Kommandant said one night.

Christoph had been invited to eat with the family after Otto's piano lesson. He nodded politely, preferring to listen rather than venture an opinion. But inside, his stomach clenched. The woman and her baby in the doorway hadn't died because of the black market or a lack of productivity on French farms. They'd died because the Germans were bleeding the city of food.

The Kommandant cut a piece of duck and dipped it in cherry sauce.

'I don't like this,' Otto said. He prodded the sauce with his fork. 'It tastes like jam.'

'Hush, Otto. Don't be rude,' Frau Schaumberg said.

Christoph said nothing. It wasn't the child's fault he didn't know that people a stone's throw away from here would give anything for a meal like this.

The Kommandant wiped his mouth on a white napkin. 'Maybe Otto has a point. I'm growing tired of French food. I want my son to experience the taste of the Fatherland.'

'But you said the French were wonderful chefs?' Frau Schaumberg ventured. 'You seem to enjoy the food at Maxim's.'

'Oh, I like oysters and champagne as much as any man, but now we have conquered Paris, it's only a matter of time before German food subjugates their cuisine as well. Food is the root of everything: our survival and identity. What do you think, Herr Leutnant?'

Christoph glanced up and swallowed his mouthful of food. 'I remember reading in the German guide to Paris how soldiers needed to be wary of the "sweet and easy life of the City of Lights". Maybe they meant the food too,' he said, ashamed of himself for outwardly chiming in with the Kommandant's views.

'Exactly. Too much of this rich French food can make a man soft.' The Kommandant chucked Otto under the chin. 'Let's see if Papa can get you some proper *deutsches Essen*.'

*

The next day, the Kommandant went to meet a group of high-ranking officials for lunch at Maxim's, taking Christoph with him. He sat with the other assistants, on hand to take notes or supply facts. He wanted to get back to the quiet sanctuary of his office. Even so, he kept half an eye on the kitchen door in case Sylvie appeared.

After the officials had eaten, the Kommandant told the story of Otto and the sauce that tasted like jam. Christoph listened, wincing at the Kommandant's self-important tone.

'Trouble is, good staff are hard to come by,' the Kommandant said. 'My head chef hasn't got a clue about German food. We're short-staffed in the kitchen.'

'The talented French chefs have either fled to Vichy or are prisoners of war in Germany,' SS-Sturmbannführer Rodert said. He was a tall man with soft, small hands that looked too effeminate to conduct interrogations and oversee activities at Avenue Foch.

'I told the head chef he needs to find another sous chef by the end of the week. If they know any German recipes, so much the better.'

There's a female chef in Avenue Foch who claims her grandmother was from the Alsace,' SS-Sturmbannführer Rodert said. 'We've confiscated her recipe book to check if she's an agent keeping notes in the guise of recipes. It's full of all our old favourites, along with some French recipes. I spent a pleasant hour perusing it yesterday.'

'Is she part of the resistance?' the Kommandant asked.

'I doubt it, but we're still investigating. The recipes seem sound. She works here at Maxim's, actually.'

Christoph's ears pricked up.

'How interesting,' the Kommandant said. 'Perhaps it's the woman who cooked that dessert for us a couple of weeks ago. Go and find out, Herr Leutnant.'

Christoph got to his feet and went straight to the kitchen, hoping it wasn't her. The head chef was leaning on the countertop looking through some menus.

'*Bonjour*. The Kommandant wondered if Mlle Sylvie is here today?' Christoph said.

'No, Herr Leutnant. Mlle Sylvie was arrested two days ago.'

Christoph's blood ran cold. He couldn't imagine that fierce young woman in a cell. It made him sick to think of it. 'What happened?'

'She was getting cloves for Sauerbraten. She never came back so I sent one of the staff to enquire, and that's when we heard. She's done nothing wrong. All she's interested in is cooking,' the chef said.

Christoph returned to the table and reported back.

'*Wunderbar*,' the Kommandant said. 'A pretty chef who can make crème brûlée and Sauerbraten. What more could a man want? Send her over this afternoon.'

'But the investigations have not yet been concluded,' SS-Sturmbannführer Rodert said.

'Very well, conclude them yourself as you see fit,' the Kommandant said. 'I'll be able to test the veracity of her story through her cooking. If she really had an Alsatian grandmother, I'll know it from the way she cooks Sauerbraten.'

13

Lisette

June, 1942 – Paris

At first light on the third day after being arrested, Lisette was hauled back into the interrogation room. She trembled as she walked. All night she'd lain awake. Had Hélène given her away under duress? Nausea cramped her stomach as she sat down. It was a different man today, of higher rank, Lisette guessed by the uniform. He stood with a light behind him, a tall, thin shadow, holding a file.

'I'm SS-Sturmbannführer Rodert,' he said. 'Please sit.'

Lisette did as he instructed. What was going on? A general? Her legs felt weak. This didn't bode well.

'Why were you in that building?' SS-Sturmbannführer Rodert asked, with no preamble.

'I told your colleague: the head chef sent me to get cloves.'

'And how long have you known Hélène?'

Lisette squirmed under his quick-fire interrogation. *Stay calm.*

'I don't know her,' she said.

The SS-Sturmbannführer leaned over the table, the light glinting on his glasses. 'And Seraphin, what about him?'

'I know no one of that name either,' Lisette said. Had she replied too quickly? The SS-Sturmbannführer was staring at her. Her insides quailed. *Oh God, please let me not buckle.* 'I was just trying to find the man who sold cloves.'

'Did you come across anyone in the building when you were there?' the SS-Sturmbannführer said, straightening up.

Lisette slowly let out her breath. This she could answer. 'There was a girl playing on the stairs.'

The general glanced at the file. 'What was she doing?'

'Arranging buttons,' Lisette said. She could picture the girl, as clear as day. 'By size and colour.'

The SS-Sturmbannführer slapped the file closed.

'Well, it seems you have luck on your side,' he said. 'The woman we arrested didn't mention you.'

'I can go free?' Lisette couldn't believe it. She only hoped Hélène would be as fortunate.

'Not exactly. The little girl couldn't say for certain which apartment you'd been to. We want to keep an eye on you. The Kommandant needs a cook over at his quarters in Le Meurice. You're to start straight away.'

'But I work at Maxim's, I can't just leave.'

'Oh, but you can. The Kommandant's man has come to collect you. You're lucky the Kommandant likes your cooking.' He gave Lisette her papers back.

'And my recipe book? Can I have that too, please? I'll need it if I'm to cook for Herr Kommandant.'

'Leutnant Baumann has it,' SS-Sturmbannführer Rodert said. 'It's out of my hands now.'

Lisette recognized the lieutenant the moment she saw him. It was the soldier who had come into the kitchens in Maxim's. She said nothing and kept her eyes down while he signed the paperwork, wondering if he recognized her too.

The soldier at the desk handed him a package. '*Das Rezeptbuch*,' he said. Leutnant Baumann nodded.

'Please, may I take it?' Lisette said.

To her dismay, Leutnant Baumann slipped the book in his pocket. '*Pardon*,' he said, 'I'm under strict instructions to keep it with me.' He glanced at the door. 'Shall we go?'

Lisette followed him, quickening her pace as he crossed the road and headed into the Tuileries. She balled her fists as she walked, cursing his authority. The book was hers. He'd no right to keep hold of it.

A commotion caught her eye. Off the main path, down an avenue, two German soldiers had cornered a young girl. The girl was crying as they jostled her. Lisette glanced at Leutnant Baumann. Hadn't he noticed, or didn't he care?

'Nothing is worse than active ignorance,' she muttered. The moment the words were out she regretted them, wishing she could take them back.

'That's from Goethe,' Christoph said, curiosity rather than anger in his voice. He studied her face. Lisette held her breath. Was he going to haul her back to Avenue Foch?

'Wait here,' he said.

His boots crunched on the gravel. The soldiers, startled by his appearance, let go of the girl. He spoke in calm, measured tones and sent them on their way. The girl scurried off. Leutnant Baumann returned to Lisette, a deep frown on his forehead.

'Come on,' he said. 'We'll be late.'

Lisette glanced at him. He'd only acted because he had

89

been shamed by her words. But she was surprised that he *had* acted, and curious that he could feel shame. She hadn't believed any of them capable of it. It still lingered in the red flush on his cheeks.

When they reached Le Meurice, Leutnant Baumann took her straight to the Kommandant and handed him the recipe book. The Kommandant sat at his desk, thumbing through the pages, and eyed Lisette.

'A fascinating book. You certainly have an interesting array of recipes, Mlle Sylvie. Of course, the proof is in the pudding.'

His lips curled in a smile, framed by his black moustache. He clearly thought he was charming. Lisette glanced at Leutnant Baumann. He stood by the Kommandant's desk, eyes on the ground.

'For dinner tonight, I want Sauerbraten and potatoes. I'll know if your story is true by how good the food is.'

Lisette hesitated. 'Pardon me, Herr Kommandant, but there won't be enough time to marinate the beef properly.' Her grandmother had always maintained that the beef needed at least a few days to soak up the flavours.

The Kommandant waved his hand. 'I want it tonight. Use your skills as a chef and make it work.'

'Very well, Herr Kommandant,' she said. 'Please may I have my recipe book so I can make it?'

The Kommandant smiled. 'Why of course,' he said, holding it out to her.

'*Merci.*'

'There's one more thing,' the Kommandant said. 'Herr Leutnant, you will accompany Mlle Sylvie to the kitchens.

Until her cooking skills are proven, I don't want her to leave the hotel.'

The kitchen at Le Meurice was bigger than the one at Maxim's. Three chefs were at work helping the head chef preparing food. They stared as she walked in with Leutnant Baumann.

'M. Dupont, Mlle Sylvie will be cooking for the Kommandant tonight,' Christoph said to the head chef.

M. Dupont nodded. 'The Kommandant told me about the situation.' He glanced at Lisette. 'Whites are over there, the larder is at the back. You can work at that counter.'

Lisette went over to where he pointed. Leutnant Baumann followed her like a shadow. Would she never be rid of him? She went to the larder to fetch vinegar, bay leaves, cloves and peppercorns, then took a joint of beef from the fridge. Just like Maxim's, there was no shortage of food here.

She propped the recipe book up against the scales, her mind working all the while. She had to get in touch with Seraphin. As she cooked, heating up the vinegar in the saucepan, and sprinkling in the cloves, peppercorns and bay leaves, her mind darted over the possibilities for escape.

She placed the beef in a roasting pot and poured over the hot broth. Ideally, it would marinate for much longer, but there were only a few hours before the Kommandant expected his dinner, so she would have to make the best of it.

She picked up the bag of potatoes. They needed scrubbing and peeling. An assistant in Maxim's usually did jobs like that.

'Can I help?' Leutnant Baumann said.

His voice startled her.

'There's no need, I can manage,' Lisette said. 'But thank you.'

'Like you did with the bandage?' He glanced at her hand and smiled. It lit up his face. 'I'd like to do something rather than just stand about.'

'All right. Thank you,' she said, and handed him a knife.

Occasionally, she glanced at him. The peel spiralled off the potatoes. He worked deftly while she pan-fried the beef then added the onion and breadcrumbs to the vinegar broth. She tasted it with a teaspoon, wincing at its blandness. She went back into the pantry and found some beef stock and white wine, added them and tasted again. Much better.

'May I taste it?' Leutnant Baumann asked.

She handed him the teaspoon.

'Remarkable,' he said. 'It tastes just like my mother's.'

So that was it. All this talk of wanting to peel potatoes. He was homesick. Was this what Seraphin had meant about being open to finding the cracks in the Germans' beating hearts? The thought sickened her.

Sylvie simmered the broth and stirred in some flour, fighting her anger. Johnny couldn't feel homesick any more. There would be no more letters about his hopes for the future. No more kisses snatched on the platform after one of his short periods of leave. Johnny would never taste his mother's cooking again, let alone a home-cooked meal in the house Lisette had dreamed of sharing with him. None of the Germans, not even Leutnant Baumann, deserved an ounce of her compassion.

At dinner, the Kommandant tasted the food and smiled.

'*Perfekt*,' he said, 'given the circumstances. Your cooking is every bit as exquisite as you are. Isn't that right, Herr Leutnant?'

'Yes, Herr Kommandant.' He caught Lisette's eye, then looked away.

The Kommandant pushed back his chair and went over to Lisette. She kept her eyes down. His shiny boots came nearer.

'I'll inform Avenue Foch that you're staying with us,' the Kommandant said. 'We can keep an eye on you here and get the benefit of your wonderful cooking skills.'

He reached out and touched her cheek, his thick, full lips curled in a smile.

'Otto will be pleased you're here,' he said. 'As am I.'

Lisette forced herself to smile. It took all her self-control not to pull away. This move to Le Meurice wasn't part of the plan, but she'd have to turn it to her advantage. Somehow, she needed to establish contact with Seraphin and continue her work for the SOE.

14

Julia

June 2002 — Bonn

Julia dreamed that she was on the stage again, her hands chained to the piano yet still unable to play. She woke up. Sweat beaded her chest. She was in Christoph's house. Thank God, it was just a dream.

'Julia!' Christoph called her name.

She grabbed her kimono and headed straight to his room, searching for the light switch. Christoph blinked in the brightness.

'I think it was her,' he said, 'in my dream.'

'Who?' Julia pulled a chair close to the bed.

'The woman from Maxim's who cut her hand,' Christoph said, struggling to sit up. Julia helped him. His hair was askew and his eyes were confused. 'I woke up and something clicked into place. I remember being sent to collect her. It was a building, somewhere in Paris.'

Paris. Christoph had never talked about the war with Julia, and she'd been too polite to ask. Now she wondered what part he'd played.

'There was a date on the Sauerbraten recipe: 1942. Is that when you went to the building to collect her?' she asked.

'It must have been,' Christoph said. 'The Sauerbraten you cooked reminded me of it. It was like a dream, but

I know it happened.' His voice sounded firmer, his eyes bright with the memory.

'Where was this building?'

Christoph rubbed his forehead. 'Let me think. It was near the Arc de Triomphe, one of the streets off there. There's a Paris guidebook on my bookshelves. Let's have a look in there.'

Julia found the guidebook, flicked through and found the Arc de Triomphe, streets spiralling off it like spokes from the centre of a wheel.

Christoph put on his reading glasses and peered at the page. His face paled. 'There' – he pointed – 'that's where I collected her.'

'Avenue Foch,' Julia said. 'What was that?'

Christoph shivered. 'The interrogation headquarters of the SS. I recall that the soldier who handed me the recipe book was wearing their distinctive collar patches.'

Julia rubbed her eyes, trying to keep up. 'Wait a minute, are you saying that the recipe book belonged to the woman you had to collect?' she said. 'The woman who made the crème brûlée?'

'Yes,' Christoph said. 'She used the recipe book to make Sauerbraten for the Kommandant, the same meal you cooked last night.'

Julia considered his words. If Christoph recalled this woman having the recipe book, then that meant . . . suddenly she was wide awake.

'So that means that the woman you remember must be Sylvie?' she said.

Christoph gripped her hand as if the pieces were coming together. 'Yes,' he said. 'Sylvie, that was her name.'

The dedication at the front of the book suggested a loving relationship. But this information, of how they first met, was unsettling. Sylvie and Christoph had been on different sides of the war.

'After you collected her from Avenue Foch, where did you take her?' Julia asked.

Christoph glanced at the map again. 'Down here,' he said, tracing his finger along the route, 'because, yes, look, I remember walking through these gardens, the Tuileries, until we reached . . .' He stopped. 'Here, the Hôtel Le Meurice.'

He let the guidebook drop into his lap as he stared at Julia. 'Of course,' he said. 'The Kommandant sent me to get her from Avenue Foch.'

'Who was the Kommandant?'

The Sauerbraten seemed to have unlocked a trail of memories. Christoph didn't have the full picture but, little by little, with Julia's questions and the map, the fog appeared to be clearing.

'I worked for him in Paris at Le Meurice,' Christoph said. 'Of course, that was it, the Kommandant wanted his son to taste proper German food. That's why he told me to fetch her. He wanted her to make Sauerbraten for his son.'

'So you must have got to know Sylvie at Le Meurice,' Julia said.

'When he tasted Sylvie's food the Kommandant decided to keep her as his cook. But I'm not sure what happened after that . . .' The excitement in Christoph's voice began to fade. 'I can't go any further, Julia. It's all foggy again.' His eyes clouded over, his faced pained with distress. 'What's happening to me, Julia? Why can't I remember it all?'

Julia patted his hand. 'It'll come – you just need to rest. You're still not back to your full strength.'

He lay down, still unsettled. 'Why should this matter, Julia? Why, out of all the things in the war, should I remember Sylvie?' He fussed with the bedcovers, plucking at a fold. 'I feel guilty, but I don't know why.'

'Maybe we should tell Daniel about this too, see what he thinks.'

'No.' Christoph's face was panic-stricken. 'Please, I beg you, he mustn't know any of this, not yet.'

'But he's your son, we can't keep him in the dark.' He might know what had happened to Christoph during the war.

Christoph clenched her hand. 'You have to respect my wishes on this, Julia.'

'All right,' she said, 'I will for now. But you might need to tell him if these recollections continue.'

'Thank you,' Christoph said, relief washing over his face. 'I wish you weren't going so soon. I want you to stay longer.'

Julia had always been the one who'd relied on Christoph's support. Now, he was pressing her to stay.

'Oh, Christoph, I can't,' she said. 'I fly out to Prague the day after tomorrow.'

'But I need to return, to remember it all,' Christoph said, reaching for her. 'Sylvie was important, I can sense it.'

Julia stroked his hand, feeling torn. She had obligations to Sebastian. 'Things seem worse late at night. Let's talk in the morning.'

'Very well,' he murmured, his eyes closing, 'but I know what I need to do.'

She stayed until he was asleep. His words tugged at her heart. He needed her. He wanted her to stay, but Prague loomed on the horizon like a black cloud. She couldn't back out now. But that was another worry. Her hands had still not fully recovered. The stiffness came and went. No matter how hard she practised she couldn't seem to get rid of it. Julia's chest constricted. She had no idea how to solve either Christoph's problems or her own.

The next morning, Julia went into the garden, a cup of coffee in her hand. A breeze wafted her kimono against her legs. God, she was tired. She'd slept badly. After settling Christoph, she'd gone back to her room and written down his recollections in a notebook. It seemed important to keep track of them.

Could she stay longer? It was tempting. She'd never wanted to stop working before. But now . . . maybe a break *would* help her hands. She had to face the awful fact that she still wasn't ready to play. The thought of going on stage in Prague terrified her. Her stomach tightened at the thought of missing another concert. It could damage her career. But so could messing up in front of an audience again.

She wandered over the lawn and down past the hedge, coming unexpectedly across Daniel, a trowel in his hand, pulling out weeds. He wore shorts and a black T-shirt, a sheen of perspiration at the base of his throat. He stood up.

'Oh, hello. What are you doing?' Julia said.

'I thought I'd tidy up the garden a bit and then Papa can sit out when he's feeling better.'

'That's nice of you.'

Daniel smiled. 'I can be nice, you know . . .' He plucked

some honeysuckle from the heap of cuttings. 'You loved the smell of this, remember?'

He passed her the flower. For a brief second, their fingers touched. A jolt ran through her, memories flooding back from before. Sitting in this garden with Daniel six years ago, honeysuckle filling the air, when he asked her to come out for a drink. Did he remember it all as vividly as she did?

Julia turned towards the house to hide the flush on her cheeks. 'I'd better start packing.' She was leaving the next day.

'Wait.' He touched her arm briefly.

Her eyes met his. Time spooled backwards. Daniel trying to make amends for his initial unfriendliness. She swallowed. Would she have done things differently if she'd known how it would all turn out? Guarded her heart, perhaps, instead of letting him in, even a fraction?

'I heard Papa calling out for you in the night,' Daniel said. 'Was everything all right?'

Julia hesitated. She didn't want to lie to him, but Christoph had expressly told her not to mention anything about his Paris memories or the recipe book to Daniel.

'He was disorientated,' she said. 'Malnutrition can do that. The doctor explained that the effects of not eating and drinking properly might linger for a while.'

'I'm worried, Julia. If it is dementia . . .'

'I tried to broach the subject with him the other day, but he was adamant he didn't want the tests.'

Daniel nodded. 'I suppose he's frightened.' He jabbed the trowel into the ground. 'I wish I could talk to him about it.'

99

Julia thought guiltily of the memories Christoph had shared with her last night. Daniel would be furious if he knew they were hiding something from him. Even back in 1996, he'd been upset by her closeness with Christoph.

'It was nice of you to make that meal for him. He enjoyed it.' Daniel held his hand up against the sun. 'I'm curious, though. What made you want to make Sauerbraten? It's such a traditional German recipe. My Oma used to cook it on the farm when I stayed with her.'

'Christoph must have mentioned it,' Julia said quickly, hoping he'd leave it at that. 'I've been trying to think of things that would tempt him to eat.'

Daniel raised his eyebrows. 'But where did you get the recipe from?'

Julia's mind went blank. She should have anticipated his questions, but with everything going on and the lack of sleep, he'd caught her off guard. Then she remembered Hilde's cookery books on the kitchen shelf. 'One of your mum's books.'

Daniel nodded. 'Good thinking.' He glanced at her. 'You always were thoughtful. Perhaps that's why he called out for you and not for me last night.' His eyes betrayed a look of hurt.

'He's probably just got used to me being here the last few days,' she said, hoping to reassure him. 'It'll be you he's calling out for when I leave for Prague.'

'Yes, I suppose so.'

'Daniel, I hope you don't mind me asking, but how long do you think you can stay?' Julia asked. 'What if something else comes up at work?'

Daniel sighed. 'It won't. The company's making cutbacks.

The day after Christoph collapsed, I had a meeting with my boss to try and convince him to keep me on. But I found out yesterday that I've been made redundant.'

So, that was the reason he'd asked her to stay. 'Gosh, that's terrible, I'm sorry, Daniel.'

'I suppose they knew my heart wasn't really in it.'

'Still, it must be a blow.'

Daniel shrugged. 'Not really in the scheme of things. I'm hardly destitute. I'll find another job. I've seen much worse suffering out there in the world. Being made redundant is nothing compared to that.'

'What do you mean?'

'I was an aid worker in Pakistan two years ago when the drought was at its peak. Livestock died in their thousands, crops failed, people were starving. It was heartbreaking to see farms that had been around for generations just disappear.'

This was a different side to him. Julia had imagined his travels were all about having fun. 'It must have been hard to witness, but I guess it puts things into perspective.'

'It does,' Daniel said. 'So I promise, you don't have to worry. I'll look after Papa when you've gone.' Daniel put his hand over his heart, like a soldier swearing an oath, and smiled.

Warmth stole through Julia. That smile. The one that made her heart somersault. She'd never expected to see it again.

'Thank you,' she said.

Christoph had a new lease of life about him. He got dressed and came down to lunch, humming as he sat down at the table. Julia was amazed to see the change in him. He still looked weak, but there was a renewed vitality in his eyes.

'You seem so much better,' Julia said. It was such a relief to see a glimpse of the old Christoph.

'I feel much better,' Christoph said. 'I meant what I said last night. Your cooking has started something in me. I need to go back and find out what happened. I need to uncover my memories of the past. There is too much left hazy and unfocused.'

'Find out what?' Daniel said, coming into the kitchen.

He'd showered and changed, his wet hair slicked back. Julia swallowed and looked away. She took the reheated Sauerbraten out of the microwave and put it on the table.

Christoph glanced at Daniel. 'I'm feeling restored by Julia's cooking, and that's made me want to explore things from my past, while I'm strong enough.'

Daniel sat down. 'Your past?' he said warily. 'I'm not so sure that's a good idea. Let's focus on the present and get you on the mend first, shall we?'

Christoph twisted his glass of water. 'Did I ever tell you about Paris?'

Julia stiffened. Was he about to tell Daniel about the recipe book?

'What about Paris?' Daniel said, his voice tight. The words hung in the air between them, full of a meaning that Julia didn't understand.

'I was stationed there during the war,' Christophe said.

Daniel's shoulders slackened. 'Well, you mentioned it occasionally. You never liked to talk about the war, which I could understand. It wasn't a war to be proud of.'

Christoph nodded. 'No, it wasn't. But that's why I want

to revisit that time again, to understand what really happened, my part in it all. I suppose you could call it a kind of balancing of the books, before it's too late.'

Daniel reached out and squeezed his father's hand. 'There's no need to talk as if there's hardly any time left. You had a scare, that's all. I think the past is best left well alone. For all our sakes.'

'But if he wants to talk about it,' Julia said, 'surely there's no harm.'

Daniel glanced at her. 'The thing is, I spoke to the doctor earlier. She thinks he should have those tests.' He turned to Christoph. 'It might help if we knew what's causing your memory lapses.'

Christoph frowned. 'I'm not having lapses,' he said.

'You just said everything was hazy and unfocused. Please, Papa, let's not ignore this,' Daniel said.

'Well, of course it's hazy, I was in Paris nearly sixty years ago. It's not dementia, it's old age that's bothering me.'

Daniel glanced at Julia and shrugged.

'Perhaps Daniel's right,' Julia said gently. 'You need to find out why it's happening.'

Christoph shook his head and frowned. 'Is this about the house?' he said to Daniel.

'The house?'

'I got your letter. I haven't forgotten that. You want to sell it.'

'I thought you hadn't read it. You never replied.'

Christoph sighed and sat back in his chair. 'Downsizing is the last thing I want to think about now. This house is where I've lived for years, it's where you grew up. I don't want to leave here.'

Daniel leaned forward, elbows on the table. 'I know, and I don't want you to worry about any of that at the moment, but if you're struggling to cope, somewhere smaller might help. I had someone round to look at the house yesterday, just to see. It's gone up in value. You need only release some of the equity, not the whole lot, and . . .'

'Daniel, maybe now's not the time,' Julia said.

'It's all right, Julia,' Christoph said, patting her hand. He turned back to Daniel. 'I did think about your proposition, and I *have* decided to take some money out of the house . . .'

'You have?' Daniel said.

'This health scare has shown me that I need to get things in order.'

Daniel looked at his father closely. 'What do you mean?'

'I'd like to spend some time with you,' Christoph said. He glanced at Julia. 'With both of you.'

Hadn't she explained this last night? 'Christoph, I can't stay much longer. Sebastian is expecting me in Prague tomorrow. He's organized it all.'

Daniel stared at her. 'Are you still with Sebastian?'

'He's my manager, yes.'

Daniel straightened his shoulders. 'I see.'

'It's not up to Sebastian,' Christoph said. 'Your hands need a break. Sometimes going in the opposite direction can bring you back.'

'Maybe,' Julia said. The thought of a break *was* appealing. She was coming round to the idea. She hadn't taken a rest for years. Perhaps it could be a chance to realign things and come back stronger.

'If Julia's staying, then you won't need me,' Daniel said.

'Of course I do,' Christoph said. 'Tell me what this venture is you're planning.'

Daniel pulled at the collar of his T-shirt. 'I'd like to try and buy the old farm,' Daniel said. 'I promised Oma that I would if I ever got the chance. And it's up for sale.'

'Ah,' Christoph said. 'The farm in Effelsberg. Now I understand.'

'Is that where you grew up, Christoph?' Julia asked.

'Yes, Hilde's land adjoined ours, but we had the prettiest house overlooking the fields and woods. Why did we end up selling it, Daniel?'

'Mama said it was because you needed the money from the sale of the house to pay for Oma's nursing-home fees,' Daniel replied. He turned to Julia. 'Papa's mother, my Oma, lived there until she was in her late eighties. I went to stay with her every summer, and I loved being there. I was heartbroken when the farm was sold. I told her that I'd try and get it back. Mama left me some money, but it's tied up in this house.'

Christoph pushed his plate away. 'I'll think about selling this house, but on one condition . . .'

'What's that?' Daniel said.

'That there's no more talk about tests, and you come away with Julia and me. There are places I want to see before I get too old. We can talk about the farm and see if you still want to buy it when we get back.'

Julia looked up startled. *Come away with Julia and me.*

'Really?' Daniel said 'You'll consider it?'

Christoph nodded.

'You never mentioned anything about us all going away,' Julia said.

Christoph rubbed his temples. His white hair was thin in the sunlight. 'I want to go back to Paris. I need to see it all again.'

Daniel looked concerned. 'I'm not sure Paris is such a good idea, Papa.'

'Please, Daniel, I want to find myself before it's too late. I know you're not keen on going there, but I need to remember.'

'That's what you really want, is it?' Daniel asked. 'A trip to Paris so that you can come to terms with the part you played in the war?'

Christoph nodded. Daniel sighed and glanced at Julia. She looked away, conscious that there was more to Christoph's desire to go to Paris than simply that. Clearly, Christoph didn't feel this was the right time to tell his son about the recipe book.

'But you're still weak, Christoph,' she said. 'You need to rest.'

Christoph sat up, a determined look in his eye. Julia caught a glimpse of the young man he'd once been. The young man who Sylvie would have known.

'I can rest at Le Meurice,' he said. 'My mind is made up, I want to go, and I need you both to take me.'

Schweinsohren

250g flour
125ml water
250g butter
a pinch of salt
100g sugar
Cinnamon
Figs
Walnuts

1. Pre-heat the oven to 200°C.
2. Mix the flour, water, butter and salt and knead to make the pastry.
3. Sprinkle with sugar and roll into a rectangle, a quarter of an inch thick.
4. Grind the cinnamon, figs and walnuts together in a pestle and mortar.
5. Spread the mixture over the pastry rectangle.
6. Mark a line along the centre of the length of pastry and roll each of the long sides to the middle.
7. Sprinkle again with sugar.
8. Cut into slices.
9. Place on a baking tray and bake for 15–20 minutes, turning the slices halfway through.
10. Remove from the oven and leave to cool.

15

Julia

July, 2002 – Paris

Julia opened the window. The Tuileries Gardens blossomed in front of her. Sandy yellow paths intersected rows of ornamental trees. The morning sun lit up the stone buildings and grey-leaded roofs of the Louvre.

She'd never stayed anywhere like Le Meurice before. The room was enormous: a double bed and armchairs arranged around a coffee table. She'd hung up her clothes on padded hangers, unpacked her toiletries, and now . . . well, now came the difficult task of phoning Sebastian to tell him she wasn't coming to Prague.

After an agonizing wait, he answered.

'Julia,' he said. 'Please tell me you're at the airport.'

'Actually' – she steeled herself – 'I'm in Paris.'

A sharp intake of breath. 'What?'

'I'm staying at Hotel Le Meurice in Paris. We arrived this afternoon.'

'For heaven's sake, what are you doing there?'

'I've come with Christoph to look after him.' Her voice faltered; please let him understand.

'But all the publicity. Tickets sold.'

Julia bit her lip. 'I know, but the stiffness keeps happening.'

'You said it was improving.'

'I know, I'm sorry, I hoped it would, but my hands need a rest, and Christoph needs my help to get back to his old self. I can't play yet, Sebastian.'

Sebastian sighed. 'I think you're making a mistake. By running away, you'll only make things worse.'

His words echoed the doubts in her head. Her mother's voice too: 'Don't be a quitter. I gave up the piano when you were born, and look where that's left me.' But running counter to this was Christoph's advice that sometimes it was better to stop.

'I'm sorry, Sebastian. I don't want to disappoint you. But there's no way I can go on stage in Prague.'

She heard him shuffling papers on his desk. 'I guess I could get Tanja to do Prague. She's free.'

'Tanja?' She was another one of his clients, an up-and-coming pianist from Estonia who was extremely talented. Julia had a sickening moment of regret.

'She's playing flawlessly right now,' Sebastian said.

'Don't say that.'

'What do you expect me to say? I'll have to spend the next few hours sorting out the cancellation. If Tanja wasn't available, it'd be much worse.'

'I know,' Julia pressed the phone against her ear. 'I'm sorry.'

'If you really think it will help, maybe this rest is worth a try. But you have to promise to come back in time for the next concert in Salzburg.'

'I will,' Julia said, hoping against hope that she wouldn't have to break yet another promise. Sebastian had been understanding, but she feared his patience would run out soon. 'Thank you.'

'What are you doing in Paris anyway?'

'Christoph wanted us to bring him here.'

'Us?' Sebastian's voice became alert. 'Who else is there with you?'

Damn, she hadn't meant to tell him. 'Daniel. It's a chance for Christoph and him to spend some time together.'

'I see. Well, I hope it all turns out the way you hope.'

She put the phone down and buried her head in the pillow. Oh God, was she doing the right thing? It was tempting to snatch up the phone and ring him again. The thought of Tanja taking her place was unbearable. But how could Julia go on stage knowing there might be a repeat of what happened at Wigmore Hall?

She breathed out. It was done. There was no going back. She was free for a while longer. She wouldn't worry about Salzburg yet. Instead, she'd put the piano out of her mind and concentrate on cooking.

Later, she went to see Christoph. He was sitting in an armchair in his hotel room, resting after the journey.

'Did you find a class then?' he said. Christoph had suggested getting some professional help with the next recipe.

'The receptionist has recommended a pâtisserie that does lessons,' Julia said. 'I've taken the plunge and booked a place for this afternoon. We're making palmiers. It's the closest I'll get to making a Schweinsohren in Paris.'

'Marvellous.'

'Will you be okay while I'm gone?'

Christoph's old, battered suitcase stood next to the

wardrobe. He hadn't brought much with him, just some clothes and the guidebook.

'I'll be fine,' he said. 'Hopefully, Daniel will keep me company.'

Julia glanced at the interconnecting door to Daniel's room. 'Have you told him about Sylvie and why we've really come to Paris?'

Christoph sighed. 'No, I think he'll disapprove.'

'Why?'

'He was close to his mother. I doubt he'd want me to try and remember a woman I knew from the war. Besides, he's never liked talking about the past.'

'He'll think we're conspiring.'

'There's nothing to tell him yet, just scraps and fragments,' Christoph said. 'Let's wait and see.'

'Did anything come back to you when we walked into Le Meurice?'

She'd watched Christoph's face as he climbed the front stairs and entered the lobby. He'd looked bewildered at the high ceiling and smartly dressed concierge.

'Yes,' he said. 'But everything's so different now. Back then, there were soldiers going in and out, not tourists. It was a strange place to work. The hotel had been designed for leisure and opulence, and there we were, at the Kommandant's bidding, managing the occupation of France.'

Being here again seemed to have helped Christoph's memory.

'It sounds like Sylvie found it strange too. I found this written by the recipe for Schweinsohren,' Julia said, opening the pages of the book. '*You were with me when I made these, Christoph. Things weren't friendly between us. We were on opposite sides, even then.* Do you remember her making the Schweinsohren?'

'No,' Christoph said. 'I just know she made an impression on me. That day in the Tuileries, when I helped a girl who was being harassed by the soldiers, I wanted to show Sylvie I was a decent person. I don't know why her opinion mattered, but it did.'

He glanced at Julia. 'Speaking of which . . . is everything all right between you and Daniel? You were very quiet on the journey here.'

Julia shrugged. She'd glanced at Daniel as he drove, his strong hands firm on the steering wheel, and experienced such a sense of longing. But there was nothing safe to say to Daniel that didn't remind her of the past.

'It's complicated,' she said.

'I know, but could you try and be friends with him, for my sake?' Christoph said. He looked tired: his eyes were tinged with purple.

Julia had no desire to make this trip any harder for Christoph. She reached over and squeezed his hand. 'Of course.'

Pâtisserie Claude was situated on the quai de l'Hôtel de Ville. The shop window was filled with an array of intricately decorated pastries. Julia's nerves doubled as she opened the door. There was no way she could make anything so exquisite. A young man wearing whites and a chef's hat welcomed her.

'*Bonjour*, you must be Julia,' he said, consulting his list. 'I'm Claude. A pleasure to meet you.'

'I'm afraid I'm a complete beginner,' Julia said, anxious he should know her limitations from the off.

Claude smiled. '*Pas de problème*. That's what I'm here for.' He handed her an apron.

Julia put it round her waist and fastened the straps. At least he seemed friendly. She glanced around. Two older couples, ready and waiting with their aprons already on, smiled encouragingly.

'*Bien sûr*,' Claude said. 'Let's begin with making the puff pastry.'

Julia took a scraper and rolling pin and got to work making the dough as per Claude's step-by-step instructions. Flour puffed all over her apron, making her sneeze. The next task was to wrap the dough around a block of butter. Claude came over to check how things were going.

'*Fais attention*. Your butter is getting too soft,' he said, hovering at her elbow.

'Sorry,' Julia said, flustered. 'What shall I do?'

'Wrap it all in cling film and pop it in the fridge. We're going to take a break anyway.' He winked. 'And relax, you're doing okay.'

Julia tried to relax, but it was difficult. Her perfectionism kept getting in the way. Claude's filling for the palmiers was different to Sylvie's recipe. Instead of joining the rest of the group, she stayed inside to consult the recipe book.

'What's that?' Claude said. He had two cups of coffee and handed one to Julia.

'An old recipe book,' she said. 'I'm making the recipes for a friend who was here during the war. The food helps him to remember those years. At the moment, it's all a bit of a mystery, so we're hoping that being back in Paris and continuing to make the recipes will help put the pieces together.'

'*C'est interessant.* May I see?' He took the recipe book and glanced at it. 'Who is this friend of yours?'

'My piano mentor. He's very old now and struggles to recollect it all,' Julia said. 'I'm not much of a cook. That's why I've come here. I'm desperate to see him at peace with the past.'

Claude's eyes softened. 'Ah, my grand-mère was the same. She struggled to remember her life. By the end, she didn't recognize me.'

Julia sighed. 'The doctor has mentioned the possibility that it might be dementia. I feel like time isn't on our side. I just have to keep going with the recipes and see where it leads us.'

'So that's why you're here today,' Claude said, handing back the book.

'I wanted to make Schweinsohren,' Julia explained. 'They're like palmiers, except, in this recipe, there's a different filling. Cinnamon, figs and walnuts.'

'A delicious combination,' Claude mused. 'I've never tried that before.'

'There are notes in the margins. Look at this one. *If it hadn't been for the Schweinsohren, you wouldn't have walked me through Paris. Do you remember the dried lavender? I wonder if you have it still.*'

'Sounds intriguing,' Claude said. 'It's a German recipe, isn't it?'

Julia glanced at him. 'Yes, my friend, Christoph, he's German. He was here during the occupation.'

'It was a difficult time for France. Even now, for Parisians, discussing the occupation is – how shall I put it? – very complicated.'

Julia nodded. 'Christoph feels a tremendous amount of guilt and shame for the occupation. I wonder if trying to regain his memories is a way of atoning, somehow.'

'Well, he sounds like an interesting man,' Claude said, taking a sip of his coffee. 'Do you know who wrote the recipes?'

'I only know her first name. Sylvie. Christophe can't remember how he ended up with the recipe book, but judging by the dedication, I imagine it was a gift from when he was stationed here in Paris.'

'So, she was French. I do love a mystery.' Claude glanced at his watch. 'Sadly, I need to resume the class. Don't tell the rest of the group, but I'll help you make your filling.'

At the end of the session, Julia had a box of palmiers wrapped in pink ribbon ready to take back to Christoph. Thanks to Claude, they'd turned out quite well.

Claude tucked his business card under the ribbon.

'Christoph is lucky to have you helping him with the recipes. I wish I could have tried something similar with my grand-mère. Where are you both staying?'

'Le Meurice.'

Claude gave a low whistle. '*Très chic*,' he said. 'I worked there for a while. The head chef, Pierre Dupont, was *my* mentor. With your permission, I'll let him know the project you're working on. His father worked at Le Meurice during the war. Pierre might be interested in what you're doing.'

'Thank you,' Julia said. 'You've been so kind. I really am a hopeless cook.'

'Everyone has to start somewhere. If I can do anything else, let me know. You have my number.'

Julia smiled gratefully. 'Thank you. You've been so kind.'

The cooking session had lifted her spirits. And Claude's friendliness had made her feel ready to tackle the rest of this trip and hopefully discover more about Sylvie. She set off down the street, humming to herself. Maybe this break would be good for more than just her hands.

There was no sign of Christoph in the hotel lounge. They'd arranged to meet at six. It was nearly half past now. Panic gripped Julia. She shouldn't have left him for so long. Then she saw Daniel reading a book, a bottle of beer on the table.

'Where's Christoph? Is he all right?' she said.

Daniel closed his book. 'Don't worry. I took him for a walk and that wore him out. He's resting upstairs.'

Julia let out a deep breath and sat down. 'Thank God. I thought something had happened.'

'I *can* look after my own father, you know.' Daniel's tone was a touch defensive.

Julia's chest tensed. She hadn't meant it as a criticism. 'I was worried, that's all.'

Daniel's shoulders relaxed. 'Sorry,' he said. 'I just feel bad that I wasn't there when he collapsed. You handled it amazingly. I'm not sure I'd be so calm.'

'How is he?'

Daniel leaned back in the chair. 'I was looking forward to spending some time with him, but he seemed distracted. I'd hoped to talk to him about the farm, and his memories of growing up there. I thought it might be something we had in common, as I spent so much time there as a child, but he wasn't really listening. He kept talking about lavender. How he needed to find some.'

Lavender. That's what Sylvie had referred to in the notes by the recipe. 'Maybe he can't focus on the farm right now.'

'I know, but I thought that's what this trip was about, a chance to talk.'

Julia twisted the pink ribbon around her finger. The gap between Christoph and Daniel never seemed to lessen.

'I'm sure that will come. You just need to be patient. He's still recovering.'

'Yeah, he was really tired when we got back.' He glanced at the box Julia was holding. 'What's in there?'

'Oh, I made palmiers. I thought Christoph might like them. You can try one if you like.'

Daniel shook his head. 'No thanks, they don't really go with beer, but I'm sure they're lovely.' He glanced at Julia. 'So, why are you doing all this cooking? For someone who was so averse to the kitchen, you're spending a lot of time on it.'

Julia shifted uncomfortably on the chair. The recipe book was in her bag, like a secret incendiary device. The longer they went on *not* telling Daniel, the more she dreaded what his reaction might be. But at least she could tell him the other reason why she was cooking.

'It's partly to do with the piano,' she said. 'Before I came to Bonn, I played in a concert in London and messed up spectacularly. I'm hoping the distraction of cooking will help and give me something else to focus on other than the piano.'

Daniel put his beer down. 'You messed up?' he said, his face filled with concern. 'What happened?'

Julia frowned. It was hard to relive it again. 'My hands seized up. In front of everyone, I just got up and ran off the stage.'

'Do you know what caused it? Can anything be done?'

Julia flexed her fingers and shrugged. 'It's not physical – I had it all checked out. My sister thinks I've been overdoing it since Mum died.'

'Your mum died? I didn't know that,' Daniel said quietly. 'I'm so sorry.'

'It hasn't been easy,' Julia admitted. 'But then, you know how it feels. You lost your mum not long ago too.'

'It's tough,' Daniel said, glancing down. 'I miss her.'

'Were you with her when she died?'

Daniel nodded. 'I spent days sleeping on a chair by her bedside. She didn't give up without a fight. It was painful to witness.'

Julia sighed. 'I wasn't even there when Mum died. I was on tour. I still feel terrible about it. The piano was always a refuge, but then this thing with my hands started happening. Christoph thinks I've pushed myself too hard.' She smiled ruefully. 'Cooking is a way of taking the pressure off.'

'And is it helping?' Daniel asked, leaning forward.

'I don't know, I'm staying away from the piano for now,' Julia said. 'In some ways, it's quite nice to forget about playing for a while.'

Daniel raised his eyebrows. 'I never thought I'd hear you say that. The piano was everything to you, over and above anything else.'

His eyes fixed on hers. The air seemed to still. Julia's mind flicked back to 1996. Her dedication to the piano had been the nub of all their arguments.

'Well, things change,' she said, glancing down at the table.

'It was electrifying to hear you play. I really hope you can sort it out.'

The seriousness of his voice unnerved her. 'Well, this

time, I can't blame anyone but myself for messing up on stage,' she said, attempting to deflect his solemnity with humour. 'There was no drunken man snogging his ex-girlfriend in the front row.'

It was supposed to be a joke about the recital he'd ruined back in 1996, but it came out all wrong. That was the problem with being around Daniel. The pain of what had happened between them was never far away.

Daniel's face blanched. 'Julia, I'm so sorry. Every time I remember that night, I'm filled with shame. I behaved appallingly.'

'I don't know why I said that,' she said hurriedly. 'I didn't mean to bring it up. Just forget it, okay?'

'No, you're right to mention it,' Daniel said. 'It was awful. I'd had way too much to drink, and I just wasn't thinking straight. I wish I could rewind time and do it all differently. It wasn't anything personal against you.'

Julia frowned. That wasn't how she remembered it. She didn't want to start an argument, but she wasn't going to let Daniel get away with brushing off the incident. The pain of it was still raw, even after all these years.

She raised a questioning eyebrow as she replied. 'You deliberately stared at me after you'd kissed her. It felt personal.'

Daniel reddened. He straightened his back. 'What about that night at the beer garden when you spent all night talking with Hans?'

'Daniel, you were with Kat. I had no one else to talk to – it was hardly anything romantic. You can't compare the two situations.'

He pressed his palms against the table. 'Whenever we got closer, you edged away again.'

'It wasn't like that,' she protested.

'Yes, it was. After that night when you made the fondue, you went all distant. You like to blame the whole thing on me disrupting your recital by kissing Kat. But the fact is, you used the piano as an excuse to push me away.'

Heat flared in Julia's chest. It hadn't been like that at all. He was remembering it all wrong.

'No, I already had my doubts that time I saw you coming out of Christoph's music room . . .' She stopped just in time. He'd been counting the money in his hand. He'd shoved it in his back pocket when he caught sight of her on the stairs.

'Saw me what?' His eyes searched her face.

She couldn't face going over it. She choked back the emotion and cleared her throat. 'Nothing. Forget it. Now isn't the time.'

He shook his head. 'That's what I mean. It's never the right time with you.'

Julia swallowed, blinking back tears. She didn't know what to say. It was impossible to try and make him understand. She took a deep breath. 'Let's just leave it, Daniel. I'm thinking of Christoph. Maybe you should too.' She knew the words would upset him, but it was the only way to end the conversation and veer away from the unspoken truth which could hurt them both.

16

Christoph

July, 1942 – Paris

The trees by the Seine swayed in the light breeze. Somehow, summer had arrived, despite the war. The trees would be in full leaf at home too, on the avenue that linked his family's farm with Hilde's. Lotte would be out in the fields with their mother. Even though she couldn't speak, Christoph and his mother had grown to understand her noises and gestures. Summertime always filled her with delight.

Christoph undid the top button of his shirt; the heat was stifling. He'd walked further than usual so that he could get some new sheet music for Otto from a shop in the rue de l'Université. Now, with it rolled up under his arm, he headed towards the Seine.

Sylvie's words still troubled him. *Nothing is worse than active ignorance.* It echoed the inner critic inside of him: the one who failed, every day, to act. Worse still had been the look of contempt on her face. For reasons he couldn't fathom, Christoph wanted her to think well of him.

As he neared the river, where couples were strolling and fishermen cast out lines into the water, he heard strange wailing noises fill the air.

'What's going on?' Christoph asked one of the fishermen.

'It's the Jews in the velodrome,' the man said. 'It's been going on for two days now.'

Le Vel' d'Hiv. Christoph hadn't realized he was so close. He'd heard the Kommandant discussing the fiasco of the French round-ups: how the French were finally making good on their promise to deliver up the Jews by herding thousands of them into the velodrome before transportation out of Paris. Christoph had blanched inwardly when he'd heard the news. Now, drifting on the light breeze, that gut-wrenching sound he could hear was the suffering of everyone trapped inside.

It was unbearable. Christoph wanted to stop his ears, to drown out the noise of all those voices, all that pain. He turned around, quickening his pace, walking towards the Eiffel Tower, away from the sound, as fast as he could.

But the wails rang in his ears; he couldn't escape them. He shivered despite the heat, crossing the Tuileries, where people sat on benches and pigeons pecked at the gravel as if nothing untoward was happening on this bright July day.

Without warning, Christoph's stomach heaved. He vomited on the grass. An old woman walking past looked at him with disgust. He wiped his mouth. His work for the Kommandant researching farms in Normandy had nothing to do with what was happening in Le Vel' d'Hiv. But it was part of the same chain; mere links separated him from such atrocities. He felt the weight of it, choking him.

Christoph tried to compose himself. He was late for the piano lesson. He knocked on the door of the Kommandant's apartment, the taste of bile still in his throat.

Frau Schaumberg opened it, her face streaked with tears, Otto by her side.

'Is everything all right?' Christoph said.

'*Nein, nichts ist in Ordnung,*' Frau Schaumberg said. She wiped her eyes with a lace handkerchief. 'The Kommandant wants Otto to learn how to make Schweinsohren. I can't go down to the kitchens with all the staff staring at me, but the Kommandant insists.'

Otto tugged Christoph's jacket. 'Papa says they're delicious and that I can eat as many as I like.'

Frau Schaumberg pulled at her handkerchief. 'It's too humiliating.'

The cries from Le Vel' d'Hiv still echoed in Christoph's mind. He struggled to feel sorry for Frau Schaumberg and her petty worries in the light of what he'd heard that morning. But he couldn't show this. Besides, he had some sympathy for her subservience to the Kommandant's commands.

'But I want to go,' Otto said, stamping his foot.

Frau Schaumberg turned to Christoph. 'Would you mind taking him, Herr Leutnant, instead of doing the piano lesson?'

Christoph hesitated. Sylvie would be there. He wasn't sure if he wanted to see her again. Especially not now, when he felt so low. It would only remind him how hateful his position was here. But he couldn't refuse a request from the Kommandant's wife.

The kitchen hummed with heat and activity. Saucepans steamed. M. Dupont was overseeing two assistant chefs who were plucking some chickens. He talked loudly, above the noise of the boiling pans. It contrasted with the cold efficiency of the hotel atrium. Christoph inhaled the aroma of fried onion. Strange, how life went on.

'Apologies for interrupting,' Christoph said. 'The Kommandant wants someone to teach Otto how to make Schweinsohren.'

Sylvie came out of the larder, her arms full of potatoes.

M. Dupont nodded. 'She'll do it. No doubt she'll have that Schwein thing in her book.'

That was the last thing Christoph wanted. 'No, don't worry, we'll come back another time.'

But Otto was crossing the kitchen to Sylvie, babbling in German. The other chefs smiled, amused. Christoph followed, feeling foolish.

'I'm sorry,' he said. 'I didn't want to bother anyone, but the Kommandant's wife insisted.' This was as awkward as he'd feared.

'It's fine,' Sylvie said, giving him a brief smile. 'I know how to make them. They're like palmiers.'

She turned to Otto. 'Schweinsohren?' she said. '*Tu et moi?*' She tapped his nose gently and smiled.

Otto smiled back, relieved. '*Ja, bitte,*' he said.

Sylvie fetched her recipe book and looked up the ingredients, then they mixed them into a dough. Christoph stood back and watched them roll the pastry flat and spread the filling on top, enchanted by her patience. Sylvie showed Otto how to roll the pastry into the centre from each of the long sides, while the hustle and bustle of lunch preparations went on around them.

It was soothing to observe her at work. Christoph felt his heart slow and the knots in his stomach loosen a little.

The sound of her voice drowned out the cries he'd heard from Le Vel' d'Hiv, for now at least. Her gentleness to Otto reminded him that kindness still existed.

When the pastries were in the oven, Sylvie gave Otto a glass of water and some left-over pastry to play with.

'How long will they take?' Christoph asked, hoping to engage her in conversation.

Sylvie took the bowl and spoons to the sink and turned on the tap. '*Quinze minutes*,' she said. 'I'll make sure they don't burn.'

'You're good with him,' Christoph said.

'He's just a child.'

She scrubbed the bowl with a wire brush. Suds dripped from her hands. The scar on her hand was fading.

'Have you settled in at Le Meurice?' Christoph asked.

Sylvie shrugged. 'As well as can be expected. I have a room with a view of Paris, but I'm not allowed to leave the hotel by myself.'

'*Pardon*, I didn't think . . .' He was an idiot. The question had been clumsy, given the circumstances. Sylvie wasn't here by choice but by the Kommandant's orders.

'It's okay, it's not your fault.' She yanked the plug and the water gurgled away.

'Ah, here you all are,' the Kommandant said, striding through the kitchen.

Christoph saluted, cursing the Kommandant's arrival. He'd wanted to say more to Sylvie, to undo his blunder, but the chance had gone.

'You've been busy.' The Kommandant glanced at Sylvie. 'The smell of cinnamon reminds me of Christmas back home. I presume this is from your recipe book?'

'Yes, Herr Kommandant. We used preserved figs from the head chef's uncle's orchard for the filling. They'll be ready soon.'

'Can I go and tell Mama how I made it?' Otto asked. The Kommandant ruffled his son's hair and nodded. Otto gave a quick wave to Sylvie and hurried out.

The Kommandant folded his arms. 'So, you really are a chef with mixed German and French heritage. A lucky find here in Paris.'

Christoph recognized that tone of voice – warm, playful, knowing – he'd heard the Kommandant use it on other women. He watched anxiously.

'Thank you, Herr Kommandant . . .' Sylvie hesitated, twisting her hands. 'I wonder . . .'

Intrigued, the Kommandant stepped closer. He *was* interested in her. Christoph could tell by the way he thrust his shoulders back.

'What do you wonder, my dear?' the Kommandant said, his voice soothing.

'If it's at all possible, I'd be very grateful if I could fetch my belongings. The boarding house where I was staying isn't far from here.'

'Indeed,' the Kommandant said. 'What is it that you need?'

'A few clothes and keepsakes. I have a sprig of dried lavender that hangs on my bed. The smell reminds me of my grandmother's garden. Just like the cinnamon reminds you of home.'

Christoph held his breath. She was too bold, but the Kommandant apparently liked her audacity. Had there been something almost flirtatious in her words? The Kommandant seemed to think so.

'Ah, lavender,' he said. 'Its scent is more conducive to sleep if tucked under the pillow. It depends on how deeply one wishes to sleep.' His eyes ran down the length of her body.

Out of nowhere, a ball of fury threatened to break loose in Christoph. He clenched his fists, forcing himself to calm down. He'd seen the Kommandant flirt with dozens of women. Why should he care this time?

'Very well then,' the Kommandant continued, 'as you have argued your case so eloquently, you can visit your old boarding house. Leutnant Baumann will escort you after breakfast tomorrow morning.'

After he left the kitchen, Christoph collected a letter from Hilde from the reception desk. Christoph's heart sank at the sight of her handwriting. He took it up to his room to read.

Lieber Christoph, she wrote

> *My father has paid for the repairs to your mother's house. She was most grateful. We'll all be one big family when you finally get home.*
>
> *It's a pity we couldn't get married during your last leave. I know it was short, but we could have managed it. Your desire to wait, to give me a 'proper wedding', has been admired by everyone in the village except me!*
>
> *Your sister misses you. When I have time, I go and visit her, but it's impossible to get any sense out of her.*
>
> *Write soon and tell me how much you miss me.*

Christoph looked out over the rooftops of Paris. Hilde's words about his sister made him uneasy. They were too much like the taunting Lotte had received at school but couched in a jolly tone. He didn't know how he could counter it. The fate of his family's farm and Lotte were now dependent upon the generosity of Hilde's father and his friends in the party.

He picked up the pen to reply but heard a noise. It came from above. Barely a sound, really. More like a door softly closing. Christoph listened again, but there was nothing.

The hotel was set out on six floors. Above the grand reception rooms and offices lay the state bedrooms and the Kommandant's apartment. Higher still were three floors of bedrooms for the staff, with the women on the lower of these floors and the men in the two floors above. Christoph's room was on the men's floor that lay almost at the top of the building and above that were storerooms in the eaves. The noise must have come from the storerooms. Maybe it was bats.

Christoph had never been in there, but sometimes he went to the very top of the building, to the old rooftop garden and glasshouse restaurant. They had been abandoned since the start of the war for fear that lights would attract the Allied bombers. Sometimes Christoph went up there to play the restaurant piano in the moonlight, preferring to play unnoticed rather than in the Kommandant's apartment. The rooftop piano was battered and a little off key from the damp, but Christoph enjoyed those moments when he felt alone.

Now, he tossed the pen aside impatiently. He didn't know what to write. He could never hurt Hilde. He'd made a promise. If he went back on it, he'd only despise himself more.

17

Lisette

July, 1942 – Paris

Leutnant Baumann waited in the lobby. Lisette had hoped to go to the boarding house alone and somehow get word to Seraphin of what had happened. Instead, she was obliged to have an escort. The lieutenant seemed to crave some acknowledgement of his humanity. She refused to give in to such a need. A man like Leutnant Baumann had fired the bomb that had sunk Johnny's boat. She lifted her chin and walked downstairs; he would get no empathy from her.

Christoph crossed the rue de Rivoli and into the Tuileries. Lisette walked next to him in silence, not questioning the diversion. She inhaled sweet, scented air under the shade of the chestnut trees.

At this time of day, before the midday sun had risen, women were out with their children, sitting wearily on iron chairs around the pond, watching them play in the gravel. The women's faces were pinched with worry. One woman glanced up at Lisette, scowling when she saw her walking next to a German soldier. Lisette pursed her lips, wishing she was alone.

Just before they went through the gate and out on to the street, Leutnant Baumann stopped.

'I wanted to say earlier that I understand how trapped you must feel,' he said.

His eyes regarded her earnestly. Was he serious? He had no idea how trapped she was here.

'Thank you,' she said, trying to keep her voice even, 'but I'm not sure you can truly understand.'

'Because I'm the enemy?' he said.

'I didn't say that.' She glanced around the gardens. They must look odd standing here, and she didn't want to attract any further attention. 'Let's just keep walking.'

'You didn't need to say it. I know I'm one of thousands of men who belong to the German army and, collectively, we *are* the enemy of France. I was in the Hitler Youth too, just like everyone else. I had to swear an oath of allegiance to Hitler,' he said, his face flushed. 'But I did it out of necessity. To protect my family. None of this is my choice. I was conscripted. We shouldn't be here, I don't want to be here, and after what I've seen and heard, I don't believe in what my country is doing.'

His eyes were moist with tears. His face white with anguish. Lisette floundered. Surely he knew that such a speech, if overheard, could have him court-martialled. She needed to calm him down and get to the boarding house. People were staring. He looked so wretched it was unbearable.

'Herr Leutnant, I'm sorry if what I said offended you.'

'You didn't offend me,' he said, breathing out a sigh. 'It's me who has offended you. I've stood by, so many times. Even yesterday, when I heard the suffering in Le Vel' d'Hiv, I walked in the other direction. I don't know how to fight against it. Forgive me.'

Lisette bit her lip. Christoph's compassion unnerved her, but it was dangerous.

'Please,' she said, trying to soothe him, 'don't concern yourself. It's not your fault. You're just a soldier following orders.'

'It's not that simple,' Christoph said. 'I'm trapped here too. My sister, Lotte, is what the Nazis call a "degenerate". She doesn't fit the mould of a perfect, German fräulein. If I deserted, they would punish her, and my mother.'

Lisette wished he would stop. With every word he uttered, her certainty faltered. She didn't want to hear all this. It made things harder. Black and white, good and bad. That's what she needed things to be.

'Herr Leutnant, I don't want either of us to get in trouble for being out too long,' she said. 'Can we please just get my belongings?'

It had been a mistake to talk to him. He wasn't like the others, and that raised questions in her mind, questions that didn't belong in a war. He *was* the enemy, and nothing would change that.

Christoph's face closed over; his emotion suppressed. 'Of course.'

Lisette asked Leutnant Baumann to wait outside the boarding house while she went up to her room. She'd leave a note for Seraphin; he must be wondering where she was by now. She unlocked the door and stared in shock. The room was in disarray: mattress slashed, drawers flung out of the chest, floorboards prised up.

She had barely registered the situation when someone grabbed her arm.

'Did you give names?' It was Seraphin. His voice possessed a harshness she'd never heard before. He pressed her up against the wall.

The weight of him squashed her ribcage, his hands circled her neck. What the hell was he doing? She tried to push him off.

'Nobody walks out of Avenue Foch and into a job at Le Meurice,' he hissed. 'Only a traitor.' His hand squeezed, cutting off the air to her lungs.

'I gave them nothing,' Lisette said, gasping for breath. 'How could you think that?'

Seraphin's hold tightened. 'Hélène was executed. Did you know that?'

'No.' Nausea rose in her throat.

'Then why did they release you?' His piercing blue eyes searched her face.

'Apparently my crème brûlée was the talk of the town,' she said.

His grip slackened. 'What?'

Lisette rubbed her neck. 'They sent the Kommandant's right-hand man, Leutnant Baumann, to collect me from Avenue Foch and take me to Le Meurice. They've put me to work as a chef in the kitchens. Leutnant Baumann has been instructed to keep an eye on me, but I can't work him out.'

'What do you mean?'

'On the way here, he got very emotional and told me that he doesn't believe in what Germany is doing. It's like he wants my sympathy. It's unnerving.'

Seraphin considered her words. 'Interesting. The Kommandant's a very important man in Paris. The intelligence that passes through Le Meurice would be extremely valuable.'

'I know,' Lisette said. 'I've already considered that.'

Seraphin pulled over a chair. 'Here, sit down. I'm sorry about the rough treatment. But I couldn't take any risks. I've been waiting here for you to come back.'

'You really thought I'd turn traitor?' Lisette said.

'No, of course not, I know how much you hate the Germans, but I had to check. I spoke to my contacts in London yesterday. We agreed that if you were still on our side, then we must continue to make the most of you. This is too good a chance to miss.'

'What are my orders?' Lisette said.

'Ah,' Seraphin smiled, 'remember what I said about exploiting the cracks in German hearts. I know that you excelled at clandestine missions in your training. That's what this will be.'

'You mean spying?' Lisette said. 'I thought the SIS took care of that.'

'The Secret Intelligence Service has got involved, given your circumstances. For now, they want you to stay put at Le Meurice, gather as much information as you can, and use any means necessary to get it.' He smiled. 'You know, I happen to think very highly of you and your skills.'

'I won't shirk my duty.'

He patted her hand. 'Good. This intelligence will be of the highest importance. What you've told me about Leutnant Bauman presents you with the perfect opportunity. But it will take all your nerve to carry it out.'

Lisette looked at him closely. 'There's no limit to my nerve.'

'In that case, this is what you must do. You need to cultivate this Leutnant Baumann's affection. Be courteous, seductive and bleed him of secrets.'

Lisette swallowed. 'I'm not sure I'm capable of that.'

'Think of all the people you'll be helping,' Seraphin said. 'I know it will be difficult, but this is what you're trained for: to use whatever means you have at your disposal to disrupt the Nazis.'

Lisette nodded. He was right. 'I understand,' she said, thinking of the lieutenant's words in the Tuileries, how he had exposed his true feelings to her. 'Sabotage isn't just blowing things up. It's possible to sabotage a man's heart too.'

'Exactly,' Seraphin said.

This was the mission of a lifetime, but she wondered how she could pretend to like Leutnant Baumann, given how much she hated the country he was from. The image of Johnny rose up in her mind, the thought of how much he'd loved her. Perhaps this was the best way to punish the Germans: by putting her hatred aside and finding her way into the secret cracks in Lieutenant Baumann's heart.

Potage Fontanges

75g soft unsalted butter
1 onion, chopped
2 leeks, chopped
225g sorrel, chopped
1 iceberg lettuce, chopped
3 sprigs chervil, chopped
450g split peas, soaked
2 medium-sized potatoes, chopped
1.5 litres of rich stock
Salt and pepper
2 egg yolks
250ml crème fraîche
8 bread rolls

1. Cook the onion, leeks, sorrel, lettuce and chervil in 50g of the butter on a low heat.
2. Add the peas, potatoes and stock.
3. Season with salt and pepper and bring to the boil.
4. Cover and simmer for two hours, stirring regularly.
5. Beat the rest of the butter into a smooth cream and add the egg yolks and crème fraîche or double cream.

6. Pour the mixture into a tureen and add the soup.
7. Serve with freshly baked rolls.

18

Julia

July, 2002 – Paris

Julia slept badly. The argument with Daniel went round and round in her head and she awoke in her room at Le Meurice feeling tired.

She opened the window and breathed in the cool morning air. She leaned on the windowsill, remembering that night when she and Daniel had broken into the open-air swimming pool in Bonn. 'I'll go in if you do,' he'd said. The water had been cold, but the first touch of his skin was warm. He'd swum closer and closer until there was almost no water between them. Then Kat and the others had turned up, and Daniel had drifted away.

Now, Julia shivered and closed the window. Her relationship with Daniel was littered with broken moments like these. Despite wanting to do her best for Christoph, Julia feared there was no way to mend the cracks between her and Daniel.

The sumptuous breakfast room at Le Meurice was flooded with light and decorated with ornate gilded mirrors and low-hung chandeliers. Soothing music played. Wealthy tourists discussed the coming day's excursions, and business travellers ate alone and read the newspapers. Julia ordered a black coffee and eggs. Christoph wanted only toast.

'I didn't sleep well,' he said. 'I was remembering the awful things I witnessed in Paris.'

Julia got out her notebook ready to jot down his recollections. 'What kind of things?'

'Le Vel' d'Hiv, as we called it,' he said, his voice heavy. 'The French police, on the orders of the Germans, used the velodrome by the river to round up Jews, and one day, during that terrible week, I was nearby. I'd never heard such terrible cries of human suffering.'

Julia frowned. 'I remember learning about that in history. Thousands were held in that sweltering place, then sent by train to be murdered in concentration camps. It's sickening.'

'It is,' Christoph said, his eyes filled with pain. 'While I was in Paris, getting to know Sylvie, millions of Jews were being sent to their deaths. The shame of that will haunt me for ever.'

'What else do you remember?' she asked, pouring coffee from the heavy silver pot. It was interesting to learn about this part of Christoph's life. She'd only known him as her piano mentor. She tried to imagine him when he was young, an enemy soldier in Paris, with all the atrocities going on around him, but it was hard to equate this with the mild-mannered old man in front of her.

'More than I expected,' Christoph said. 'Maybe it's because we're here, in Paris, or because of the delicious Schweinsohren you made. I remember that after Sylvie made the Schweinsohren for Otto I escorted her back to her boarding house to get her things.' He sighed. 'I made such a fool of myself trying to convince her I knew that it was wrong, the German occupation of Paris.'

Julia wondered what Sylvie had made of this. Christoph had obviously been sensitive about his position in Paris, but it wouldn't have detracted from the fact that he was a German soldier, working for the Kommandant in a city where he didn't belong.

A tall man in whites came over to the table. He was grey-haired with friendly crinkles around his eyes.

'*Pardon*,' he said, smiling broadly. 'I hope you don't mind me interrupting. Claude rang me yesterday. I'm Pierre Dupont. Head chef at Le Meurice.'

'Ah yes, Claude mentioned you,' Julia said. 'This is Christoph.'

'The man who is reliving his past,' Pierre said. 'My father was head chef here during the war. You might remember him. Jean Dupont.'

Christoph looked perplexed.

'Jean.' His gaze drifted off into the distance. 'I don't think I do. I'm sorry.'

'It was so long ago,' Julia said.

Pierre nodded. 'Of course. You might not recall him, but my father always spoke highly of you. He claimed you were the only decent German he'd met during the war.'

Christoph's eyes widened. 'Really? He said that. How extraordinary. I wonder what I did to deserve that accolade.'

Pierre shrugged. '*Lieutenant Baumann*, he'd say, *a special man*. If I asked why, he'd tell me that keeping secrets had kept him alive during the war and he wasn't about to start blabbing now. Not even to his own son.' He frowned. 'He was interrogated and imprisoned, you see.

139

He was accused of some plot here at the hotel. It scarred him for life.'

Christoph laid down his napkin. 'Did your father ever mention a woman called Sylvie? She was a chef in his kitchen.'

'Sylvie?' He thought for a moment. 'I'm afraid not. She's the woman who wrote the recipe book, is that right? That's what Claude told me. Such a fascinating story.'

'She was so sad that day,' Christoph said.

'Which day?' Julia said.

'When we walked back from the boarding house. I carried a box of her things. She was like a painting in the rain. All the colours had run out of her.'

Pierre sighed. 'That is what it meant to be French and suffer the occupation,' he said. 'My father described how the life went out of the city.'

'I felt so helpless,' Christoph said. 'I wanted to make her smile.'

'Well, you must have done something right,' Julia said. She took the recipe book out of her bag. 'Look, the next recipe is potage fontanges. She writes: *How strange to talk about future dreams in the middle of a war, and to C, of all people. The notes make the music. The vegetables make this soup. Both conjure memories.*'

'Potage fontanges was my father's recipe,' Pierre said with a delighted smile. 'She must have learned it from him. I know it off by heart. I'll teach you it,' he said to Julia. 'I insist.'

'That would be marvellous, thank you,' she said.

'But you must source the ingredients yourself,' Pierre

said. 'My father always maintained that the vegetables must be chosen by the cook.'

'Oh,' Julia said, 'of course. I'll find a supermarket and get everything we need.'

Pierre frowned and wagged his finger in mock consternation. '*Non*,' he said. 'You need to visit Marché Maubert by boulevard Saint-Germain. They sell fresh vegetables from all the best farms around Paris.' He smiled at Christoph. 'Now, I must get back to the kitchens. It's been a pleasure to meet you both.'

Julia put the recipe book back in her bag. This was incredible. She'd be cooking in the same kitchen where Sylvie had worked. She looked up and saw Daniel striding over.

'Who was that?' Daniel said to Christoph.

'The head chef. He's going to teach Julia an old recipe for vegetable soup,' Christoph said.

'How come?'

'It seems Julia has an admirer at the pâtisserie, and he got in touch with Pierre,' Christoph said.

'An admirer?' Daniel glanced at Julia.

'Claude was just being kind, that's all,' she said, her cheeks reddening.

Daniel opened the menu. 'I see.' He glanced at Julia, and then Christoph. 'So, is this cookery lesson from the head chef all part of helping to heal Julia's hands?'

Julia looked down at her plate, preferring to let Christoph answer.

'Of course, and hopefully it's having a good effect,' he said.

'I'm just puzzled. Where are all these recipes coming from? There doesn't seem to be any plan or pattern to what Julia makes.' Daniel eyed them both. 'Unless there's something I'm missing.'

Julia felt his stare on her. She brushed some crumbs off the tablecloth. 'There's no real plan,' she said, trying to keep her voice light.

'So it's just a lucky coincidence that the head chef of Le Meurice is so willing to help?' Daniel said, his brow creased.

Julia and Christoph exchanged a furtive glance. Julia felt caught in the middle. She couldn't say anything. This was Christoph's secret to tell, not hers.

'I don't know what you mean,' Christoph said firmly. 'But if you want to help, Julia needs to buy some ingredients from Marché Maubert, and you'd be the ideal person to go with her.'

Julia's stomach contracted. 'No, it's fine, I'm sure I can find it.'

She'd much rather go alone. The thought of being in Daniel's company without Christoph there as a buffer was unthinkable. But Christoph seemed intent on forcing them together.

'You might find it useful, Daniel. If you're serious about farming, it'll give you a feel for what happens at the point of sale. Unless, of course, you're not that serious about farming after all . . .'

'You know I'm serious,' Daniel said. 'I've worked at farms in every country I've been to.'

'All the more reason to go and help Julia then.' Christoph folded his napkin.

Father and son stared at each other, neither willing to back down.

Daniel sighed. 'Fine, I'll take her.'

It took a ridiculous amount of time to decide what to wear to the market. Julia tried on many different outfits. In the end, she opted for jeans and a white shirt. Her nerves were worse than before she went on stage. Why was she so petrified of being alone with Daniel? She stared at her reflection in the mirror. *Get a grip. It's only Daniel.*

He was waiting by the hotel reception desk, his expression unreadable.

'You don't have to come,' she said.

He raised his eyebrows. 'Try telling that to my father. He seems to want to get rid of me.'

'No, he doesn't. I'll be fine on my own, honestly.' That wasn't quite true, but she'd do her best. How hard could it be to pick out vegetables?

'I'm sure we can be civil to each other for a couple of hours,' Daniel said with a wry smile.

Julia met his eyes and swallowed. She wasn't so sure. But if he could be sensible about it, then so could she.

The little square was full of stalls laid out in rows, with striped awnings and sides. Vendors called out their wares in sing-song voices, and customers haggled over prices. Several women had gathered by one of the charcuterie stalls and were discussing the merits of the produce on offer, the occasional cackle of laughter rising into the air.

'Do you have a list?' Daniel said.

'Yes, it's in here somewhere.' She fished it out of her

bag. The sooner they got the shopping done, the sooner they could go back to the hotel. 'I suppose it's just a case of finding the vegetables.'

He smiled at her, apparently amused by what she'd said. 'It's not that simple. You need to consider the smell, the texture, how long ago it was picked, what sort of soil it was grown in.'

'And you're the expert on this?' She squinted in the sunshine.

'Actually, yes I am.'

To Julia's surprise, it turned out that Daniel really did know what he was doing. He took the list and systematically made his way around the market.

Julia watched as he picked up vegetables, held them, smelled them, and defied the haughty gaze of the stall-holders to return them if they weren't good enough. He was knowledgeable about the best type of onions and which potatoes would hold their firmness in a soup. He even managed to find chervil and sorrel – two items that she had no idea how to identify. Soon, all the ingredients had been gathered.

'Let me get you a coffee to say thank you,' Julia said impulsively. 'I'd never have managed that without your help.'

She found a table outside a café and bought them each a coffee and pain au chocolat. The warm pastry flaked over her jeans as she bit into it. She brushed it off and glanced at Daniel, suddenly curious.

'Where did you learn all that?' she asked, gesturing to the market.

Daniel stretched out his legs under the table. 'All over the place. Big prairie farms in America, a dairy farm in

Italy, fruit farms just outside Bonn, and one year, harvesting olives in Greece. I used to help sell the produce too.'

'But you grew up in a city. How come you have this passion for farming?

Daniel sighed. 'Oma's farm. The first time I went, I didn't want to go. I must have been six or seven years old. Things were very tense at home between Mama and Papa. Maybe they wanted me out of the way, or perhaps I was too much of a handful for the whole summer holidays. Anyway, Papa dropped me off and stayed the night before heading back to Bonn, and I was left with Oma.'

'What was she like?'

Daniel smiled, 'Sharp as a pin, despite her age, and physically fit from being outdoors. She didn't dwell on my homesickness. She simply took me out to the vegetable garden and told me about each plant, and then marched me out into the fields to learn about the cows. Before long, I was filling up the watering can and weeding between the potatoes and getting up at 5 a.m. to milk the cows.'

Daniel gazed up at the sky. Julia sensed these memories were precious to him.

'I just remember such a feeling of calm,' he continued. 'The warm earth on my fingers, the scent of the leaves, the birds singing. I was left to my own thoughts. Oma didn't *need* me like Mama did. I didn't have to try to work out her moods. We worked alongside each other, and that's where I learned to love farming.'

'Have you ever tried growing your own vegetables?'

'Of course, don't you remember?' Daniel caught her eye and she blushed.

Of course she remembered. He'd taken her to the

allotment he tended for an old neighbour. She remembered his arms wrapped around her as they sat on the bench, bees buzzing on the sweet williams, the scent of honeysuckle and the taste of him on her lips. It had been a few days before the recital.

'It was a beautiful place,' she said.

Daniel smiled. 'The most peaceful place in Bonn.'

At least it had been until Daniel asked her to go on holiday with him after the recital and she'd said no. Her career was only just taking off, she couldn't just up and leave. He hadn't understood why the piano was so important to her. She looked at him now, and wondered if he still felt that way.

'Why do you like farming so much?' Julia asked, hoping to steer the conversation to more neutral territory. 'It seems like hard work: always going over the same patch again and again.'

Daniel shrugged. 'It's a bit like practising the piano, I imagine. All the hard work is worth it when the plants grow and you harvest the fruit and vegetables. It's the same with the cows, taking care of them year after year in return for milk and meat.'

'If you buy your family's old farm, are you intending to stay put?' Julia asked.

Daniel eyed her with a sceptical smile. 'Are you asking because you're interested or because Papa wants to know?'

'Because I'm interested. I don't talk to Christoph about you.' She glanced at the market square, conscious that this wasn't quite true. 'I just wondered if you really want to settle down and live there. You're not exactly renowned for your ability to stay in one place.'

Daniel leaned his elbows on the table. 'Some of the happiest times of my life were spent at that farm. Helping to bring in the hay, felling trees in the wood, harvesting the orchard.' He smiled. 'It probably sounds strange, but I've reached the point where I don't want to keep travelling. I want my own place. Land that's mine. Somewhere that means something.' He paused and glanced at her. 'A home.'

It sounded idyllic. Julia wasn't sure she'd ever felt like that about a place. The house had felt hollow after her dad had gone. The emptiness came with her even when she moved out, following her to her rooms at college and each hotel room while on tour. Even her own flat couldn't really be called home. One day, she dreamed of having somewhere to put all her books and music, perhaps even a grand piano. But she couldn't imagine it happening.

'Those are good reasons for wanting the farm,' she said. 'You should tell Christoph, explain it to him too.'

'I did try the other day, but he was too preoccupied to take it in.' He smiled. 'You know, it's ironic to hear you, the touring pianist, asking me about settling down.'

'Yes, well,' Julia said, glancing at her hands. 'I'm not a touring pianist right now, am I?'

Daniel rubbed his temples. 'I'm so sorry, I forgot that you've got your own worries.'

He reached over and touched her arm. The weight of his hand sent heat coursing through her veins. She looked up. Something in his eyes seemed to reach out to her. Only that morning, she'd remembered the night swim, and the startling sensation of his proximity in the water. Now, she felt it again across the table.

'Whenever I heard you play,' he continued, 'it eclipsed everything else. You have such a talent. It's awful to see you like this.'

'The trouble is, I don't know who I am without the piano,' she said helplessly.

'I wish I could help you remember,' Daniel said.

His compassion was too much. Julia couldn't bear his kindness, nor the warmth of his hand. She slid her arm out from under his touch, trying not to notice the hurt look on his face as she moved away.

She stood and gathered up the bags. 'Come on, I think we've got everything. Pierre will be waiting for me.'

Daniel's eyes settled on her. For a moment she thought he was going to revisit the subject of the piano. But he got up, seeming to think better of it.

'All right, let's make a move,' he said. He reached over and gently took the shopping bags from her. 'Let me at least carry these, and give your hands a rest.'

Julia stared around the pristine kitchen. Everything looked so sleek and modern now, but here, in this very space, Sylvie would have made the potage fontanges all those years ago. Pierre held Sylvie's recipe book open, his finger marking the page. He peered at the writing.

'*Regarde ici*,' he said. 'She's scribbled something. *JD might be a hard taskmaster, but he knows how to combine vegetables. Don't always go for the obvious choice, he says.*' Pierre looked up at Julia and smiled. 'JD must stand for Jean Dupont, my father. He taught me the same thing. How strange that he never mentioned her.' He gave the book back. '*Allez*, let's get started.'

In Pierre's hands, the knife moved in a blur until all the vegetable were chopped into neat pieces.

'That's incredible,' Julia said.

Pierre shrugged. 'Well, I couldn't play a piano concerto, so I guess we all have our talents. Now, that needs a couple of hours to simmer,' he said. 'Why don't we make some rolls to go with it?'

Later, under Pierre's guidance, Julia mixed butter into a smooth cream, then beat in some egg yolks and crème fraîche. She tipped the mixture into a soup tureen and then poured the hot soup over it.

'*Voilà*, it's all done,' Pierre said.

Julia carried the tureen into the dining room, where Christoph was waiting. An image from the market stole into her mind. Daniel holding a lettuce, peeling back the leaves, one by one, to check the freshness. There had been such gentleness in his hands. Recalling the gesture, it made her breath catch. The tureen wobbled on the tray. She put out her hand to steady it. Of all the things to remember from this day, how strange that she should remember that.

19

Christoph

July, 1942 – Paris

Christoph carried Sylvie's box of possessions from the boarding house to Le Meurice. It wasn't heavy: some clothes, a hand mirror, and the dried lavender perched on top. She was different somehow. He noticed her glance at him from time to time.

He wanted to say more to her. About how he'd grown up hearing that France was the enemy: how it threatened Germany's western border and had ensured that the Treaty of Versailles ruined the German economy after the Great War. To tell her that since he'd been here, he'd come to see things more clearly. But it was obvious that his outburst in the Tuileries had made her uncomfortable.

'Did you get everything you wanted?' he asked eventually.

'No, not everything.'

A gust of wind blew the lavender on to the pavement. Christoph bent down to pick it up.

'It might be better in your bag,' he said, holding it out to her.

Sylvie shook her head. 'Leave it. It doesn't matter.'

Christoph slipped the lavender into his pocket. 'I'll look after it, then. Just in case.'

She watched him, a sad look on her face. 'Thank you.'

They started walking again. Emboldened, Christoph kept talking. 'My sister, Lotte, loves lavender. My mother taught her how to sew and make a lavender cushion to scent her drawers.'

'My mother taught me that too,' Sylvie said with a smile. 'How old is Lotte?'

'She's nearly sixteen, but inside she's probably younger than Otto. Mama says that she often sits at the piano, confused about where I am. She'd enjoy making those pastries you made with Otto. Gentle activities with her hands always soothed her.'

'What's wrong with her? If you don't mind me asking.'

'She got ill when she was two,' Christoph said as they walked along the street. Sylvie seemed different to how she'd been on the way here. Less pensive, more willing to talk. 'Up to then, she'd been developing normally – crawling, walking, starting to talk. But some bacterial infection affected her brain. She was never the same afterwards.'

'That must have been terrible,' Sylvie said.

He detected a hint of compassion in her voice.

'Yes, my mother and father were distraught, but we had to be strong for Lotte's sake. I was suspended from school one day for hitting a boy who'd teased her.'

'She's lucky to have you as her brother.'

Christoph glanced at her. There was definitely a change in her. Her eyes had softened. As they reached the steps of Le Meurice, he wondered why.

*

A few days later, Christoph was teaching Otto how to play 'Für Elise'. The boy kept making mistakes and grew agitated.

'Let's take a break,' Christoph said.

'But I've nearly got it,' Otto said.

Christoph smiled. 'You need to learn when to stop. Sometimes, our hands need time to digest what we've learned. Listen, while I play it.'

The notes were as familiar as the paths around the farm. Halfway through, Otto tapped his arm. Sylvie stood in the doorway, holding a tray on which stood a large tureen.

She placed it on the table and wiped her hands on her apron. 'I heard you playing. It sounded beautiful.'

'Thank you. It's my sister's favourite piece,' Christoph said. Something in the way she looked at him caught his attention. 'Otto, can you go and wash your hands, please.'

'Do you have any other siblings?' Sylvie said, standing aside to let the boy pass.

'No, just her. She's enough of a handful, my father used to joke. But, of course, he loved her.' It was strange talking to Sylvie like this. Any moment, he expected her to close herself off, but her expression was open and interested.

'You talk about him in the past tense,' Sylvie said.

'He died two years ago. Lotte misses him terribly.' Christoph smiled. 'He was a great teller of fairy-tales.'

'He sounds nice.'

'Do you have any brothers or sisters?' he asked, eager to keep her talking.

'No, there's just me,' Sylvie said with a sad smile. 'It's probably for the best. My father didn't like stories.'

Otto ran back in, shaking his hands dry. Christoph wanted to ask more, but Sylvie was already on her way out of the room.

'I hope you enjoy the soup,' she said, then added tentatively, 'it was nice to talk to you. There's always coffee brewing on the stove, if you ever want one.'

She gave a half-curtsey and left the room.

Christoph stared at the space where she'd stood. What did she mean, *coffee brewing on the stove, if you ever want one*? Was it an invitation to visit the kitchens? To visit her? He rubbed his chin. Or was he reading too much into it?

He sat down to eat with Otto. The soup tasted like springtime; of the small vegetable patch his father had kept behind the barn. After the funeral, Christoph had harvested the last vegetables his father had planted. His mother had made a soup, just like this one. It was like a gift, a promise that even though death had come, life still sprang from the ground.

He didn't see Sylvie for a few days, but that didn't stop his mind wandering to thoughts of her. Even now, late at night, he couldn't sleep, turning over their conversations in his mind. To distract himself, he thought about work.

There was a lot to do. The Kommandant had told him to organize a shipment of food by train from Paris to Köln. Coordinating the deliveries of produce from the farms around Paris took time.

'No one is to know about this,' the Kommandant had said. 'Just get the food to Paris, and the army will take care of the rest.' Christoph felt uneasy about the whole thing. Technically, his work was harmless: he wielded a pen, not a gun. But the effect of this shipment would cause suffering and more deaths from lack of sustenance. He'd seen the queues outside the empty shops. Food was growing scarcer.

In the silence of his ruminations, Christoph heard a sound from above. A low moan. He listened intently. There it was again, accompanied by the creak of a joist. Christoph sat up. It sounded like someone was up there.

Christoph decided to investigate. He got out of bed and silently climbed the stairs to the sixth floor of the hotel. The noise came again, from somewhere inside the storerooms. Christoph hesitated. Perhaps he should leave well alone. He remembered the child's face at the window after the round-up. This time he was determined not to walk away.

Christoph tried the door handle. It was stiff, but with a firm shove the door opened. He crept in, closing the door behind him.

He was in a vast, gloomy space filled with discarded furniture. Moonlight trickled in from a tiny window. In the corner, behind a stack of boxes, lay a young man in rags. His face was pale and covered in sweat. The man's eyes grew huge at the sight of Christoph in his German uniform. He looked about eighteen, thin and frail.

'Don't hurt me,' the man whispered. He pushed himself back against the wall.

'I won't, don't worry.' Christoph glanced around the room. The man was clearly hiding up here. There was a torn patch on his jacket, the stitching frayed. A yellow star,

Christoph suspected; it would explain why he was hidden away like this. But who had hidden him here? And why the hell did they think it was a good idea to hide a Jew in Le Meurice, right under the nose of the Kommandant?

Christoph knelt down. The man drew back.

'I want to help,' Christoph said gently.

The man shrank away from him. 'You're a soldier.'

'Ignore my uniform – I'm not like them. My name is Christoph Baumann. I'm from a farm near Bonn and I'd much rather be playing the piano than being in this war.'

The man smiled warily. 'I hope that's true.'

'What's your name?'

'Why should I tell you?' The man winced, clearly in pain. Christoph glanced down. One trouser leg was rolled up and a bandaged tied around his shin. Dark red dried blood stained the white fabric.

'What happened?' Christoph asked.

'Nothing,' the man said.

'Look, I promise, I'm not going to hurt you. You have my word.' The man's lips were dry. 'You're dehydrated. I'll get you some water. I'll be back in a minute.'

He moved stealthily back to his room and filled a glass with water from the carafe on the chest of drawers. Carefully, he carried it back up to the storeroom. When he reached the corner where the man had been, it was deserted.

'I've got the water,' Christoph called softly.

The storeroom was thick with silence. He didn't want to search the place: that would only frighten the man and make too much noise. Christoph placed the glass on one of the crates.

'I'll leave it here, then,' he whispered.

There was no reply. Christoph went back to his room and got into bed. He lay there, wondering if he'd catch a sound from above. But there was nothing. The man, if he was still up there, must be lying just as still as Christoph, holding his breath in fear of his life. Christoph's eyes began to close. Someone in the hotel must know the man was up there. But who?

20

Christoph

July, 1942 – Paris

The next day, after a late lunch, Christoph was one of the last to leave the dining room. A detritus of half-eaten meals and plates lay strewn around.

'Oh, I beg your pardon. I thought everyone had finished,' Sylvie said, coming in with a tray.

'No, it's fine,' he said.

She'd passed through his dreams the last few nights. He'd woken, puzzled. During the day, he thought about visiting the kitchens, as she'd suggested. But something held him back. Guilt about Hilde. A fear that Sylvie was just being polite. But now she was here. Standing right in front of him.

'How are you?' he asked.

She stood awkwardly by the door, gripping the tray. 'I'm well, thank you.'

'What are you making today?'

'Potage fontanges, like I made for you and Otto. M. Dupont wanted me to add eggs and crème fraîche this time, to thicken it. I've never tried that before, but it works well.' Her voice was animated, then she stopped and bit her lip. 'Sorry, I'm talking too much.'

'I like it when you talk about cooking. It's infectious.

Like when you cooked with Otto. He loved making the Schweinsohren with you.'

Sylvie smiled. 'That's how I learned with my grandma. Side by side in her kitchen. It's the best way to understand how a recipe works.'

Her shoulders relaxed. The strain in her face lessened. Her passion for food gave her such pleasure. Just like the piano had given him.

'What did you mean the other day about your father not liking stories?' Christoph asked.

Sylvie put down the tray. 'He preferred to drink, and it made him unpredictable. I learned to stay out of his way and I left home as soon as I could.'

'Is that why you came to Paris?'

'Yes. He never liked me cooking, said I made too much of a mess.' She smiled ruefully.

'And your mother, did she agree with him?'

Sylvie sighed. 'She had to.'

'You must miss her, and your grandmother too.'

'My grandparents were killed when their village was bombed,' Sylvie said. 'But my mother and father are still there.'

Christoph felt hot with shame. 'God, I'm so sorry, Sylvie. I don't know how you can stand here talking to me. It's barbaric what we're doing, the lives that are being lost, and all for –'

'Shush,' Sylvie said, glancing at the door. She shook her head. 'I appreciate your sympathy, but you need to be careful.' She smiled shyly. 'I wouldn't like anything to happen to you.'

Christoph glanced at her, startled by the warmth in her voice. 'Do you mean that?'

Sylvie reached out and touched his arm.

'I like talking to you. Promise you'll come and see me in the kitchen.'

Hope flared inside him. 'I promise,' he said.

That night Christoph ventured back up to the storerooms. He'd put some bread rolls in his pocket to bring for the man. The room was in darkness. He'd brought his flashlight this time.

'It's me – Christoph,' he whispered.

Christoph ducked his head where the ceiling sloped and made his way over to where the young man had been.

The blankets, the bucket, even the glass Christoph had left, were nowhere to be seen. Christoph frowned. The man had been injured. He couldn't be far away; that leg had looked too painful.

Quietly, he searched the storerooms, which went back a long way. Christoph stole in between old beds, tables and chairs covered in dustcovers until he reached the far end, a rough brick wall. Retracing his steps, he cast the flashlight left and right, until, near one of the beds, a glint caught his eye. It was the glass. So he was still here.

'I've brought some bread,' he whispered. 'I'll just leave it here.'

There was no reply. But the silence seemed to vibrate. The man was listening, Christoph could feel it. Perhaps weighing up whether to trust him or not. Christoph waited a moment longer.

'I'll bring some more food tomorrow,' he said to the empty, dark space.

Perhaps if he kept coming, the man might grow to trust him in time.

The next day, Christoph ventured into the kitchen, as M. Dupont was out. Sylvie made him a coffee, then opened her battered recipe book and added some notes.

'What are you doing?' he asked.

'I like to keep it up to date. That's what my grandmother taught me. *Let the recipes evolve.*'

'Where did your grandparents live?' he asked.

'In Normandy. A smallholding in the country. I loved being there. They worked hard, night and day, and not a scrap of food was wasted.'

Christoph thought of the maps in his office, the farms he had to inspect and hold to account. According to the Kommandant, the farms were under German control now: the food belonged to the German nation. But Christoph's father had taught him that food belonged to the soil that it had grown in, to the hands that had tended it.

Sylvie removed the light, papery skin of an onion and began to chop. Her fingers held the knife so lightly yet moved so fast.

'May I ask you a question?' she said.

'Of course.'

'What did you do before the war?'

'I went to agricultural college,' Christoph said, 'but I never wanted to take over the farm. I hoped to become a concert pianist.'

'Hoped?' Sylvie said. She tipped the chopped onion into the frying pan.

'I was accepted into the Bonn Music Conservatory, but then I had to sign up for the army.'

Sylvie put down her knife and considered his words.

'You *could* still go,' she said, 'if the war ever ends.'

Christoph thought of Hilde, of the life that awaited him when he returned. She wanted him to work on the farm with her father and brothers. 'I'm afraid I'll be taken in a different direction now.'

Sylvie stirred the softening onions. 'That's a shame,' she said softly, glancing at him.

Christoph's blood quickened. A wave of desire washed over him. He had to be careful. He stood up and drained his coffee.

'Well, I must get back to work,' he said.

Now that he had her good opinion, he was afraid of what it meant. He shouldn't let this friendship continue, for Hilde's sake. But he didn't know how to stop it.

21

Lisette

July, 1942 – Paris

It was four in the morning and it was Lisette's turn to make bread for the day. She pummelled the dough with her fist. She wasn't comfortable with the idea of seducing Leutnant Baumann, but he wasn't like the other men, the ones who wanted a woman for the night and an audience for their bravado and swagger. She remembered how he'd slipped the lavender into his pocket; he seemed to crave a connection on a deeper level.

She sprinkled some more flour on to the marble board. The disconcerting thing was that she *had* started to value Christoph and see beyond his uniform to the man inside.

A noise by the door startled her and the Kommandant appeared. 'Ah, Mlle Sylvie, I saw the light was on and thought perhaps M. Dupont was here.'

'No, I'm sorry, Herr Kommandant, it's only me.'

'So I see.' He walked over to the table. His boots clicked against the tiles. He loomed above her, hands clasped behind his back. He was renowned for needing little sleep, going to bed late and rising early, which meant the staff never knew when he might appear.

'Can I help you with anything, Herr Kommandant?' she said. Perhaps he was hungry, or Otto needed a drink.

'Yes, I believe you can,' he said, a smile playing on his lips. 'I've never seen your hair properly. It's always hidden under your chef's hat or tied up. Please, take it down.'

Lisette held her breath. Was he serious? He stared at her, waiting. She reached up and took off her hat. Then, with unsteady hands, she unfastened her French plait.

'Ah.' The Kommandant reached out and held a strand between his fingers and twisted it tightly. 'Just as I thought. Beautiful hair. Such a shame you hide it away.'

Lisette swallowed, her mouth dry. His power pulsed towards her. No one would hear her if she cried out. He was the Kommandant. Whatever he wanted, he could take.

'*Bonjour, Sylvie.*' One of the assistant chefs, Guillaume, bustled in. Then he caught sight of the Kommandant. 'Oh, *pardon*, Herr Kommandant.'

The Kommandant let go of her hair. His expression turned cold. 'Tell M. Dupont to come and see me when he arrives,' he said.

The head chef was often with the Kommandant. There were whispers among the kitchen staff that M. Dupont was a collaborator, creaming off the spoils of black-market deals and keeping his ear out for the Germans.

'Yes, Herr Kommandant,' Lisette said.

Her legs were weak. The Kommandant frightened and repulsed her. He embodied everything she despised about the Germans. The contrast between the Kommandant and Leutnant Baumann was stark. And yet, in some ways, the lieutenant's humanity, his genuine warmth, made him seem more unnerving.

*

A few days went by and there was no sign of Leutnant Baumann. Lisette worried that her flirtation with him had been too subtle. In the lull between breakfast and lunch, she made coffee and pain au chocolat and crept upstairs to his office.

She found him sitting at his desk, surrounded by papers. He brushed back his fringe and smiled, his eyes seeming to light up at the sight of her.

'I thought I'd bring the coffee to you this time.' She placed the tray on his desk.

'Thank you,' he said, leaning back in the chair. 'This is a very pleasant surprise.'

Sunlight came in through the window, illuminating the gold-embossed spines of books on the shelves. She glanced at the titles. They were all in German. Agricultural texts on farming and animal husbandry.

'So, this is where you work?' she said.

'Yes. Not as nice as your kitchens, but at least it's quiet.'

She glanced at his desk. 'It looks like you're busy. Is that why you haven't been to see me?'

The edge in her voice was deliberate. She needed to notch things up a little, or Seraphin would grow impatient. It worked. Leutnant Baumann fixed his eyes on her, his cheeks reddening.

'I've been thinking about you,' he said. Then, after a heartbeat, 'In fact, I've been thinking about you a lot.'

The intensity of his gaze was disconcerting. Lisette went to the window. Military lorries and cars stood parked in rows in the courtyard, a reminder of where she was.

'There's never much time to talk, is there?' she said. 'Even now, M. Dupont will be wondering where I am.'

She took a deep breath and glanced at him. 'I've been thinking about you too, but . . .'

'It's all right, I know what you're going to say. I'd like to get to know you better, but I suppose it's out of the question.' He smiled sadly.

Now was the moment to make things clear to him. She wasn't sure if she had the guts to do it. But the thought of the opportunity to gain intelligence and how important it could be to the war effort made her continue.

'I never said it's out of the question. In fact, I'd like that very much.'

Christoph stared at her. She swallowed, her mouth dry. Had he understood the meaning of her words?

She didn't dare stay around to find out.

'Enjoy the coffee,' she said quickly, and fled into the corridor, her heart racing.

The next day, Lisette was the last one in the kitchen. M. Dupont had retired for the night, claiming a headache, and left her to do the dishes.

Usually, she didn't mind being alone. But recently, being alone had become troublesome. She replayed the scene in Leutnant Baumann's office. Pretending to flirt with him was one thing. But there remained a guilty sensation that she'd enjoyed it too.

Lisette dried a saucepan. In the silence, she heard a rustle by the back door. She went over to look. A slip of paper had been pushed under it. Lisette picked it up. It was a receipt of some kind, but the miscellaneous items didn't make sense: *bar of soap, loaf of bread, one tin of sardines, pyjamas.* Under 'supplier', it read: *Jacques M.* She put the receipt in her pocket, then drew back the bolt and opened the door. The narrow side street was dark and empty.

'What are you doing?'

Lisette swung round. Leutnant Baumann stood by the stove. She could tell he meant nothing by the question, but her stomach tightened as she answered.

'It's a beautiful night,' she said. 'I went out to see the stars. I'm tired of being in this place all the time.'

'In that case, come out to dinner with me on Friday night,' Leutnant Baumann said. The words came out in a rush. 'I mean, why not? It would make a change.'

'The Kommandant won't let me.'

'All taken care of,' Leutnant Baumann said. 'The Kommandant agrees that your behaviour has been exemplary. He said we should start treating you like an employee rather than a prisoner.'

'There was no need to speak to him,' she said, 'but thank you.'

Since that morning when she'd been making bread, the Kommandant had been a few times to the kitchens to speak with M. Dupont. He had made a point of lingering near where Lisette worked. He had watched her, and she couldn't help but worry that he suspected her too. At least now, from what Leutnant Baumann had said, she'd gained his confidence.

'The Kommandant can't make his dinner reservation,' Christoph said, 'so he gave it to me. Would you like to come?'

Her efforts at flirtation had worked. He'd asked her out to dinner. The agent side of her knew this was an opportunity. More familiarity with Leutnant Baumann would give her the chance to extract more information from him. But the woman in her was afraid. Here in the hotel, she knew her role: but out there, in a more intimate setting, the lines might blur.

'Don't worry if not,' he said, reading her hesitancy. 'I just thought, after what you said the other day . . .'

Lisette touched the lapel on his jacket. 'I meant what I said. I'd love to come.'

This was like jumping from the aeroplane again. She was stepping into unknown territory: accepting an invitation for him to take her out. She was determined to do anything to save her country. But deep down, she knew that this was more than just a new venture for her as a spy. She was entering uncharted waters as a woman too.

The next day, M. Dupont was in a temper. The meat supplier hadn't turned up.

'The Kommandant has guests for lunch tomorrow,' he said. 'Guillaume, you'll have to visit rue Clément.'

Guillaume had a tray of burnt pastries in his hand. 'The oven's playing up. Someone else will have to go.'

M. Dupont cast his eye around the busy kitchen. Knowing she was now permitted to leave the hotel alone, Lisette came forward.

'I can go. I've prepared the sauce. The vegetables are peeled and ready,' she said.

She wanted to show the receipt she'd found last night to Seraphin.

'All right,' he said. 'Hand this list to the butcher. No time-wasting.'

'Understood.' Lisette tucked the list into her recipe book and stashed it in her bag.

The soldiers on the door of Le Meurice asked her where she was going. For a moment, she thought the Kommandant's new instruction about her being free to go out had not been passed on. But when she explained her errand, they moved aside.

Outside, she inhaled deeply. She'd go and find Seraphin first, and then deal with the supplier at rue Clément. She crossed the road and felt the sunshine on her skin. It struck her how empty and quiet the city was. Women passed by with haggard faces. German road signs had replaced French ones. Soldiers and checkpoints littered the streets. She pulled her coat more tightly around her. Having witnessed the Kommandant's arrogance, she knew the city had every reason to be fearful.

Café Lille looked out on to the street. Here on the Left Bank, the tension of occupation existed, but it was not so intense. Perhaps it was because of the students who rushed around with books and bicycles, still studying for a future they hoped would return.

Lisette sat at a table by the window. The coffee was bitter and grazed her throat. Seraphin leaned his bike up against the wall and crossed the road, a camera case slung over his shoulder.

'Nice to see you,' he said, coming over to her table. 'I hope work is going well.'

She knew he wasn't referring to her cooking.

'He's asked me to go out to dinner with him.'

'Marvellous.' He sat down and ordered a coffee. 'Extract all the information you can. But be careful: don't let your feelings get involved.'

'I know my duty. I see the cracks in his heart, but I don't climb inside.' At least, she was trying not to.

Seraphin smiled. 'Very good. See, already you've overcome your weakness. But being *sans cœur* has its advantages in a situation like this. There's no better person for the job. You will not easily give your heart away, *n'est-ce pas*?'

Lisette shook her head. 'I'm not sure I have one to give.' She passed him the receipt. 'Do you know what this means?'

Seraphin unfolded it beneath the tablecloth and frowned. 'Where did you find it?'

'Someone pushed it under the kitchen door. I didn't see who delivered it.'

Seraphin scrunched the receipt up and shoved it in his jacket pocket.

'It's nothing,' he said. 'Jean Dupont is using the black market to stock Le Meurice, that's all. He must be taking a payment off every transaction. That man is a menace, getting involved in things he doesn't understand. Be careful of him.'

'He's always consulting with the Kommandant. I think the Kommandant likes having a talented Frenchman in his pocket.'

Seraphin took a sip of coffee and glanced round the café.

'They're all using the black market – the French and the Germans,' he said, his voice bitter. 'We pay the Germans reparations, and they use our money to buy French food and keep it to themselves. At least, that's what I suspect.'

'But the people are starving.'

'Indeed.'

'Leutnant Baumann has something to do with the

Agriculture and Food Supply Department. He must know about this.'

Seraphin leaned forward. 'That's why your role is so important. If we had proof of what the Germans are doing, and could sabotage their efforts, it might make people act.'

Lisette leaned closer. 'What do you want me to do?'

'I've heard they're planning a large shipment of produce out of Paris. Find out when and where.'

Lisette nodded and drained her coffee.

Whatever strange affinity she'd felt towards Leutnant Baumann, it wouldn't stop her from achieving her mission. There were more serious things at stake. Paris was being strangled. Ensconced in Le Meurice, with endless supplies of black-market ingredients, she'd been in danger of forgetting that until she'd walked through the streets and seen it again for herself. Beguiling Christoph was simply a means to an end. Christoph *was* the enemy; nothing could change that.

Canard à la Rouennaise

1 duck, with giblets
lardons
6 onions, finely chopped
1 teaspoon each of salt and pepper
¼ teaspoon mixed spices
4 shallots, finely chopped
500ml red wine
25g unsalted butter

1. Preheat the oven to hot.
2. Take the liver from the selection of giblets and mince with the lardons and onions.
3. Season the liver, lardons and onion mixture and use to stuff the duck.
4. Truss and roast for 30 minutes.
5. Remove the duck when slightly browned and cut into pieces.
6. Arrange the pieces of duck on top of the stuffing mixture and shallots.
7. Crush the duck with a press or mortar to extract the blood.

8. Mix the blood with the red wine and pour over the duck.
9. Roast the duck for 20 minutes or until the sauce thickens, and serve.

22

Julia

July, 2002 – Paris

Julia sat with Christoph on a bench in the Tuileries, sparrows pecking the gravel at their feet. The scent of lavender wafted on the air. Christoph's face was haggard. He was up one minute – buoyed by the latest recollections – and down the next, saddened by the fact that his mind could go no further.

'Sylvie was a chink of light in the darkness. I loved talking to her. If she was prepared to give me the time of day, perhaps I wasn't beyond redemption,' he said. He rubbed his forehead. 'What was I doing, Julia? I had a fiancée back in Germany, but I'd invited Sylvie out to dinner. In the middle of a war filled with atrocities. I don't know what made me do it.'

Julia thought of Daniel. The pull towards him was magnetic, despite everything that had happened. 'Maybe you couldn't help it.'

'The feelings I had were so strong,' He gripped the top of his walking stick. 'The memories aren't enough; they make me miss her.'

Julia bit her pen. She'd made notes while Christoph had been talking about how he'd got to know Sylvie. 'Coming to Paris was supposed to help you, not make you feel worse.'

Christoph turned to her, his eyes moist. 'Oh Julia, it's not that simple. Now I've begun to remember, I want to know it all.'

Julia stared at her notebook. The memories were a jumble of recollections. Things came to Christoph in a rush or with painful slowness. Sometimes he lingered on a particular detail: the maps in his office, or the way Sylvie chopped onions at lightning speed. At other times, he spoke with a burst of fervour.

'Perhaps it's time to involve Daniel,' she said, twisting the pen in her hand. 'I think he suspects something.'

Christoph sighed. 'If you tell him, this whole thing will have to stop.'

'But why?' Julia asked. 'It all happened so long ago, before he was born, before you were even married.'

'I was here in Paris with Daniel once. I don't know where the memory fits in, Julia, but he must have been little because I recall the feel of his hand in mine as we walked through the streets, our closeness. But something must have happened. We were never so close again. For some reason, Paris became a place I never went to or mentioned.' He shook his head. 'I'm thankful he even agreed to come here. We have to keep the recipe book a secret, Julia, please. I don't want to stir up an argument I can't remember.'

Julia nodded. 'I will, but only if you promise to have those tests done when we get back to Bonn. We need to understand what's going on inside your mind.'

Christoph's head drooped. She hated to insist, but the recollections were clearly distressing. 'Very well,' he said, 'if you promise not to say anything to Daniel, I'll do the tests.'

Julia gazed at her sprawly handwriting and unruly sentences. She wondered what it all meant and where it was leading. One thing was certain, they couldn't stop now.

Later in the afternoon, while Christoph slept, Julia went to Bar 228 in Le Meurice and ordered a gin and tonic. The alcohol relaxed the tension in her shoulders. Among the frescoes, dark wood and painted ceiling she was tucked away from the world outside. Soft jazz played in the background and elegant couples sat chatting on deep leather chairs.

This next recipe was complicated. Canard à la rouennaise, duck in red wine sauce. Julia wasn't sure how to approach it. It was beyond her capabilities, and she was wary of arousing Daniel's suspicions.

Julia sipped her drink and studied the notes Sylvie had written in the margins. Her handwriting was splattered with dark red droplets.

First meal I ate with C. Dinner at La Tour d'Argent. Always wanted to try this dish, and it's their speciality.

What had Sylvie felt: a Frenchwoman in occupied France, having dinner with a German soldier? Women who had affairs with Germans were punished after the war: their hair shaved off, their shame visible to all. Is that why Christoph felt guilty? It was impossible to know until he remembered more.

'Hello.' Julia heard a voice behind her. 'Can I sit down?'

It was Daniel. Julia slid the recipe book off the bar before he could see it and tucked it into her bag. 'Yes, of course.'

'What are you doing?'

'Just contemplating my next cooking adventure.'

Daniel ordered a beer. 'What are you planning to make this time?'

'Canard à la rouennaise,' Julia said, 'but it's out of my league. It needs a special contraption to squeeze the duck carcass.'

'I've heard of that,' he said. 'Isn't it a speciality at La Tour d'Argent?'

That was the restaurant Sylvie had mentioned. 'Have you been?'

'No, but someone at work went on his honeymoon and he raved about it.'

'Oh,' Julia said. 'Do they still make it?'

'I believe so. He said it was a long-standing tradition there.' He smoothed the condensation off the bottle. 'We could take Christoph, if you like. I'm not a fine dining expert, but if it would help this culinary odyssey you two seem to be on, I'd be happy to accompany you.' He hesitated. 'Unless you'd rather go without me.'

'What makes you say that?'

'You and Christoph are as thick as thieves; you always have been. I saw you both chatting today in the Tuileries. It looked very intense.'

Julia thought guiltily of Sylvie's recipe book, of the deeply personal memories that Christoph had shared with her. 'It's not like that at all.'

Daniel shrugged. 'Well, that's how it feels sometimes.' He tilted his head to one side. 'Look, can I ask you something?'

Julia nodded, wondering what was on his mind.

'I know this sounds crazy, but all these recipes you keep thinking of, are they coming from a specific book?'

Julia stared at him. Her breath grew shallow. 'What makes you think that?'

Daniel turned the beer bottle and thought for a moment.

'When Mama was dying, she was fixated on some recipe book, said it had almost ruined their marriage. She described the tatty old cover and handwritten recipes and warned me that, for Papa's own peace of mind, it was all best left in the past. She told me she'd hidden it, somewhere he'd never find it.'

Julia's heart beat faster. Hilde had known about the recipe book; she must have put it in the cupboard, and now it was sitting in Julia's bag. Her stomach twisted at the thought of lying to Daniel. She was torn between wanting to tell him the truth and her loyalty to Christoph.

'I'm just making things I hope Christoph will eat, things that might remind him of his past here in Paris, or his upbringing in Germany. That's why I'm looking for more traditional dishes,' she said, choosing her words carefully. 'The canard à la rouennaise caught my eye because it's made using such an unusual method.'

'That's all?'

'Yes,' Julia said, trying to hold his gaze.

Daniel breathed out. 'Okay, sorry, I just had to check. I don't want him to stumble on anything that would upset him.'

'No, of course not. Me neither.' She took a gulp of the gin and tonic, hoping the subject was closed. 'I think Christoph would like it if we all went to that restaurant.'

Daniel glanced up. 'All right, see if he wants to go. If I'm around, I'll come too.'

'Where else would you be?'

He smiled. 'Don't worry, I'm not going far. I'm heading out to Normandy tomorrow to see an organic farm. That trip to the market got me thinking. I need to do some research.'

'What kind of research?' She liked this side to Daniel, his passion about his future.

'When I was travelling in India I went to an amazing organic farm in Chennai. It started off as a village farm making organic cheese from the cows and buffalo that grazed there, but eventually the city sprawled around it.' He sighed. 'I was sceptical at the time about whether they'd survive. I'd done my college course in food production, and organic was seen as niche and low yield, but they're still going today.'

'So, if you bought the farm in Effelsberg, you'd want to make it organic.'

'Yes, seeing that market yesterday made me realize that I have a real vision for it. At the time, travelling was just a way of escaping from place to place, but when I look back at the knowledge I picked up, it's all linked to farming sustainably, growing quality produce.'

His enthusiasm sparkled in his eyes. Julia smiled. 'It sounds like you're on a mission.'

'Yeah, I don't want people to think I'm all talk and no action,' he said with a grin. 'I'm determined to make you think well of me, Julia.'

She looked up slowly and met his eyes. His proximity radiated around her, sending a ripple of warmth across her skin. Her breath tightened.

'Why do you care what I think?' she said.

He reached over and lifted a strand of hair from her cheek. 'Because we both know this thing between us isn't finished,' he said. 'That's why.'

It was impossible to look away. Julia's heart thudded. 'I'm not sure we can turn the clock back . . .'

A familiar voice called across the bar. 'Julia, at last! They told me I'd find you here.'

It was Sebastian, a holdall in his hand, sunglasses on his head.

Daniel's face went white and he swiftly moved away from her. 'What's he doing here?'

'I don't know . . .' Julia's head was spinning. Sebastian and Daniel hadn't seen each other since the recital. The recital was supposed to mark the start of her career. She had played the piece she'd been practising for weeks, but when she had caught sight of Daniel kissing his ex-girlfriend Kat in the front row she'd frozen. It was Sebastian who had hauled Daniel, drunk and belligerent, out of the auditorium.

Now, Sebastian kissed her on both cheeks and nodded curtly at Daniel.

'I'm only in Paris for a few hours,' he said to Julia. 'I have a flight back to London at midnight. I thought I'd spend some time with my favourite client in between.'

'I can't believe you're here,' Julia said. 'How did it go in Prague?' She glanced at Daniel. His jaw was clenched. *We both know this thing between us isn't finished.* Had he really just said that? Sebastian's arrival had caused the moment to evaporate.

'It was great. Tanja did brilliantly. What are you doing tonight? I'd like to take you out to dinner.' He glanced reluctantly at Daniel. 'You too, Daniel, with Christoph, if he's well enough.'

'We were just talking about trying to get a table at La Tour d'Argent,' Julia said.

'Perfect. I'll book a table for four and hope that Christoph can come too,' Sebastian said. 'Now, let's have another drink. Two white wines, please, and Daniel, another beer?'

Daniel eyed up Julia's gin and tonic and raised an eyebrow at Sebastian's presumptuousness in ordering her wine. 'No, thanks. I need to check on Papa.' He banged his beer down and strode away.

Sebastian glanced at Julia. 'Did I interrupt something?'

'No, your timing was perfect.'

Julia took a last swig of her gin and tonic. She needed to come to her senses. This break was supposed to be about sorting herself out and resting in preparation for the next part of the tour, not to mention supporting Christoph. Things were too complicated with Daniel, no matter how much she might wish otherwise.

Julia checked her reflection in the full-length mirror before she left the hotel room. Her dress was electric blue with diamante cuffs and, normally, it gave her courage. Tonight was about taking Christoph to the restaurant where he'd had his first date with Sylvie. But it was impossible not to be nervous about how Daniel and Sebastian would get on.

Sebastian was waiting for them in the bar of La Tour d'Argent. He kissed Julia and turned to the barman. 'Can I order some champagne, please? Four glasses.'

'Not for me. I'll just have a beer,' Daniel said, his hands in his pockets.

'Of course,' Sebastian said.

There was no eye contact between the two men, save a brief nod of greeting. Julia felt the tension, particularly from Daniel, who sipped his beer and glanced around the room.

'It's good to see you again, Herr Baumann.' Sebastian shook Christoph's hand and handed him a glass of champagne. 'I'm glad to see you're looking well.'

'That's Julia's doing,' Christoph said.

Sebastian smiled and passed Julia her glass, clinking it with his own. 'I remember when I first heard Julia play. She took my breath away. She still does. There was one concert, in Madrid, when she surpassed all my expectations.'

Julia tried not to catch his eye at the mention of Madrid.

'That's exactly what I thought the first time I heard her play.' Christoph smiled. 'I'd sworn not to take on any more students, but with Julia, I just knew she was special.'

Julia blushed, feeling the warmth of Sebastian's gaze. It was hard not to wonder what Daniel made of it all. She wished the waiter would hurry up and take them to their table.

'Julia tells me you've been very understanding about her taking a break,' Christoph said.

'I know how hard she's been working. It's not an easy time to stop, but I trust Julia to know her own mind. She's remarkable.' Sebastian raised his glass to her and smiled.

Daniel made a noise, something between a snort and a cough.

'What is it you do now, Daniel?' Sebastian said, turning to him. 'Last I heard, you were knee-deep in the prairies.'

Daniel shrugged and leaned against the bar. 'Farming's my passion. And travelling.' He took a long swig of beer, gripping the bottle tightly.

'How nice to have the freedom,' Sebastian said pointedly.

Thankfully, the waiter came to take them to the table, bringing the champagne bottle in an ice bucket. Daniel carried his half-finished bottle of beer. Julia took Christoph's arm and helped him into the chair. The huge bay windows of the La Tour d'Argent revealed a view bristling with rooftops. In the distance, purple clouds bruised the sky. Christoph stared for a moment, taking it in.

'I remember this view.' He glanced at Daniel. 'I had dinner here once, back in the 1940s. The skyline was different then, not so many streetlights and high-rise buildings.'

'How did you come to be at such a fancy restaurant?' Daniel asked, leaning back in his chair. 'I thought you were just an administrator.'

Julia looked over at Christoph. How would he answer that question?

'Someone up the chain of command couldn't make their reservation, so I went with a work colleague.'

Daniel seemed to accept this explanation.

'What was it like in Paris back then?' Daniel asked.

Christoph smoothed his tie against his shirt. 'I didn't like being here as an occupier. Even though I had a desk job, I witnessed some horrific things on the march to France, and while I was here. I felt deeply uncomfortable about what the Nazis were doing.'

'When were you here?' Sebastian asked. The waiter poured the rest of the champagne.

Christoph frowned and glanced at Julia. 'Help me out,' he said. 'The dates aren't quite so fixed in my mind.'

'Well, you recall being around when the round-ups at Le Vel' d'Hiv took place,' Julia said. She turned to Sebastian and Daniel. 'He was walking nearby and heard the cries of the people inside. The round-up of Jews happened in July 1942, so he must have been here then.'

'My God,' Sebastian said. 'That's awful.'

'It was unimaginable what those people went through,' Christoph said, his voice heavy with sorrow. 'There was nothing I could do. I knew I felt deep shame about being here in Paris, but now I understand why. It's a memory I wish I could forget.'

Daniel's brow creased with concern. 'That's a lot for you to process, especially when you're just recovering.' He glanced at Julia. 'You need to be careful about what memories are triggered by Papa being here.'

'I can't decide what he's going to remember and what he'll forget,' Julia said, sensing his criticism. 'If that was the case, there are a few memories of my own I'd happily erase.'

She locked eyes with Daniel. He must have known she was referring to the recital. The shame of that night – not only professionally, but emotionally – had stayed with her for a long time. The studio had been filled with musicians, and a potential manager, Sebastian. It wasn't so much that he'd been kissing Kat that put her off her stride, it was the look he gave her afterwards. As if he wanted to hurt her for choosing the piano over a relationship with him.

Daniel looked down at the table. 'I'm sure we've all got things we'd rather forget.'

'It's helped, talking to Julia,' Christoph said. 'I don't feel so confused by everything. We're taking it slowly, remembering it bit by bit.'

'Well,' Sebastian said, stroking Julia's arm. 'Perhaps it's a good thing she's missed the Prague concert if having her here is helping you, Christoph.'

Daniel cleared his throat and signalled to the waiter for another beer. As soon as it came, he downed most of it in one go.

Sebastian glanced at Julia and raised his eyebrows. She knew what he was thinking: this was like the recital, when Daniel had drunk too much. But something was bothering him, she could tell.

'Take it easy,' she said, hoping to smooth the waters.

'Sorry,' Daniel muttered.

The waiter arrived with a trolley. The press, containing the cooked carcass of the duck, stood in the centre. The waiter twisted it and the metal crushed the duck, sending blood trickling out.

Sebastian grimaced. 'Amazing that something so brutal can taste so good. They'll use the blood to make the sauce for the meat. It's delicious.'

The waiter wheeled the trolley back to the kitchen for the final stage of cooking.

'I'm glad I didn't have to make that,' Julia said. 'Thanks for arranging a table.'

Sebastian kissed her hand. 'Anything for you.' She knew the gesture meant nothing. He always did it before she went on stage. But Daniel was staring at her, consternation in his eyes.

She tried not to notice. This was Christoph's evening. Music tinkled in the background; voices murmured intimately. She wanted to imagine what it would have been like for Sylvie and Christoph all those years ago, but Daniel's presence was like static in the air.

Daniel stood up. 'I'm sorry, but I'm not feeling great. I think I'll go back to the hotel.'

'What's the matter?' Christoph said, alarmed.

Daniel placed his napkin down. 'I'm sorry, Papa, I just can't do this. I thought coming to Paris was about you and me reconnecting, but sitting like this, listening to you talk, I'm not really sure why I'm here.'

'But . . .'

'Sorry, Papa.' Daniel headed towards the stairs.

Sebastian ordered another bottle of champagne. Julia looked at the empty seat. She couldn't leave it like this. 'Sorry, I'll be back in a minute.'

She caught up with Daniel in the street. A half-moon shone down between gaps in the buildings. Cars sped by: a river of red tail lights in the night-time traffic. It was raining.

'Daniel!' she called. He turned round. He'd forgotten to bring a jacket and his shirt was splattered with raindrops. 'What's going on? This was supposed to be a nice evening.'

'Until Sebastian showed up.'

'He got us the table. It was kind of him.'

'It's not just that. I just couldn't bear to sit there any

longer and feel like the outsider with my own father. I should know these details of his past. He should have told me.' Daniel pushed his hair back. In the streetlight, his face was half in shadow. 'Paris isn't a good place for us. It never was.'

'I think he's just wary of making things worse between you,' Julia said. 'Don't just give up. That's not like you.'

'Isn't it?' Daniel said. 'Look, maybe you're right. We can't turn back the clock.'

'Then why did you say we're not finished, in the bar earlier?'

He gazed at her, his eyes pained. 'I don't know. I thought maybe something was still there. But after Sebastian arrived it seemed a foolish idea.'

'Why does he bother you so much?'

'I've seen how he looks at you. Something's happened between you two, I can tell.'

Julia hesitated. What could she say? It was just one stupid kiss last year. It didn't mean anything.

'I knew it,' Daniel said. 'The moment I saw him at the recital – successful, handsome, charming – I knew I never stood a chance.'

'Daniel, that's not fair. You had other people too.'

'In fact, I knew the day we first met that I could never fully capture your attention.'

'What do you mean?'

'We were waiting with the little lost girl in the station office in Bonn while everyone looked for her mum. We played Hangman to distract her, do you remember? It was fun, and I thought you and me had a connection, but you kept looking at your watch as if you had somewhere else to be.' He paused and drew in his breath. 'I wrote the last Hangman for you as a message, but you never finished guessing it. The little girl's mother showed up, and gathered her in her arms, and when I asked if you wanted to know what the Hangman phrase was you said you didn't have time. You couldn't get away from the station fast enough.'

'It wasn't like that!' Julia said, frustrated. She'd had no idea that Daniel was Christoph's son at that point; she hadn't even known his name. Julia had felt the connection too, from the moment his eyes had met hers when they'd teamed up to look after the girl. But by the time the girl's mother arrived, Julia was already two hours late to meet Christoph. No matter how tempted she was to stay and get to know this handsome stranger, Julia couldn't risk starting off on the wrong footing with her new mentor, Herr Baumann.

'If what you'd written was so important,' she said, 'why couldn't you have just told me what it said? We're not children, Daniel, playing games of Hangman. Sometimes you have to say what you want directly.'

Daniel wiped the rain from his cheek. 'But even after you made the fondue and we kissed, I was never sure how you really felt. I wondered if something had happened to change your mind.'

Julia blinked in the rain. Something *had* happened to make her doubt him, even before the debacle of the recital.

'I don't know how to explain it. It was just . . .' She remembered back to that morning. The dim light of the hallway. It had been just a few days after they'd talked late into the night, sharing the fondue and their first kiss.

'I saw you coming out of Christoph's music room with a handful of cash, hiding it in your back pocket. And then later, I heard you and Christoph arguing. He seemed to be accusing you of stealing it.'

'You were spying on me?' Daniel's eyes narrowed.

'No, of course not.'

'That's what it sounds like.' He pressed his hand against his forehead. 'So, all this time, you've believed I was a thief. Even before I messed up at the recital, you'd made up your mind about me. Jesus, I never stood a chance with you, did I? You'll always think the worst.'

'What am I supposed to think? The letter, the estate agent, the equity for the farm. These might be the last years of his life, and all you want is his money. You were never there for him, Daniel. You were always gallivanting around the world and only came back when you needed help.'

As soon as she'd said it, Julia knew she'd gone too far. It was all in the past. Why couldn't she just leave it there?

Daniel's cheeks were pinched, his eyes blazing. 'If that's your opinion of me, then I really don't know what the hell I'm doing here.'

He turned and strode off, his shoulders hunched against the rain. Julia stared helplessly. It was too late to take her words back now.

23

Christoph

July, 1942 – Paris

The night before he was due to take Sylvie out for dinner Christoph went up to the storerooms. He had some ham and crackers, wrapped up in brown paper, and a jug of water. He checked the corridor and went out on to the stairs. They were deserted. Hardly anyone ventured up here.

The storerooms smelled musty. Every time he came up, there was no sign of the man, but the food he'd left always disappeared. This time, however, Christoph sensed a shift in the room.

'Hello?' he whispered.

He made his way to the back, and there, laying crouched in a foetal position, was the man. He was clutching his stomach and looked very pale. Christoph knelt by his side.

The man groaned. Christoph noticed a plate, some left-over food on it, by the old bed. He recognized the floral pattern. The head chef ate his meals from this set of plates, while the rest of the staff had plain white ones. Only M. Dupont had access to the cupboard where the plates were kept. That meant it must be M. Dupont who'd brought the young man up here and was keeping him hidden.

'Let me guess,' Christoph said. 'You had poached egg and haddock, didn't you? The egg must have been off.

M. Dupont usually makes sure everything is perfect but perhaps he was having a bad day.'

The man looked at him, terrified. Christoph knew he'd guessed correctly.

'It was M. Dupont who brought you here, wasn't it?' Christoph said gently. He'd never have thought the taciturn M. Dupont would have been responsible for bringing this Jewish man into the hotel.

'I can't say,' the man said, shivering.

Christoph took one of the dust sheets off the crate and placed it over him. 'If I was going to report you, I'd have done it by now. But I don't intend to.'

The man looked at him warily. 'Why not?'

'What's happening here is wrong. I want to help you if I can.' He knew it was mad to risk his life like this. But he couldn't turn his back on the man now he'd spoken to him and seen the pitifulness of his situation.

Christoph passed him a glass of water. 'What happened to you?'

The man sat up, still pale, but more composed. 'I was at my friend's house when the police came. They took us away in a van. There was no time to tell the rest of my family. We were taken to Le Vel' d'Hiv.'

'You were there?' Christoph said, horrified.

'It was like hell,' he said. 'There were so many people; they were pushing busloads of us towards the entrance. I was herded along with hundreds of others. I caught a glimpse inside and made a run for it in the commotion.'

'Is that how you hurt your leg?'

'Yes, the place was chaotic. Thank God it was the

French in charge and not the Germans. I went down the first street I could find, over a wall and into someone's garden. I smashed my leg on a trellis as I went down.'

'You're lucky to be alive.'

'Luck is all we have now.'

Christoph calculated how many days it was since the Le Vel' d'Hiv round-up; the man must have been here since mid-July. Two weeks at the most. 'How did you get to Le Meurice?'

The man rubbed his forehead. 'I waited until it was dark then hobbled out and made my way to M. Dupont's house. He's involved with the Éclaireurs Israélites de France. He thought hiding me right under the nose of the Kommandant was the safest place I could be. Once my strength is up, I hope to join my family again.'

Christoph frowned. This was a serious situation. If the man was caught . . .

'I'm sure M. Dupont will take care of you,' Christoph said. 'Tell him Leutnant Baumann is willing to do what he can.'

Christoph twisted his watch strap. Half past six. She wasn't going to come. He'd been a fool to expect it. He'd been sitting alone at Le Tour d'Argent for half an hour, thinking about the hideaway in the storerooms and his plight.

Then he saw Sylvie at the top of the stairs. She wore a brown coat and a red dress with a black belt. Her hair was free of the chef's hat and fell in dark waves over her shoulders.

'I'm sorry I'm late. They closed the metro,' she said.

The waiter took her coat. Christoph readjusted his thoughts. She hadn't stood him up. She was here.

'Don't apologize,' he said. 'It's the army's fault the stations keep closing. Would you like white wine?' He caught the waiter's eye. '*On prendra une bouteille de Sancerre, merci.*'

'Where did you learn such fluent French?' she asked.

Christoph shrugged. 'I had a tutor. His views would be spurned now, but he believed in language as a way to keep the peace.'

'He would have got on with my grandmother. She taught me a smattering of German for the same reason.' Sylvie said. Her eyes darted around the room. 'You wouldn't think there's a war on, or even an occupation. Everyone seems so at ease.' She touched the silver cutlery, frowning.

'And yet it's impossible to forget what's going on,' Christoph said. 'You might feel happier to be seen with me if that were the case.'

Sylvie glanced around the room. 'It *is* rather strange to be here.'

'You don't have to stay if it makes you uncomfortable,' Christoph said. 'There's no obligation.'

Sylvie blushed. 'Perhaps, Herr Leutnant, we can pretend that the war isn't happening, just for a moment.'

Her voice sounded strained, as if she was trying to be jolly but her heart wasn't in it.

'Could you call me Christoph instead of Herr Leutnant?' he said.

Sylvie glanced at the menu. The waiter poured the wine. 'If you like,' she said, 'Christoph.' She bit her lip as she read through the starters and main courses.

To put her at ease, Christoph asked, 'What would you

recommend from the menu? The Kommandant told me to try the salmon mousse, but I can't stand that kind of thing.'

'There's only one dish you can have at La Tour d'Argent,' Sylvie said. 'Canard à la rouennaise. My grandmother used to talk about it. It's rather expensive, though.'

'Don't worry, I have plenty saved up,' he said. 'Your grandmother must have been a remarkable woman.'

The candlelight shone in the rich curls of Sylvie's hair.

'She was. She taught me everything I know.'

'Do you have any other family members?' Christoph said. 'I mean . . . is there anyone significant?'

He winced inwardly at his clumsy question.

'I was engaged to be married,' she said, 'but my fiancé was killed in the fighting.'

'I'm sorry, I . . .' Another loss suffered at the hands of the Germans. 'What happened?'

Sylvie took a sip of wine. 'He died at sea. His parents got a telegram and then sent me a letter. I was in Paris at the time, the wedding dress was bought, he had leave booked. Everything seemed set. Of course, I'd seen it happen to others. But I never expected it would happen to me.'

Christoph didn't know what to say. He couldn't console her, not when his fellow countrymen were responsible. Instead, Christoph remembered how his mother had consoled him when his father died.

'What is your happiest memory of him?' he said, asking the same question his mother had asked him.

Sylvie looked at him, startled. 'I don't know. I've tried not to think about it. There were so many.'

'If you could pick just one, what would it be?'

Sylvie brushed back her fringe.

'I think it would be the day we got engaged. We were in the city, in Paris. He was on leave. For most of the day, it was awkward and unhappy – I couldn't stop thinking about how little time we had left. But near the end, it started raining. We ran under the trees near the Eiffel Tower, and there was a band playing in the bandstand. He asked me to dance, a big smile on his face, and suddenly, time stopped. I can still recall the song.'

'What was it?' Christoph said. He sensed her mood lifting as she spoke. Transported back to that time.

'Oh, a beautiful classic by Lucienne Boyer, "Parlez-moi d'amour", that my grandmother used to sing as she cooked.' Sylvie smiled, then sighed. 'Anyway, by the end of the song we were soaking wet and he'd gone down on one knee in all the mud and asked me to marry him.'

'That's a wonderful memory,' Christoph said. The faraway look in her eyes made him feel forgotten. Sylvie had been in love, and the Germans had killed that promise. He felt a twinge of doubt that he could ever make her care for him.

Sylvie shook her head. 'I'd rather not talk about him any more, if you don't mind.'

'I'm sorry. It must have been awful . . . losing him.' He searched for the right words. 'I feel responsible somehow.'

'It's not your fault. But if it wasn't for the war . . .' She blushed. 'Sorry. Put my words down to the fact that I was supposed to be married but I'm not.'

Sylvie took another sip of wine. Her hand shook. Christoph wanted to reach out, to feel the pulse on the underside of her wrist, but he resisted.

'I don't mind,' he said. 'The more you speak to me like that, the more human I feel.'

Sylvie glanced at him. 'Then maybe I should do it more often.'

Christoph gazed into her steady blue eyes. He swallowed. 'Yes, I'd like that.'

He thought of Hilde's letters. Of the money poured into his mother's farm by Hilde's father. These should be the things that held him back. But as he looked across the table at Sylvie, he knew that they would not.

At half past ten, they left the restaurant. The curfew was in place from nine in the evening until five in the morning, but because Christoph was a German soldier he was permitted to escort her back to Le Meurice. The street was empty and dark. The moon shone on the Seine, making a white pathway over the water.

'Here, you should have this.' He handed Sylvie the customary Tour d'Argent postcard with the serial number of the dish they had eaten there on it.

'Thank you,' she said, tucking it into her bag. 'My grandmother had one just the same. The meal was an anniversary gift.'

'I've enjoyed this evening very much,' Christoph said.

'So have I.'

Sylvie's skin glowed in the light and it made him catch his breath.

'What are you thinking?' he asked.

She smiled. 'You've asked so many questions about me. I haven't had a chance to ask you any.' She stopped walking and leaned against the stone parapet overlooking the river. 'Like, what do you do in your office all day?'

He shrugged. 'I'm affiliated to the Agricultural and Food Supply Department. We're overseeing food production. I haven't visited any farms yet. They're just coordinates on a map. But I will.'

'When?'

'Next week. I'm going to check a farm in Normandy that's using the new crop planning we've given them. There are lots of mouths to feed, so my department wants to make production more efficient.'

Sylvie sighed. 'People would kill for a morsel of what we tasted tonight.'

'Yes, I fear that times are hard for Parisians, especially with plans to reduce rations and most of the food going back to Germany.'

'I see.' Sylvie looked back to the river.

Christoph gripped the stone rail. He'd been insensitive. Times might be hard for the French, but not for the officers and soldiers of the German army. He thought of the man in the storerooms, surviving on leftovers from the kitchens. The Germans lived in another world, while the rest experienced food shortages and hunger.

'I'm sorry. I shouldn't have said that,' he said.

Sylvie linked arms with him. He smelled linen and soap on her skin.

'I'm not ready for the night to end just yet,' she said. 'Could we have a drink in your office?'

Christoph dissolved at her touch, at the warm press of her body next to his. It didn't take long to answer.

'Yes, of course.'

24

Lisette

July, 1942 – Paris

It was the wine that made her act so boldly, the urge to find out some intelligence that would make a difference to the war. But sabotaging a man's heart was easier said than done. Lisette wondered if she had the guts to see it through, especially with the memory of Johnny's proposal still lingering in her mind. It hadn't happened in Paris, of course, but in Green Park in London. The rain, the song, the bended knee in the mud had all been true, but the location she'd given Christoph was a lie. His kind questions had got her to reveal more than she'd planned, despite still keeping her identity a secret.

Christoph went to find some wine and glasses. While he was gone, Lisette scoured his desk. Maps lay interlaced with papers. Farms had been circled on a map. She caught sight of a telegram, only partly revealed under a book:

Betrieb Lebensmittelzug
Abfahrt 19:00 07. August Orléans nach Paris, Gare de Lyons
Abfahrt 03:00 08. August Paris, Gare de Lyons, nach Köln

The rest was obscured. Lisette swallowed. Here it was. The proof Seraphin had been looking for. Quickly, she memorized the times of the train that would be taking food from Paris to Germany.

She glanced at the door. He'd be back any minute. She walked towards the mantelpiece.

Boot heels clicked in the corridor outside. Firm, commanding: it didn't sound like Christoph. The door opened, and there stood the Kommandant.

'I saw a light on. What are you doing in here?' he asked.

'Leutnant Baumann has gone to fetch wine glasses.'

The Kommandant glanced at her dress, taking in the curves of her body.

'Ah,' he said, raising his eyebrows. 'You've been out to dinner. How much prettier you look dressed as a woman instead of as a chef. I'm glad he was able to make use of my dinner reservation.'

'It was kind of him to take me, Herr Kommandant.' A blush crept over her cheeks.

'Of course, and kind of you to go. Perhaps you will be kind to me also?'

His words slid like butter into a hot pan. Lisette pulled her coat across her chest.

'Kommandant.' Christoph returned, two glasses in his hand.

'It seems you have made a friend at last,' the Kommandant said. 'We all need friends in times like these.'

'Yes, Herr Kommandant.'

'Enjoy your evening.' The Kommandant took one last lingering look at Lisette, then closed the door behind him.

Christoph put the glasses down. 'What did he want?'

'He saw the light on and came to investigate. For a

moment, I thought he was going to have me arrested for snooping.'

Christoph poured the wine. 'And were you snooping?' he asked with a smile.

'No, of course not,' she said, forcing a laugh.

Christoph smiled. 'It seems to be the night for unexpected visitors. I came across M. Dupont in the kitchen. Said he was looking for something, a receipt from a supplier.'

Lisette stiffened. That receipt was in Seraphin's hands now. 'M. Dupont is a law unto himself,' she said. 'Look, perhaps I shouldn't be here.'

She couldn't do this. The dinner. The walk home. The Kommandant assuming she was Christoph's fancy woman. She'd got the information about the train. There was no reason to stay any longer.

'Don't go, not yet, There's something I want to show you.' He took her hand. 'If it helps, I have a fiancée back home, so you're quite safe with me, I promise.'

His eyes were deep black in the half-light, his hand soft against her own. The smell of his cologne filled the air between them. A fiancée. He'd never mentioned her before. His behaviour with Lisette had suggested he was a free man. The fact that he was engaged should have made her feel protected, but she felt both safe *and* in peril, the two opposing emotions vibrating in her at once.

'Please. Just come to the roof garden,' he said. 'No one will know.'

Lisette followed him upstairs. She couldn't pinpoint the impulse which had made her say yes, but she hoped it was the draw of more information to take back to Seraphin.

They reached the roof garden, high above Paris. Christoph led her to a conservatory in the centre. Tables and chairs stood stacked in a corner. It smelled musty and neglected. Christoph flung off dust covers and revealed an old upright piano.

'I come up here sometimes to practise,' Christoph said, sitting down on the stool. 'I want you to see that not everything that comes from my country is bad. Some of it is beautiful.'

Lisette pitied him. He wanted to be free of this terrible role that history had assigned to him, but it could never be.

'I don't think . . .'

He was already playing. Something sentimental and sad. She'd heard this piece before. It was beloved by her grandfather, played on his record player during her summer stays in France.

'The "Moonlight Sonata",' she whispered.

Each note was a petal falling. Christoph's hands rippled over the keys. He possessed an incredible talent.

All too soon, the piece ended and the music died away. Lisette longed to hear it again. Everything had seemed so simple while Christoph was playing.

'I love that piece,' she said.

'Sometimes I imagine what I could have been had this war not started. I hope the opportunities aren't lost for good.' He looked bereft, his shoulders hunched.

Lisette wanted to comfort him. It would have been inhumane not to. But the reality was that the war had changed everything.

'No one is going to come out of this war and go back

to being the same person they once were,' she said. 'But it's up to us to make the right choices, to still hold on to what was precious to us. For me, that's cooking. For you, it's the piano. You mustn't let your talent die. Keep practising. Keep believing. Life might take you in a different direction, but if you truly love the piano, then you might find your way back to it.'

'If you say it, Sylvie, maybe I can believe it.'

He invested her with a power she didn't possess. Worse still, he trusted her. 'I wouldn't set too much store in what I say,' she said.

He came over and kneeled in front of her.

'But I do. You make me feel like anything could happen. And it has. I'm up here on the roof playing the "Moonlight Sonata".' He laughed, sounding carefree. 'I've been cautious so far, but now I feel reckless.' He took hold of her hands. 'Come with me to the farm in Normandy. I know you'd love to see the countryside again. La Ferme Villiers-le-Bâcle. It's not far from Rouen, surrounded by woodland. I'll say you're my translator, or assistant, or whatever. But please, come.'

His cheeks were flushed. The idea was unthinkable. She'd be alone with him. Far away from here.

'The Kommandant would never allow it,' she said.

'He won't know. He's off to a conference in Vichy. We won't leave until he's gone.'

'And what about M. Dupont and the kitchens?'

'You're owed some time off.'

'I don't know,' she said, nervously.

'I'll arrange separate rooms. There won't be any impropriety, I promise. I enjoy your company, how you challenge me,' he said, squeezing her hand. 'Please, I don't usually do this kind of thing, but tonight it just feels right.'

Lisette stared at him. What could she say? She'd played the part of liking him so well, that it had led to this. Perhaps he'd regret this impulsive gesture in the morning. But somehow, looking at his shining eyes, she doubted it. She couldn't refuse him. Not after she'd led him on this far.

She smoothed the folds of her dress. 'All right, then.'

She tried to tell herself this would help the resistance, that she could gather more intelligence to bring back to Seraphin. But she knew it was more than that.

Two days later, Lisette met Seraphin in a queue outside the bakery. He stood behind her. Queues were one of the few places where people were permitted to gather.

'Dinner was productive then?' Seraphin whispered.

She nodded.

'And?' Seraphin said.

'He hinted that rations are to be reduced,' she whispered, anxious not to be overheard.

'I suspected as much,' Seraphin said. 'It's all going east. We're surrounded by fertile land, but nothing is coming to Paris unless it's to fill the Nazis' plates.'

'He's involved in monitoring farms. Increasing production. Crop plans,' Lisette whispered.

'Anything else?'

'Yes,' she said. She'd saved the best piece of information till last. 'There's an *Essenszug* leaving Paris on the eighth of August from Gare de Lyon at 3 a.m., heading to Köln. It will be loaded with produce for Germany.'

'You've done well,' Seraphin said. 'Keep that gentleman

friend of yours on side, all right? I'll contact you with further instructions.'

'He wants me to go with him to inspect a farm in Normandy, La Ferme Villiers-le-Bâcle, near Rouen,' said Lisette. 'I've said yes. It could be an opportunity to learn more, but I wanted to check with you.'

Seraphin nodded. 'You were right to accept. The closer you get to him, the more he'll tell you.'

'I think so. He is quite unguarded in what he says, for a German soldier,' Lisette whispered. 'I think the war and the occupation weigh heavily on his conscience.'

'That's good,' Seraphin said. 'The more cracks, the more opportunities for you to penetrate his secrets. You're doing well, Lisette. I know maintaining a facade like this is asking a lot of you, but we're all impressed with how you're doing.'

'Thank you.' Coming from a seasoned agent like Seraphin, that meant a lot.

'In fact,' Seraphin whispered, 'now that I know you're heading that way, I may have an errand I need you to run while you are there. An important drop-off.'

She was about to reply when two soldiers arrived and started asking the people in the queue for their papers. One man, ahead of them in the line, held his out for inspection, but it was not to their satisfaction. They dragged him, struggling and crying, out of the queue.

The man's shoes came off as they pulled him along. He cried out in pain as his bare feet bounced over the cobbles. Lisette watched, helpless and disgusted.

'Whatever it is, I'll do it,' she said.

Brathähnchen

1 tablespoon cooking fat or unsalted butter
1 bunch wild sorrel, chopped
1 bunch lemon thyme, chopped
1 chicken
Salt and pepper
10 shallot onions, peeled and halved

1. Pre-heat the oven to 200°C.
2. Mash the butter with half the chopped wild sorrel and lemon thyme and salt and pepper.
3. Loosen the chicken skin and rub some of the herb and butter mixture under it.
4. Stuff the cavity with shallots and remaining herbs.
5. Rub remaining herb and butter mixture over the outer skin.
6. Roast the chicken until golden brown and crispy-skinned.

25

Julia

July, 2002 – Paris

After the argument with Daniel, Julia walked back to La Tour d'Argent. Sebastian and Christoph did not question her, but threw the odd concerned look in her direction while they chatted. She ate her duck in silence, wrapped in her own thoughts.

Sebastian left at ten to catch his flight. Julia went with him to get his coat.

'I'm sorry if I made things worse,' he said. 'I just don't like the fact that Daniel's here with you, not after how he's behaved in the past.'

'Oh, Sebastian,' Julia said. 'You can't look after me all the time.'

'No, but I wish I could.' He cupped her cheek. 'If I wasn't your manager, would that make a difference?'

Julia shrugged. 'In Madrid, yes, it probably would've made a difference. But now ... my head is in such a muddle with everything. I need you as my manager right now. Nothing more.'

Sebastian put on his coat. 'I guess that'll have to do,' he said. 'And speaking as your manager, have you been able to keep up the practising while you're here? I can arrange a practice room at the Conservatoire if you need it.'

Julia shook her head. It had been bliss to forget all about the piano for a while and lose herself in Sylvie's recipes. 'I'm giving my hands a complete break for now,' she said.

'Don't leave it too long.' He kissed her cheek. 'Take care, Julia. I'll see you in London next week and help you prepare for Salzburg.'

Julia returned to the table.

'Well, that was quite an evening,' Christoph said.

Julia sighed. 'Having Daniel and Sebastian in the same room wasn't a good idea.'

'There's definitely a bit of rivalry there,' Christoph said with a chuckle.

'Nonsense.' Julia blushed. 'They don't like each other because of what happened at the recital.' She glanced around the restaurant. 'At least we can talk now they've gone. I've been longing to ask if you remember coming here with Sylvie.'

Christoph sat back in his chair. 'I do remember. Being here was the start of something. Maybe I didn't realize at the time, but I was falling in love with her.'

'Was she falling in love with you too?'

Christoph took a sip of wine. 'I'm not sure. We sat over there, by the window. She wasn't at ease with me here. But later, when I took her up to the rooftop garden at Le Meurice, she seemed to soften.'

Julia got out her notebook and wrote down what he said. 'Why did you take her up there?'

Christoph shrugged. 'I wanted to take us somewhere that felt far away from the roles we played in the war. I played the "Moonlight Sonata" for her. For a moment, while I was playing, I believe we forgot what had brought us there. At least, she agreed to go away with me.'

Julia stopped writing. 'Go away with you? Where?'

Christoph shook his head, looking uncertain again. 'I'm sorry, Julia. I don't know.'

Julia patted his hand and gestured to the waiter for the bill. 'Don't worry. Perhaps it will come back to you in the morning.'

Julia sat by the window of her hotel room in her blue dress, staring at the Eiffel Tower. Christoph had gone to bed hours ago, but she couldn't sleep. The notes of the "Moonlight Sonata" echoed in her head. She picked up Sylvie's recipe book and thumbed through the pages.

The next recipe was Brathähnchen, a simple peasant dish of chicken and vegetables. Underneath, Sylvie had written: *Cooking for two at La Ferme V-L-B in Normandy is different to cooking for unseen guests in a hotel kitchen.* What did V-L-B stand for?

A tentative tap sounded on the door. Julia slid the recipe book under her pillow and went to answer it. It was Daniel. He looked dishevelled in the harsh light of the corridor, his clothes still damp from the rain.

'Is Sebastian here?' he said.

'No, he went to the airport to catch his flight.'

Relief flooded Daniel's face. 'Can I come in?'

'I don't know . . .'

'Look, I'm really sorry about tonight. I shouldn't have left like that. What you said to me on the street, about the money. I'd like to explain.'

Something in his voice made her hesitate. She didn't want to turn him away. 'All right. Come in.'

He sat down by the window and Julia sat opposite him. The lights of Paris spilled across the darkness like jewels. He leaned forward, resting his elbows on the table.

'You were right. I did take the money. But it wasn't what you think.'

'What was it then?'

'It's not easy to explain. I've never told anyone. You see . . .' He hesitated, tapping his fingers against the wood. 'I took the money for Mama.'

'Hilde?' Julia said, startled.

Daniel rubbed his temples. 'I loved her, but she was troubled. Do you remember the night she burst in on us when we were kissing? How unstable she was?'

Julia recalled how Hilde had cried. Up until that moment, the night had been almost perfect. Julia and Daniel had ended up in his room, eating the fondue she'd struggled to make. He'd told her that he couldn't stop thinking about her, and her heart had thudded as he'd moved closer, his eyes deepening. The kiss had barely started when Hilde barged in.

'I thought she was upset because I was in your room,' she said. 'She seemed to resent me being there, as if Christoph had gone too far by inviting me to stay.'

'No, it was more than that. Don't you remember what she said?'

Julia nodded. It was said with such bitterness. *Pianists take and take and never give back until one day you have nothing left.* Hilde's barely disguised animosity towards Julia hadn't helped Julia's relationship with Daniel either. Her disapproval had spilled over on the night of the recital when she'd told Julia that it was her own fault Daniel had disrupted things, that Julia had led him on. Julia recalled the curl of cigarette smoke from Hilde's mouth as she delivered these barbs in the garden. She seemed to believe she was saving her son from a life like her own: that of being unloved and neglected in favour of the piano.

'Since I was ten or so, she suffered from depression,' Daniel said, his brow furrowed. 'The crux of it seemed to be that she felt Papa never really loved her. When he was away teaching, she always feared the worst, that he was having affairs, being unfaithful. She never trusted him, and it ate away at her. No matter how much he tried to reassure her, or I tried to comfort her, she would slip into a black mood that never seemed to shift.'

'She burdened you with all that?' Julia said. No wonder Daniel's relationship with Christoph was complicated. Hilde's distress would have turned him against his father, and maybe it had contributed to Daniel's attitude towards Julia as well.

'That's why I needed the money, you see.' Daniel pressed his fingers together and bit his lip. Clearly it was hard for him, admitting all this.

'Daniel, if it's too much . . .'

He shook his head. 'I want to tell you. She self-medicated, you see, as a way of coping.'

'What do you mean?'

'Papa wasn't tight or anything, but she'd often run out of money. She didn't want Papa to know. She bought the pills privately. When she didn't have enough cash, I took the money for her.'

So that was it. The furtive, guilty look. It all made sense.

Julia remembered Hilde's fierceness when it came to Daniel. 'She was very protective of you. I remember her telling me after the recital that you deserved compassion. That she hadn't told you the half of it, but that you knew enough to be wary of the past.'

Daniel glanced away. 'I always had my suspicions about his unfaithfulness, but because he was away so much I never knew for sure.'

Julia thought of the recipe book. Hilde had been aware of its existence; she must have seen the dedication from Sylvie at the front. She wasn't sure if Daniel had made any connection between Christoph's supposed unfaithfulness and the recipe book, which Hilde had told him about when she was dying. Tentatively, she probed further. 'Did Hilde ever tell you about anyone specific?'

Daniel glanced at her quizzically. 'Why do you want to know?'

'I just wondered if it was all conjecture or if she had someone in mind.'

'It's funny you should ask,' Daniel said, 'because when she was dying, and going on about that recipe book, she did tell me never to let him track down someone called Sylvie. Apparently, she was the woman who had written the recipes. Mama said . . .'

'What?' Julia leaned forward in the chair, not daring to breathe.

Daniel hesitated. 'I should probably talk to Papa about it, when we're back in Bonn and he's feeling better.' He rubbed his chin. 'It'd be hypocritical for me to get upset about him telling you his memories and leaving me out, then doing the same thing.'

Julia sucked in her breath. Daniel clearly knew something.

He stood up. 'There's something I'd like to show you.'

'It's late . . .'

'Please.' He held up a room card. 'I asked the receptionist if there was a piano you could try, and she said you could use the one in the rooftop suite as there's no one staying there right now.'

'I'm not sure.' She *did* want to see the rooftop, the place where Christoph told her he had played for Sylvie, but seeing it with Daniel was another matter.

'Please come. They call it the Belle Étoile penthouse suite, and it has a grand piano.'

He clearly didn't realize the rooftop was connected to Christoph's past. Julia couldn't miss the opportunity to see it and this gesture was Daniel's way of making amends. 'Okay, I'll come,' she said.

The hotel was quiet, the lights dimmed. They took the lift to the top floor, and arrived in a marble hallway. Daniel slotted the card in and the door opened on to an enormous room, with a glass table, white sofas and a Steinway grand piano on a white rug.

Averting her eyes from the piano, Julia followed Daniel out to the jasmine-scented terrace which wrapped around the entire suite. Paris lay below, a city of lights.

Sylvie and Christoph had stood here too, but back then the city had been shrouded in darkness.

'Why don't you try the piano?' Daniel said softly. 'It'd be a chance to see if all the cooking is helping your hands.'

Julia's stomach knotted. 'No, I couldn't.'

But she glanced back into the living room and saw it there: the lid open, inviting her to touch the gleaming black and white keys.

'Take all the time you need. I know this must be hard,' Daniel said. 'I'll be out here if you need me.' He moved along the balcony, tactfully leaving Julia alone.

The piano had always been a kindred spirit. It offered opportunities and possibilities for her imagination, her talent, her future. But Julia had become frightened of it. The only possibility she foresaw was that of failure.

Still, she couldn't resist going in and sitting down on the stool. She rested her hands on the piano keys. There was no sound up here: the traffic, the crowds, even Daniel, were all lost to a silence that cried out to be filled with music.

She gave in. The opening bars of the 'Moonlight Sonata' came to life. She closed her eyes, the melody pulsing through her bloodstream. She saw Christoph in her mind's eye, and somewhere, Sylvie, listening. She wanted to play for them.

Then her fingers tensed. Images from the London concert flashed before her eyes: the searing spotlight, the hushed audience, the notes mangled and damaged. The music crashed to a halt. She closed her eyes and fought back the tears. After a few moments, she heard Daniel's footsteps behind her.

'Are you okay?' he said.

'I'm sorry. I can't play any more.'

'Is that what happened in London?'

Julia nodded. She couldn't bear to speak about it. Daniel seemed to understand. He came over, and she shuffled along the stool, making room for him to sit down.

'Papa used to play that piece,' he said. 'I'd sneak in and listen.'

'I thought you didn't like the piano.'

His face was hidden in shadow, but Julia was conscious of every contour of his body, just a whisper away from hers.

'The piano took Papa away from me.'

'It can swallow you up,' Julia said. 'The practice, the performing. People get tired of sharing you with music until, one day, they're gone, and it's just you left with the piano.'

Daniel turned towards her in the darkness. 'Is that what happened to you?'

Julia closed the lid. 'In some ways, yes.'

'What about Sebastian?' His voice whispered in the shadows.

'He's my manager, Daniel, nothing more. I've told you that already. There's nothing between us.'

'But he'd like there to be?'

Julia shrugged. 'He would. But I don't, and I've made that very clear to him.' She looked at Daniel. His eyes were deep pools. There was so much unsaid. She looked away. 'To be honest, there hasn't been anyone really, not since . . .'

Not since you. The unspoken words sank in. Her life had been all about the music for the last six years, and now the music had deserted her.

'I'm sorry about what I said tonight,' Julia said. 'I should've known there was more to what I saw.'

'I'm sorry too. I've worked hard since Mama died to

find a rapport with Papa, but it's hard. We were close when I was little, but then later, when I was eight or nine, after a trip here, to Paris, he seemed to retreat. I could never work out why. And then, with Mama and her worries about him being unfaithful, I found myself taking sides, and he became even more distant. I see you sitting with him, talking, and I wonder why he can't talk to me like that. I suppose this trip has reminded me of the distance between us and how Paris seemed to play a part in that.'

Julia shifted her feet against the pedals. 'We talk about the past, that's all.'

'I've never dared ask him about the war. I always assumed his reticence meant he'd done something shameful. When the German soldiers returned home, it was all about keeping quiet. There were no heroes' tales like the British had.'

'You could start to ask, like you did in the restaurant,' Julia said. His eyes caught the moonlight, the shadows deepening his face.

A breeze blew in from the balcony and made the curtains swell.

'Do you think he'd want to come with me to see the farm?' Daniel said. 'He was the one who told me about it. When I was little, he talked about this place called La Ferme Villiers-le-Bâcle that he visited in Normandy during the war, and how beautiful it was. I think it reminded him of the farm at home.'

Julia held her breath. 'What did you say the farm was called?'

'La Ferme Villiers-le-Bâcle.'

The farm to which Christoph had taken Sylvie: *La Ferme V-L-B.*

Julia's heart raced. 'I'm sure he'd like to go.'

'And will you come too?'

She rubbed her arm. 'Maybe you two should have some time together.'

Daniel shook his head. 'I can't imagine being on my own with him. We'd run out of things to say. We need you there too.'

Daniel's car rattled along the road. The suburbs dwindled into countryside. Green, flat fields lay under a huge blue sky. Christoph sat in the front next to Daniel. He'd been full of enthusiasm for this trip, delighted that Daniel had suggested it. 'What a coincidence that you remembered me talking about it,' he said. 'I would love to see it again.' Now he peered out of the window, and Julia longed to ask him how he felt about returning.

Two hours later the car turned up a dusty track, passing along an avenue of trees and through an open gate towards a stone farmhouse, its windowpanes painted blue. At the sound of the engine, a middle-aged woman wearing knee-length denim shorts and a white blouse, and a stocky man in overalls came out to meet them.

'*Bonjour*,' the woman said. 'I'm Monique, and this is my husband, Raymond. *Enchanté*.'

'Hello, I'm Daniel. This is my father, Christoph, and Julia . . .' He tailed off, clearly unsure of how to introduce her. Julia smiled and shook hands with them both.

'Thank you for agreeing to see us,' Daniel said.

'It's our pleasure. There's nothing I like more than discussing the farm,' Raymond said. 'We don't get many visitors out here.'

'My father was here briefly during the war,' Daniel said. 'That's how I'd heard about it.'

'Yes, Monique said you'd mentioned that on the phone. How remarkable. What were you doing here?' Raymond asked Christoph.

'Oh,' Christoph said, glancing furtively at Julia. She knew he wouldn't want to mention anything about Sylvie. 'I'm ashamed to say I was here on official business for the Department of Agriculture and Food Supply. I wasn't proud of my role.'

Monique touched his arm. 'It's in the past now,' she said. 'Does it look very different to you?'

'I think I remember the buildings,' Christoph said. 'I believe I stayed in that cottage over there. There was a millpond too, I think.'

Raymond nodded. 'Why don't we have lunch down there, Monique? I'll show Daniel and his girlfriend around the farm. We'll start with the crops and then visit the dairy.'

Julia's cheeks flushed. 'Oh, no, we're not . . . I'm not his . . .'

Daniel's face was bright red too. 'Julia is my father's friend; he was her mentor. Both my father and Julia are concert pianists.'

'Ah,' Raymond said, 'my apologies. Then it's just you and me for the tour.'

As Daniel and Raymond set off down the track, Monique gestured behind the old stone cottage that looked like it was used for storage. 'Would you like to sit by the millpond while Julia and I make the lunch?'

'Oh yes,' Christoph said. 'If you don't mind.'

He stared at the cottage as they walked past. Monique led the way along a narrow path. It was fringed with nettles and foxgloves. The air grew cooler. Soon they came to a clearing where the millpond lay, reflecting the sky. Set back from the water was an area where the grass had been mown short. A wooden table and chairs stood in the shade. Christoph gazed at the pond. He looked back at Julia, his eyes moist.

'It's very peaceful here,' he said.

'Yes,' Monique replied. 'It's one of my favourite spots. I used to swim here as a little girl.'

Christoph sat down on one of the chairs.

'I need to pick some wild sorrel and finish the chicken,' Monique said to Julia. 'Would you like to help me?'

'Will you be okay here, Christoph?' Julia asked.

Christoph nodded and closed his eyes. 'You go. I'll be fine. I have my thoughts to keep me company.'

Monique took a different path back to the house, stopping to pull out some wild sorrel as she went. The air was pungent with the smell of the rich green leaves.

'It's a family recipe,' Monique said, 'from during the war. A chicken dish with wild sorrel. I've forgotten how we came to know it, but I've always thought it tasted delicious.'

Julia thought of the recipe in Sylvie's book. Could it be the same one?

'Did your grandparents tell you anything about that time?' she asked.

They were back at the farmhouse now. The heavy oak door opened into a large kitchen with a low ceiling. Bunches of dried flowers and bay leaves hung from the eaves. A long wooden table stood on the terracotta-tiled floor.

Monique took the chicken from the fridge.

'A little,' she said. 'There were stories about the Nazis intercepting contraband items that were dropped by the British in these parts. One brave young Frenchwoman was shot dead in the woods not far from here.'

Julia stared at Monique. Her heart nearly stopped beating. *One brave young Frenchwoman*. What if that woman was Sylvie? Surely Christoph would have remembered that. She felt a tremor of apprehension. How would Christoph cope if the memories had a tragic ending?

'Please can you chop these shallots in half?' Monique asked, handing Julia a bag of onions and a chopping board and knife.

Monique went to fetch lemon thyme from the kitchen garden. Julia tried to concentrate on peeling the onions. It couldn't have been Sylvie who was shot, Julia reasoned – she had been a chef, and she had come to Normandy with a German lieutenant. But Sylvie had been interrogated before. Perhaps there was more to Sylvie than Christoph could recollect. As Monique chatted on while they prepared the lunch, Julia tried to shrug off her sense of unease.

An hour later, when lunch was ready, Monique and Julia carried the lunch things out to the millpond. Christoph woke blinking in the sunlight at the clatter of plates, cutlery and wineglasses. The sleep had done him good. He looked up with interest when Daniel and Raymond also arrived at the table, eager to hear what Daniel had discovered.

Monique served the chicken with heaps of green salad

and new potatoes dripping with golden butter. Raymond uncorked the wine and they began to eat.

Julia could see by Daniel's face that he'd had a good morning. He was brimming with ideas. Christoph asked him what he'd seen, and Daniel turned towards him as he ate, explaining about crop rotations and organic soil certification. Christoph listened intently. The effect of Christoph's attention on Daniel was transformative. The frown that usually hovered between his eyes disappeared.

'It's like this chicken, Papa,' Daniel said. 'You can taste that it hasn't been tampered with or constricted in its growth. It's the same with organic milk. Raymond said I could do a course in organic farming to top up what I already know.'

Christoph leaned back in his chair and smiled at Daniel. 'I'm sure you could. Would the farm in Effelsberg need a lot of work to turn the non-organic soil back to its natural state?'

'There's a bit of preparation needed,' Daniel said. 'Planting clover seems to be the key to rewilding the soil. The cows could then graze on natural ground.'

Raymond topped up the wine glasses. '*Je suis impressionné par lui,*' he said, patting Daniel on the shoulder. 'He's remembered everything I told him. I used to teach agriculture at the Caen-Normandy University. It always stands out when a student is interested.'

'Except, I'm thirty-two,' Daniel said. 'I hope I haven't left it too late.'

'*Ce n'est jamais trop tard.* From what you've told me, travelling all over the world and working on farms has taught you a great deal. You can distance learn and start farming at the same time. I can tell you've got farming in your blood.'

'Well, it never flourished like this in me. I never went back to farming after the war,' Christoph said, glancing at his son. 'This is Daniel's own talent. I'm very proud of him.'

Julia held her breath at Christoph's unexpected declaration. She knew how much it would mean to Daniel. Daniel dipped his head, clearly moved. 'Thank you,' he said.

Daniel glanced at Julia; the fullness of the moment was stored up in his eyes and shared briefly with her. For once, she knew exactly what he was thinking. It was like they were back at the beginning, eyes meeting by the bench in the train station, and all the old hurts were washed away.

Julia blushed and looked away at the millpond dappled by sunlight. What would have happened if Daniel's mum hadn't come in when she had that night? Julia swallowed. Daniel was right. There *was* something unfinished between them. But she wasn't sure she dared risk her heart again.

26

Christoph

August, 1942 – Normandy

Christoph sat at his desk, finishing off last-minute preparations before the trip to Normandy. The week had passed quickly and finally it was here: he was going to spend almost two days with Sylvie.

The Kommandant had driven off in a cavalcade of vehicles to his meeting, his wife and son at his side. Before he left, he told Christoph that General Winkler, Head of the Production and Supplies Division, would be arriving soon. 'We will hold a special dinner on his arrival,' the Kommandant had said. 'Show him what German hospitality looks like at Le Meurice.'

Now all that remained was for Christoph to speak to M. Dupont and let him know that he was taking Sylvie with him. He telephoned through to the kitchens, asking him to come up to his office. He was still debating whether to say anything about the young man in the attic when M. Dupont knocked on the door.

He stood awkwardly by Christoph's desk. Christoph motioned for him to sit down.

'I wanted to let you know that I'm taking Sylvie with me to Normandy for a couple of days,' Christoph said.

'That's fine. We'll manage.' M. Dupont regarded Christoph carefully. 'Is that all?'

'No,' Christoph said, finding the words. 'I wanted to talk to you about someone else. I think you know who I mean.'

M. Dupont's jaw clenched. 'Possibly.'

'If there's anything I can do to help, you must let me know.'

'I see,' he said. 'May I ask why you're taking such an interest? You could have advanced your career by reporting it.'

Christoph leaned closer. 'I have a sister, a little younger than the man in the attic. She doesn't fit the Aryan mould. Life has been very difficult for her. My mother keeps her indoors, out of sight, but we never know when the doorbell will ring and someone will try and take her away. I can't help her right now, but I can help that man you're hiding.'

M. Dupont took in his words. 'I appreciate that,' he said, 'but your silence is all we need. The fewer people visiting the storerooms the better; it will only draw attention to his hiding place. For now, that's the best way to help him.' He nodded. 'And please, call me Jean. Thank you for keeping this a secret.'

After he'd gone, Christoph thought about what Jean had said. He was prepared to do more than just be silent, but perhaps for now that was all they needed.

Sylvie waited in the lobby, clutching her bag. A fluttering feeling stirred in Christoph's veins. In his room upstairs was a letter from Hilde. She'd written about plans for the wedding. With each sentence, another link in the chain was forged. But for the next two days, he'd pretend the future didn't exist.

He took Sylvie's suitcase and put it in the boot of the car. He'd been allotted a Volkswagen Kübelwagen to visit the farm. Sylvie climbed into the passenger seat.

'So, it looks like we're off,' Christoph said.

Sylvie nodded. It was hard to tell if she was glad to be going or not. She stared straight ahead and fiddled with the clasp on her handbag. Christoph started the engine and the car spluttered to life. He reversed out of the courtyard and drove on to the rue de Rivoli. Well, she was here, which was something, and that was all he could rely on for now.

The farmer's wife had allotted Christoph a small one-roomed cottage adjacent to the main farmhouse. There'd been some mix-up and the telegram to say that a female translator was coming with him hadn't been received. The farmer's wife pursed her lips and looked Sylvie up and down.

'Is there anywhere else I could sleep?' Sylvie said. One half of the cottage was a kitchen with a basic stove, table and chairs. The other half, separated by a curtain, contained a double bed.

The woman sniffed and shrugged. 'Non. We've got my sick mother in the spare room, and three children in the other. I can bring some extra blankets and a camp bed. My brother-in-law and his wife had no complaints when they lived here. But now she's got the baby she's gone back to live with her mother.'

'Thank you, I'm sure we'll manage,' Christoph said. 'I was hoping to see the fields now, if possible?'

'My husband is at the market. He'll be back this afternoon,' the woman said, folding her arms.

'May we have a wander around in the meantime?' Sylvie asked.

The woman frowned. 'There's a path to the millpond, best to stick to that. I've left food in the cupboard.'

'Thank you,' Christoph said.

'She hates me,' Sylvie said after the farmer's wife had gone. 'She probably thinks I'm a Parisian woman of the night.' She glanced around the room, her face disapproving of it all. 'Besides, you don't really need a translator. Your French is superb.'

'I'm sorry,' Christoph said. 'I can take you back to Paris if you like.'

Sylvie gave him a brief smile. 'We're both sensible adults. We'll just have to make the best of it.'

The room felt intimate. He'd never shared a space like this with anyone. Their suitcases stood side by side near the stove.

Sylvie clearly felt it too. She cleared her throat. 'Let's go and find the millpond she mentioned.'

The woods were filled with foxgloves, and wild sorrel grew in among the trees. The footpath twisted and turned until it opened out by a rundown mill. The stream rushed through a channel before slowing down and entering a millpond fringed with trees.

They stood for a while, listening.

'It's so peaceful.' Sylvie let out a contented sigh.

Christoph took his jacket off and laid it on the ground,

flattening the long grass. He sat down, hoping she might relax here, and, after a moment's hesitation, Sylvie sat down beside him, arms clasped around her knees.

'What do you hope to do after the war?' Christoph said. He reclined on one arm, looking up at her. She was beautiful, so near, yet out of reach.

'After the war? I can't imagine it ending,' she said. 'But if it does, it depends on what the world looks like. I'd like to try and follow my dreams. Everyone should have that chance. But when this war ends, things will be very difficult, for so many people. So much damage and destruction has been done.'

'Yes,' Christoph said. He and Sylvie were on opposing side. For the war to end, there'd have to be a winner and a loser. If the Germans won, and Hitler had his way in Europe, the consequences didn't bear thinking about. And if the Allies won, what would that mean for him, on the wrong side of history?

'But if things ever go back to normal,' he continued, 'what do you imagine doing?' She was so near he wanted to reach out and stroke her arm, but he resisted.

The tension in her face eased a little. 'I'd open a restaurant and run it myself. Ristorante La Casa in Rome would be my inspiration. I've heard it's incredible,' she said. 'And do you still intend to go back and study the piano in Bonn?'

'I thought I did. I can't imagine doing anything else, but now . . .' The aspiration sounded hollow to his ears. Thousands of people had been displaced and killed, families torn apart, cities ruined. In such a world, what use was a concert pianist?

Sylvie turned towards him. 'If it's at all possible, you should pick up where you left off. Promise me you'll do that.'

Christoph smiled, amused by her fervour. 'I'll try. And you must start that restaurant.'

She bowed her head. 'It sounds unreal, doesn't it? The war is like a night that stretches on and on, and the worst thing is, there's no telling when the end is coming or if we'll be here when it does.'

He glanced at the curve of her lips, the little scar above her eyebrow, the tiny pulse in her neck. She smelled . . . familiar. Like nobody else, yet utterly known.

'Sylvie, if we do survive, and it does end, then you and I –' He stopped, filled with an impulse to tell her something, yet what it was, he didn't know.

'Let's not spoil the day by talking about what ifs.' Sylvie glanced at the pond, clearly uncomfortable with the direction of the conversation. 'Let's go for a swim. Freshen ourselves up after the drive here.'

Christoph swallowed his words. Now clearly wasn't the time. 'It looks pretty cold.'

'Come on. Diving into cold water is like being reborn.'

'All right,' Christoph said with a smile. 'But if I catch pneumonia, I'll blame you.'

Sylvie went behind a bush to get changed. Christoph took off his uniform. It was a relief to feel the air on his skin instead of the itchy fabric. He plunged in.

'Come on,' he called, shivering in the water. 'This was your idea.'

Sylvie came out from behind the bushes. His eyes widened. Dressed in just her plain undergarments, she was more beautiful than he could have imagined. In one fluid movement, she dived beneath the surface. When she emerged, her hair sleek against her skin, she was smiling.

'Do you feel reborn?' Christoph said.

'Yes,' Sylvie said. 'And you?'

'Things have never felt clearer.'

He drifted towards her, closer and closer, until there was barely anything between them. Christoph felt as if the war had been washed away. Briefly, his arms encircled her waist. Sylvie held his gaze for a moment, then laughed and wriggled free, diving under the water. She surfaced and swam away from him. He watched as droplets cascaded from her arms and caught the light like molten glass.

27

Lisette

August, 1942 – Normandy

Christoph's eyes were closed. Sunshine covered him in a bronze haze. Lisette could still feel the burn of his arm around her waist. When they had climbed out of the pond, Lisette knew without even glancing at him that it was all he could do not to touch her. His restraint sparked up a tiny, exquisite flame inside her that she'd never experienced before.

With Johnny, it had been the opposite. Growing up together in the red-brick street, they'd known everything about each other. It seemed only natural that they should kiss, and later make love and, not long after that, get engaged. It was only after he died that Lisette wondered, in the long, wretched nights, if they had really desired each other, or if it had all been too inevitable.

Christoph, however, upset her equilibrium. Differences so deep she'd thought they were etched in stone had blurred. Sitting beside him now, she felt unlike herself. Woodpigeons cooed in the trees. A breeze whispered through the grass and made her shiver.

Whatever existed between her and Christoph – and she was thankful it was only a whisper – she couldn't let it affect things. She was here for a reason. Seraphin had given her instructions. She had a duty to her country.

'Meet Marie at the old mill near the farm. She's a member of the local resistance,' he'd said, when they'd met in the café the day before. 'The drop-off is at one in the morning. Bring back a package for me. Tinned tomatoes. Understand?'

She'd nodded, relieved to have a mission to concentrate on.

That evening, Christoph went with the farmer to see his fields. Lisette laid out the plucked chicken and the wild sorrel she'd picked on the way back. She thumbed through the pages of her recipe book until she found the one she was looking for. Brathähnchen. One of her grandmother's favourites.

The ritual of preparing the chicken worked its magic and calmed Lisette's nerves. There was no lemon thyme available so she chopped a little extra of the sorrel. Cooking always had this effect. She heard her grandmother's voice speaking the instructions. *Loosen the chicken skin and rub some of the herb and butter mixture under it.*

While the chicken cooked, Lisette slipped the paring knife into her pocket. It would come in handy for the drop-off early tomorrow morning. She'd need something to open the tomato tin and extract whatever it was that her superiors in London had hidden inside.

'That smells delicious,' Christoph said when he returned. His presence upset the balance. The room became charged with possibilities.

'Why do you have to inspect what they're growing?'

Lisette said. Her tone was conversational, but she knew Seraphin would want to know.

Christoph uncorked a bottle of white wine and filled two glasses. 'French farms aren't productive enough for the Reich. At least, that's what those in authority say.'

'They've always made enough for the French,' Lisette said firmly.

'I know,' Christoph said. Lisette detected the strain in his voice. 'It's wrong that all this food should be plundered from France and taken to Germany.'

He was more sensitive than other Germans she'd come across, at Maxim's and in Le Meurice, who didn't think twice about taking French food. But still, it was impossible to ignore that he was here in Normandy to facilitate the removal of produce that could go to feed the hungry in France. 'Yet, still it's happening,' she said.

'I know,' Christoph said. 'In fact, General Winkler, Head of the Production and Supplies Division, is arriving soon, the Kommandant told me. No doubt he'll want to discuss it all. There's to be a special dinner when he arrives.'

'What will he discuss?' Lisette asked lightly.

'I'm not sure of the details, but overall production issues, I expect,' Christoph said. 'The Kommandant says that certain crops are said to be of "first importance". The army needs more oilseed to replace fuel that we can no longer get from North Africa. Instead of wheat waving in the fields, Hitler wants to see sunflowers.'

'Sunflowers?' Lisette said. 'Such happy flowers. I can't imagine them being used for war.'

'No, but they grow quickly. I persuaded the farmer to

plant more of his fields with sunflowers. There will be hectares of yellow dancing in the breeze.'

Lisette shuddered at the thought. Here she was, in the company of a man who had just convinced – or, more accurately ordered – a French farmer to grow produce that would aid the enemy's war effort. She got up and went to the cupboard to get a candle, hiding the anguish on her face.

Lisette lit the candle and placed it on the table, forcing a smile. 'See, I was right. You had no need of a translator.'

It had grown dark outside, and the candle gathered the room around them, drawing them closer.

'I'm sorry, I can see you're upset. I wish I didn't have to follow orders, but if I deviate from what's expected, the Kommandant will know. It could affect my family.'

'I know,' Lisette said. She understood the bind he was in.

'This meal is delicious,' Christoph said, clearly making an effort to lighten the mood. 'You're a remarkable cook. Being here with you, talking like this . . .'

His eyes shone in the candlelight and he looked straight at her. Heat rushed through her body. It came from some unthinking, heedless part of herself. She took a gulp of wine.

'Tell me about your fiancée,' she said.

The word 'fiancée' fell like cold water and took the shine out of his eyes.

'Better not,' Christoph said. 'It doesn't put me in a good light.'

Lisette almost regretted asking. He looked so sorrowful. But it had cooled the unexpected desire she'd felt between them, so she persevered.

'Why not?'

Christoph rested his knife and fork on his plate.

'Because I made a promise in haste rather than in love, and that's never a good thing. It's not her fault. Hilde is simply herself and, in some ways, that's comforting.' He sighed. 'I wonder if I'd have asked her to marry me if it hadn't been for the war . . .'

He gazed at her, leaving the words unsaid. Lisette read his mind, the suggestion he was making. This task she'd been given was turning into more than just seduction. She felt as if they were hovering on the edge of something far deeper. Flustered, she picked up the dish of left-over chicken.

'I'll take the rest of this to the farmer's wife,' she said. 'She might rethink her bad opinion of me.'

Outside, night was falling. Lisette leaned against the cold stone of the cottage wall. This trip was even harder than she'd thought.

The farmer's wife softened a little at the sight of Lisette and the Brathähnchen. She didn't invite Lisette into the house but gave her a brief nod of thanks. Through the open door, Lisette saw a couple of dogs and the children by the fire. Satisfied that nothing here would impede her mission in the early hours of the next morning, she parted from the farmer's wife with a smile.

Christoph insisted on sleeping in the camp bed. Lisette took her suitcase and went behind the sheet, pretending to change. She sat down on the bed and listened while he moved around the room, clearing up the table, shaking out the bedding. Would he ever settle down? She couldn't leave until he was sound asleep.

Eventually, she heard the clunk of his belt buckle on the floor. Lisette held her breath. The camp bed creaked as he got into it.

'Good night, Sylvie,' he said.

'*Bonne nuit*,' she replied.

Lisette looked up at the eaves crisscrossing the ceiling. Were Christoph's eyes open? Her whole body tensed at the thought of him just a stone's throw away. It became so unbearable that she nearly said his name just to break the silence. Then she heard a soft snuffle that deepened into a snore. Thank God. He'd fallen asleep.

His deep breathing became regular. The darkness thickened. Slowly, Lisette stood up. Christoph didn't stir as she tiptoed past him and out of the cottage.

It was strange to be out at night in the empty yard. The missions in Paris were done in daylight, in the hustle and bustle of the city. If anyone saw her out and about at this time of night, it would immediately raise suspicions.

The farmhouse shutters were closed. The dogs whined. Lisette licked her finger and tested the direction of the wind. Thankfully, it was blowing away from the house, so hopefully the dogs wouldn't pick up her scent.

She found the path through the woods. The moon shone, giving enough light to see by. Boughs creaked overhead. At night, she'd be safer out in the open. SOE training had taught her that: less chance of ambush. But there was no other way to the mill.

She reached the pond. Only that afternoon, she'd sat here with Christoph. An owl hooted in the abandoned rafters of the mill. Lisette stayed in the shadows close to the wall. The minutes ticked by. Then, from behind the mill, a flurry of pigeon wings.

A few metres away, a female voice whispered. 'Are you here to see the bats?'

'*Oui*,' Lisette replied, remembering the phrase Seraphin had given her. 'And the other nocturnal creatures.'

A young girl, twenty perhaps, came out of the shadows. She wore black trousers and a brown workman's jacket. Her hair was tied back in a scarf and she carried a rucksack on her back.

'I'm Marie,' she said, with a brief smile.

She handed Lisette a spade, put her fingers to her lips, then pointed away from the millpond. Lisette gripped the rough handle and followed her through the trees.

Lisette had been trained in Scotland for drop-offs. How to use lights to make a temporary runway. The necessity of speed and caution. But this was the first time she'd done it outside of practice. She'd be relying on Marie's local knowledge.

After a mile or so of walking in silence through the forest, they came to a vast clearing. Lisette assessed the area. The ground was soft, which meant the parachutes could easily be buried, and the trees were far enough away to enable the plane to see their lights.

'Well done,' she said to Marie. 'This is an excellent spot.'

'Let's get the flashlights in place,' Marie said. 'The plane will be here soon.'

Marie and Lisette pressed the lights into the ground: *Three white lights in line, 100 metres between each light*, as the SOE handbook instructed. Then they ran back into the cover of the trees to wait.

'How many times have you done this?' Lisette whispered.

'Three or four. Once for an agent drop-off, the rest for supplies,' Marie said. 'I used to play in these woods as a child: I know every inch. My brothers are prisoners of war in Germany. I wanted to do something to help.' She glanced at Lisette. 'And you?'

'Apart from when I was parachuted into France, this is my first time at a drop-off. I've been in Paris.'

Marie shook her head. 'I prefer the countryside. There are more places to hide. The Boche can't cover a vast forest like this.'

Lisette thought of Le Meurice. 'In Paris, we hide in plain sight. It doesn't matter where we fight, so long as we resist.'

Marie nodded. 'On this we can agree.'

Up above, an engine hummed. This was the most dangerous part. Lisette knew the noise of the engine would attract attention. They had to get the delivery as soon as it landed and disappear before anyone could trace their position.

Marie flashed a recognition signal. Up ahead, the aircraft whirred, low enough for them to make out the open door, from which a light flashed in answer.

'Get ready,' Lisette said.

Just visible in the moonlight, a small parachute on which a canister was suspended fluttered down. It landed with a muted thud on the earth. Then another came, wide of the mark. The wind picked up and blew it towards the woods, where it got tangled in the trees.

The plane circled, then headed away.

'I'll get the parachute and the canister from the tree,' Marie said. 'You kill the lights and get the other one.' She threw her rucksack down at the bottom of the tree and climbed up the branches.

Lisette switched off the flashlights, then cut the strings of the parachute with the knife and folded it up into a bundle. Using the spade, she buried the parachute in the soft earth, and took the canister and flashlights back into the safety of the woods. She stowed the lights in the undergrowth. Inside the canister, she found the tin of tomatoes Seraphin had spoken of. She stuffed it into her pocket.

'Marie,' she whispered, venturing over to the tree. 'Have you got it?'

'Nearly. Stay hidden and keep watch.'

Lisette pressed herself against the tree trunk. Far in the distance, a light caught Lisette's eye. A dog barked. German voices carried on the wind.

'Soldiers are coming,' Lisette said urgently.

'I'm not leaving without the supplies,' Marie whispered from high up in the branches.

Flashlights bobbed through the trees. Lisette guessed there were two soldiers, but they'd be armed. Time was running out.

'Leave the canister and come now.' She couldn't see Marie, but she heard the rustling of branches.

'It's nearly free. Don't worry about me, just go.'

'No. I'm not leaving you.'

The dogs barked, louder this time. They were getting nearer. Adrenalin sped through Lisette's body. There would be no explaining this away. Right now, they were sitting ducks.

'My foot's tangled in the damn string,' Marie whispered.

The dogs whined. Had they picked up a scent? Lisette remembered her SOE training: *Help the arrested agent to escape only if it can be done without prejudicing the security of the organization.*

Sod that, Lisette thought, heaving herself into the branches. I'm not going without her. She found Marie halfway up the tree. With a swift movement, she sliced through the parachute strings with her knife, freeing Marie's leg. 'Down, now, and run for it.'

They jumped down and ran through the trees, away from the clearing, branches whipping their faces. One of the soldiers gave a shout. Seconds later, a shot fired. Lisette ducked but, beside her, Marie fell to the ground with a cry. She'd been hit.

Another shot rang out. Marie cried out in pain. Lisette crouched down. God, she'd been struck in the neck. Blood gushed from the wound. Marie pushed her away. 'You have to go,' she gasped.

Lisette hesitated. She could take on one soldier perhaps, but not two that were armed. The mission had been to collect the package for Seraphin. She had that in her pocket. Above all else now, she had to keep it safe, but not at Marie's expense.

'Take my hand,' Lisette implored.

Marie shook her head. 'I beg you, go now,' she cried, 'or it'll have all been in vain.'

Lisette stared into Marie's eyes for a moment. She was clearly in pain, unable to run. Her face was very pale with the loss of blood. 'I can't abandon you.'

Marie cupped Lisette's face. 'I won't survive this. I want you to escape and keep fighting for France.' She winced in pain. 'Give me your tablet. I know you have one. Let me finish this now before they can torture me.'

Lisette nodded, unable to bear the truth of what Marie was saying. She was too young to be dying like this, but to let her fall into the hands of the Germans and have her pain prolonged was unthinkable. Lisette cut the hem of her skirt with the knife and placed the rubber-coated cyanide pill in Marie's hand.

'Run,' Marie said, putting it into her mouth and biting hard.

The soldiers were nearly upon them. Lisette's SOE training kicked in and she tore herself away and ran. She fled through the trees, Marie's words ringing in her ears, and stopped only when she reached the millpond.

Lisette gasped, trying to catch her breath, blood thumping in her ears. As far as she could tell, no one had followed her. Her stomach churned as her mind relived the anguish of the last few moments.

There was no time to dwell on it now. She had to work quickly. Lisette gouged open the tomato tin with the knife. Peeling back the jagged metal, she found a small vial inside and stuffed it into her pocket. She threw the tin and the knife into the millpond and made her way back along the path, her body trembling with shock and fear.

The farm was just as she'd left it: silent and sleeping. She crept in, the wood making a faint creak as she trod, and stole back through to the half of the room where Christoph lay sleeping.

Her hands shook as she changed into her nightdress.

She buried the vial at the bottom of her suitcase. Christoph's breathing remained steady.

Terrible images flashed through Lisette's head: Marie's screams, the shots, the sickening feeling of being unable to help her, the terrible finality of the pill. It was horrific, all of it – those soldiers were barbarians, no better than dogs themselves. Lisette choked back a sob, but another came, just as fierce.

'Sylvie?' Christoph whispered. 'Are you all right?'

In that moment, the accent of his voice linked him to the soldiers. 'I'm fine,' she said, through gritted teeth.

'Are you sure?'

'Yes, go back to sleep,' She gripped the sheets with her fists.

But she heard him get up and walk over. He pulled the sheet aside. In the moonlight that glowed through the curtains, she saw his chest was bare, the pyjama trousers gathered close around his hips.

'What happened?' he whispered. 'Did you have a bad dream?'

The whole war was a nightmare: all the losses, the sacrifices. But what had happened to Marie was not a dream. The fear and terror in her eyes had been real. Lisette couldn't hold the anguish back. She began to cry – anger and sorrow mixed together.

Christoph came over and sat down on the bed next to her. Lisette drew back. 'Don't come near me.'

'I don't understand,' he said. 'What have I done?'

'I can't bear it any more,' Lisette said, her breath ragged, her words coming out between sobs. 'I hate this war. I hate what you're all doing to this country. Those I've loved are gone, and for what? They're dead, Christoph. Nothing will ever bring them back.'

Christoph stared at her, pain in his eyes. 'Oh, Sylvie.'

'I know you feel differently to other German soldiers, you show compassion and kindness and hate it too, but that's just words. Those sunflowers aren't just crops. They're fuel for planes and tanks and more killing.' Lisette buried her head in her hands.

Christoph sighed. 'I see,' he said. 'What I've done today is wrong. I fool myself that it's just farming, but it's more than that, isn't it? It's people's lives.'

'It's worse than that,' Lisette cried. 'Do you know what they're doing? There is a death camp in Poland, killing thousands of Jews, every minute, every hour, even as we speak. So many people are dying, Christoph.'

Christoph nodded. 'It's unspeakable, shameful, inhuman . . .' He struggled to find the words. 'I hate what my country is doing, Sylvie. You must believe me.'

'Do you?' Lisette said.

'Yes,' Christoph said desperately. 'I abhor this discrimination on the basis of race, sexuality or mental or physical disability. My sister is one of them, remember, an "idiot" whose life is deemed unworthy. Even before the war started, there were enforced sterilization and euthanasia killings in Germany of the mentally ill and others. I hate it as much as you do.'

Lisette nodded, sensing his torment, but what did it count for? The gulf between his role in the war and hers couldn't have been greater. Until this moment, Christoph had been asleep in his bed while Lisette and Marie had been out in the woods.

'I'm so sorry,' Christoph said, desperation in his voice. 'Maybe I can reduce the farmer's quota of sunflowers and we could bring some food back with us to distribute.'

'No. That would put you in danger. There's nothing you can do. That's the worst thing about it all.'

'The worst thing is seeing you in such pain and not being able to take you in my arms,' he said softly.

Lisette drew in her breath. In the tenderness of his voice lay the crux of her torment. She could hardly bear the truth of it. At this very moment when she felt such rage and despair against the Germans for what they'd done – to her grandparents, Johnny, Hélène, Marie, to everyone in this war – she longed for Christoph, of all people, to comfort her.

He was so close she felt the warmth emanate from his skin. Every muscle in her body ached to feel his arms around her, to lose herself in the safe harbour of his embrace.

'Sylvie . . .' He gently touched her chin and lifted her head up to meet his eyes. The depth and connection that met her gaze took her breath away. 'I know that I am everything you hate, everything you despise, and that I shouldn't have brought you here. But, despite how impossible it all is, I'm falling in love with you.'

Lisette struggled to fight the desire welling inside. 'Please, just hold me,' she said, her fingers trembling, not daring to acknowledge what he'd just said.

Christoph pulled her close. Something stirred within her: molten, burning, urgent. His hand slid down her back, leaving a trail of heat. His eyes were hungry, full of need, a need she shared.

In that moment, she was neither Lisette nor Sylvie. She was nameless, lost in longing and hoping to forget the horrors of the woods.

At the first touch of his lips Lisette gasped with the exhilaration of being close to him, her skin burning, their tongues entwined.

There was no more pretending, no more waiting. He was here. He pressed against her, his chest hard and firm, his hands slipping under her nightdress. She moved closer, desperate to feel his skin against hers.

He paused just inches from her face, and looked into her eyes. 'If you don't want this, Sylvie,' he said. 'Just tell me.'

Of course she wanted it. Every fibre of her being craved him. But at his words, her doubt and the horror of the night flooded back.

'No, not like this,' she said.

She summoned all her strength and pulled away. This was madness, driven by her need to obliterate the memory of what had happened to Marie. Nothing else. Seraphin had told her not to lose her heart. Christoph was part of a mission. That was all. If she gave herself to him, it had to be as an agent, carrying out a task. Not as a woman overcome by desire.

'I'm sorry,' Christoph said. 'I shouldn't have kissed you.'

Lisette straightened her nightdress and took a deep breath. 'It's not your fault. Just forget it.'

Christoph stood up, his face flushed. 'Sleep well, then. No more bad dreams.'

Christoph went back into the shadows, his bare feet padding over the floor to the camp bed. Lisette lay down and pulled the covers over her, trying erase the thought of him from her mind.

Something had happened tonight. Some line had been crossed. But as her eyelids sealed shut and sleep overcame her, Lisette had no idea if the step they'd taken would be irrevocable or simply a dream that would fade and be gone by morning.

28

Julia

July, 2002 – Paris

The journey back from Normandy had been peaceful. Julia had sat in the back of the car while Daniel explained more about his plans for the farm to Christoph. Now, the interconnecting door between Julia's room and Christoph's was ajar. Daniel was getting Christoph ready for bed, their companionable conversation continuing.

Julia liked hearing their voices. She'd deliberately left them to it, not wanting to get in the way. She opened a bottle of wine that she'd ordered to be sent to her room and poured a glass, sitting by the window. Her mind was full of the visit to the farm.

While Monique had washed the dishes and Raymond and Daniel had gone to see the orchard, Christoph had talked for a long time, his eyes closed, conjuring the recollections of his trip with Sylvie to the farm one by one. He remembered the moment they'd kissed and then she'd pulled away. Julia had breathed a sigh of relief. He made no mention of a Frenchwoman being shot and killed in the woods, which meant that it couldn't have been Sylvie.

Julia sighed. It was hard to believe, but in two days she was due to go home. Back to the cold little flat, to feeling sick with fear about her hands. The concert in Salzburg in a week's time loomed on the horizon.

It wasn't the stiffness of her hands that frightened her most, it was the realization that she'd lost her love of playing. She took a sip of wine and gazed at the rooftops. She had no idea how to bring that love back.

'Christoph says goodnight,' Daniel said, coming to the door. 'I think I've worn him out with all my talk.'

Julia smiled. 'He's loved it.' She glanced to check the recipe book was out of sight. It was hidden in her bag on the table.

'I suppose I'd better turn in too,' Daniel said.

'You could join me for a drink,' Julia said, 'if you want to.'

'I do.'

Julia filled a glass for Daniel. He'd caught the sun from being out in the fields.

'It was a beautiful farm,' she said. 'I could have stayed there for ever.' She rubbed her hands. If only it were possible.

'You're thinking about the piano,' Daniel said.

'Actually, I'm trying not to think about it, but sometimes that makes it worse.'

'What was that tune you were humming on the way back?'

The day had spun a melody in her head. She hadn't realized she'd been humming it out loud.

'I made it up. I used to write music when I was younger, but I ended up focusing on grades and performances.'

'You wrote something with Christoph that first time you came to Bonn,' Daniel said, taking a drink of his wine.

'Yes, inspired by Eberhard Müller, I wrote my own ending for Mozart's unfinished "Fantasia No. 3 in D minor".' It had been exhilarating to get to know the piece and then compose a new section.

'I remember. I heard you practising it. It sounded incredible,' Daniel said. 'You should write it down – the tune you hummed in the car. What inspired it?'

'The farm, I suppose. The peacefulness, how much Christoph enjoyed seeing it all again. It must've been an oasis of calm during the war.'

'A last respite before he was sent to fight in the east,' Daniel said.

Julia sat up. This was news to her. 'I didn't know Christoph was sent to Russia. When was that?'

'No idea,' Daniel said. 'He always clammed up when the subject of Russia arose. They needed every man out there by the end of 1942.'

Nineteen forty-two. That was the year he'd met Sylvie. What had happened for Christoph to be removed from Paris and sent to Russia? 'Didn't you ask him?' she said.

Daniel shook his head. 'I told you, I wanted to know more, but he never wanted to talk about it. I only remember that snippet about the farm.'

Julia felt a shiver of foreboding. If Christoph went to Russia, it meant that he and Sylvie must have had to part. How would Christoph cope if the memories broke his heart, perhaps all over again?

'Well, we know he survived,' Daniel said with a wry smile, 'or he wouldn't be here today. And nor would I.'

'No,' Julia said. But what about Sylvie? What had happened to her?

Daniel swilled the wine in his glass. 'I've been thinking about what you said the other night. How I should have been more direct instead of trying to send you a message in a game of Hangman. I'd like to tell you what that hangman said now, if you'll listen.'

He glanced at Julia, his eyes impenetrable. Warmth stole into her core. 'I'll listen,' she said, catching her breath.

'Do you have any paper?'

Julia ripped off a sheet from her notebook and handed him a pen.

'Promise you won't laugh,' he said.

He wrote down the blanks: _ _ _ / _ _ _ _ _ / _ _ _ _ / _ _

'I won't make you guess,' he said, raising his eyebrows. 'I seem to recall it was the little girl doing all the guessing anyway.'

In capital letters, he filled in the blanks: H-A-V-E/D-I-N-N-E-R/W-I-T-H/M-E. He clicked the pen closed and glanced at her shyly.

'That's what you wrote?' Julia said. 'The first day we met?'

'Yes, well, you disappeared in a taxi, only to reappear as Christoph's student. The moment came and went.' He paused. 'I regret not being more direct.'

'And now?' Julia asked, her breath shallow.

The air around them tightened. His eyes dimmed as he contemplated her. 'And now I'm going to do what I should have done back then, right before everything got complicated.'

He reached out and took Julia's hand. His thumb stroked along her palm. The movement passed like a current through her body. She swallowed, unable to move. He leaned in towards her and his lips touched hers, the contact enflaming her mouth. She moved closer. Her elbow nudged her bag. It slid off the table. Julia caught the handle just in time, but the contents fell on to the floor: pens, her purse, chewing gum, make-up. Then she saw it: the recipe book. Her heart stopped. Glancing up at Daniel, she could tell that he'd seen it too. The colour drained from his cheeks.

He reached down and picked it up. Julia's heart went cold. There, in his hand, was Sylvie's recipe book. He opened the front cover and stared at her.

'I don't believe it. This is the book, isn't it? Tatty brown cover, handwritten recipes. You've had it the whole time.'

'Daniel, please, I can explain . . .'

'Where did you get it from?'

The intimacy and warmth had evaporated. Julia felt sick.

'I found it,' she said. 'On a shelf, under the stairs. I didn't know what it was at first, but when Christoph refused to eat anything I thought I'd try some of the recipes.'

Daniel flicked through the pages. As he saw the recipes, realization dawned.

'This is why you've been taking such an interest in cookery,' he said, his voice hollow. 'Every meal is here. Why didn't you tell me?'

'I wanted to, but Christoph was afraid you wouldn't understand.'

Daniel shook his head. 'I thought you were evasive when I asked you if the recipes were from a specific book.

I told you that Mama had mentioned a woman called Sylvie.' He screwed his eyes closed. 'How could you have kept this from me?'

Julia's chest tightened. 'When you told me about your mum and the recipe book the other night I realized you'd be upset. But it wasn't my secret to tell. Christoph's recollections are helped by the recipes. He wants to remember what happened with Sylvie.'

Daniel put the book down, pain in his eyes. 'This has to stop, Julia,' he said. 'Mama told me to protect him from this part of his past. She made me promise not to let him track down Sylvie. I don't want him to get hurt.'

'That's not your decision,' Julia said, gently. 'It's Christoph's book, his memories.'

The interconnecting door opened. Christoph stood there, his face half full of sleep. 'What's going on? I heard voices.'

'Daniel's found Sylvie's recipe book,' Julia said. 'I'm just trying to explain –'

'I can't believe you kept this from me, Papa,' Daniel said, in anguish. 'You don't know what you're getting yourself into.'

'That book is mine,' Christoph said. His face was pale, his breath laboured. 'If I want to use it to regain my memories, then that's what I'll do.'

Daniel's face was grave. 'I'm sorry, Papa, I can't let this charade continue, not when you're going to get hurt in the long run.'

'What are you talking about?' Christoph stared at him.

Daniel put the book down. 'I know what happened to her, to Sylvie.'

Julia stared at Daniel in disbelief. She'd never expected that he would hold the key to Sylvie's fate.

'How?' Christoph said. He winced and clutched his stomach.

Daniel guided Christoph to a chair and knelt beside him. 'Mama told me when she was dying,' he said. 'She described the recipe book and told me to protect you from the past.'

Christoph stared at Daniel. 'But why would Hilde do that?'

'Because she knew that finding out what had happened to Sylvie would upset you deeply.'

'Why would it upset him?' Julia said, holding her breath. 'What happened to her?'

Daniel glanced at Christoph, hesitating. 'Are you sure you can't remember all this, Papa? There was a letter, tucked in the recipe book, addressed to you. You must have read it years ago and put it there.'

'I don't know,' Christoph said, his hands twisting anxiously. 'The memories of my time in France are coming back one by one, but this . . . it must've happened later. I don't remember a letter. What did it say?'

He stared at Daniel, his face ashen.

'If only you'd told me what you were doing, I could have prevented all this,' Daniel said, distressed. 'There's no good way to tell you this, but perhaps it will stop all the searching.' He took a deep breath. 'Mama said that the letter was from a private investigator. You must have hired him after the war and asked him to track down Sylvie.'

'And?' Christoph said. 'Did he find her?'

Daniel bit his lip. 'No, but he discovered what happened to her.'

'Tell me,' Christoph said.

Daniel clasped his father's hand. 'He found out that Sylvie had died. In 1942. During the war.'

Julia couldn't believe what he was saying. Sylvie. Dead.

Christoph blinked. 'What?'

'I'm sorry, Papa. She didn't make it. Mama told me the letter said that she died at the camp in Drancy.'

Christoph stifled a sob, his face grey. 'Stop, don't say any more.'

Julia felt a wave of despair. 'Daniel, are you absolutely sure?'

'I'm sorry, Julia. Mama was adamant that's what the letter said.' He turned to his father. 'I had to tell you, Papa. It's better that you know the truth.'

'*Nein*,' Christoph spluttered, his face screwed up with pain. 'You're doing this to punish me.'

'No,' Daniel said, aghast. 'I'd never do that. I didn't want to come to Paris, remember, but I came for you. I had no idea this was about Sylvie.'

Christoph gasped for breath, clutching his throat. Julia rushed towards him. He collapsed in her arms, fighting for air.

'Ring an ambulance,' she cried.

Daniel scrambled for the phone. Christoph's breath grew more ragged, his grip on Julia's hand weaker.

'Julia, believe me, I didn't mean for this to happen,' Daniel said.

Julia couldn't answer. All she could think about was Christoph. She couldn't bear the thought that his last memory might be Daniel's voice telling him the news of Sylvie's death.

29

Christoph

August, 1942 – Normandy

Morning came. Christoph had been waiting for the sun for hours. He'd kissed her. That's all he could think about. The memory of it wove a tight band around his heart. He longed for her to wake, for the chance to show her that his foolish mistake hadn't ruined things between them. But that was a lie. The kiss had changed everything inside of him.

Light seeped through the curtains. He heard voices in the farmyard, fists hammering on the farmhouse door. He got up and peered out of the window.

'*Aufmachen! Lass uns rein!*'

Two soldiers stood in the yard, guns over their shoulder.

The door opened. The soldiers wrenched the farmer outside.

'Show us where they're hiding!' one of the soldiers yelled.

The farmer shook his head. '*Je ne sais pas.*'

The farmer's wife came to the door, her children clinging to her skirts. One of the soldiers seized the youngest child, a girl with tangled brown hair, and held a gun to her head.

Until now, Christoph had simply watched the scene unfold. It was all happening so quickly. But the gun aimed at the child flicked a switch inside him.

'What's going on?' Sylvie said, coming to the window.

'Stay here.'

Christoph went outside, heart pounding. He wanted to pull the girl free, but he avoided looking at her. He strolled over, as if at ease.

'Who are you?' one of the soldiers asked.

'Leutnant Baumann, Administration Assistant to Kommandant Schaumberg. I'm here on a production research project for the Kommandant,' he said. The soldier lowered his gun a little. 'Has something happened?'

'There was a drop in the woods. One of the traitors escaped. Last seen running towards this place.' The soldier nodded to the farmer's family. 'We need to question them.'

'I've been here all night. There's been no disturbance,' Christoph said. 'I'd have heard something.'

'Even so,' the other soldier said, waving his pistol at the farmer and his wife, 'they must know something.'

'They don't speak German,' Christoph said. 'Let me talk to them in French.'

He turned to the farmer. '*Avez-vous vu quelqu'un ici hier soir?*'

'*Non*,' the farmer replied. 'Everybody knew the Kommandant's man was coming to stay. Even our neighbours have avoided us.' He glanced at his daughter. The little girl's face was frozen with fear. 'Don't let them kill her.'

'They don't know anything,' Christoph said to the soldier. 'Who'd hide here, where a German official is staying?'

The soldiers looked at each other, weighing up his words.

'Now, unless you want me to take your names and report you to the Kommandant for wasting time,' Christoph continued, 'I suggest you get going. *Sofort.*'

The soldiers left, muttering to each other, casting a backward glance at the farmyard.

'*Merci*,' the farmer's wife said, clutching Christoph's hand. 'I don't know how to thank you.'

'We're having pancakes,' the little girl said, tugging at his sleeve. 'Come and have some.'

Christoph glanced at the cottage and saw the faint outline of Sylvie's head at the window. The farmer's wife followed his gaze. 'Bring her too,' she said.

Christoph walked back to fetch Sylvie. His legs were empty, as if all his power was spent. Only now did he realize how dangerous his intervention could have been for all of them.

Sylvie stood by the table.

'You saved her,' she said.

The shadow of the eaves made it hard to see the expression on her face. But her voice was warm like a blessing. She seemed to hesitate, then she ran towards him.

The full length of her pressed against him, her thighs, the soft swell of her breasts, her mouth touching his lips and setting them alight. He clasped her close, his body still smouldering from the night before, ignited once again by her touch. He grabbed a fistful of her hair, savouring the thickness. Her scent engulfed him, the kiss deepening, the warmth spreading. Her hands slid under his shirt, her nails grazing his skin. He groaned.

'Sylvie,' he said huskily. 'We can't, not now. They want to give us breakfast. To say thank you.'

Sylvie's chest heaved as she caught her breath. God, he wanted to take her to bed and explore every inch of her. He kissed her swollen lips, desire breaking over him again.

She pulled away and smoothed down her nightdress. 'We'd better not get carried away then,' she said.

At the sight of her smile, playful and teasing, Christoph nearly lost control. He clenched his fists and swallowed. 'We'd better not,' he said.

He stepped away and waited while she got dressed, longing to slip behind the curtain that divided the room. Today, they'd be returning to Paris, to the constrictions of Le Meurice. This taste of freedom, of being simply himself, would be impossible to forget. He had no idea if it could continue back in Paris. But, for Sylvie, he was determined to try.

30

Lisette

August, 1942 – Normandy

Lisette watched Christoph with the farmer's daughter. He'd taken his notebook out of his pocket and was playing Hangman. The little girl frowned with concentration as she tried to think of the letters.

The farmer's wife had asked Lisette to write out the recipe for the roast chicken. She carefully copied it from the recipe book on to the back of an envelope the woman had given her.

Lisette's body was still flushed from where Christoph had touched her. Watching him outside, negotiating with the soldiers, a sudden realization had struck her. That kiss the night before, after she'd returned from the drop, hadn't been a mistake. She'd wanted it. A need for him had been building for weeks. There was no specific moment when it had started. Perhaps it had been since that first meeting, in the kitchen at Maxim's. She'd fought it all this time. So, when he had walked back to the cottage the instinct to run to him was overwhelming.

She touched her lips, still tingling from that kiss. Her body ached to be near him again. He glanced up at her. No smile, just a smouldering look that told her he felt the same.

The farmer's wife came and sat next to her.

'Your soldier saved our lives,' she said.

Lisette nodded. 'Yes. Only he's not my soldier.'

The woman looked at her. 'I think he is.' She sniffed. 'I'm not one to judge, but you should be careful.'

Lisette tore her gaze away from Christoph. The woman's face was full of concern.

'I am careful,' Lisette said. 'I'm here as his translator, nothing more.'

'I've seen the way you look at him,' she said. 'You know, the woman who was shot is dead. She was a young girl from the village. Barely out of school, but she did her duty.'

Lisette's heart lurched, seeing Marie's face in her mind. But she couldn't admit that she already knew Marie's fate. 'My God, that's terrible,' she said, her voice trembling.

'I heard she wasn't acting alone,' the woman said, raising her eyebrows.

Lisette drew in her breath. 'Where did you hear that?'

The woman glanced at Christoph. He was trying to guess the letters now.

'We're not ignorant, you know,' she said, her voice still low. 'Just because we live in the country, it doesn't mean we're not resisting too.'

'I see.' Did the woman know Lisette was an agent? It was impossible to tell. Lisette finished off the instructions for making the roast chicken. 'There. It's all written down.'

'*He* may be good,' the woman said, jerking her head towards Christoph. 'Who knows? But the rest are rotten. Is that what you want? To risk everything for a German soldier? There's more at stake, as you well know.'

Lisette shivered. She knew it was dangerous. Seraphin

had asked her to seduce Christoph, not to fall in love with him. Those kisses had touched her heart in ways she hadn't known existed, but she could never betray the trust the SOE had placed in her.

Christoph stood up and came over, tucking his notebook into his pocket.

'We'd better be heading back to Paris,' he said. 'Thank you so much for breakfast.'

The farmer's wife nodded. 'We are forever in your debt for what you did today.' She glanced at Lisette. 'Stay safe in Paris.'

Lisette thought over the woman's words as they travelled back along the country roads. Every now and then, Christoph glanced over and squeezed her hand. Lisette smiled back, but her heart was heavy. The woman was right. Lisette was an agent, here to do her duty and nothing more. Seraphin had picked her for this task because she was *sans cœur*. From now on, she needed to be more careful.

31

Christoph

August, 1942 – Paris

Two days after they returned from Normandy, Christoph came up to his room to write to his mother. It had been raining all morning but now the sun shone through the windowpane.

He sat at the desk. Three days ago, he'd swum in the millpond with Sylvie. Two days ago, he'd held her in his arms. Yet, since being back at Le Meurice he hadn't spent five minutes alone with her.

Rekindling that sense of freedom had proved impossible. Christoph had been handed a new list of farms to identify on the map. Sylvie was always in the kitchen, too busy to talk. Tonight, he decided, when she was clearing up, he'd try and get her alone.

He sighed and sat back in his chair. How could he describe this situation to his mother? Someday, there'd be a reckoning between what he felt now and the life he'd left behind. But he wouldn't think about that yet.

A short tap sounded on the door. Christoph opened it, and there was Jean.

'I need your help,' he said. 'The leg is infected. I've been up to the storerooms and dressed the wound, but it'll need a new dressing and I've got a couple of days off. It'll look suspicious if I'm here. Will you do it?'

Christoph didn't hesitate. 'Of course.' He took the bandages from Jean and a bottle of disinfectant.

'*Merci*,' Jean said.

'Thank you for trusting me,' Christoph said.

Jean scowled. 'I'm not sure I do, not yet. But *he* does. And that's enough for me.'

At ten o'clock that evening, Christoph headed down to the kitchen, hoping to see Sylvie. The kitchen was empty and silent. The stainless-steel worktops shone.

'Sylvie,' he whispered.

He found her round the corner, near the larder. She was plunging saucepans into a sink full of water. She turned, deep in thought, a frown etched between her eyes.

'Oh, you startled me,' she said.

'I wanted to see you. Is it a bad time?'

'No, of course not.' Her voice was brisk. She scrubbed the pot with a brush.

It was like starting over, getting to know her again. And yet, she'd kissed him, twice. Kisses that had kept him awake, burning with desire, ever since.

'Is everything all right?' he said, touching her arm.

'Of course.' But she still didn't look at him.

'I've hardly seen you since we came back. Things aren't the same here as they were at the farm.'

Sylvie lifted the pot on to the draining board.

'I've been busy, that's all. The farm was a beautiful interlude, but we've both got work to do here at Le Meurice.' She glanced at him, her expression guarded.

He couldn't bear the politeness of her tone. 'Then let me take you out to lunch tomorrow,' he said.

'I'm sorry, I can't tomorrow. Perhaps the weekend after. Things might be quieter then.'

Christoph's heart snagged on her words. Was she making excuses? She rubbed her hand across her forehead, leaving a blossom of foam in her hair.

'What are you doing tomorrow?' he said.

'Now that the Kommandant is allowing me to leave the hotel, I thought I'd catch up with an old friend.' Sylvie wiped her hands on her apron. 'I'm sorry. It's been so busy here and I . . . well . . .'

'An old friend?' His chest flared with possessiveness. Who was this old friend? Were they male or female? Why would Sylvie prefer to spend her precious time off with this person instead of him?

'You're having second thoughts,' he said, thinking desperately of their kiss. She'd been quiet on the journey back, but he had thought she was just tired.

Sylvie finally looked at him. 'No, I don't regret what happened, it's just . . . I'm not sure what should happen now.'

Silence filled the space between them. So that was it. She was as nervous as he was about what it all meant.

'Sylvie . . .' Christoph brushed the foam away. He cupped her head and drew her towards him in a kiss.

Sylvie responded, her mouth warm against his, but then she drew back.

'It's all happening too quickly,' she said.

'Then come to lunch. We can just talk,' Christoph

said. He took her hand. 'Or I could come and meet your friend too.'

Sylvie frowned. 'No, I'm sorry.' She twisted her hand away and turned back to the sink. 'I'd better get on.'

Christoph woke the next morning to an empty day. He hadn't slept well, troubled by Sylvie's evasiveness the night before. She was like a waft of smoke he couldn't catch. Always that feeling of her being just out of reach. He got dressed, a sense of foreboding pulsing in his head. The question had been vexing him all night – was she really meeting an old friend, or was that an excuse? He splashed his face with cold water from the jug. He couldn't bear it any longer. He had to find out.

He waited by the door of his office, which had a view of the hotel reception. There was no sign of her at nine o'clock. By ten o'clock, he felt conspicuous. His head still ached from the thoughts swirling round his mind. This was nonsense. Worse still, it was demeaning. He was about to creep back to his room when Sylvie appeared.

She walked out of the hotel and turned left, heading down the rue de Rivoli towards the Louvre. Keeping well back and sticking to the other side of the street, Christoph followed, feeling ridiculous, but insecurity drove him on. At the metro, she stopped to show her papers, then got on a train. Christoph jumped into one of the other carriages, craning his neck at every stop to see where she got off.

Christoph nearly lost her in the station. By the time he caught up, she was stepping into a café in a little cobbled square. He watched from a distance, under the shade of a chestnut tree, as she took a seat by the window.

For a few minutes, nothing happened. Then Sylvie stood up, a cautious smile on her face. A man had arrived, tall, good-looking, with piercing blue eyes. They embraced, a kiss on each cheek. The man held her a fraction too long for Christoph's liking.

They sat down, drawing their chairs close to each other. The man touched her hair, pulling a strand out of her eyes. Sylvie glanced at him, smiling. Christoph watched them talk. They seemed absorbed, close . . . *intimate*. Had she ever talked to Christoph so intently? The man put his arm around her shoulders.

Christoph leaned back against the wall. So she *had* been lying. Nausea filled his stomach. Sylvie had been an anchor to his true self. Now, seeing her like this with that man, he was adrift again.

32

Lisette

August, 1942 – Paris

Lisette crossed the street and headed to the café. She hadn't liked lying to Christoph, but what else could she do? She'd seen his face fall and knew what was crossing his mind. The farmer's wife's warning circled her thoughts. The feelings he'd unleashed in her were dangerous.

The café was busy but she managed to find a table by the window.

'What are you looking so earnest about?' Seraphin said when he arrived.

'Nothing,' she said, forcing a smile. She couldn't tell him the thoughts that swirled inside her.

He kissed her on each cheek. She slipped the vial into his pocket as they embraced.

'What happened with the train?' she asked in a low voice.

They sat close together so they could whisper. The café was so crowded the noise drowned out their words.

'We blew up the tracks; the train never made it to Köln. It's lying on its side in a French field.'

'That's good,' Lisette said. 'One less train to feed the German troops.'

'How did you get on with your Boche? I hope the trip

to Normandy hasn't turned you into a double agent?' He tucked a strand of hair behind her ear with a teasing smile.

'Of course not,' she said. 'I'd never betray my own country.'

'I know you wouldn't.' Seraphin patted her hand and moved his chair closer. 'But perhaps you are a double agent of the heart?'

He was so near the truth that she panicked. Did it show in her face?

Seraphin smiled. 'A crazy idea, *ne'est-ce pas*? Besides, I know you're *sans cœur*, that's why you're perfect for this job.'

She smiled. How wrong he was. But she was trying to fight her feelings.

'Did you hear what happened to Marie?' Lisette said.

Seraphin nodded and stirred his coffee, a solemn look on his face. 'She didn't make it. And we almost lost you too.' He cupped her cheek. 'Every time I see Estelle and say goodnight, I think how I'd feel if my daughter was an agent in the field. You're doing something very brave, Lisette. I'm proud of you.'

Lisette nodded, warmed by his affirmation. But she couldn't help thinking of the others. Hélène. Marie. Twice now, others had perished while Lisette had escaped. The guilt was unbearable. Even more reason to shut Christoph out of her heart.

'I want to do more,' she said, her jaw tight. Something to atone for the sin of falling for Christoph.

'Oh, you will.' He leaned in. 'Did Leutnant Baumann tell you that an important visitor is coming from Berlin?'

'Yes, I was going to tell you. General Winkler. Christoph

said there's going to be a dinner. But how do you know this?'

'You're not my only agent, Lisette. General Winkler is Head of the Production and Supplies Division. Most of the food that gets shipped out from France is heading east to the troops in Russia. He's come to talk about stepping up production for a last push. But you're going to disrupt their plans.'

'I don't understand.'

Seraphin put his arm around her shoulder, leaning his head closer to conceal what he was saying.

'At the lavish dinner at Le Meurice,' he whispered, 'you'll make one of the courses. The vial will be the secret ingredient.'

'What's in it?'

'Poison,' Seraphin whispered. 'It's too dangerous to leave at the hotel. But I'll find a way to return it to you when the time is right. Pour it into the mixture. That's all you need to do. By the time they're choking on their own vomit, you'll have fled.'

'It will kill them,' Lisette murmured.

'What's in that vial is deadly stuff.' Seraphin said. 'All that canoodling with your German suitor will have paid off when he feels his throat tighten and the air deplete in his lungs.'

Lisette blinked, taking in his words. 'But . . .'

Christoph's death on her hands. She could never harm him. Unexpectedly, he'd crept into her empty heart. Yet that is exactly what Seraphin was asking of her.

'This is for you,' Seraphin said.

He slid a pair of keys across the table, each with a brown label fastened to it. Written on the labels was *Apartment 14.*

'The apartment is on rue Pastourelle,' Seraphin continued. 'A safe place to go after the dinner until we can fly you out of France. There's a spare, in case. Don't worry, no one uses the place, and if you take food for the concierge, he'll turn a blind eye.' He smiled. 'In one fell swoop, you'll kill the whole dining room full of Germans.'

'Why not target General Winkler?' Lisette's mind scrabbled for alternatives. 'Your plan is too risky.'

'Don't tell me you're getting faint-hearted. You could get the Légion d'Honneur for this.' Seraphin's face was etched with urgency. He gripped her hand. 'You owe it to Marie and Hélène. Not to mention Johnny and your grandparents. Oh yes, I know the SOE said hatred was your weakness, but now's your chance to turn it into a strength.'

The next day, Lisette rose early and washed her face. She hadn't slept well. Her orders were to carry out Seraphin's plan and leave France, but how could she do it without risking Christoph's life?

She got dressed for her morning shift, shivering in the cool air. In five days, she'd have to leave France and never see Christoph again, and he may very well be dead by then, though she'd do everything to try and avoid it. That same recklessness she'd felt at the farm returned. If she was never going to see Christoph again, what harm would it do to act on her emotions? To give in and let him love her. Lisette glanced in the mirror and touched her cheek. Even the thought of it made her burn.

She'd just finished dressing when there was a tap at the door. The Kommandant stood in the corridor, filling every corner of the narrow space.

'Aren't you going to invite me in?' he said.

Lisette stood back and let him pass. What was he doing here? He filled the room like a thick, grey fog. He took off his gloves and laid them on the bedside table.

'So, I hear there was an irregular occurrence while I was away.' He raised his eyebrows. 'An unauthorized companion went with Leutnant Baumann to the farm. I know it was you. I've spoken to the head chef.'

'I'm sorry, Herr Kommandant. Leutnant Baumann asked me if I wanted to see the countryside.'

The Kommandant rubbed his chin. 'The countryside, eh? It seems he got caught up in a search of the farmhouse. You can tell me. I've read the reports.'

'Leutnant Baumann cleared up the problem, I believe.'

The Kommandant smiled. 'A knight in shining armour. I can imagine how his chivalry touched your heart. But you see, they never did catch that other person. It would have been better if Leutenant Baumann had let them search the farm, don't you think?'

Lisette steadied her breathing. 'It wasn't up to me, Herr Kommandant,' she said.

'And yet you didn't reveal yourself to the soldiers. Nobody mentioned you in the report, which struck me as strange.'

Did he know about her involvement in the drop? Or was there something else he wanted?

He went to the window and undid the catch. 'Such an interesting view. Come over here and see.'

She hesitated. The Kommandant held out his hand and ushered her into the space before him. She stared at the Louvre and the Tuilleries. He stroked her hair.

'Since reading the report, I've been intrigued. What is it about Leutnant Baumann that has beguiled you? He's such an ordinary fellow.' His breath trespassed on her skin. 'I'd look after you much better than he does.'

He bent down and kissed her neck.

Lisette ducked out of his grasp. 'You're mistaken about Leutnant Baumann and me, Herr Kommandant. I had a fiancé, you see, and I'm loyal to his memory.'

The Kommandant smiled. 'I admire loyalty, up to a point. But sometimes it's better for one's own survival to be a little disloyal. Don't worry, I won't give up on you. My wife and son are departing soon for Germany. I'll need some company then.'

He bowed, and left her, closing the door behind him.

The room felt different. It smelled of his cologne, his arrogance. Her skin had been stained by his lips. She wanted to bathe in scalding water and rid herself of his scent.

She stood by the window and let the breeze blow over her. She hated him. She didn't care if he died at the dinner. But Christoph had to live. Somehow, she'd ensure he didn't eat the poisoned food. Lisette was determined to take whatever goodness she could find in the war and, for these last few days in Paris, make it her own.

That night, after her shift ended, Christoph was waiting outside her room.

'I need to speak to you,' he said, his face serious.

Lisette closed the window, pulled the black-out curtains and switched on the lamp on her chest of drawers. It was strange having him this close, knowing that it was only a matter of days before she'd never see him again.

'I'm glad to see you,' she said. 'I'm sorry we couldn't spend yesterday together.'

She reached out to take his hand, but he moved away.

'You didn't look sorry,' he said.

'What do you mean?'

'I saw you in the café. With that man. You said you were meeting a friend. It certainly looked friendly.' His face was pained and angry. 'If you wanted me out of the picture, why not say so? There was no need to lie.'

Lisette didn't know what to say. She'd lied to him, but not in the way he imagined.

'Oh, Christoph, it wasn't like that. You could've come into the café. Seen for yourself.'

Doubt showed in his face.

'What do you mean?' he said.

'I *was* meeting a friend.' Her mind worked quickly. 'Marcel was my fiancé's best friend. They grew up together. In fact, it was Marcel who introduced us, because my fiancé was too shy. I like to meet him from time to time. He knows stories from when they were little. It comforts me to hear them.'

How easily the lies came, but that was what she'd trained for.

Christoph bit his lip, digesting what she'd said. 'He's not your lover, then?'

Lisette took his hand. This time he didn't pull away.

'He's not, I promise. Never has been and never will be.' At least that part was true.

Christoph let out a huge sigh.

'Oh, Sylvie,' he said, clasping her hands, 'I'm sorry. At times, you seem distant. I thought the worst. I'm so ashamed.'

Lisette cupped his cheek with her hand. A fierce desire to protect him burned inside her.

'Whatever happens,' she whispered, 'finding you has been an unexpected gift.' She swallowed, determined to get the words out. 'There are a thousand reasons why this shouldn't happen, but we have to make the most of it.'

'Do you really mean that?'

Lisette nodded. She'd still do her duty. But why not take this gift while she had the chance? She pulled him close and ran her fingers through his hair. He responded urgently, his lips merging with hers. The room dimmed. The kiss cleansed everything – the lies, Seraphin's plan, the Kommandant.

Christoph pulled away, his eyes shining. 'Then let's –' He stopped mid-sentence.

He stared at the bedside table. 'What are those?'

Lisette followed his gaze. The Kommandant's black gloves.

'Christoph, it's not what you think,' she said.

Doubt tumbled back into his eyes. He let go of her. 'First the man in the café, now my superior.'

Lisette's arms stiffened. 'He came here to question me about the farm. You know what the Kommandant is like.'

'It says a lot that you're happy for a man like the Kommandant to occupy this room.'

'Stop it, Christoph,' she said. 'How can you be so hateful? That's not the kind of man I thought you were.'

Christoph didn't answer. He walked out and slammed the door shut. Lisette cried out in frustration. There were only five days left. Five days before she had to leave him for ever. How could she make him avoid the dinner if he no longer trusted her?

Fonds d'Artichauts Farcis

6 artichokes
6 slices of poitrine fumée (smoked streaky bacon)
2 tablespoons vegetable oil
2 onions, chopped
4 shallots, chopped
1 clove garlic, chopped
450g mushrooms, chopped
1 tablespoon puréed tomatoes
¼ teaspoon salt
125g unsalted butter
375ml stock
225g breadcrumbs

1. Trim the leaves from the artichokes.
2. Wrap the artichokes in the poitrine fumée and secure with string.
3. Cook in boiling water for about 20 minutes until the hearts are soft, then remove from the water.
4. Heat oil in a frying pan and cook the onions, shallots, garlic and mushrooms for 5 minutes.
5. Add the puréed tomatoes and salt.
6. Cook for a further 5 minutes.

7. Add the stock and cook for a further 10 minutes.
8. Remove the string and fill the artichokes with the vegetables.
9. Sprinkle with breadcrumbs and place under the grill until breadcrumbs begin to brown.

33

Julia

August, 2002 – Paris

Julia stretched her legs and tried to find a comfortable position. The waiting room at the Hôpital Saint-Antoine was almost deserted. She'd been here for hours. There'd been no sign of Daniel. With only room in the ambulance for one person, he'd told her to go with Christoph.

The doctor came over. 'Julia, is it?' he said, consulting his notes. 'I understand you were with Christoph when he was brought in?'

'Yes, how is he?'

'We've managed to stabilize him,' he said, 'but he's still very weak. We think he suffered a severe panic attack. Do you know what might have caused it?'

Julia thought of Daniel, telling Christoph that Sylvie had died. 'He'd just received some distressing news, and then he struggled to breathe.'

The doctor jotted something down on the clipboard. 'His white blood cell count is high. I'd like to do some more tests. You mentioned last night that he'd recently been discharged from hospital in Germany?'

'Yes. He collapsed with malnutrition and dehydration. And he's been suffering from confusion and memory loss. Could this be connected, do you think?'

'Possibly,' the doctor said. 'I'll see if we can get his notes from Bonn. Meanwhile, I need to keep him here, until we know the underlying causes for his weakness. He's complaining of a pain in his stomach. Then perhaps we can transfer him back to the hospital in Bonn once he's stable.'

Julia went to see Christoph. He lay ensconced in pillows. Tubes ran from his body into machines that hummed and flickered with lights.

'Julia, is that you?' He tried to smile, then winced, clutching his stomach.

'How do you feel?' Julia said.

'It doesn't matter,' he said weakly. 'Just tell me he's wrong. Tell me she could still be alive.'

Julia took his hand. 'I don't know. Daniel seemed very certain.'

Christoph closed his eyes. 'I'd know if she'd died, Julia, I'm sure of it. We have to find out. If only I could remember her surname . . .'

'Christoph,' she said gently. 'You need to stay here until you're well enough to be transferred to Bonn. I've got to head back to the UK soon.' She stroked his hand; his skin was as thin as paper. 'We might have to stop our search for now.'

Christoph's face skewed with pain. He clutched her hand. 'But you *must* stay. I can't stop now. I remember having a terrible argument with Sylvie. I was so jealous of a man she met in the café, of finding the Kommandant's gloves in her room. It wasn't the same after Normandy and I said some terrible things. Please. I need to know what happened next.'

'Oh, Christoph,' she said, torn. 'I promised Sebastian I'd go back and get ready for Salzburg.'

These were excuses, and she knew it. There might be demands on her time, contracts to be honoured, a career to salvage, but the thought of abandoning Christoph caused a dull ache in her chest.

'I need your help, Julia,' Christoph said.

He winced and clutched his stomach again. Julia couldn't bear it. The news of Sylvie's death had raised more questions than it had answered.

Daniel had been standing outside the hospital, hunched by the bike racks, hands in his pockets. Their brief kiss flashed in his mind. If he hadn't caught sight of the recipe book, what would have happened next? But he *had* seen it, and it was as if the kiss had never happened.

'How is he?' he said, once inside the hospital. 'I've been up all night, worrying.'

'You should have come with us. I've just been speaking to the doctor. They think last night was a panic attack, but they're concerned about the results of his blood tests, and he's got a terrible pain in his stomach. They want to look into it further.'

'It was awful last night,' Daniel said.

He looked wretched, but if Daniel hadn't told Christoph about Sylvie, he wouldn't have collapsed. 'The doctor said that it was shock that made him panic. He couldn't cope with what you told him, Daniel.'

Daniel stared down at his feet. 'I was trying to protect him.'

'He's in hospital, Daniel. Your words put him here.'

His eyes darted up. 'That's unfair. I had to tell him.'

Julia gripped the strap of her bag. 'Not like that. It was such a shock.'

Daniel rubbed his eyes; they were smudged with shadow. 'I feel terrible. But I couldn't keep it from him,' he said. 'I wish you'd told me the real reason we were in Paris. You led him on and got his hopes up about Sylvie. Not me.'

'I didn't get his hopes up,' Julia said firmly. 'There was no expectation of what we'd discover. I was enabling him to process the memories in his own time. You catapulted him into a reality he wasn't ready for.'

Daniel sighed. 'Yes, I see that now. I just wish I'd known what you were both doing.'

'Did your mum mention anything about Sylvie's surname? I wondered if it was on the letter. At least, if we knew that, we could check about her death.'

'I'm sorry, Julia, I don't remember,' he said, glancing at the floor. 'I just want all this to stop. Our family has been through so much: you don't know what it was like being the only child of two unhappy parents. It's just Papa and I left now. He's very old, Julia, and who knows how long I have left with him. I just wanted to spend some peaceful, happy times with him. I didn't want all this strife from the past to reappear and unsettle everything again.'

Julia's heart constricted.

'I understand it must have been hard, but like you said, we don't know how long he has left. If he wants to use this time to remember, we have to support him.' She glanced at the hospital. 'Look, I'm heading back to the hotel to get his things before we check out tomorrow. Could you sit with him while I'm gone?'

Daniel nodded, his brow creased. 'Of course. I'd like to tell him I'm sorry for how it all came out last night.'

Christoph hadn't brought much to Paris. Julia folded his shirts and placed them in his suitcase, followed by his trousers, a couple of jumpers and the guidebook of Paris. Soon the wardrobe was empty.

As she lifted the lid of the suitcase, something slid in the lining. Julia worked her fingers around the edges and found a rip where the stitches had come loose.

She took hold of what felt like string and pulled. Out of the hole came a luggage label, from which dangled a small iron key. The writing on the fob read: *Apartment 14.* Next to the words was an ink drawing of a shepherd's crook.

What did it open? A chest, a door, a house? Why was the key in the lining of Christoph's case?

Questions flickered through her mind. Was the key connected to Sylvie?

The telephone in Julia's room rang. She clutched the key in her hand and went to answer it. It was her sister, Anna.

'Where have you been?' Anna said. 'I kept ringing last night, but they said you weren't in. I've been worried sick.'

Julia caught sight of her face in the dressing-table mirror. She had dark rings around her eyes, and her hair was scrunched up in a messy ponytail.

'I'm sorry, I was at the hospital. Christoph collapsed again.'

'Oh my goodness, Julia. Is he all right?'

Julia sighed. 'No, not really. He's going to be in there for a while.'

'What will you do?' Anna said. 'Are you still planning to go to Salzburg?'

'I told Sebastian I'd come back and start practising, but I'm not sure it'll do any good.'

'What do you mean?'

Julia swallowed hard.

'I've fallen out of love with the music.' There, she'd said it. 'Or rather, it's fallen out of love with me. I'm terrified of playing, Anna. How can I go to Salzburg feeling like that?'

Her throat tightened with a sense of loss. She wanted to play at her best and be respected for it. But now, it seemed that was impossible.

'Besides,' Julia continued, swallowing her tears, 'I don't know if I can leave Christoph now.'

Anna was silent for a moment. 'Don't tell Sebastian any of that,' she said. 'It might jeopardize your career if he knows how you really feel about music.'

'What shall I do then?' The thought of Sebastian turning up again in Paris, on top of everything else, was unbearable.

'Surely Tanja can cover one more concert. The music world will respect you for looking after Christoph – he was your mentor, after all,' Anna said. 'Tell Sebastian you'll be back in time for the Elisabeth competition recording. Even better, he can arrange for you to do that in Bonn. You have to at least try and get through the first round. Just don't burn your bridges. You've worked too hard to throw it all away.'

Julia bit her thumbnail. 'I can't tell Sebastian I'm missing another concert. He'll go crazy.'

'Then let me to speak to him. Don't come back until you're ready. You concentrate on Christoph and I'll sort Sebastian out.'

A weight rolled off Julia's shoulders. 'Thank you, Anna.'

Julia put the phone down. She unfurled her fingers and looked at the key. Perhaps the search wasn't over yet.

34

Julia

August, 2002 – Paris

Christoph lay in the hospital bed, his eyes cloudy and weak. Julia had returned and found Daniel sitting awkwardly at Christoph's side, a plate of food on the table.

'Have you spoken to the doctor?' Julia asked him.

'Yes, he explained what you'd already told me. We're in a bit of a limbo until they do the tests. They've given him some painkillers for his stomach ache. I did try and persuade him to eat something, didn't I, Papa? But he's been asleep most of the time.'

'I'm sorry, I'm not hungry,' Christoph murmured.

'That's okay. We just want you to get better.' He leaned closer. 'I really am sorry about how I told you about Sylvie. I just thought it was for the best.'

Christoph patted his hand. 'I know.'

'Maybe you can stop all these recipes and memories now,' Daniel said gently.

Christoph sighed. 'It's not that easy. Knowing that she died makes me want to know how and why it happened.'

Daniel nodded. 'I'm not sure that's a good idea, but you don't have to decide now. There are other things we need to sort out. I need to find somewhere to stay now the booking at Le Meurice is almost up and Julia's heading back to the UK.'

'Actually, I'm not sure I'm going back yet,' Julia said.

Daniel's eyes flew to meet hers. A mixture of hope and wariness. 'How come?'

'I don't want to leave Christoph,' she said, nodding towards the bed.

'Ah, right, of course,' Daniel said. 'What about your next concert though? You've already given up so much to be here.'

Julia gave a small smile. 'I think I underestimated the problem with my hands,' she said. 'The fact that I can't rely on them is a symptom of something more.'

Christoph touched her hand. 'That's what I meant when I said that music flows from the heart to the hand and on to the keyboard.'

Daniel nodded. 'So, it's like your heart isn't in it any more? I wish there was something I could do.'

Julia shrugged off his sympathy, not wanting to dwell on it now. 'You could find somewhere we can both stay, more reasonably priced than Le Meurice. And close to the hospital.'

Daniel smiled. 'Now that I can do.' He kissed his father's cheek and gave him a hug.

'See you soon, Papa.' His eyes met Julia's. 'I'm glad you're staying.'

As the door clicked shut, a twinge of guilt lodged in Julia's chest. She'd hoped to get a moment alone with Christoph so that she could ask him about the key. But once again, it meant going behind Daniel's back. Julia took the key out of her bag.

'I found this in the lining of your suitcase.' Julia took the key out of her bag and handed it to Christoph.

He stared at it, turning it over in his hand. 'I recognize the feel of this.' He peered at the label. 'Apartment 14. What's that?'

Julia opened Sylvie's recipe book.

'I thought the key might be linked to Sylvie, and I was right. The next recipe is for fonds d'artichauts farcis. Sylvie wrote: *Ate this with C the first time we stayed in the apartment. Our haven.*' She pointed at the key. 'It must be for the apartment she mentions.'

'I don't recall an apartment. The last thing I remember is slamming her door closed,' Christoph said wearily. 'I was so foolish. Just when she'd finally come round to wanting to know me better, I ruined it all.'

'But this suggests she did forgive you,' Julia said. 'Why else would she have gone to the apartment with you? Maybe I can find out where the apartment is.'

Julia couldn't explain why she felt hopeful. There was no address, nothing to go on. But the key – so small and compact – signified something real. 'Let's keep going until we've tried everything.'

Christoph squeezed her hand. 'Thank you, Julia. I want to find out the truth more than anything.'

Julia rang Claude from a windy street, feeding cents into the phone box. There was no one else she could think of. She explained about the key and her hope that the next recipe would help Christoph remember the apartment. He told her where to buy artichokes and shallots and said she could use his kitchen. She arrived with bags of ingredients, her fingers aching from the weight.

'Thank you,' Julia said, heaving everything on to the table, 'I can't tell you how grateful I am. Hopefully the fonds d'artichauts will revive his memory.'

'*Bien sûr*. I'm glad to see you again. If I can help find this long-lost apartment, I'll consider it a job well done.' He inspected the artichokes. 'How is Christoph doing?'

Julia shook her head. 'Not good. He's very weak. I'm worried about his mental state too.'

Claude took out a chopping board and a sharp knife. 'You need to start by trimming the artichokes.' He laid them on the table. 'Did this illness come on suddenly?'

'He's been unwell for a while, it seems, but he was refusing tests. We thought he was getting better, but he found out that Sylvie died during the war. Daniel, his son, told him, and Christoph had a bad turn once he heard the news. It must have been shocking to hear.' Julia began to chop, hacking through the ends of the fibrous stalks. 'I wish Daniel had waited for a better time, but I suppose he felt he had to say it.'

Claude filled up the kettle and set it to boil. 'It's not always easy for fathers and sons.' He handed her some slices of poitrine fumée. 'Here, you need to wrap the artichokes in this.'

While the artichokes boiled, Julia and Claude chopped the onions, shallots, garlic, and mushrooms and put some oil in a frying pan to heat.

'What will you do if you find the apartment?' Claude asked.

'I hope it'll tell us what happened next. Why Sylvie died. At least that would be closure.'

She wasn't sure how she'd explain it all to Daniel. She hadn't intended to make this recipe behind his back, but what else could she do? He'd made his feelings about it clear.

Julia tipped the chopped ingredients into the oil and shook the pan. Claude smiled.

'You've grown in confidence,' he said.

Julia stirred in the puréed tomatoes and salt. 'It began as a way of helping Christoph, but I'm starting to enjoy cooking.'

'When you cook for someone else, the way you're making this, it's always an act of love.' Claude shrugged. 'At least, that's how I think of it.'

'I suppose it is.'

When the artichokes were ready, Claude put them in a box and handed it to Julia. 'Whatever happens, whether you find the apartment or not, at least you'll have tried.'

Julia stepped out of the pâtisserie and into the street.

When you cook for someone else, the way you're making this, it's always an act of love.

Had Julia ever played the piano that way? For someone else as an act of love? It had started like that: playing was the only certain way to make her mother smile. But as the years went by and the bar was raised higher, her love for the piano had been replaced by something else. Obsession, devotion, desperation. Julia clutched the meal she had prepared. It felt good to make something out of love again, whatever the outcome.

Daniel was in the waiting room when Julia arrived.

'He's just having his bedding changed, so I thought I'd wait out here.' He glanced at the box in her hands. 'What's that?'

Julia held it protectively. 'It's just something I made for Christoph to encourage him to eat.'

Daniel stared at her. 'Is this from the recipe book?' She nodded. 'Oh no, Julia, we talked about this. No more digging up the past, for Papa's sake.'

'But Christoph wants to continue,' Julia said, desperate to convince him. 'Even if Sylvie did die, he wants to remember it for himself.'

Daniel shook his head. 'I'm really worried about what that might do to his mental state. Papa's fragile as it is. He needs to concentrate on getting well, not chasing ghosts from the past that will stir up the anguish for him even more.'

'I know, Daniel. I understand your concerns, but these are his wishes.'

Daniel pressed his hand against his chest. 'We need to protect him from any more heartache, especially now, when he's physically weak,' he said. 'We don't even know the extent of what's wrong with him or how ill he really is. We can't carry on with this wild-goose chase. We both know it ends badly.'

Julia understood his point of view; she really did. But why couldn't he understand that this was Christoph's decision? She took the key out of her pocket.

'I found this in Christoph's suitcase. It's for an apartment that Christoph visited in the war. He wants me to find it.'

Daniel threw up his hands. 'I don't believe it. You just don't let up.'

Julia clasped the key. 'I know you don't want me to do this, but I've promised Christoph I will carry on helping him.'

'It was the same six years ago. The two of you have such a bond, and even now you think you know what's best for him. All the things you had in common with Papa, how much he admired your talent. *She's like the daughter I never had*, that's what he said, and I was the son he never wanted.'

'He never said that.'

'He did, Julia, I heard him. My window was open. He told you I wasn't good enough. I know what he thinks of me.'

Julia's heart contracted as she looked at Daniel's pained expression. She'd been sitting in the garden with Christoph. He'd known that there was something between her and Daniel. He'd wanted to warn her to be careful. 'I'm not saying that Daniel isn't the right one for you,' Christoph had said, 'but it needs to be someone who'll support you in your career. I want the best for you, Julia, you're like the daughter I never had.'

'Oh, Daniel,' Julia said now, impatiently. 'He was talking about my career. He didn't want me to lose sight of things. You must let this anger go. If Christoph wanted to keep you in the dark, it's because he knew how you'd react.' She tried to get it through to him. 'Your father could be dying; he wants to remember his past and you need to stop thinking of yourself. Christoph doesn't want to be protected from his memories. Can't you see that?'

Daniel looked at Julia. 'I don't know,' he said, taking a deep breath. 'Mama made me promise not to let him track Sylvie down. It's not just the anger I need to let go of, it's my sense of obligation to her too. I'm not sure I can do that.'

'Well, I suggest you try,' Julia said. 'Otherwise you might come to regret not helping him with this journey.'

35

Christoph

August, 1942 – Paris

Christoph stood in the corridor outside Sylvie's room and tried to catch his breath. What had he done? Seeing the Kommandant's gloves had made him lose all reason. She'd opened her heart to him and he'd thrown it back in her face.

Christoph glanced at Sylvie's door. Maybe it was best if they both calmed down. He'd find her later and apologize. Besides, he'd promised Jean that he'd change the dressing on the young man's leg today, and it was already late.

Up in the storeroom, the man's face was paler than usual. He sat against the wall, his leg straight out in front of him.

'How are you feeling?' Christoph asked.

'A bit better,' he said. 'I feel like my temperature has gone down.'

Christoph touched his forehead. 'It seems normal to me. Let's have a look at your leg.'

The cut on the man's shin was still raw, but it smelled all right, which was a good sign.

'I'd say another week and it will be much better,' Christoph said, tying the new bandage firmly. 'Any idea when Jean intends to get you out?'

The man rolled his trouser leg back down. 'Soon. He's made contact with my family. They're hiding in a village in the Loire. The plan is to get over the border into Switzerland, once I have joined them.'

Christoph thought of the journey ahead. It was fraught with peril.

'What were your family doing here in Paris?' he asked.

'We came in 1940 from Belgium, four months before Hitler invaded. We never expected the Germans would follow us all the way to Paris.'

'It must have been terrible,' Christoph said. His country was responsible for so much upheaval. He wished there was an end in sight.

'It's been unbearable. The laws, the restrictions, gradually strangling us. I can't stand feeling like I'm not normal, as if I don't have the right to even be here.'

Christoph bowed his head. 'It's us Germans who shouldn't be here.'

The man gripped his hand. 'It doesn't matter what you say, you're just one among thousands. Sometimes, I think it's not worth living, slowly suffocating up here.'

Christoph couldn't bear the emptiness in his voice. 'You've already come this far. Just a bit longer and you'll be free, I'm sure of it. You have Jean's support, and mine too. Don't give up.'

The man nodded. 'Thank you, Christoph. If some Germans are like you, then maybe there is hope.'

'I'd love to know your name, if you'd be willing to tell me.'

The man drew in his breath. 'I'm called Jacques. Jacques Morgenstern.' He looked up at Christoph, fear in his eyes. 'Do you promise you won't tell anyone?'

Christoph saw the morning star in his mind's eye, rising over the fields near the farm on a snowy winter's dawn. The star was clear and bright, the air icy and fresh, so different from this dark, stifling attic.

'I promise,' he said. 'You're going to get out of here.'

Jacques smiled wryly. 'Am I supposed to trust the word of a German soldier?'

Christoph shrugged. 'Not ordinarily, but this one you can. I guess you're not much younger than me . . .'

'I was eighteen in March. My father gave me a blessing, in secret, at home. And my mother asked me what I wanted for the year ahead.' Jacques shook his head. 'I wish the war would end and I could carry on with my life.'

The sadness in his voice pained Christoph. Jacques' life had been reduced to this dark place.

'I hope with all my heart there will be a future for you,' Christoph said. 'What do you want to do when all this ends?'

Jacques thought for a moment. 'Nothing spectacular. I'd like to travel, see the world, get rich and then get married.' He grinned, and his eyes lit up briefly. 'My mother said I always went for the impossible girls, the ones who were out of reach. I'd like to find a woman like that one day and win her over.'

Christoph's heart contracted at the hope in his voice. 'Then I pray you will.'

The next morning, Christoph went downstairs to see Sylvie. After talking to Jacques, he knew that life was too precious to waste with suspicion and arguments. He strode towards the kitchen, but in the hotel lobby a soldier called out to him.

'Herr Leutnant, the Kommandant would like to see you in his office.'

Christoph pictured the Kommandant peeling off his gloves in Sylvie's room. Nausea filled his stomach. But there was no avoiding him: Christoph had to go when summoned.

The Kommandant sat in his leather chair. He didn't invite Christoph to sit down.

'I've received a report about the incident at the farmhouse,' he said.

Christoph frowned. 'I wouldn't say it was an incident, Herr Kommandant, more a misunderstanding.'

'Ah, well, that depends on how you look at it. The soldiers' superior wasn't happy that one of my men had got involved. I was very displeased to find my name mentioned. So yes, I'd call it an incident.'

Christoph nodded. 'I see. I apologize, Herr Kommandant.'

'You overstepped the mark, Herr Leutnant, taking that woman from the kitchen with you without my permission. There was no mention of Sylvie in the report. Where was she when all this happened?'

Christoph's cheeks grew warm. 'The message about her attending hadn't reached the farmer's wife, I'm afraid. We were forced to share the same quarters, but nothing untoward occurred.'

The Kommandant stroked his thumb along the edge of the report. 'You were perhaps seeking to impress her by addressing the soldiers in such an offhand way.'

'No, Herr Kommandant.'

The Kommandant stood up, his face stern.

'I find myself rather interested in Sylvie. I want to get to know her . . . exclusively, if you understand me, but she seems rather friendly with you.'

Christoph's heart pounded in his chest. 'Sylvie has a mind of her own.'

'Indeed. So, you'll stay out of my way?' The Kommandant fixed his gaze on Christoph. 'I know how much your family back in Germany relies on you, especially your sister.'

Blood roared in Christoph's ears. The veiled threat towards his family enraged him, but he couldn't show it.

'You *will* stay away from her,' the Kommandant said, his eyes narrowing.

In the silence, Christoph swallowed hard. Damn the Kommandant for putting him in this position. How could he choose between Sylvie and the safety of his family?

'If that's what you want, Herr Kommandant,' he said.

'Normandy, in a hovel,' the Kommandant said with a smirk. 'It shouldn't take long to convince her that I can offer more. When you go to the Loire next week to inspect the next farm, I want you to go alone, is that understood?'

Christoph bowed his head. 'Yes, Herr Kommandant.'

It wasn't until the evening that Christoph was finally able to go and find Sylvie. He found her scattering herbs into a frying pan of vegetables.

'I need to talk to you,' he said.

'More accusations?' she said.

'I'm sorry, I don't know what came over me. I was wrong to accuse you. Can you forgive me?'

Sylvie gave the frying pan a vigorous shake, then banged it down on the hob. 'I'd rather die than have anything to do with the Kommandant.'

Christoph pressed his palms together.

'I know,' he said. 'I knew it the minute I walked out of your room.'

'Then why didn't you come back?'

'I don't know. I was too ashamed of being jealous and jumping to conclusions. I'm sorry, Sylvie.'

He didn't mention Jacques. Better that she didn't know.

'You need to remember who I am. I'd never deceive you with someone else,' she said.

'I know. I would have come sooner, but the Kommandant summoned me,' Christoph said. 'He's set his sights on you and forbidden me to get in the way.'

Sylvie's face blanched.

'He thinks he can win you over,' Christoph said in a pained voice.

'He's mad.'

Christoph bit his lip. 'What you said before about making the most of our time together, did you mean it?'

'Yes, of course.' Her eyes seemed to brim with unspoken words.

'I want to be with you too,' he said, reaching for her hand. 'But the Kommandant will be keeping an eye on me. There's no privacy here.'

Sylvie took a deep breath. 'Not at Le Meurice,' she said. 'But there is somewhere we could go.'

He stared at her. 'Where?'

Sylvie reached into her pocket and took out two keys.

'There's an apartment. Not far from here,' she said. 'My grandmother used to rent it out. It's empty now. We can meet there. The Kommandant will never know.'

'You'd go there with me?' Christoph said. 'Despite the risk?'

Sylvie took his hand and pressed it to her heart. 'Can you feel that?' she said.

The thud of her heart pulsed against his hand. He felt the soft curve of her breast too.

'I feel it,' he said.

'That's what this is about. Life. Living. We can ignore it and stay safe or take a chance.'

'I don't want to ignore it.' He swallowed hard.

'Then meet me there, tomorrow.' Lisette gave Christoph one of the keys. The brown fob read: *Apartment 14.*

'Where is it?'

'Rue Pastourelle. Here.' She took a pen from his pocket. 'This will help you to remember.' She drew a shepherd's crook on the label.

He smiled. 'Wherever you lead, I'm bound to follow, is that how it is?'

Sylvie didn't return his smile. 'Perhaps you won't always be able to follow me,' she said, 'but at least we'll have something to remember.'

She put the key into his pocket and slipped her arms around his waist. God, how he wanted her.

'But no more accusations,' she said. 'I wouldn't be doing this if I didn't want to be with you.'

'I promise.'

He smelled rosemary on her skin, the scent of remembrance. She held him tight.

'Until tomorrow,' she said, and the weight of the hours was in her voice.

36

Lisette

August, 1942 – Paris

Lisette walked briskly to the apartment. Thoughts criss-crossed her mind like a shuttle working on a loom. She had to balance Seraphin's plan to poison the dinner with her desire to prevent Christoph from coming to any harm. The Kommandant's attentions complicated things, but she wouldn't let them distract her. The apartment would provide a temporary refuge for her and Christoph. The thought of meeting him there, the promise of what would happen, sent warmth sliding down her body. The kisses had only been the start.

When she arrived, an elderly concierge sat in the courtyard reading a newspaper.

'*Bonjour,*' Lisette said. 'I'm renting number fourteen.'

'These apartments change hands every five minutes,' the concierge complained. He rustled the newspaper. 'We like it quiet here.'

'I like it quiet too.' She laid some eggs on the table, purloined from the larder, as Seraphin had suggested.

He glanced up and smiled, clearly appreciating the gift. 'Top floor on the right.'

The apartment was tiny, but it was enough. There were four rooms: a bedroom overlooking the courtyard, a tiny bathroom and a kitchen which opened on to the living room.

Lisette put her bag on the table and took out the ingredients she'd brought from the hotel. She set a pan of water to boil on the stove.

Nerves made her hands tremble. He'd be here soon. Was she doing the right thing? If Johnny's loss had taught her one thing, it was that moments like these were to be treasured.

She wrapped the artichokes in slices of poitrine fumée, secured them with string, and plunged them into a deep pot of boiling water. Then she heated some oil in a frying pan and fried the onions, garlic, mushrooms, and shallots. Something to eat afterwards. Lisette swallowed, light-headed at the thought of what was to come.

At last, the doorbell rang. Christoph was here. She checked her face in the mirror, her cheeks flushed, and opened the door.

It was like seeing him for the first time. He stared at her with such longing it took Lisette's breath away. He strode towards her and gathered her up in his arms.

'God, the minutes went so slowly,' Christoph said, his fingers teasing her hair. Her scalp tingled with pleasure. 'I just wanted to be here with you.'

Lisette's body unfurled. All this time, all this waiting. She pressed against his firm chest. He groaned and backed her up against the wall of the hallway. His kisses enflamed her, undoing all her senses. She could feel how much he wanted her.

She led him to the bedroom at the back of the apartment, amazed at her own boldness. His hands touched her skin and a flame burned within her.

He gently turned her around, then undid the zip at the

back of her dress. She stepped out of it, feeling the heat that radiated from his stare.

'You're beautiful,' he said. He kissed the slope of her shoulders, the swell of her breasts, unfastening, clasp by clasp, her brassiere.

'Your turn,' Lisette said. She opened his belt buckle and unbuttoned his shirt. He yanked his trousers off. She ran her hands over his chest, feeling the warmth of his skin.

'Are you sure you want this?' Christoph said.

Lisette nodded, filled with urgency. In three days' time, she'd never see him again.

'More than anything,' she said.

Christoph picked her up and laid her down on the bed. She saw fragments of him: the light in his eyes, the curve of his nose, the shadow at the base of his neck. Longing overwhelmed her. She drew his body against hers. He groaned and kissed her, kisses that seemed endless. He was so near, growing closer and closer until, at last, she gasped, opening to let him in, heat burning, wanting him deeper and deeper.

He drove himself into her. She moved against him, his moans answering hers, building to a crescendo. The world shrank to a place of murmurs and shudders: a molten core between them. The delay in it erupting was exquisite. When it came, bursting over her like a wave, it was beyond anything she'd ever experienced. She cried out, holding on to him as the aftershocks of pleasure rippled between them. Gradually, her breath subsided.

'I didn't know it could be like that,' Christoph said.

Lisette ran her fingers over his collarbone. 'Nor did I.'

He kissed her, long and slow. She closed her eyes and curled up next to him.

'Sylvie,' Christoph murmured.

'Hmm.' She was aware of nothing but the sensation of his body against hers.

'Thank you.'

Later, she woke, throbbing and aching, her body filled with a new kind of contentment. She rolled over. Christoph wasn't there. She frowned, put on her shirt and went to look for him. He was already awake, sitting at the kitchen table, his jacket hung over the chair, a letter in his hand. He gazed at her, a look of anguish on his face.

'What's wrong?' she said. 'Has something happened?'

'This letter arrived from my mother. I was on my way to meet you here when it was delivered. I put it in my pocket, and I've only just read it now . . .' His voice trailed off, and his face was ashen. 'It's the most awful news, Sylvie.'

Lisette sat down. 'Tell me, what is it?'

'Last week there was a round-up in the village. Until now, they've left my sister alone. But this time, soldiers came banging on the door. My mother tried to stop them, but they hauled Lotte out.'

'Oh, Christoph, that's terrible.'

'But what's worse, Sylvie, is that she couldn't answer their questions.' He screwed the letter up in his hand and banged the table with his fist. 'My mother was ordered to prepare a suitcase of clothes, and say goodbye, and the bastards took her away.'

Lisette put her hand to her mouth, shocked. 'Can anything be done? Could you speak to the Kommandant?'

Christoph took a deep breath. 'He won't do anything. I know his views on the matter.'

'What do you mean?'

'He's said many times that it's better for the nation to be "purified of these useless lives in order to ensure that our race thrives and remains the strongest".' Christoph clenched his fists. 'You know, I've never bought into that ideology, Sylvie, never. Somehow, I thought Lotte would be safe. She's a kind, thoughtful girl who never did anyone any harm.'

Lisette squeezed his hand.

'Try not to lose hope,' she said.

She gathered him in a silent embrace. A feeling of urgency drove through her. Time was rushing by, not just for her and Christoph, but for everyone they loved.

'Is it right that I should want you now, in the middle of all this desolation?' Christoph whispered.

Lisette cupped his face in her hands. 'I think seizing moments like this is the only way to cope.'

Muscheln

2kg mussels
1 glass of white wine
Salt
Peppercorns
Bay leaves
Butter
1 onion, chopped

1. Clean the mussels.
2. Tip the mussels into a large pan with a tight-fitting lid.
3. Add the wine, salt, peppercorns, bay leaves, butter and chopped onion.
4. Set the pan over a high heat and seal with the lid.
5. When the pan starts to steam, cook the mussels for 3–4 minutes, shaking from time to time until they open.
6. Serve with the pan juices as a broth.

37

Julia

August, 2002 – Paris

The sorrow of Lotte's plight stayed with Christoph. Julia held his hand as he told his memory of that day in the apartment, tears streaming down his face.

'Who were they to decide whose lives were useful or not?' he cried. 'Lotte had her own gifts, different to others, but valid nonetheless. In the brutal world of the Nazis, no one credited her talents.'

'Perhaps Lotte survived. There might be some way to find out.' Lisette didn't want Christoph to fall into despair. The news about Sylvie's death was now compounded with the tragedy of Lotte's removal.

'We have to,' Christoph said. 'I need to know. She shouldn't have been taken, Julia. The Nazis were monsters.' He pushed away the remains of the artichoke and closed his eyes. 'Is it awful that I should have experienced such happiness with Sylvie when Lotte had been taken?'

'You'd found love,' Julia said. 'Who could blame you? The apartment must have been a special place.'

'It was,' Christoph said. 'There was nothing remarkable about it. But being there with Sylvie made it magical.'

'Can you remember where it was?'

Christoph shook his head. 'It looked just like any other

stone building. I don't think it was far from Le Meurice, though, just a few streets away.' He thought for a moment. 'I do remember a pair of dragons carved in the stonework above the door.'

'That might help,' Julia said. But it was difficult to know where to start looking.

'Show me the label again,' Christoph said. He stared at the drawing of the crook. Then his eyes widened.

'Of course,' he said. 'She drew it on to remind me of the name of the street. It's a shepherdess's crook. Rue Pastourelle. I joked that I'd follow her wherever she led me.'

'That must be it!' Julia exclaimed. She jotted the name down in her notebook. 'I'll have a look for it in that guidebook.'

'You have such faith, Julia, but I'm losing hope.' His eyes filled with tears. 'If she died, and I survived, then I didn't follow her, did I? And I've let Daniel down too. I should have told him about the recipe book, and why we'd come to Paris. If I had, we might have been doing this search together. He might have understood.'

Julia didn't know how to reply. The relationship between Christoph and Daniel was more complicated than she'd imagined. If Daniel wanted to engage with Christoph's search for his past, then it was up to him to step forward. Julia tucked the key in her pocket. She needed to find the apartment.

While Christoph slept, Julia went to the hospital café to consult the map at the back of the Paris guidebook. She bought a cup of coffee and looked up rue Pastourelle. Her finger traced the grid reference. There it was: about forty minutes' walk from Le Meurice. Might the apartment still be there?

Julia looked up. Daniel was striding towards her, a determined look on his face. Julia closed the map and gathered up her notebook. Her heart raced: she was in no mood for his negativity about Christoph's memories. She stood up, ready to leave.

'Wait, Julia,' Daniel said. 'I'm here to apologize.'

Julia hooked her bag on her shoulder. 'I've nothing more to say to you. Christoph remembered where the apartment was, and I'm going there.'

He gestured to the chair. 'Please, just hear me out.'

Julia sat down, a sceptical look on her face. 'What's going on?'

'I've walked miles along the river, trying to imagine what Paris was like when Christoph was here. The Nazi flags, the military vehicles, the barricades, and checkpoints. He was part of a terrible force that took over the city and eliminated its freedoms, even its identity.'

'And?' she said impatiently.

'Yet, in amongst all this, some woman called Sylvie, a Frenchwoman, came to care for him so much that she gave him that book of recipes with a dedication that suggests their relationship was more than just friendship.' Daniel shook his head. 'In spite of everything that was happening to Paris, Sylvie must have seen something in Papa that made her like him, made her love him even. Regardless of which sides of the war they stood on.'

Julia felt a tremor of hope. Was Daniel starting to understand at last?

Daniel leaned forward. 'You were right, Julia. This is Papa's story, not mine, or Mama's. I've been trying to control what comes out of the past, but I can't. It *is* extraordinary to think Papa and Sylvie found love despite what was happening around them. I shouldn't feel threatened by what happened between them. It was long before my parents were married, or I was born.'

'Exactly,' Julia said, so relieved to hear his words. 'It doesn't change your parents' marriage or your childhood. Sylvie's from the past. I think remembering her is a way for Christoph to remember himself.'

Daniel reached out for Julia's hand. His skin was warm and his touch awakened a familiar ache inside. 'I want to help Papa with exploring the recipes. I'm sorry I didn't understand before.'

Julia smiled. 'He'll be so glad. You're a part of this too.'

'I've checked us out of Le Meurice. Our suitcases are in the car. There's nothing to stop us going to the apartment right now,' Daniel said. 'Let's do this search together.'

Hope inflamed her heart. 'Are you sure?' she said.

A rare, unguarded smile caught his eyes. For a moment, he looked just like he had at the station in Bonn. Julia realized this wasn't just about Christoph and Sylvie. It was about her and Daniel: moving on from those events six years ago.

'I'm sure,' he said.

38

Julia

August, 2002 – Paris

Rue Pastourelle was a twenty-minute drive from the hospital in the third arrondissement. Cream-coloured stone buildings rose four or five storeys high, and as they slowly drove along the street Julia noticed that one of the buildings had two dragons carved above the doorway.

'That must be it.' Julia twisted the key in her hand. 'What if no one's there? Or they don't let us in?'

Daniel glanced at her. 'Are you having second thoughts?'

'It's just that it will be strange to see something that up to now has been a memory in Christoph's head. Why, are you?'

Daniel rubbed his forehead. 'It's like going back in time.' He glanced at Julia. 'I'm glad you're here. I'd never have come here on my own.'

Daniel parked the car and they got out. Julia pressed the intercom and explained to the concierge that they needed to enquire about apartment fourteen. She was prepared to explain more but, to her surprise, he buzzed open the door. Julia and Daniel went in and found themselves in a small courtyard. Small trees in pots stood along its edges.

The concierge shuffled out of a ground-floor apartment and stared at them suspiciously. 'Can I help you?' he said.

'Hello,' Julia said. 'I know this is a strange request, but we're tracing the memories of someone who visited this place in the 1940s, and wondered if there's any chance of asking the current occupant if we can please view apartment fourteen.'

The concierge frowned. 'What do you want with apartment fourteen?' he said.

'This man's father,' she said, gesturing at Daniel, 'stayed there during the war.'

'It would mean a lot to him if I was able to see it,' Daniel said. 'He's not well, you see, he's in hospital, and I'd like to be able to help him make peace with the past.'

'Ah,' the concierge said, his face softening. 'It's important that the younger generation respect the past. I take it from your accent that your father was on the other side?'

'Yes,' Daniel said, 'and no one could be more ashamed of that than my father. We wouldn't stay long. Just a quick look around.'

Julia held up the key. 'This is the key he used to open the apartment.'

The concierge's eyes widened. 'I didn't know anyone else had one. Nobody has stayed there for years, not since I've been working here. It's always been empty.'

Daniel and Julia exchanged a glance.

'So no one's living there now? Did you ever meet the owner?' Julia asked.

'No,' the concierge said. 'A solicitor wires the money over for the rent and my wife keeps it clean.'

'Then, please,' Daniel said, 'could you show it to us?'

'There's not much to see,' the concierge said. He looked them up and down, seemingly deciding to trust what they said. 'Come on then, follow me.'

He lumbered up the steps. At last, they reached the top floor.

'Well, here we are. I hope you find what you're looking for.' The concierge nodded and headed back downstairs.

'Do you want to open the door?' Julia asked Daniel. By rights, this moment belonged to him.

He shook his head. 'You do it.'

He seemed nervous, as if Sylvie might be waiting behind the doorway. Julia put the key in the lock and opened the door.

She stood on the threshold, taking it all in. The door opened on to a narrow hallway, a black and white runner covering the wooden floor. A pockmarked mirror hung on the white wall and underneath it stood a small side table. The apartment smelled empty and forgotten.

Julia walked down the hallway and opened each door, Daniel following behind. The neat little bedroom contained a double bed and a mahogany wardrobe full of wooden hangers. The bathroom was tiny. The apartment reminded Julia of a guest house: spartan and neutral, with no personal touches.

She glanced around the kitchen.

'That's odd,' she said, pointing to the kettle and the oven. 'Someone has definitely used this place since the 1940s. Look at the fridge too.'

'Not exactly the latest models, though,' Daniel said.

He opened the door to the living room. The oak-framed

sofa and armchairs were from the 1940s, but the upholstery looked like it had been patched up. An upright piano stood by the window, a fringed lampshade on top of it.

'You know what we should do?' Daniel said.

'What?'

'Instead of looking for a cheap hotel to stay in while Papa's in hospital, we should ask the concierge if we can stay here.'

Julia looked around the room. 'You want to stay here, where your father stayed with Sylvie?'

'I know it sounds odd, but somehow being here makes me feel closer to him. This place was a refuge from everything that was happening in Paris. Perhaps Sylvie represented some kind of haven for him too.'

'It's quite antiquated,' Julia said, 'and a bit musty.'

'I can get some fresh bedding and supplies,' Daniel suggested, 'and I'll give the place a quick spruce-up with a duster.'

'What makes you think the concierge will allow it?' Julia asked.

'I'll go down in a minute and offer to pay him in cash. I bet he won't refuse.'

Julia thought for a moment. It would be incredible to stay in the apartment, but staying here with Daniel? It was so small and intimate.

As if reading her mind, he smiled. 'Don't worry, I'll sleep on the sofa.'

Julia blushed. 'I wasn't . . .'

'And we'd better get some food so we can make the next recipe. What are we making?'

Julia liked the way he said *we*. He was really making an effort to get involved in this search. He held her gaze, reminding her of what had happened just before the book went tumbling to the floor, spooling back to that moment in Le Meurice when he'd kissed her. Julia swallowed and looked away.

'Muscheln,' she said.

The concierge was happy to let them stay there for a cash payment. He pocketed the money and asked to see their passports, insisting that he make a note of their passport numbers.

'I like to do things by the book – well, sometimes,' he said with a wink, 'just in case the mystery owner should ever enquire, but I doubt anyone will bother you. The place has lain empty for decades. The gas and electric should work, but the phone line has been disconnected. You can use mine if you need to.'

Later, before they got back to the apartment with the shopping, they stopped at the concierge's apartment to call Christoph. The concierge went to watch television in the living room, leaving Julia and Daniel in the hallway. Julia spoke to the nurse in charge first. She passed on the telephone number in case of an emergency, then waited for Christoph.

The line crackled. 'It's me, Julia,' she said.

'Did you find it?' Christoph said. His voice sounded far away.

'Yes.'

'What's it like?'

'Old-fashioned. There's an upright piano in the living room. I can't imagine how you got it up the stairs.'

'A piano?' Christoph said, vaguely. 'I don't remember that. Is there any sign of Sylvie?'

'Not yet. A few objects suggest that someone lived here a couple of decades ago, but there's no clue as to who that was.'

'Will you be all right there alone?'

'Oh,' Julia said, her face growing hot, 'I'm not alone. Daniel's here. We're going to stay here now we've checked out of Le Meurice.'

'Ah, that's good.' He coughed. 'Well, let me know how you get on. Before you go, can you put him on for a minute?'

Daniel put the handset to his ear.

'*Hallo, Papa,*' he said. '*Ja, natürlich.*' He glanced at Julia. '*Sicher.*'

He put the phone down and sighed.

'What did he say?'

'That he's glad I'm getting involved, and to look after you.' His voice sounded flat.

'That's good, isn't it?'

'He sounded factual, like he was ticking things off a list before it was too late. There wasn't much emotion behind it.'

'He's exhausted.'

Daniel shrugged. 'Maybe. It's not like I've given him any cause to invest in our relationship, but maybe that will change now I'm helping you.' He gave her a brief smile.

They thanked the concierge and went up the stairs to

the apartment. While Daniel went back down to get their suitcases out of the car, Julia put the shopping away.

By the time Daniel came back, lugging the two heavy cases, Julia was lifting a box out from the back of one of the kitchen cupboards.

'Look what I've found,' she said. She heaved the box on to the table. 'A pile of musical scores. Isn't that typical?' She glanced at the box. It looked promising. 'Let's have a look before we start cooking.'

'But I'm starving,' Daniel said. 'I'm not sure I can wait until we've cooked something. We could just get a takeaway.'

Julia shook her head and smiled. 'A few months ago, I'd have said yes. But I've started to enjoy cooking. These recipes aren't about getting fed. They're about reconnecting with the past. And it's been soothing to use my hands for something other than playing the piano. You can nibble on a baguette while we cook.'

Daniel glanced at the recipe book. 'You're right. The recipe book is why we're here.'

'Exactly.' She picked it up. 'This is the recipe for mussels.'

Daniel peered at Sylvie's handwriting. 'What does that say?'

'It says: *Good for taking your mind off things. Use white wine in the broth. Afterwards, leave time for love.*'

'I see.' Daniel smiled slowly. 'And are we following this recipe to the letter?'

Julia blushed, her eyes mirroring his spark. 'Let's just focus on the cooking, shall we?' She set the mussels in a large bowl full of water.

Daniel opened a bottle of wine and poured two large glasses. Julia gulped hers down, glancing at him. A sense of expectation hovered in the room.

Daniel rolled up his sleeves, his tanned forearms flexing in readiness. 'What shall I do?'

'You could slice the onions,' Julia said, handing him a knife and a chopping board.

'I've always wanted to do this.' He steadied the knife and attempted to cut the onion at lightning speed. Pieces went all over the counter. He smiled sheepishly. 'It looks easier on TV.'

'Maybe you just need more practice,' she said. His smile was infectious. It was fun cooking with Daniel.

Julia squeezed past him to the bowl of mussels. For a moment, her body pressed against his.

'Sorry,' she said, blushing.

He smelled so familiar; that woody, fresh scent that was like a second skin. She glanced at him. In the tiny kitchen, he was close enough to touch, close enough to . . . She drained the mussels, pushing the thought away.

'What shall I do with these onions?' he said.

Julia checked the recipe book. 'If you could find a large saucepan with a lid and a heavy base. We need to fry them.'

His arm brushed her waist as he moved past her, sending a charge through her body.

'There's not much space, is there?' he said, reaching into the cupboard and taking out a casserole dish.

He added some oil to the dish and heated it up, then tipped in the onions and leaned against the counter. His eyes swept over her like a breeze.

'Do you remember in Frau Linden's allotment when I asked you to come away with me?' he said.

Julia's breath tightened. Why bring that up now?

'Yes,' she said hesitantly.

'I imagined us doing stuff like this: hanging out, cooking, seeing places.' He took a sip of wine. 'But I think you thought I was trying to drag you away from the piano.'

Julia added the salt, peppercorns, bay leaves, butter and a glass of wine to the pot, pondering his words. She didn't want to remember that day.

'I was nervous about the recital. I couldn't think beyond it,' Julia said. She wiped her hands on the tea towel. 'The piano was my passion. I'd devoted my life to it. You didn't seem to understand that.'

'I was too blinded by what I wanted,' Daniel said. 'I should have supported you more. It must have been a big deal to come to Bonn and study with Papa. A lot of pressure too, with the recital and everything.'

Julia tipped in the mussels, stirred them with a wooden spoon and pressed the lid down firmly. 'It might have made a difference if you'd acknowledged that at the time,' Julia said. 'Instead, you issued an ultimatum: the piano or you. I'd only just met you. My dreams of a piano career had been with me all my life.'

Daniel nodded. 'Yes, I'm sorry I was too immature to see that. There was a lot I didn't see. It took me far too long to realize how well respected Papa was in the music world. I only saw him perform once or twice; I can barely remember it. It seemed such a chore at the time. I wish I'd appreciated it more.'

'I never got the chance to see him live, but I used to

listen to his recordings for hours in my bedroom,' Julia said. 'Meeting him after the concert in Frankfurt was amazing, and when he wrote to invite me to stay with him in Bonn I literally screamed the house down with excitement. My sister, Anna, thought I'd gone mad.' She smiled, remembering back. 'I'd left music school a few years before, college friends were getting recording contracts and deals, but my career had stalled. Christoph's offer to mentor me was a dream come true. My mum was over the moon. It made all the difference.'

They were both silent for a moment. Julia wondered what things could have been like if Daniel *had* understood all this sooner.

'Well, for what it's worth,' Daniel said, as if reading her thoughts, 'I think I do get it now.'

He came over and lifted the lid of the casserole dish. 'It looks like they're ready. You should taste the juices,' he said, dipping in the wooden spoon. 'After all, you're the head chef in this operation.' He held her chin and gently placed the tip of the spoon on her tongue. 'Is it good?'

His touch on her skin was electric. She couldn't tear her eyes away from him. She nodded. 'Maybe a little more salt.'

For a moment she thought he was going to bend down and kiss her. But he seemed to think twice. He cleared his throat.

'Better not let it go cold. I'll set the table, while you add the salt and plate up.'

'Okay,' Julia said. Being near him was harder than she'd thought.

Daniel unearthed a candle from a drawer. The flame flickered on the table. He managed to tune the radio.

Classical music played. A breeze came in through the open window. They sat down. There was silence for a moment while they both ate a few mouthfuls.

'We did it,' Daniel said, clinking his glass against Julia's. 'They taste delicious. I enjoyed cooking them.'

'Me too. Although I did fear for your fingers when you were slicing those onions.' Julia smiled at him. His eyes were bright in the candlelight.

'I once tried diving for wild oysters in Sweden,' Daniel said. 'The water was so clear, you could see miles down.'

'I bet it was freezing too. Did you catch any?'

'A couple, but the instructor found most of them. It was an incredible experience. We ate them afterwards – they tasted like Guinness – with hunks of bread.' He took a sip of wine. 'Have you ever been to Sweden?'

Julia raised her eyebrows. 'I've performed at the Konserthuset in Stockholm. But sadly there was no time for wild oyster diving. Or to see the northern lights. I was on a flight out to Sofia two days later.'

Daniel nodded. 'You've travelled too, but in a different way. Maybe you could go back and visit these places at a more leisurely pace. There's this tiny village called Särkimukka by the Lainio River. There's no light pollution and the view of the aurora borealis is breathtaking. You're surrounded by forest and snow – it's like being at the end of the world.'

'One day I'd like to see it.' Julia got a glimpse of how much fun it would be to travel with Daniel, to spend time seeing these places with him. She wondered if he felt it too.

'I hope you will,' Daniel said, his gaze lingering on her. He topped up her glass. 'Can you believe we're sitting here like this? After six years, you're finally having dinner with me.'

Julia smiled. 'It's been a long time.'

After the meal was finished, Daniel filled the sink with soapy water while Julia carried the bowls and glasses over.

'Once,' Daniel said, 'when I was little, Papa covered a glass in bubbles and rubbed his finger around the rim. The room was filled with the most amazing sound.'

He tried it with one of the wine glasses. A perfect note sang out.

'You try,' he said to Julia.

She rubbed the glass but couldn't make the sound.

'Like this . . .' Daniel said.

He stood behind her and took hold of her hand. The length of his body pressed against her back. Time seemed to stand still. Gently, he guided her fingers over the rim until a note hummed.

'That's amazing,' she said.

Daniel turned her around to face him. His eyes were dark and serious.

'When you wouldn't come away with me, I said you were selfish, do you remember?'

'Yes.' Hearing the words, it hurt all over again.

He clasped her hands. 'It was me who was selfish. I was stupid and young and angry at the world. I took that out on you because I once again saw someone I loved turning away from me, but I was the one pushing you. I'm so sorry, Julia. I want to show you I've changed, that I do understand the mistakes I made. I want there to be only good memories between us from now on.'

That argument had been the prelude to what happened at the recital. It was hard to just forgive and forget.

Julia glanced down at the linoleum floor. 'I don't know,

Daniel, I can't just forget how you treated me at the recital, or before that. I believe you want to do things differently this time, but you have to realize I need to take this slowly. It's not easy for me to let people in once, let alone twice.'

She eased herself out of his arms and glanced at the table. The candle had nearly burned down.

He nodded, taking in her words. 'Of course. I don't want to put any pressure on you, not like I did last time.'

'It wasn't just you,' Julia said. 'I realize that I did prioritize the piano over everything else, which didn't help. Then you stirred up all these feelings in me and, back then, I didn't know what to do when there was so much else going on. There's just a lot of bad memories.'

'Well, I don't want you to worry right now. You've done so much for Papa, and you've got the problem with your hands weighing on you. I just want to be here for you, and hopefully, over time, you'll see you can trust me.'

'I hope so, Daniel,' Julia said. 'I want to.'

He touched her shoulder. 'Come on. I'll clear the kitchen up and you go and get some rest.'

Julia smiled and squeezed his hand. 'All right. Thank you.'

As she left the kitchen, she glanced back at him. He had already turned back to the sink and was washing the bowls. Julia felt a tiny bud of hope. Perhaps it would be possible to get over the past and start again.

39

Christoph

August, 1942 – Paris

Christoph woke with Sylvie in his arms. It was their second visit to the apartment in as many days. She smelled of parsley and cloves. Last night, he'd helped her cook mussels, opening the tiny kitchen window to let out the steam. They'd drunk half a bottle of white wine he'd brought from Le Meurice. They shouldn't have stayed over. But after making love, it had been tempting to lie in each other's arms and sleep, to pretend the world outside didn't exist.

He brushed back her hair. She opened her eyes and smiled.

'I don't want to leave,' Christoph said.

She stroked her hand across his arm. 'Then let's not.'

Out there, things were bleak. He'd had no luck convincing the Kommandant to help with Lotte. His heart cracked every time he thought of her.

'We could steal away,' he said. 'Leave France and go somewhere there isn't a war.'

Sylvie rolled on to her front to look at him. Her bare skin shone in the early-morning sunlight. 'There's nowhere to go. We're on borrowed time.'

Christoph nodded. Borrowed, but precious nonetheless. He could hardly believe she was here, lying beside him.

'Time drags when you want it to go fast and speeds up when you want it to slow down,' he said, smoothing his thumb over Sylvie's palm.

Sylvie's hand suddenly closed over his own, gripping it tight. 'I wish I could stop time right now.'

He stroked her cheek. 'Tell me, what's on the menu for this special dinner?' The date of General Winkler's arrival had been confirmed for Monday, but the Kommandant was already getting everything in order.

Sylvie rested her head on her elbow. 'Salmon mousse choux pastries to start, followed by chicken and then Sachertorte. I'm in charge of the salmon.'

Christoph pulled a face. 'Why did you choose salmon mousse? I told you I didn't like it when we went to Le Tour d'Argent.'

Sylvie shrugged. 'I'll make a salad, just for you, with a special dressing.'

He drew her towards him. 'I might be brave enough to try the salmon if it's made by you.'

'No, don't do that,' she said quickly. 'I don't want you to eat anything you don't enjoy. Promise me. Eat the salad instead.'

Christoph smiled. 'All right, though I don't know why it matters so much,' He sighed. 'After the dinner, I'll be going to the Loire. I wish I could bring you with me, but the Kommandant has expressly forbidden it.'

'I wish I could come too,' Sylvie said. She gave a brief smile, restless suddenly. 'Come on. We can't put it off any longer. We need to head back before someone realizes we're both gone. You go first. I'll follow later.'

*

The hotel was quiet when Christoph returned. He went straight to his office, relieved that there was no sign of the Kommandant. Horns beeped outside and Christoph went to the window to investigate. A cavalcade of five black motor cars drew up in the courtyard, Nazi flags fluttering on the front of each car.

The Kommandant climbed out of one, dressed in full military regalia. He opened the door on the other side, and another man got out, General Winkler, Head of the Production and Supplies Division. Christoph recognized him from pictures in the newspapers. What was he doing here? He wasn't due to arrive yet.

Minutes later, the Kommandant burst into Christoph's office.

'Where the hell were you?' he said, tearing off his gloves.

'It was my morning off,' Christoph said, the words already prepared.

'If you'd prefer to be fighting out in the east, I can arrange it,' the Kommandant said. 'You should be at your desk.'

'I know, I'm sorry, Herr Kommandant. What's going on?'

'General Winkler has descended on us three days early,' the Kommandant said. 'That man delights in making my life a living hell. A flight from Berlin was available, so he took it. We've just got back from the airport.'

Christoph almost felt sorry for the Kommandant. General Winkler was a notorious taskmaster. He oversaw all the shipments from west to east. There were endless telegrams and instructions regarding the quota of food and supplies.

'He's come to investigate the train that was derailed last week,' the Kommandant said. 'He's gone to his room to rest, and then this afternoon he intends to question the French police about the incident.'

He stopped pacing the room and stood by Christoph's desk.

'We'll have to bring the dinner forward to tomorrow, seeing as he's got here early. He wants to fly back to Berlin in two days. It seems that things are building up for a push eastwards.'

'Yes, Herr Kommandant. Should I postpone my trip to the Loire?' He didn't want to go and leave Sylvie.

The Kommandant shook his head. 'No, it's business as usual, as far as I'm concerned. You can head off the morning after the dinner.'

'Yes, Herr Kommandant.'

'Now, General Winkler's security team needs to conduct a thorough search of the hotel. SS-Sturmbannführer Richter is in charge of the security detail for him. You'll ensure SS-Sturmbannführer Richter finds his way around, yes?'

A sick feeling gripped Christoph's stomach. A search of the hotel. What about Jacques, alone in the attic? 'Yes, of course.'

Bile rose in Christoph's throat. General Winkler's security team would most likely be SS troops. Christoph might have been able to divert ordinary soldiers from the attic, or at least told Jean to get Jacques out of the building, but with the SS things would be more complicated.

The Kommandant waved his hand. 'Don't stand there gawping. SS-Sturmbannführer Richter's waiting for you.' With a brief salute, Christoph retreated.

*

Le Meurice prickled with nervous energy, soldiers going back and forth through the front entrance. In the lobby, a tall, thin man with three burly henchman beside him, glanced at Christoph impatiently.

'You're the chap showing us round? I'm SS-Sturmbannführer Richter,' he said. 'Everything has to be checked to ensure the hotel is secure.'

'Of course,' Christoph said. 'I'll take you to the cellars.' As far away from Jacques as possible.

SS-Sturmbannführer Richter pointed to the stairs. 'I always start at the top.'

Reluctantly, Christoph was obliged to lead the way upstairs. He didn't want to be part of this. And yet, here he was, taking these men to the place where Jacques was hiding. His mind was blank with fear. He couldn't think how to stall them or warn Jacques. He only hoped that Jean had got there first.

Eventually, they reached the door to Jacques' hiding place. Christoph could hardly breathe. One of the soldiers took a crowbar out of his bag.

'It's just a storeroom,' Christoph said.

'We can't be too careful,' SS-Sturmbannführer Richter said. 'Not when the General's safety is at stake.'

The door broke and splintered. Dust filled the air. SS-Sturmbannführer Richter and his men switched on their torches. Christoph followed the flashlights as they swept around the attic. To his overwhelming relief, there was no sign that anyone had ever been there.

The soldiers searched every inch of the attic, lifting the waterproof lining and unhooking tiles to see if anyone was on the roof. Eventually, SS-Sturmbannführer Richter gave the order to stop.

'Nothing,' SS-Sturmbannführer Richter said. 'Although you might need to let the Kommandant know there could be rats. I spotted some droppings along the skirting board.'

'Yes, Herr SS-Sturmbannführer, of course,' Christoph said, relieved that rats were SS-Sturmbannführer Richter's only concern. The soldiers had been very thorough, throwing off dustsheets and overturning furniture. It was evident that Jacques was no longer up here.

SS-Sturmbannführer Richter moved on, instructing the soldiers to search the women's quarters. They checked in wardrobes and under the beds. Room by room, the soldiers worked their way through the staff quarters until they came to Christoph's room.

'Here, allow me,' Christoph said, unlocking the door. 'This is my room.'

SS-Sturmbannführer Richter went in. He nodded at the neat bed and desk.

'I understand you're the Kommandant's right-hand man,' he said.

'Yes, Herr SS-Sturmbannführer, his administrative assistant.'

SS-Sturmbannführer Richter opened the bedside-table drawer and smiled at the bundle of letters.

'Someone waiting for you back in Germany?' he said.

'Yes, Herr SS-Sturmbannführer. My fiancée.'

'Well, this all seems to be in order,' SS-Sturmbannführer Richter said. 'As the Kommandant and General Winkler are on the next floor and we do not want to disturb them, we'll do the cellars next. The head chef can take us. Thank you for your assistance.'

SS-Sturmbannführer Richter clicked his heels and left. The door closed, leaving Christoph alone in the room.

At that moment, he heard a faint noise. The hairs on the back of his neck stood up. It was coming from under the bed.

'Jacques, *c'est toi*?' he whispered.

Jacques wriggled out, his body held in tension, as if he might disintegrate at will if his survival demanded it.

'What the hell are you doing here?' Christoph said. He locked the door. Christ, if the SS had found him here, they'd both be done for.

'Jean brought me when he heard the cars arrive. It was the only place he could think of.'

'Jean will be with SS-Sturmbannführer Richter now.'

'Can you help me then?' Jacques asked, his voice hoarse.

'Of course,' Christoph said without hesitation.

Ever since Lotte had been taken, Christoph had known he had to take a side. He could no longer ignore what was happening around him. What a fool he'd been to think he could glide through the war staying neutral. He looked at Jacques' quivering hands. He couldn't help Lotte, but he could help Jacques.

'This place is swarming with SS,' Christoph said. 'You can't stay here. You need a safe place, a refuge . . .'

There wasn't much time. If they left now, while SS-Sturmbannführer Richter and his soldiers were in the cellars, there might be a chance. Christoph rifled through his wardrobe.

'Here,' he said, handing Jacques a spare uniform. 'Put this on. I know a place where you can hide.'

40

Lisette

August, 1942 – Paris

Lisette walked briskly along the Seine. She was late to meet Seraphin. Christoph's scent was all over her body. There'd been no time to wash. She'd tossed the mussel shells into the bin and hurried out. Everything was fragile. There wouldn't be many more moments with Christoph. Soon she would leave France for ever.

Seraphin was waiting in the shade of a chestnut tree in the Tuileries, his camera in his hand. 'If anyone asks, I'm taking pictures of the Tuileries to send to my mother, who is too ill to visit Paris any more.'

'Is that true?' Lisette asked.

'Not quite.' He smiled. 'But she always did love this spot.'

They set off strolling around the garden. Every so often, Seraphin stopped to take a photo of the flowers in the borders.

'I've got something to tell you,' Seraphin said, his face grave. 'General Winkler has come early. To accommodate his new schedule, the dinner will be tomorrow instead of on Monday.'

Lisette stiffened. Tomorrow. That meant she only had one more day with Christoph. That was no time at all.

'I'm not ready,' she said. 'It's too soon.'

Seraphin glanced at her. 'But you know what to do. It's simply a matter of doing it sooner rather than later. And then, you'll be on your way back home.'

Home. England. Lisette couldn't imagine it. Strange as it sounded, Paris had come to feel like home. But this ending was inevitable. Her time here had been part of a mission, nothing more. Christoph had never been part of the equation. She strengthened her resolve. There was one last task to carry out, and she would use all her skill and determination to do it.

'You can count on me,' she said.

'I know I can. Your professionalism has impressed me throughout. I'm going to miss working with you.' Seraphin lifted up the camera. 'May I take a photo of you? A proper one this time, not for identity papers. I'd like something to remember you by, and then, one day, I can tell my daughter about all the things we did during the war.'

Lisette smiled. 'I'm sure Estelle will be very proud when she hears about your work.'

Some passing soldiers whistled appreciatively as Lisette stood next to a bed of pink and white roses. She couldn't bear to look at the camera. Instead, she gazed towards Le Meurice, wondering where Christoph was and what he'd be doing. The thought of him made her smile and, at that moment, she heard the shutter click.

'*Magnifique.*' Seraphin nodded to the soldiers and linked arms with Lisette. 'They'd never suspect we're plotting the downfall of their superiors,' he whispered.

Lisette had been going over the plan in her mind. 'There's one problem: I don't have the vial yet,' she said. 'I gave you the poison for safekeeping, remember?'

'It was delivered to Le Meurice yesterday.'

'Not to me.'

'You're not our only contact in the hotel; it went to another agent there. As per protocol, I can't tell you who. I didn't want to risk you having the vial any sooner. Your German chap makes it too dangerous. But once the cooking starts, you'll find it in among the ingredients, don't worry.'

Seraphin stopped in the shade of the chestnut trees, his face grave. 'There's something else I need to tell you. The plan with the poison is a delicate balancing act. If anything should happen, if we can't use the vial as intended, then I'm afraid I must ask one last thing of you.'

The breeze moved the trees and the scent of roses wafted through the air. 'What's that?' Lisette said warily.

'This order has come from London. It's not my choice, and I know how hard it will be. But I have no doubt you have the strength and capabilities to see it through.' He paused. 'You see, if the plan fails, you've been instructed to move on to the Kommandant.'

Lisette froze. 'What?'

'We know he's interested in you. If for some reason the plan goes awry, that's what you must do. Cast off Leutnant Baumann. Cultivate a relationship with the Kommandant. The information he carries would be even more vital for our aims. Surely you can see that.'

Lisette stepped back. Seraphin's face was impossible to read.

'I don't understand,' she said. 'I'm carrying out the plan tomorrow. Then I'm leaving France. That's what we agreed.'

Seraphin nodded. 'Yes, of course, that is Plan A. But as

I've learned to my own cost, you always need a fall-back plan. The Kommandant is your Plan B.'

Lisette shuddered. Stay in Paris. End things with Christoph. Begin a romance with the Kommandant. Seraphin was overestimating her abilities and her sense of duty if he thought she was capable of that. 'The plan will work. It has to,' she said.

Seraphin touched her cheek. 'I hope it does, for your sake. But if it doesn't, I'm sorry, but you must follow orders and become the Kommandant's mistress.'

Extra soldiers had been posted on the door of Le Meurice. Lisette showed her papers and they let her in without a smile. Le Meurice had become even more dangerous; eyes watching everywhere. Lisette kept her head down and went straight to the kitchen. Her mind scrambled to make sense of Seraphin's words. There was no knowing if the plan would go ahead or not. She had to stay alert.

The staff were huddled in a group, complaining in nervous voices.

'We'll never be ready in time,' Guillaume, one of the chefs de partie, said.

'What's going on?' Lisette took off her coat and hung it behind the door.

'That chap Winkler is in Paris, so the dinner is tomorrow,' Guillaume said. 'The SS are turning the place upside down. They're in the cellar now. M. Dupont has the lucky job of showing them round.'

The SS. Lisette's stomach turned cold. 'We'd better get on with sourcing the ingredients then, and prepare what we can today.'

Lisette tried not to think about the vial: to whom it had been delivered or when it would be passed on to her.

The staff followed her lead and got to work. When Christoph came into the kitchen with a soldier, no one batted an eyelid. They were used to his visits. Lisette didn't notice him until it was almost too late. Christoph held the young man's sleeve, as if directing him. The man looked petrified and the uniform was ill-fitting.

'Christoph,' she said.

He put his fingers to his lips and kept on moving. Christoph and the young man went past Lisette and through the back door, out into the street.

Lisette frowned. She hadn't seen the young soldier before, and he hadn't looked well. She wondered when Christoph would be back. She fetched some flour, butter and eggs and started to prepare the choux pastry, puzzling over it all.

'Stop what you're doing,' a voice shouted, 'and don't move.'

Lisette froze, pastry stuck to her fingers. Soldiers swarmed the kitchen dressed in black uniforms, led by a tall, thin man. 'That's the man who was searching the place,' Guillaume whispered. 'SS-Sturmbannführer Richter.'

In among the group was M. Dupont, jostled and pushed by two armed men. The Kommandant strode behind, his expression grim.

'You have a traitor in your midst,' SS-Sturmbannführer Richter said.

Time slowed down. The blood drained from Lisette's face. She leaned against the counter to steady herself.

SS-Sturmbannführer Richter pointed at M. Dupont

and the soldiers shoved him forward. 'He is a member of the resistance and is intent on murdering the guests as they eat.'

Lisette's heart went cold. *You're not our only contact in the hotel.* She'd suspected that the head chef was a collaborator. He was always friendly with the Kommandant and had special privileges in the hotel. But M. Dupont must have been the agent Seraphin had been talking about, the one to whom he had sent the vial.

The soldier aimed his gun at the back of M. Dupont's head. His face was white and covered with sweat.

'What's going on, Herr SS-Sturmbannführer?' the Kommandant said, standing by the kitchen door, a deep frown on his face.

'Your head chef planned to poison us all,' Major Richter replied. He held up a vial. 'We found this on his person. A few drops in the meal and the guests would have been severely ill within hours or possibly even dead.'

The poison. If M. Dupont had the vial, then he knew it was destined for Lisette. Her stomach lurched. He knew enough to implicate her.

'It seems you've not been as assiduous in your preparations as General Winkler would have hoped,' SS-Sturmbannführer Richter said, enjoying the Kommandant's discomfort. 'I'm arresting the entire kitchen staff and taking them for interrogation.'

Lisette glanced at the back door. A soldier was already stationed there.

'Of course,' the Kommandant said, 'but I can vouch for one member of staff here.' The Kommandant swivelled his eyes towards Lisette and smiled.

'Mlle Sylvie will stay,' he said. 'I need her to create the most splendid dinner Paris has ever seen. She's the only one talented enough to do it, now you've arrested that man. Don't worry, she's been interrogated recently, so I know she's clean.'

'Very well,' SS-Sturmbannführer Richter said. 'Keep her. The rest are coming with me.'

He kicked M. Dupont with the toe of his boot. Lisette turned away. Another agent brought down in front of her eyes. It was too much to bear.

One by one the kitchen staff were taken away. The air was bitter with fear, and some were weeping. Soon the kitchen was empty. How prescient Seraphin's words had been. *If something happens, if the plan with the poison goes wrong, you must move on to the Kommandant.* A cold weight settled in her heart.

Before she could clear her thoughts, the Kommandant came over, smug with the role of being her protector.

'So,' he said, 'it's in your hands now.'

'But I have no staff. I can't do the dinner all by myself,' she said.

'I don't mean the dinner. You can call in some help from Maxim's. I'll pay double what they earn. No, I mean the situation between us. SS-Sturmbannführer Richter would have taken you too if I hadn't spoken. One good turn deserves another, don't you think?'

Lisette took a deep breath. Her mind raced at double pace. She was here to fight the Germans. She'd followed orders to the last, apart from falling in love with Leutnant Baumann. Now she had to put that aside. Seraphin had ordered her to foster a relationship with the man standing in front of her. The man leaning towards her and pressing his thin lips against hers. Her mind told her that she should do her duty, but the Kommandant's breath was sour, his hand rough. She couldn't bear it.

'I'm sorry, it's just . . .' she said, pulling back.

The Kommandant stared at her, displeased.

'I will repay you. I want to. It's just . . .' Lisette scrambled for excuses. 'I'm in shock. So much has happened, and now I must prepare for the dinner. I don't want to let you down.'

The Kommandant's face softened. He gripped her hand and pulled her closer.

'I understand,' he said. 'You're overwhelmed. After tomorrow's dinner is complete, we'll have more than enough time for each other.'

He pressed her close and kissed her cheek. She shuddered inwardly.

'My beautiful Sylvie,' he said. 'It will be worth the wait . . .'

Eintopf mit Bohnen und Kartoffeln

150g lardons
2 onions, chopped
500g potatoes, sliced
Parsley, chopped
Salt and pepper
500g tomatoes, sliced
750g green beans, chopped

1. Preheat the oven to 130°C.
2. Fry the lardons and onions and place in a cast-iron pot.
3. Layer the potatoes on top, and sprinkle with parsley, salt and pepper.
4. Layer the tomatoes on the potatoes, and again sprinkle with parsley, salt and pepper.
5. Add the beans and pour in boiling water until the contents are immersed.
6. Cover with a lid, place in the oven and cook for two hours.

41

Julia

August, 2002 – Paris

Julia woke in the double bed. Someone was knocking at the apartment door. She was about to get up when she heard the door open and a man speak.

'Good, you're up.' It was the concierge. 'The hospital rang and asked me to let you know that your father is having an MRI scan today.'

Julia sat up. An MRI scan?

'Oh, I see,' she heard Daniel reply. 'Thanks for letting us know. I'm sorry you had to come all this way up.'

'Not at all,' the concierge said. 'I hope he's okay.' Julia heard the door close.

A sweet and salty smell filled the air. Lardons and onions. She rubbed her eyes. Daniel must be cooking. She got up, put on her cardigan, and went to find him.

The kitchen was a hive of activity. A frying pan hissed on the hob and there were chopped beans and parsley strewn on the table. Daniel glanced at Julia across the kitchen. The intimacy and tensions of the night before came rushing back, but she pushed them away.

'Did you hear the concierge come up?' he asked.

'Yes,' she said, pulling out a chair and sitting down. 'An

MRI. That's good, I suppose, that they're investigating everything.'

'He'll be okay. He has to be,' Daniel said. He stirred the onions and lardons. 'I got up this morning and decided to make the next recipe for him.'

Julia glanced at him, surprised. Last night, she'd wondered if he'd meant what he'd said, but he seemed to be making an effort. She peered over at the recipe book on the counter. 'Is it Eintopf mit Bohnen und Kartoffeln?'

'Yes, it's nearly ready to go in the oven.'

'He'll be delighted you made this,' she said. 'We can take him some later.'

Daniel nodded. He tipped the potatoes into the pan then leaned against the counter and smiled. 'You were humming something in your sleep. I heard you when I got up to get a glass of water.'

Julia pulled the sleeves of her cardigan over her hands. 'Really? I fell asleep thinking of a melody. Maybe it was that.'

He came and sat down opposite her. 'Do you think you could play it?'

Julia pushed back some loose strands of hair. 'I don't know. Why?'

'In the allotment, after I called you selfish, you said that the piano was your life. That it had been more constant than anyone.' He held her gaze. 'After everything that's happened with your hands, it makes me sad to think of that. It must be so hard not being able to play.'

Julia couldn't bear the pity in his eyes. 'It is.'

'What if you tried playing your own tune?' Daniel said.

'Maybe that would make a difference. You won't be confined to the melodies of others.'

'I don't know.' It was strange to hear these insights from Daniel. He must have really been thinking about it all.

'You could use the piano here. I can go in the other room, or out for a walk. I won't disturb you.'

His hands, resting on the table, strong and firm, were almost close enough to touch. Julia swallowed.

'I don't want you to go anywhere,' she said. Better say it now, before the moment was over. 'It's not *you* that brings back bad memories, it's the pain of what might have been that does.'

Before he could answer, Julia went to the piano. Doubts about playing sprang up inside her. What if she wasn't ready? The tune had faded in her mind. Her palms became clammy.

Then, she glanced up and saw Daniel, watching her calmly, without expectation or judgement. Whatever she played or didn't play, it would be okay, his eyes seemed to say. Her breathing slowed. The melody returned. She knew how to begin.

As she played, Julia was aware of a blissful calm. It had been years since she'd experienced this. These were her own notes. As a result, her hands didn't falter once. When the music ended and Julia came back down to earth, Daniel's voice broke the silence.

'That was extraordinary,' he said, kneeling by the piano stool. 'You shouldn't be breaking your neck trying to compete with other pianists. You should be composing your own music.'

'Do you think so?' Julia said.

She closed the piano lid gently. Who knew how long the fluency in her hands would last?

Daniel touched Julia's cheek. 'I feel it too, you know, the pain of what might have been. Maybe it's time we did something about that . . .'

Julia sucked in her breath. There it was: the warmth of his voice, the light in his eyes. She'd been longing for this affirmation, and now . . . He slid his hand up her arm, shivers spreading across her skin.

'Julia,' he said. He was so close, and there was nothing she wanted more than the touch of his lips on hers. At last, his lips touched hers. The kiss was gentle at first, exploring, teasing. Then it grew deeper, their tongues entwined. A flame flared in Julia.

'Should we be doing this?' she whispered, some rational part of her brain still switched on.

'Don't think too hard, Julia. Just let it happen, like the music . . .'

He took her hand, his eyes smouldering. She followed him to the bedroom. There was nothing to stop them this time. For six years, she'd waited for this.

He closed the door and turned to face her. It was just the two of them, finally, together in this room. He moved towards her and she wrapped her arms around him, desperate to feel his body against hers.

'I thought this would never happen,' Daniel whispered, kissing the soft skin on her neck.

She shrugged off her cardigan, smiling with the pleasure of his touch. 'Me too.' She ran her fingers through his hair.

His pupils were black with desire. One by one, he undid the buttons on her nightshirt and let it drop to the floor.

He gazed at her in wonder. 'My God, Julia, you're beautiful.'

He lifted her up, and laid her on the bed, then bent down and kissed her, gentle kisses that sent delicious tremors across her skin.

Julia drank in his scent, feeling her way with her hands across his shoulders. He moaned, his hand kneading her back then travelling across her belly, lower, and lower. She gasped. A current sparked deep inside.

Her mind cleared of doubts. Now. Here. No more waiting. It was simple. She wanted him. As his hands moved rhythmically, she pulled his T-shirt off, savouring the heat of his chest.

'Are you sure about this?' Daniel whispered, their eyes locked, just millimetres apart.

'It's taken us long enough.' She tugged loose the buckle of his belt.

He groaned and kissed her throat. She was ready now, warm and burning, aching for him to take her. He moved above her, her legs widening to let him in. Nearer and nearer until, with a gasp, he entered her.

At each burning thrust, the world opened, her body unfurled like the petals of a flower, until he was inside her, closer and deeper than anyone had ever been before. As the room dissolved into murmurs and shadow and waves of desire, the seams of her heart came undone. She cried out, clutching Daniel, her name on his lips the last thing she heard as the moment overwhelmed them both.

Later, Daniel ran her a bath. When Julia got out, he was gone. A note on the pillow said he'd popped out to get something but he'd be back soon. He'd drawn a heart by her name. She smiled. The bed was still crumpled from where he'd lain. She bent down and savoured the scent of him on the pillow. Her stomach was rumbling so she got dressed and went to find something to eat.

The Eintopf mit Bohnen und Kartoffeln was cold so Julia heated it up on the hob. A deep feeling of wellness flooded her body. She got out two bowls and coffee cups. Regret might come later, but it wasn't clouding the horizon yet.

The front door clicked open and Daniel walked in, carrying a bag in his hand. 'I'm back,' he said, coming over and sliding a hand around her waist. 'I've bought you a gift.'

Julia glanced up surprised. 'What is it?'

Daniel took out a book of blank sheet music. 'What you played me earlier was beautiful. I bought you this so that you can write it down.'

Moved by his thoughtfulness, Julia clasped her arms around his neck and kissed him. 'Thank you, Daniel, that's so kind. I'm not sure my piece was as good as you think, but maybe it's time to try composing again.'

Daniel took off his jacket. 'The soup doesn't look too bad, considering it was my first attempt at making it,' he said. 'I'm looking forward to trying some.'

Julia moved the box of music from the end of the table to make room for the pot. As she picked it up, the underneath collapsed and scores scattered over the floor. She bent down to pick them up. Then stopped. In among the music was a photograph. A woman was standing in front of some rose bushes. She was smiling, but her gaze had drifted to the left. On the back of the photo was written *Sylvie, 1942*.

'What's that?' Daniel said.

'It's Sylvie,' Julia said. 'I found it in the box.'

Daniel leaned over Julia's shoulder to look.

Sylvie's hair was crimped and pinned up. She wore a fitted white blouse and a pencil line skirt. She was beautiful, but it was her eyes particularly that made her face shine.

'She's got a look of you. The way she's smiling, you could almost be related,' Daniel said. He took the photo out of Julia's hand and studied it closely. 'I'm sure I've seen this woman before. I recognize her face.'

'What do you mean?' Julia said.

'My God, this is worse than I'd thought,' he said, his voice strained. 'This isn't just about the long-lost past.'

Julia gripped his hand. 'I don't understand.'

Daniel moved away, struggling to compose himself. 'Do you remember I told you that my father brought me to Paris when I was eight?' He stared at the photo, breathing hard.

'Yes,' Julia said, wondering where this was leading.

'Papa and I had been to a café and were standing on the street corner. I wanted to go back to the hotel and watch TV. But he said we had to wait. A woman walked towards us. They talked. I couldn't understand what they were saying. It was all in French. But then he touched her face. It was such a tender gesture; I'd never seen him do anything like that with Mama. Then the woman looked at me.'

'At you?'

'Yes. She had tears running down her face, but she was

smiling. She gave him a package, said something to me in French that I didn't understand, and then she went.'

'You think this woman was Sylvie?'

'I know it was,' Daniel said firmly, pointing to the photograph. 'She was older than she is here, but I'd recognize her anywhere. After that trip, Papa retreated into his music. I didn't know what was going on, but the coldness and distance between my parents increased. I've always connected that woman from Paris with the reason why my parents weren't happy, I just didn't know how she fitted into the puzzle. And now, it turns out she's Sylvie, the one he wants to find.'

Julia stared at Sylvie's face. It seemed incredible that Daniel had seen her: alive, here on the streets of Paris.

'When did this happen?' she asked. 'When did you see her?'

'It must have been around 1978.'

'If the woman you saw on the street was Sylvie, then she couldn't have died at Drancy.'

'But that doesn't make sense,' Daniel said. 'Mama told me that the letter said Sylvie Dubois died in Drancy in 1942.'

Julia stared at him. 'Dubois? But you said you didn't know her surname when I asked you.'

Daniel reddened. 'I'm sorry, I was going to tell you.'

'Oh, Daniel.'

'I was still afraid of what we might discover. I should have told you sooner.' He stared at the photo, then cast it down. 'I thought we were searching for a wartime fling. Not someone he met again while he had a family.' Pain filled his eyes.

Julia stared at the photo. Whatever this might mean for Christoph, it was hurting Daniel.

'I know this is hard,' she said, touching his hand. 'It might have been a chance encounter in 1978, nothing more.'

'Or maybe they were having an affair,' he said, clearly troubled by it all. 'I want to help Papa, I really do, but that meeting happening long after the war ended changes things. I was the one who had to pick up the pieces for Mama. Instead of being allowed to be a child, I had to parent her through her anxiety and depression. The root of her fear was that Papa had been unfaithful. And now, it looks like she was right. I was always trying to convince her she was wrong, that of course he wouldn't cheat on her.'

He rose from the table and looked out of the tiny window, pressing his forehead against the glass. 'My perpetual travelling the world was an attempt to get away from the tension between Mama and Papa. I'd been putting up with it my whole life.' He turned back to her, his eyes imploring. 'Please, Julia, once Papa is well enough, can we just take him home and forget all of this?'

Julia sucked in her breath. Here it was. The moment of choice. Daniel wanted her to stop. Christoph, she knew, would want to continue. It was impossible to please them both. How could she even try? But even as she flailed for a solution, her mind was made up.

'If there's a chance that Sylvie is alive, I have to keep searching,' Julia said. 'I understand that you can't help me, and I'm not asking that of you, but in return you need to understand that I have to finish this journey for Christoph.'

Daniel's shoulders drooped. 'I know, I get that. Perhaps I just need some time to get my head around all of this.

I'm afraid that what we might discover will drive Papa and me even further apart.'

Julia went over to Daniel and touched his cheek. 'It's a lot to take in,' she said. 'but just think, this might actually bring you closer. There's been a lifetime of secrets between you and uncovering them might heal your relationship.'

Daniel shook his head. 'I don't know.' He stood up. 'Sorry. I need some time to think about all of this. Would you mind taking the soup to Papa? I'm not sure I can face him just yet after seeing that photo.'

He went off to the bathroom, thoughts weighing heavily in his eyes. Julia heard the water running. He must be reeling from the discovery. She stared at the photo. It was strange to see the face of the woman whose words she'd read in the recipe book.

What would Sylvie decide if she were faced with the choice of hurting Christoph or hurting Daniel? Julia was caught in the middle: between Christoph's memories and Daniel's recollections. She needed additional information – cold, hard facts – to decide what to do. If she went to the National Archives, maybe she could find out more.

Before she left, she hovered outside the bathroom door. She lifted her hand to tap on it, then stopped. Maybe she should leave Daniel alone for a while, let him digest things. She sighed, picked up her bag and left, closing the apartment door behind her.

The reading room in the National Archives was quiet. Julia collected the microfiche of the Drancy records for 1942 and went to find a desk. She peered at the litany of names typed in grey ink of people imprisoned in Drancy. They were too numerous to count. It was sickening to think how many had been sent to concentration camps.

Name after name scrolled by. Suddenly, there it was: Sylvie Dubois. Arrived in Drancy in September 1942. Died two weeks later of typhoid. So she'd never even made it out of France.

Julia frowned. If Daniel was correct, and the woman he saw in Paris in 1978 was Sylvie, then she couldn't have perished in Drancy. Which meant that either Daniel or the records or were wrong.

Julia sat back, trying to puzzle it out. Perhaps she needed to go further back. Why would Sylvie have been sent to Drancy in the first place? She remembered Pierre saying that his father, Jean, had been interrogated about a plot at the hotel. Could it be linked to that?

Julia went to the front desk and asked for the Avenue Foch records.

'There are reams of them,' the attendant said, as she handed over the files. 'The Nazis were nothing if not thorough.'

Julia went back to her desk and sat down with the files. She lost track of time as she focused intently on looking for any mention of Sylvie.

She found Pierre's father's records. It stated that Jean Dupont had been accused of intending to poison the guests at a large dinner for a General Winkler. Jean's interview records didn't mention Sylvie but there was another name. It caught Julia's eye because it was so unusual.

The record stated:

M. Jean Dupont, who we suspect was working for the resistance, argued that he'd been betrayed. He named a man named Seraphin. Jean accused Seraphin of being involved with the Special Operations Executive (SOE). He said Seraphin had double-crossed him. No trace of Seraphin's real identity was later found. Jean was tortured for information, which was unforthcoming, and then sent to Natzweiler.

Julia sighed. She knew from Pierre that his father had survived the war. Unfortunately, though, Jean had now passed away and Pierre didn't recall him ever mentioning Sylvie. Julia stared at the papers.

So if she wasn't arrested for being involved in the plot, what had she done? The only other time Sylvie had been in trouble with the German authorities was when she was arrested and questioned over the recipe book, also at Avenue Foch. Nothing had come of it because she'd been released to work at Le Meurice, but still, the interview notes might yield some clue.

She flicked through the papers. Sure enough, there was the account of how Sylvie had been detained. An inexperienced soldier had found her recipe book and arrested her because it contained French and German recipes. The interview directly correlated with Christoph's account of the misunderstanding, and why Sylvie had been sent to Le Meurice. But one part of the records was intriguing. Something Christoph hadn't mentioned, or simply hadn't known.

Mlle Sylvie Dubois was questioned about a woman known to us only as Hélène after leaving an apartment block in rue Clément where Hélène was found to be in possession of wireless crystals. Hélène was arrested and confessed to being an agent for the Special Operations Executive (SOE). Mlle Dubois claimed no knowledge of Hélène at all, nor, when questioned, did she know of Seraphin, the man whom Hélène said had arranged for the crystals to be delivered. Mlle Dubois was released into the hands of the Kommandant's right-hand man, Leutnant Baumann, and no further action was taken. Hélène was subsequently executed. Seraphin was never found.

Julia closed her eyes and tried to digest the information. Who was this Seraphin mentioned in both Jean and Sylvie's records? And if he had been involved in the SOE, could it mean that Sylvie was in some way connected to the SOE as well? Surely not if she'd been released and sent to work at Le Meurice. It didn't make sense.

Julia tidied the papers away and sighed. There wasn't much to go on, just that unusual name. She thought of Christoph, alone in the hospital, grieving for Sylvie, and of Daniel, alone at the apartment, hating Sylvie and what he believed she'd done to ruin his parents' marriage. The only way to help them both was to find out the truth.

Christoph was asleep when Julia arrived at the hospital. She sat and watched him, trying to think what to say. Eventually, his eyes opened. Julia took his hand.

'Christoph, I need to ask you something. During the war, did you ever hear of someone called Seraphin?'

'Seraphin?' he said. 'No, never.'

He was tired. She could see his eyelids drooping. But

she had to keep going. His memories were the only way to put the archive records into context.

'Do you remember Pierre telling us that his father, Jean, was interrogated? Did you ever suspect Jean of being a member of the resistance? I mean, before he was arrested.'

'Of course I did.' He tried to sit up, clutching his stomach. Julia bolstered the cushions behind him to make him more comfortable. 'When I discovered Jacques in the storeroom, I knew Jean had to be in the resistance.'

Julia scribbled in the notebook, then looked up. 'Wait a minute. Who was Jacques? You haven't mentioned him before.'

'No, I suppose I was so focused on Sylvie. Jaques was a Jew Jean was hiding up there. When Jean was arrested, I got Jacques out of Le Meurice and hid him at the apartment.'

Julia stared at him, astonished. 'That explains why Pierre said his father thought you were a remarkable man. You took such a risk.'

'It was the only thing to do.' Christoph reached for a glass of water. His arm was thin and weak. Julia held the glass to his lips.

'I was at the National Archives, reading Jean and Sylvie's interrogation records. The name Seraphin came up in both accounts. But, from what you've said, it seems it was a dead end.' She sighed and put down her notebook. 'Look, I've brought you some Eintopf mit Bohnen und Kartoffeln. Daniel made it.'

Christoph raised his eyebrows. 'Daniel? I thought he didn't approve of me trying to remember Sylvie.'

'He was almost coming round to the idea. But then

I found this, and Daniel told me her surname: Sylvie Dubois.' Julia reached into her bag for the photo of Sylvie. She handed it to Christoph.

Christoph stared at the image. 'It's her. Her eyes, that smile. Where did you find it?'

'It was in a box of music in the apartment,' Julia said. 'Have you seen it before?'

'I don't remember it,' he said, tracing Sylvie's profile with his finger. His eyes moistened. 'Such a gift. To see a photograph of the woman I've only glimpsed in my head. Sylvie Dubois.'

Julia opened the container of Eintopf mit Bohnen und Kartoffeln. The smell of the lardons filled the air. She handed it to Christoph. He propped the photo up against a box of tissues and took a tiny spoonful, savouring the flavour.

'Delicious. I only wish I could eat more.' He stared at the photo, drinking in the sight of Sylvie. 'I don't understand. Why has Daniel changed his mind now he's seen this photograph?'

Julia sighed. 'Daniel remembers seeing the woman in this picture in 1978, here with you in Paris. He's angry because he thinks you were having an affair with her and that's what caused your family to fall apart, and Hilde's sadness.'

'An affair? In 1978? But he said Sylvie died in Drancy.'

'That's what the records say. But if Daniel really did see her when he was a child, she can't have died. And maybe . . .' Julia hesitated, unsure whether to raise his hopes.

Christoph's eyes shone. For a moment, his age and suffering melted away.

'Maybe she's still alive,' he said.

42

Christoph

August, 1942 – Paris

Christoph sat in his office; the maps pushed aside. Without meaning to, he'd reached a turning point, not just in his thoughts but in his actions. He could hardly believe what he was contemplating. It was too dangerous, too outrageous to work. But he didn't know what else to do.

The Kommandant strode into the room and glanced disapprovingly at Christoph's idle hands.

'Everything's going well in the kitchens,' he said. 'I've been keeping a special eye on things after that fiasco with the head chef. M. Dupont had me fooled, I'll admit. Little did I think he was intending to murder us.'

'Me neither, Herr Kommandant,' Christoph said. They'd be torturing Jean for names. He couldn't bear to think of it.

'I hope you're not brooding about Sylvie.' The Kommandant glanced in the mirror and smoothed back his hair. 'When this dinner's over, neither Sylvie nor I will bother you any more.'

'I don't understand.'

'I'm being transferred back to Berlin,' the Kommandant said. He clasped his hands and drew back his shoulders. 'I've decided to take Sylvie with me. I've grown fond of her cooking and will require her skills back in the Fatherland.'

Christoph stared, unable to process what the Kommandant was saying.

'Oh yes,' the Kommandant said, with evident delight at Christoph's discomfort. 'The Service Travail Obligatoire now extends to unmarried women aged twenty-one to thirty-five. Sylvie will work as my personal chef.'

'I see,' Christoph said, forcing the words out.

'It's all worked out rather well. By the time you get back from the Loire, we'll be gone.' The Kommandant glanced round the office, at the untidy pile of maps and papers. 'For Christ's sake, Herr Leutnant, get this room sorted out. General Winkler is a stickler for orderliness.'

After he'd gone, Christoph went to the window. The car he'd taken to Normandy was parked next to General Winkler's entourage. He already had the keys in his pocket, ready for an early start the next day. He glanced at the boot. It was deep enough for several suitcases. Surely a stowaway could fit as well.

He rubbed his temples. It would only work if he got Sylvie out of the hotel first, as soon as dinner had been served. Tonight, the whole of Le Meurice would be feasting in the dining hall. By ten o'clock, everyone would be stuffed full of Sylvie's delicious food and half gone with alcohol. He could walk her to the apartment once the main course had been served. She and Jacques could hide out there while he came back to Le Meurice. Then, as already planned, he would set off in the car to the Loire early in the morning, picking up Sylvie and Jacques on the way.

Christoph opened his desk drawer. He had a sheaf of documents verifying his authority to inspect the farm. No one would dare question a German official with all the right paperwork, nor would his car be searched.

Christoph stuffed the file into his briefcase, trying to compose himself. He needed to calm the storm in his head if this plan had even the slightest chance of working.

That evening, the dining room was resplendent. Women draped themselves on the arms of officers. Men laughed, their gold fillings glinting in the candlelight. Christoph was seated away from the Kommandant.

The Kommandant caught sight of him and waved him over. His cheeks were flushed with champagne and he'd already wolfed down his salmon starter.

'Let me introduce you to General Winkler,' the Kommandant said. 'He's going to give a speech later. You will find it most informative.'

General Winkler was rather more composed than the Kommandant. He sipped his wine delicately.

'You'll find Leutnant Baumann a diligent worker,' the Kommandant said. 'He's researching farm production for us. Tomorrow he heads off to the Loire for two days to inspect the progress of some farms which are in the process of harvesting vast fields of sunflowers.'

'Very good,' General Winkler said, nodding approvingly. 'The oil will be a valuable resource in our fight on the Eastern Front.'

The two men began discussing the situation in Russia. Now was the time to get Sylvie out of the hotel. He could take her to the apartment and be back in time for the speeches before anyone noticed.

As he turned to go, Christoph caught sight of a man sitting at the end of the table. His hair was combed to one side and he wore a red cravat. Christoph was sure he'd seen him before. His intense blue eyes and his smile, appearing now as he talked to SS-Sturmbannführer Richter, were familiar. He looked like the man that Sylvie had been with in the café, the best friend of her fiancé. But that was impossible. Why would he be here?

There was no time to wonder. The soup course was being served: Eintopf mit Bohnen und Kartoffeln. Soon, General Winkler would make his speech. Christoph left the dining room, taking the back route via the corridors to the kitchen. Now was the moment to act.

The kitchen was buzzing with activity. Waiters traipsed in and out carrying plates of food. Sylvie was head chef now that Jean had been arrested. She had assigned each cook from Maxim's a dish to prepare. Christoph made his way towards her.

'Christoph,' she whispered as soon as he was close, 'the Kommandant came down before dinner started. He's taking me to Germany, I don't know what to do . . .'

'It's all right. Come on, we need to go,' he said, taking her hand.

'But I can't, I'm supposed to follow orders. I want to do my duty,' she said, tears in her eyes. 'It's just that this is more than I'd expected.' He'd never seen her so distressed.'

'Forget about it, the Kommandant's orders don't matter, you have to save yourself, there's no time.' He glanced around; everyone was busy. He grabbed a pot full of Topf.

'We'll take some extra food. I've got your things. I packed them this afternoon while you were down here.'

'But I need –'

'I've got the recipe book too. We must go now, there's no time to lose.'

Sylvie followed Christoph into the sidestreet. Stopping by the bins, Christoph retrieved her suitcase from where he'd stowed it.

'Where are we going?' she asked.

'The apartment. It's the only safe place I could think of.'

If tonight went to plan, that dinner would be the last thing Lisette ever cooked at Le Meurice.

He held her hand and they walked quickly through the streets. They passed soldiers jostling on the pavement. He didn't have much time. Just enough to see her safely to the apartment and then hurry back for the speeches. The concierge nodded as they crossed the courtyard and went upstairs. Outside the door to the apartment, Christoph stopped. He placed her suitcase on the floor, the pot of Topf next to it. In the distance, the sound of planes. Please God, let there not be any bombing tonight.

'I have to go back,' he said. Sylvie tightened her grip on his hand. 'Just for a few hours, until the dinner is over. I'll come back first thing in the morning.'

'They'll wonder where I am.'

'I'll make up an excuse.' He hesitated, glancing at the door. 'There's someone else here too: a Jewish man called Jacques. Jean was hiding him at Le Meurice, but I got him out when the SS came.'

Sylvie's eyes widened in the half-lit landing. 'You brought

him through the kitchen yesterday, when M. Dupont was arrested. He was wearing your uniform.'

Christoph nodded. 'Yes, there was no chance for me to explain. He was hidden in the storerooms at Le Meurice for a month, but I have a plan to get us out of occupied France.'

Sylvie clasped Christoph's hands. 'It's not right that you should risk yourself like this. Not for me. Not for anyone.'

'I had to choose a side, and I've chosen it,' Christoph said. 'I can't help my sister now, but I can help Jacques. And I can help you. I'll come back with the car, and we'll escape Paris tomorrow.'

Sylvie drew back. 'A car?' she said. 'We'll be stopped. You'll be recognized. A German soldier, a Frenchwoman and a Jewish man all travelling together. How would you explain that?'

'You and I drove to Normandy without any problems. We'll do the same again, but head south towards the Loire, and then to the border. Just like last time, you'll be my companion and translator, and Jacques will be hidden in the boot of the car.'

Sylvie frowned. 'Do you think it'll work?'

'Of course. You'll be travelling with a German lieutenant who has a cast-iron reason for going to the Loire, and documents to prove it. We'll sort out papers for Jacques once we're over the border.'

'You've got it all worked out,' Sylvie said, biting her lip, 'but you're taking a massive risk.'

'It will be worth it.' He glanced at his watch. 'I need to return to the dinner now, but when the sun rises I'll be back.'

'Then we'd better say goodbye,' Sylvie said, her voice small.

In the shadow of the landing he could hardly see her, but he knew every curve and swell. He drew her close.

'Just for now,' he whispered.

She put her arms around his neck and kissed him. It was a kiss like no other: full of urgency and yearning. Desire stirred. He longed to take her into the apartment.

'I love you, Sylvie,' he murmured, inhaling her scent.

'Oh, Christoph. I love you too.'

Her eyes filled with tears. He couldn't bear to leave her, even for a few hours. He was so close to staying, to risking everything and remaining with her. But he had to go. It was the only way to cover up her absence. It was just for a few hours, until morning, and then he'd be with her again.

General Winkler's speech had finished by the time Christoph returned. He heard the thunder of hands clapping and feet stamping and slipped back into his seat. The desserts had been cleared away and everyone was drinking coffee and liqueurs. The bombing was over in the west of Paris and, fortified by alcohol and bravado, General Winkler had decided the dinner would continue.

'Where have you been?' the Kommandant said. He leaned over Christoph, unsteady on his feet.

'Sylvie wasn't feeling well, so I helped her upstairs. I hope you don't mind. I think she's just exhausted,' Christoph said. 'She's excited about leaving for Germany. You've managed to win her over, Herr Kommandant.'

The Kommandant slapped Christoph on the back. With his belly full of alcohol and food, he was in a jovial mood.

'I knew it,' he said. 'She'll do well with me in Berlin. Good that Sylvie's getting some rest. She'll need all her strength for what I've got planned.' A smirk played on his lips.

Christoph clenched his fist, smarting at the Kommandant's words, but he didn't dare display his anger, not when he was only hours from escaping it all.

The Kommandant wound his way around the tables, chatting to guests, introducing General Winkler to others. After coffee, Christoph slipped away and went up to his room to pack.

He didn't sleep well. After the bombing had stopped, he was disturbed by vivid nightmares. When he woke up, his forehead was bathed in sweat. He checked his wristwatch. Five o'clock. He'd overslept. Sylvie would be wondering where he was. He got dressed and went downstairs. The hotel was empty except for the staff preparing breakfast.

In the courtyard, the soldier on guard asked him why he needed the car.

'I'm inspecting a farm outside Paris today,' Christoph said. 'The Kommandant's orders.' He dangled the keys in the morning sunshine.

The soldier stood aside. Christoph climbed in and started the engine. The car glided out of the courtyard and on to the rue de Rivoli. He took a circuitous route in case he was being followed. The roads were quiet. Checking his rear-view mirror to make sure the coast was clear, Christoph parked outside the apartment block.

He bounded up the stairs two at a time, his heart light with the success of the first part of his plan. He just needed to get Sylvie and Jacques in the car while the streets were deserted. Then they could be on their way.

'Sylvie,' he whispered, hurrying down the hallway of the apartment, 'Jacques, are you ready?'

His voice echoed in the silence. There was no sound, no rustle of footsteps, no one coming to greet him.

'Sylvie,' he called, louder now.

He wrenched open the door to the bedroom, then the bathroom, the kitchen. No one was there. His heart thundered in his chest.

'Where are you?'

He looked out of the window, but there was no sign of them. There was no sign of anyone. Sylvie's suitcase and recipe book had gone. Only the uniform, the one he'd lent to Jacques, lay folded on the table, and the empty pot that had contained the Topf.

Christoph sat down, his legs weak. What had happened? They'd vanished into thin air.

The front door clicked open. For a moment, his heart leapt with relief.

But it wasn't Sylvie. It was the man he'd seen at the dinner. The man who looked like Sylvie's fiancé's best friend, his eyes a stormy blue.

'So, she's deserted you too, has she?' he said in French. 'Well, perhaps it's for the best. Germany with the Kommandant would never have suited her. And sadly, a relationship with you would never have worked either.'

'Who are you? Where is she?'

'Me? I'm nobody,' the man said. 'And I've no idea where she's gone. It's out of my hands now. But I do know you're leaving Paris today.'

'What do you mean?' Christoph said. He looked over the man's shoulder. Two German soldiers stood behind him.

'The Kommandant wants you gone. Count yourself lucky it's not the death penalty for desertion,' he said. 'You've been deployed to the Eastern Front. You leave today.'

'But where's Sylvie?' Christoph said. He grabbed the man by his lapels and pushed him up against the wall. 'What's happened to her?'

The soldiers pulled Christoph away and held him in an armlock.

The man shrugged. 'She's *sans cœur*, you know. Always has been. But if I ever see her again, don't worry. I'll tell her you perished at Stalingrad.'

The soldiers shoved Christoph towards the door and dragged him down the stairs. He didn't have the will to resist. All his strength had vanished. Russia meant certain death. But, knowing that Sylvie had abandoned him without a word, Christoph didn't care.

43

Julia

August, 2002 – Paris

Christoph was overwhelmed with distress when he recalled the empty apartment and being sent to the Eastern Front. He cried out, burying his head in his hands.

'I should have stayed with her that night,' he said. 'I should never have gone back to Le Meurice.'

'Do you think she was taken?'

Christoph shook his head. 'There was no sign of forced entry or struggle.'

'Maybe she left to protect you.'

'Perhaps,' Christoph said bitterly, 'but she still left me all the same, and took Jacques too. I don't understand why they didn't wait for me.'

Nothing Julia could say consoled him. In the act of remembering, Sylvie had abandoned him all over again.

The doctor ushered Julia out of the room while the nurse gave Christoph his painkiller medication.

'We should have the results of the MRI scan soon,' the doctor said. 'Hopefully that will put his mind at ease.'

Julia glimpsed Christoph through the glass pane of the door. He was quieter now, his eyes closed. This was exactly what Daniel had feared. The search for the past was damaging the present.

Julia climbed the stairs to the apartment with slow steps. Perhaps it *was* time to stop the search, if not for good, at least until Christoph had regained his strength and got over the shock of Sylvie leaving him.

Daniel was in the living room, sorting through some papers.

'What's going on?' Julia said.

'I decided to have one last search to see if there were any other clues here in the apartment,' he said.

'Have you changed your mind then?' Julia said, sitting down on the sofa, hoping Daniel had reconsidered. 'Are you ready to find out what happened?'

'I don't know, but I knew I couldn't just sit around. Where have you been?'

Julia tucked her hair behind her ears. 'I went to the National Archives and then to see Christoph, but I'm no closer to finding Sylvie, despite scouring pages of records. Have you had any more success here?'

'Well, that's just it,' Daniel said. He passed a document to Julia. 'From what you'd said about the apartment and Christoph's memories of being here with Sylvie, I'd assumed the apartment belonged to her. But actually, it doesn't belong to either of them.'

Julia frowned. 'Who does it belong to then?'

'Auguste Seraphin Emboscier. I found a copy of the deeds in one of the drawers.'

Julia skimmed through the document. Auguste Seraphin Emboscier. That middle name – Seraphin – was the name mentioned in Jean's interrogation, and in Sylvie's. Julia's breath grew shallow.

'I think this man Seraphin is connected to your father and Sylvie.'

Daniel came and set next to her. 'How?'

'When your father and Sylvie were at Le Meurice, the head chef, Jean Dupont, was detained on suspicion of plotting to poison the guests at an important military dinner. Sylvie, out of all the kitchen staff, was spared the interrogation. Jean blamed someone called Seraphin. Jean believed Seraphin was working for the Special Operation Executive and had betrayed him. Seraphin's name came up in Sylvie's records too.'

Daniel stared at her. 'But I don't see how . . .'

'The owner of this apartment, M. Emboscier, he must be the same man.'

'It could be a coincidence.'

Julia gazed around the room. Dust tickled her nose. They were getting closer. She could feel it.

'We have to track him down.'

'I've already tried to do that,' Daniel said. 'M. Emboscier died in 1991. The solicitors informed me when I rang them half an hour ago. They've no idea how Christoph ended up with a key.'

'So who does the apartment belong to now?'

'The daughter of M. Emboscier.'

'Then we have to talk to her.' She hesitated. She was getting carried away and assuming that Daniel wanted to help. 'Have you decided what you're going to do? I mean, I'll talk to her, regardless of whether you want me to or not.'

Daniel shook his head. 'I know you will. You're strong,

Julia, and determined. That's what I admire about you. I wish I could feel the same, but maybe I'm just too close to it all.' He took her hands. 'I'll be here to support you and Christoph, but I don't want any part of the search. I'm not ready for that kind of journey, not yet.'

Julia gazed at him. She'd hoped they could do this together. Surely knowing the whole truth was the only way to repair Daniel's relationship with Christoph. 'Are you sure about that? I think that deep down you do want to know more. Why else would you have searched the apartment?'

'Because I wanted to bring this whole thing to a conclusion,' Daniel said, 'and then we can concentrate on looking after Papa and getting on with our lives.'

'This *is* our lives,' Julia said impatiently. 'And it's Christoph's too. You don't seem to realize that.'

She left Daniel and went down to the concierge's appartment to telephone the solicitor, explaining Christoph's predicament. They were reluctant to give out information but finally they relented and said they would contact Seraphin's daughter and see if she was willing to talk to Julia.

A few minutes later, while Julia was waiting anxiously by the phone, drinking a cup of coffee that the concierge had kindly made her, the solicitor rang back to pass on the address of Seraphin Emboscier's daughter, Estelle. She was apparently willing to speak to Julia. Jubilant, Julia went back upstairs to get her bag.

'Have you tracked the daughter down?' Daniel asked, hands in his pockets, hesitating by the door.

'Yes.' Julia took her bag from the back of the chair. 'Are you sure you won't come with me?'

He shook his head. 'Papa should get his results today. I'm worried about what they'll find. Couldn't you wait until afterwards?'

'No, I need to do this now. She's expecting me. There's plenty of time before we see the doctor.' She went over to Daniel and rested her palm on his chest, gazing at him intently. 'Look, I kind of understand your reluctance. This is all happening fast and it's dredging up something that's still recent in your family's past. But I honestly believe you would benefit from being a part of it, instead of watching from the outside. You never know, Estelle might provide the conclusion you're looking for.'

Julia kissed his cheek and headed down the hall to the door. There was nothing more she could say or do. It was up to him now. Estelle was waiting, and Julia was desperate to hear what she had to say.

44

Julia

August 2002 – Paris

Estelle lived in a townhouse not far from Montmartre. Julia pulled on the bell. A thin, white-haired woman in black trousers and a crisp white shirt opened the door.

'*Bonjour*. Your solicitors gave me your address,' Julia said. 'I wondered if I could talk to you about apartment 14 on rue Pastourelle.'

The woman nodded. 'You'd better come in.'

She led Julia into a high-ceilinged living room. Books lined the walls. Black-and-white photographs were displayed on side tables.

'Sit down,' she said. 'I've waited a long time for someone to come and discuss that place with me.'

'What do you mean?'

'My father's legacy is a complicated one.' Estelle sat back elegantly in the chair. 'You see, apartment 14 did belong to him. He bought it before the war. He saw what was coming. He used it as a safehouse for agents in his network.'

Julia sat forward in the chair. 'His network?'

'*Oui*, the Watchmaker network in Paris. Active between 1940 and 1943. He was a handler. Agents were recruited. Deeds were done. He got them in and out and was the main conduit of instructions from London.'

'How do you know all this?' Julia asked.

Estelle smiled. 'When I was eighteen, he sat me down and explained everything to me. He wanted me to know the dark and the light of what he'd done. There was still a great deal of blame about what had gone on: the collaboration and collusion with the Nazis. He wasn't trying to exonerate himself; he wanted me to understand and learn from it all.'

'But then, I don't understand.' Julia handed Estelle the key to the apartment. 'I found this. It belongs to Christoph Baumann, a man who'd been in the German army. It doesn't make sense for him to be connected to your father.'

Estelle looked at the key, then laid it down on the coffee table.

'Nothing with my father made sense. He was like a wea-thervane, always changing position. He was on the side of the French, of course, always. But he maintained that that meant making sacrifices and sometimes appearing to be on the side of the Germans.' She smoothed her trousers and frowned. 'It caused a lot of trouble, especially after the war.'

'Was he a double agent?' Julia asked.

Estelle looked at Julia, her eyes sharp and bright. 'Per-haps, but if it appeared as if he favoured the Germans, it was only to get their trust and gain a bigger prize.'

Julia mulled over her words. 'Was he connected with the arrest of Jean Dupont, the head chef at Le Meurice?'

Estelle closed her eyes. 'It's possible. Let's say he did betray Jean. It led to him being trusted by the Komman-dant. This would have put my father in a better position to damage the Reich.'

'It's hard to know which side your father was on,' said Julia. 'Christoph remembers your father coming to the apartment with some German soldiers. They arrested Christoph and sent him to fight in Russia. The fact that your father was the man that brought them suggests that he was willing to betray Sylvie too.'

Estelle folded her arms. Julia sensed that she had faced questions like this before. 'There was a trial after the war,' she said. 'My father showed me the papers. Along with many collaborators, he was arrested and tried for treason. Do you know who came to his defence?'

Julia shook her head.

Estelle smiled. 'The British government. They confirmed that his orders had come from London. When Lieutenant Baumann set off the following morning after the dinner in Le Meurice, the Kommandant suspected him of deserting. My father saw the opportunity to gain the Kommandant's trust, so he revealed the whereabouts of the apartment. His actions that day proved to the Germans that he was a reliable informant and enabled him to save many more lives by giving the Germans false intelligence. So, you see, nothing is ever simple in wartime.'

Julia frowned, trying to follow the connections. 'Christoph got the key from someone called Sylvie Dubois,' she said. 'Do you know how she was connected to your father?'

'Sylvie Dubois? Estelle shook her head. 'I don't recall my father talking about anyone of that name. This apartment was connected with another woman.'

'Who?'

'Lisette Munier. I met her once. She came to find my father after the war. I listened outside the door. She was angry and hurt. She'd been part of the network, another agent in the SOE, and thought that Seraphin's actions had cost her greatly. He tried to explain his motives and wanted to give her the apartment to make amends. I went in and introduced myself, wanting to see the woman who'd dared confront my father. It was 1963, I think. She was very beautiful.' Estelle smiled at the recollection. 'They stopped arguing and I brought in some wine. Lisette was very gracious to me. That's when my father told her about the apartment.'

Julia touched the base of her neck. 'But I thought Sylvie Dubois was the one who had the keys to the apartment. I've never heard of a Lisette Munier. Look,' she said, searching in her bag, 'we found this photo of Sylvie in the apartment.'

Estelle looked at the photograph. She smiled. 'Ah, my father must have taken this during the war. This is the woman I met that day. This is Lisette Munier.'

'But it says Sylvie on the back.'

'Agents hide behind many names. Sylvie, Lisette: who knows? But this was her. I know she lived there from time to time in the seventies. But when I tried to find her after my father died, there was no trace. In his will, he requested that the apartment be formally handed over to her. I had the deeds ready to sign. But it was as though she had never existed.'

Julia stared at her, dismayed. 'But then, how am I going to find her?'

Estelle shrugged. 'You won't,' she said. 'Perhaps that's what she intended. Many people do not want to be remembered for their role in the war, and that is especially true of an agent. For someone like Lisette, a name is not designed to reveal her identity. It is simply a word to hide behind.'

Shortly afterwards Julia took her leave and walked back to the hospital. She pressed the button on the traffic lights and waited for the cars to stop. Things had reached a dead end with Sylvie or Lisette or whoever she was. Love, it seemed, was not an anchor or a bond but rather something untethered, like smoke, that could drift away over the years.

A car beeped. The lights had changed. Julia waved an apology and hurried across. Daniel was waiting for her on the other side.

'Well?' he said.

Julia smiled a tight smile. 'There's absolutely no trace of her, and no clue as to which direction to take next. I'm going to have to break the news to Christoph. It's not the conclusion he would've hoped for.'

'I'm sorry,' Daniel said, 'I know how much the search meant to you.'

'That's not the point,' Julia said, tears smarting her eyes. 'It's how much it meant to Christoph that matters.'

Daniel reached out to her. 'You've done as much as you can. I may not have wanted to do the search, but that doesn't mean I'm not here for you, and for Christoph. It's going to be hard telling him, but we can do it together. I'm not going anywhere.'

Julia bit her lip. 'Do you mean that?'

Daniel gathered her in his arms, enfolding her in his warmth. 'Look, the search for Sylvie may be over, but I meant what I said in the apartment. I want us to let go of the past and get on with what comes next.'

He lifted Julia's chin and kissed her. She responded, clasping her arms around his neck, but in the back of her mind there was still a nagging doubt. If the questions about Sylvie remained unanswered, how would Daniel ever truly mend his relationship with Christoph? And if he couldn't face the past, she couldn't see how their own history would ever be resolved.

Christoph struggled to take in the news.

'But if Daniel and I met her in 1978, if that was really her,' Christoph said, when Julia had explained everything, 'surely that means something. I only wish I could remember that day, but everything after that morning when I found the apartment empty is a blank.'

'Estelle's solicitors tried to find Lisette Munier when her father died,' Julia said. 'There was no sign of her. We now know that Lisette . . . Sylvie definitely survived the war – Estelle recalls seeing her at her father's house –'

'And I definitely saw her with you in 1978 in Paris,' Daniel said. 'But despite all of Julia's efforts, there's no trace of her.' He took his father's hand and clasped it. 'I'm so sorry, Papa.'

Christoph took a deep breath. 'We don't know the truth because Sylvie never wanted anyone to know.' He looked out of the window at the scudding clouds. 'She was a liar. A spy. She probably never loved me at all, she just wanted information. No wonder I couldn't remember. When it comes down to it, there was nothing meaningful there at all.'

'You don't know that,' Julia said, resting her hand on his arm. 'She must've been in a terrible situation; caught between falling in love with you and having to do her duty.'

Daniel nodded. 'Perhaps in the end it was just easier to leave, with no explanations or goodbyes.' He glanced at Julia. 'I can sort of empathize with Sylvie feeling at a loss about what to say. It still doesn't make it right though.'

Julia nodded. 'I suppose we'll never know why she did it, because Lisette Munier cannot be traced. Mme Emboscier employed someone to try, but despite a thorough search they never found her.'

'No,' Christoph said, glancing at them both. 'Thank you for trying too. I'm so grateful for all your help.'

Daniel reddened. 'I can't take any credit, Papa. I'm trying to get over it, but that trip to Paris in 1978 was the start of the distance between us. I couldn't face the thought of trying to find the woman who'd caused such pain to Mama and drove a wedge between you and me.'

Christoph gazed at him sorrowfully. 'I'm sorry, Daniel. I wish I could remember what happened in 1978, but I can't.'

'Now the search is over, it doesn't matter any more. To be honest, I'm relieved. I don't think now is a good time to go raking over the past,' Daniel said.

Julia didn't agree, but she kept silent. There was no past to find any more, so what did it matter?

The doctor tapped on the door and came in. He stood at the end of the bed.

'I'm glad you're all here. We have the results of the tests and the MRI.' His face was grave. Julia felt a clutch of dread.

'As you know, your doctors in Bonn suspected the early onset of dementia,' he said. 'I'm afraid our tests confirm that this is the case. There are some steps we can take to make you comfortable, but it's clear that your memory is going to deteriorate.'

Christoph stared at the doctor. Julia clasped Daniel's hand.

The doctor frowned. 'I'm afraid there's more bad news. You see, the dementia could take years to progress, but in the meantime there is a more pressing health issue.' He came closer to Christoph, compassion in his eyes. 'The MRI has shown up a series of tumours. You have an inoperable cancer on your pancreas.'

'What do you mean?' Daniel asked.

'We cannot remove the tumours, given their position, and any treatments we try would only delay but not halt the spread of the cancer.'

'How long have I got?' Christoph asked hoarsely.

The doctor spoke matter-of-factly. 'A few weeks, months maybe, at the most. I'm very sorry.'

Julia stared at him. It took a moment for the words to sink in. Cancer. Inoperable.

'It's not possible,' she gasped. She'd grown so close to Christoph these last few weeks, closer than teacher and pupil. He had always been almost like a father to her. She couldn't bear to think of the world without him. He wasn't her father, she knew that, but he was the closest thing she had to one.

'There must be something you can do,' Daniel said, his voice full of anguish.

The doctor sighed. 'I understand your concern. We're hoping to transfer him back to the hospital in Bonn. You'll be able to explore options with the doctors there.'

'We'll do everything we can to fight this cancer,' Daniel said to Christoph.

Christoph shook his head. 'No, I've had my allotted three score and ten. Even if I did survive this, there's the dementia.' He sighed, resigned. 'I've reached the point where all I long for now is peace. Let's go home. It's time to let go of the past.'

Filets de Maquereaux à la Flamande

4 mackerel, filleted
2 eggs, beaten
50g plain flour
125g unsalted butter
4 tablespoons parsley, chopped
2 spring onions
½ teaspoon each salt and pepper
⅛ teaspoon nutmeg
Juice of half a lemon

1. Melt the butter in a frying pan.
2. Dip the mackerel in the beaten egg and dust with flour.
3. Fry on both sides until browned.
4. Add the parsley and onions, and season.
5. Lift out the fillets and keep warm, stir the sauce until smooth, and add lemon juice to serve.

45

Julia

September, 2002 – Bonn

A gentle breeze wafted through the music room. Christoph lay on the sofa, thin and wan. Julia cast him a worried glance. He'd lost all interest in food since they'd been back. Not even a meal from Sylvie's recipe book could tempt him. He was on palliative care now, and very weak.

Daniel was outside, overhauling the garden. It seemed to be his way of coping with his helplessness at Christoph's diagnosis. He was dutiful and attentive to Christoph's practical needs, but Julia was fairly sure that the two of them hadn't talked things over properly yet.

'Will you play me something?' Christoph asked.

'I'll try,' Julia said.

She went over to the piano. She'd lost heart with cooking too. The recipe book was stowed on a shelf in the kitchen. Daniel had been shopping for convenience food – frozen meals they could easily heat up, cold meats and cheeses, tins of soup. Julia was grateful. She couldn't face cooking at the moment.

Today, Julia played Christoph a piece by Chopin. Unexpectedly, she managed it from start to finish without stumbling.

'That was note perfect,' he said.

'Sebastian will be pleased.' He was flying over to Bonn the next day to oversee the recording of her piece for the Queen Elisabeth competition. 'But is note perfect enough? My hands felt fine, but it was like my heart had disconnected from the music.'

Christoph tilted his head. 'To play properly, your heart needs to be strong too.'

Julia closed the piano lid. 'Hearing about your love for Sylvie gave me hope.'

'And perhaps your feelings for Daniel . . . and his for you.' Christoph smiled, and his eyes twinkled knowingly.

Julia glanced at him. 'How did you guess?'

Christoph smiled. 'I may be old, but it was evident in Paris. Perhaps I was wrong to warn you off him six years ago.'

The sky had darkened. It looked like rain. Julia got up and switched on the lamp beside the sofa. 'I don't think either of us were ready then,' she said. 'And even now, I'm not sure the timing is right.'

'If you mean my illness, that shouldn't stop you.'

Julia shook her head. 'It's not just that. We've each got our own battles to face. There's my hands and the piano to sort out. Daniel's just been made redundant and will need to focus on finding a new job. And' – she hesitated – 'so much is unresolved between the two of you. I think it holds him back.'

Christoph sighed. 'I don't know how to talk to him, how to make it better.'

'He was very upset about his memory of seeing Sylvie in Paris that time.'

Christoph rubbed his eyes. 'It must have hurt to learn

that I'd been unfaithful to his mother. It's not something I'm proud of.'

'I think he always suspected something,' Julia said. 'Over the years, Hilde blamed the fact that you'd been unfaithful for her state of mind. Daniel tried to stick up for you, but you were away touring, and that drove a wedge between the two of you and he grew closer to Hilde. Finding out that it was Sylvie who you met in Paris in 1978 has really hit him hard.'

Christoph closed his eyes. 'I wish I could remember that time in 1978, and then maybe I could explain it to him. I'm afraid there's a void that I just don't know how to fill.'

Julia came over and tucked the blanket around him. 'Don't fret, there's still time.'

But she was worried. When the awful day came, the answers Daniel needed would die with Christoph. How would Daniel cope? Julia was afraid that, with everything else they each had to deal with, Christoph's passing and the unresolved wounds from the past would leave a hole in Daniel's heart too big for her to mend.

The next day, Julia left Christoph with a hot-water bottle on his stomach and Bach playing on the stereo while she went to meet Sebastian. As she was closing the front gate, Daniel came down the street, the wheelbarrow loaded with plants.

'Thank goodness I've caught you,' he said. He dusted his hands on his jeans. 'How are you feeling?'

'Terrible,' Julia replied. 'I'm dreading it.'

Daniel took hold of her hands and clasped them tightly.

'I heard you playing for Christoph yesterday. It sounded phenomenal. I'm no expert, but I couldn't detect a single fault. I bet you'll do amazingly today.'

'I'm not sure I should be going with Christoph so ill.'

Daniel drew her closer and stroked a strand of hair back from her forehead. 'Of course you should go. This is what you want, isn't it? A place in the competition? Christoph knows how much this means to you; he wants you to do it.'

'Thanks.' She glanced at the front window. 'Will you keep an eye on him? He's feeling dreadful about Sylvie and what happened in 1978. He wishes he could remember more and explain it.'

Daniel nodded. 'I know. I catch him looking at me sometimes, but he's too confused to know what to say. It must be awful to lose great chunks of your memory. He seems lost in the gaps and he doesn't know how to get out.'

Julia squeezed his hand. 'The recipes seemed to help, but I'm not sure he has any appetite for food or for remembering now.'

Daniel cupped her cheeks. 'Look, I'll take these plants to the garden and water them, and then I'll go and sit with him. I don't want you to worry. You need to focus on playing.'

Julia smiled, relieved. 'Thank you, Daniel, that would be amazing. I'd be so glad if the two of you could reach some kind of understanding.'

He looked at her, sadness in his eyes. 'I know you mean well, Julia. But I'm not sure that's possible. There's so much information still missing. Maybe it's for the best.

More details about Sylvie might make it harder for me to accept it all – the affair with Sylvie, the unfaithfulness to my mother. And I really am trying to do that, for Christoph's sake.'

'I know,' Julia said.

'Now remember,' he said, encouragingly, 'you are incredibly talented. Beethoven should feel lucky you've chosen to play his notes, when you're so good at composing your own.' He raised his eyebrows. 'And don't forget to send my regards to Sebastian.'

Julia smiled. 'I won't.'

Daniel kissed her on the cheek, then drew back with a quick smile and took hold of the wheelbarrow. Julia watched him disappear through the side gate and into the garden.

Since they'd been back from Paris he'd been affectionate but restrained, almost as if he was holding back from something more. Julia didn't know what lay behind it. But she felt a sense of hesitancy too. As if they were both wary of going too far and getting hurt. She sighed and thought of the studio performance that awaited her. At least the piano was one thing she had begun to feel a little more certain of.

The recording studio was in a converted townhouse near the centre of Bonn. Sebastian was already there, talking to the sound engineer. Julia's stomach churned. Playing in front of Christoph was one thing. Playing in front of Sebastian would be nerve-wracking.

'You're here.' The relief on his face was palpable.

'Are you angry with me for cancelling Salzburg? I'm sorry it was Anna who rang and not me.'

Sebastian rubbed his cheek. 'I wasn't angry,' he said. 'I was just disappointed that you couldn't have told me yourself. She also told me about Christoph's diagnosis. It must be awful.'

Julia had been strong for Christoph, but now, with Sebastian's concerned eyes on her, she faltered.

'I can't take it in,' she said, tears pricking her eyes. 'There's literally nothing he can do but wait until . . .' She swallowed a sob. 'He wants me to keep playing. Says it's the best gift I could give him, just to carry on as normal.'

Sebastian squeezed her arm. 'Are you sure you can do this?'

Julia nodded, thinking of Daniel's encouragement. 'But can I play with my back to the sound desk? I'm not ready to face an audience yet.'

'Of course,' Sebastian said. 'And don't worry. When the time's right, we'll build you back up, small audiences first, then larger crowds.'

Julia recorded the 'Moonlight Sonata' in a single take. She didn't think about the sound engineers or Sebastian watching from the other side of the glass. She didn't think about Daniel or Christoph. Her mind was blank. The notes were simply stepping stones taking her from one end of the piece to the other.

'That was good,' Sebastian said. He stepped over the microphone wires. 'Different to how you've played it before, but hopefully good enough.'

Julia wiped her forehead. 'You'll send it to the judges?'

'As soon as the CD's been burned.' He glanced at his watch. 'Why don't I take you for lunch to celebrate?'

'I can't,' Julia said, gathering up her bag. 'I don't want to leave Christoph for long.'

'Of course,' Sebastian said. 'I'll let you know as soon as I hear anything.'

The house was quiet when Julia returned. Christoph was asleep on the sofa. She sat for a moment, watching him. He looked peaceful enough, but he winced now and then, as if in pain.

The afternoon sun lit up the photograph frames on the mantelpiece. Christoph and Hilde on their wedding day. Daniel under a Christmas tree playing with a toy farm. Daniel looked guarded, as if he already knew more than he should.

'Julia, is that you?' Christoph murmured. 'How did it go?'

'It was strange,' she said, coming to sit beside him. 'Normally I see pictures in my head, memories and colours. But this time, there was nothing. Only the notes.'

'Music is like that sometimes. That's why it's therapeutic in overcoming grief. At least, that's what I found.' He reached for a glass of water and took a sip.

Julia considered his words. 'You think the numbness is a way of coping?'

'Yes, but if it goes on too long, that's not good. That's why I gave up performing and concentrated on teaching. Something died in me.'

'Can you recall what happened?'

Christoph shook his head. 'No, only that I stopped doing concerts.'

Julia thought for a moment. 'I remember reading an

interview you did in the *BBC Music Magazine*. It must have been 1999, because I was eighteen and I'd entered the BBC Young Musician of the Year competition. You said that, to perform, a pianist needed deep wells of emotional and spiritual energy, and that in the late seventies your energy simply dried up.'

'Perhaps I was burnt out. It happens, as you well know,' Christoph replied, glancing at Julia's hands.

'Yes, but you never returned to the stage. I always regretted that I'd been too young to see you perform. All the reviews said you had an extraordinary gift for holding the audience in the palm of your hand from the minute you began playing. I wonder why you didn't go back to it.'

Disconnected thoughts came together in Julia's mind. Something *had* died in Christoph the day he discovered the empty apartment. Perhaps 1978, when Daniel and Christoph saw Sylvie on the street corner, was another watershed moment.

'It could be linked to meeting with Sylvie in Paris that time with Daniel,' she said. 'If it were possible, would you like to remember all this, or is it too painful?'

'I do want to know, desperately, before it's too late. But I can't see how it's possible.' He flinched, pressing against his stomach. 'Could you get me my painkillers, please?'

Julia went to the kitchen and took the pills from the drawer. She was about to go back with them when she caught sight of the recipe book on the shelf. Her heart thudded as she took it down and flicked through the pages.

The back door opened. Daniel came in, wiping his boots on the mat. He caught sight of the book in her hands. 'What are you doing?'

'There are still a couple of recipes left in this book. I'm hoping they might link him back to meeting Sylvie in 1978, and maybe the events leading up to it.'

Daniel stared at her. 'I'm not sure, Julia . . .'

'We have to try.'

The next recipe was for Filets de Maquereaux à la Fla-mande. In tiny handwriting, Sylvie had written: *After what happened today, I will never make this recipe again.*

Daniel read it and bit his thumb. 'What if this meal makes things worse?'

Julia straightened her shoulders. 'We have to try, Daniel, and hope for the best. There might not be another chance to find out what happened.'

Later, after she'd settled Christoph with the painkillers, Julia cooked the mackerel. She took the fish out of the frying pan and put it on to a plate with some steamed vegetables. Daniel fetched a knife and fork. Julia felt a surge of hope that the recipe would reignite Christoph's memories and bridge the gap between him and Daniel. They carried the food through to the music room, where Christoph was just waking up.

'That smells delicious,' he said, edging himself up.

Julia put the tray on his knee.

'It's from Sylvie's book,' she said. 'I think it's important we finish what we started . . . before it's too late.'

Christoph smiled sadly. 'I appreciate the gesture, but this food won't make any difference. My memories won't go further than the day she left.'

'Just try a bit, it can't do any harm,' Daniel said, placing the cutlery by his side.

Christoph speared a piece of mackerel and chewed it slowly. He managed a few mouthfuls, then put the fork down.

'Nothing's coming back to me. I'm sorry.'

'It's okay,' Daniel said, clearly disappointed.

'Don't worry about it,' Julia said.

She felt a pang of sorrow for them both. Daniel had been too young to understand or grasp the context of what he'd witnessed in 1978, and Christoph was too ill and old now to remember. She'd been foolish to hope that Sylvie's recipe would make a difference. Perhaps it was only food after all.

46

Christoph

May, 1952 – Effelsberg

Christoph sat on the bench overlooking the vegetable patch. It was summer. His first proper summer at home since 1941. It was a miracle that he was here at all.

No German will return until Stalingrad is rebuilt, the Russians had declared. His letters home had been lost; Christoph's mother had heard nothing from him since his capture in 1944 until he had rung her from Berlin last year, in 1951, telling her, 'Yes, I'm alive. I'm coming home.'

But home wasn't the same any more. Christoph watched the oxen make their way back towards the lane. Hilde's father was bringing in the hay, as he'd done every year since Christoph left.

Lotte's absence was the biggest, most heartbreaking difference. During his time in Russia digging foundations or laying bricks, Christoph had prayed that she'd survived. Now, with more knowledge of the murders that had taken place in the concentration camps, Christoph knew that she hadn't.

Why Hilde hadn't married during the long years of his absence, Christoph didn't know. He'd come back a wreck, while Hilde had blossomed: talking of the horses, her costumes for Karneval, the future.

'When will we marry?' she'd asked the week after he

returned. She'd sat on his bed, her shoulders back, glowing with vitality.

Christoph had sighed and watched sunlight dapple the window.

'I'm not the man I was, Hilde. In all honesty, I don't know why you've waited. If you've had second thoughts . . .'

There, he'd said it. Presented her with an escape route, and himself too. He'd twisted the sheet in his hand, praying she'd changed her mind.

'Don't be silly, Christoph,' Hilde had said. 'We belong together.'

Now, a year after his return, the wedding was due to take place in two weeks. Hilde had taken care of everything. He'd been too weak, too griefstricken about Lotte to resist.

Now, he sighed and checked his watch. Hilde would be back soon. She'd gone to visit her sisters. All day he'd waited for a quiet moment to read the letter, and now that he was alone, he was afraid to do so.

Not long after he came back from Russia, when he had recovered a little, he'd contacted a man he'd heard of in Bonn, an investigator who for a fee could trace people lost during the war. Now, after months of waiting, a letter had arrived. His hands trembled. If there was a chance of finding Sylvie, he would call the wedding off.

Christoph ripped the envelope open. His eyes darted over the words.

Herr Baumann

Thank you for the money you transferred. I've returned from Paris, where I gained access to the National Archives. I found a

record of Sylvie Dubois. It stated that she died at Drancy in
September 1942 of typhoid.

It's never easy in these circumstances, but I hope you take
consolation from knowing the facts.

Best wishes
Friedrich Weber

Christoph read it again, stunned. Sylvie. Dead. The
freshness of the evening turned to dust. All the time he
was in Russia, when the thought of Sylvie had kept him
alive, she'd been dead. Her lips, her skin, her laughter – all
extinguished only months after she'd left him. Christoph's
stomach heaved. He ran to the hedgerow, just in time,
retching into the bushes.

Hilde would be back soon. Christoph wiped his mouth
and thrust the letter into his pocket. What the hell would
he do now that Sylvie was gone? What was left for him?
Sylvie's voice drifted into his mind: *You must go back and*
study the piano when the war is over. Pick up where you left off.
Promise me you'll do that.

'Christoph,' Hilde called. 'What are you doing?'

She walked over to where he sat.

'I'm just looking at the view,' he said.

She sat on his knee, her floral scent comforting, the
weight of her pressing his anguish down. For better or for
worse, he was tied to Hilde now.

'We can't stay here after we're married, you know,' he
said.

Hilde narrowed her eyes. 'What's that supposed to
mean?'

'I'm not a farmer. I never have been. Your father and brother have organized the work between them. They've no use for me.'

'They assumed you'd start work when you were ready.' She tilted her head slightly. 'Why, has something changed?'

Christoph thought of the letter. Yes, something had changed, but he couldn't tell Hilde. He'd go mad with grief living here, stifled by the farm.

'I want to take up my place at the music conservatory in Bonn,' he said. 'I'll never be a farmer, but I know I can be a good pianist and earn a living for us, for our children.'

'So that's your plan.' Hilde put her arms around his neck. 'I can't wait to be pregnant.'

Christoph held her close. This was the solution to Sylvie's death. To plunge himself into music and forget about the past. 'We'll have a townhouse in Bonn. I can make a success of the piano, I know I can.'

I can make a success of this marriage too, he thought, if I put my mind to it.

Hilde nestled against him. 'Very well,' she murmured, 'if you promise I can decorate the place from top to bottom.'

Christoph held her tight. What else could he do? If he took Sylvie out of the equation – and she was unalterably out of the equation for ever – he had a steadfast, determined woman at his side and the prospect of a promising career. He had to let go of the past and grasp the future.

47

Lisette

June, 1962 – Rome

Church bells woke Lisette at six o'clock. She got dressed in the chilly morning air. The market would be open soon.

'Signora Lisette?' the landlady said, tapping on the door.

That name. She should have given it up long ago, but she chose to keep it, changing only her surname from time to time.

'He's back,' the landlady said. 'Out in the courtyard.'

Lisette went downstairs to find him. He waited by the steps. He was thirty-eight now, but he still had traces of the eighteen-year-old she'd met in the apartment. He was the only person she knew who could make her feel light-hearted.

'Jacques,' she said, smiling. 'What are you doing here?'

'What do you think?'

'Come on, you must've given up on me by now. I'm an old woman.'

'Nonsense. You're only forty-one, and you'll never be old to me.' He kissed her cheek. 'Besides, I've had twenty years to grow up and sow my wild oats. Don't you think it's time?'

Lisette laughed, a belly laugh that made her feel, for a moment, as if all the past grief could be overcome.

Jacques had been the one constant in her life since the war. Friends and family had never understood what she'd experienced. Only with Jacques could she relax, because he'd experienced it too.

'Tell me the real reason why you're here,' she said.

'I've bought that place in Nice.' A smile brimmed on his lips. 'Builders are renovating it as we speak. Every table has a view of the Mediterranean. The kitchen is huge. All I need now is a chef.'

'I'm proud of you, Jacques. Your family must be so pleased.'

'You haven't answered my question.'

'You didn't ask one.'

Jacques raised his eyebrows. 'It's the same question I've been asking for the last five years.'

He still had a thick shock of black hair. He'd trusted her implicitly that night, following her out on to the streets of Paris. She had taken him to a man on rue Marbeuf who forged papers and produced new identity cards for them both. Travelling together as brother and sister, they'd got out of Paris in a party of fruit-pickers heading to the fields south of the city. From there, she'd used the skills she'd learned in her SOE training to get them across the country – camping in woods by day and travelling by night.

Jacques had come into his own on the road. He grew fit and healthy, tanned by the sun, his muscles strengthening from the walking and fresh food. He became her equal, taking turns to keep watch at night and learning how to hunt. He was protective when she grew tired, and when they huddled close for warmth on the cold nights she was conscious of his strong arms around her. He seemed older than his eighteen years. While she grieved in secret for the loss of Christoph, Lisette came to depend on Jacques. His optimism and humour gave her a much-needed reprieve after the trauma of leaving Paris.

Despite the terror and fear of those days, Jacques had kept his spirits up. Looking at him now, in the sunshine, he wore it well, this burden of still being alive. Lisette struggled with it sometimes.

'Jacques, I'm in charge of lunch. The markets have just opened . . .'

'All right, I'll meet you later. But it's time, Lisette, to look to the future. You know I'm right. It's what we both deserve.'

He kissed her hand. She should be flattered that such a man cared for her – Jacques was successful, handsome, kind, and the bond forged in those days on the run was unbreakable – but she waved him goodbye with a heavy heart. How many times could she say no before he never came back?

'We have a full house,' the manager at La Casa said. 'Some people have waited months for a table.'

'Don't worry. I'll give them a meal to remember,' Lisette said, putting down the bags of shopping.

She opened her recipe book and flicked through the pages. The book had been with her through it all, more constant than any person had been.

'We'll start with fresh caviar,' she said to the attentive sous chefs, 'then filets de maquereaux à la flamande, followed by poached peaches and raspberry coulis.'

As she cooked, Lisette forgot all about Jacques, and the past. She concentrated on frying the mackerel, adding the herbs and the lemon juice. Cooking was the only time she experienced a sense of calm. That was why she took on as many shifts as possible.

At the end of the meal she had to tour the tables with the manager. She answered one or two questions about the composition of the dishes, nodding politely at the diners' compliments.

At last they reached the final table, tucked away in the corner. A couple sat finishing their main course. Lisette stopped. The man. It couldn't be. Her heart pounded. The room seemed to tilt. It was Christoph.

He stared at Lisette, shock bleeding colour from his face, his wine glass held mid-tip.

'May I present the chef,' the manager said.

Lisette couldn't take it in. His hair was longer, greyer, he wore a suit, a red tie . . . but it was him.

The woman sitting opposite Christoph smiled.

'When we decided to go away for our tenth wedding anniversary, I knew Rome was the place, didn't I, Christoph?' she said in broken English. 'He insisted we have lunch at La Casa.'

Christoph put down his glass and forced a smile when his wife – *his wife* – addressed him. He was here. Alive. But he was also married. The tall, elegant woman reaching out to take his hand was his wife.

It was too much. Lisette muttered words of thanks and fled. She escaped out into the backyard, breathing lungfuls of air, heart racing with the sheer unexpectedness of seeing him here. He'd survived. All this time she'd mourned the fact that he was dead, killed in Stalingrad, so Seraphin had told her. But he was here. In Rome. Close enough to touch.

Eventually, she went back in. The restaurant was empty. She went to the table where Christoph and his wife had sat. There was a smear of lipstick on the woman's napkin. Christoph's coffee and petit fours lay untouched.

'Telephone for you, Lisette,' the manager called. 'A man asking for Sylvie. I told him there's no one of that name, so he asked for the chef.'

Lisette took it by the desk, where no one could overhear.

'Hello.'

'Sylvie.'

An avalanche started in her heart. It was really him. 'Yes.'

'I thought . . .' Christoph said, his voice breaking. 'I hired an investigator. The records in Paris said you'd been killed. If I'd known you were alive . . .'

'Oh, Christoph.' All the empty years, only to find each other like this.

'You told me about La Casa – do you remember, by the millpond?' he said. 'I'd never have brought her if I'd known you were alive and here in Rome. It was such a shock to see you standing there.'

Lisette breathed deeply. 'I looked for you too, but I heard you'd died in Russia.' All this time . . . her heart ached with the waste of it.

'Hilde's waiting for me at the hotel,' Christoph said. 'I had to ring you. I wanted you to know I'd never have married her if there was a chance of finding you. I can't bear that you're here and I can't see or hold you.'

'Please stop,' Lisette said. 'There's no use. Those years have happened. You can't change that. You're married now. That's what you've chosen.'

'Sylvie, don't say that.'

'Christoph, it's too late,' she said. This day had been bearable until now. She'd been coping. She couldn't let this moment make things worse. 'Let's just be glad we're both alive. That we made it. Forget we met today.'

'What do you mean, forget? How can I?'

'You must.'

Lisette put the phone down before she changed her mind, then grabbed her coat from the hook.

All these years, she'd lived half a life mourning the loss of him. But he was alive and married, for Christ's sake. He hadn't mourned her, he'd moved on with his life. What was she doing, treading water like this?

When she reached the *pensione*, Jacques was waiting for her. He got out of his car. The years were etched on his face, but he was still ready to follow her, to cast in his lot with hers, just like he'd done that night at the apartment.

'Shall we go for a spin?' he said.

Lisette's mind cleared. Maybe it was time.

'Jacques, are you going to ask me again?'

'You know I am,' he said. 'And this time, it's not just my hand I'm offering, it's a restaurant too. We'll make an amazing team; I know we will. My grandmother knew it. For her, Lisette, for her memory, marry me.'

At the mention of his grandmother Lisette's eyes filled with tears. That tiny, fierce woman who'd given Lisette a second chance at life.

'I'll marry you, Jacques,' she said. 'Let's leave for Nice tonight.'

Jacques enfolded her in his arms. She choked back tears. Jacques must never see them. For him, today was the start of a new life. For Lisette, it was the end of an old one.

Citron Pressé avec Lavande

English lavender
150g granulated sugar
Water
Juice of 6 large lemons

1. Mix the lavender with the sugar.
2. Pour into a saucepan and cover with water.
3. Bring to the boil and stir, then remove from heat and leave to steep for 30 minutes, then strain into a jug.
4. Strain the lemon juice into the jug.
5. Add water, and serve sprinkled with lavender.

48

Julia

September, 2002 – Bonn

For two days, after trying the Filets de Maquereaux à la Flamande, Christoph stayed in his room, drifting in and out of
sleep. He seemed to have deteriorated. The nurse who came
daily to check on him told Julia these kinds of setbacks were
normal at this stage. Daniel and Julia took turns sleeping in
the chair, keeping watch, while the other got some rest and
took care of the house. We're like ships passing in the night,
Julia thought. She blamed herself for cooking the recipe,
wishing they'd heeded the warning that Sylvie had written.

On the third morning after Christoph had got worse,
Julia awoke, stiff and aching.

'Christoph,' she whispered. 'Are you awake?'

'*Ja.*' His voice was weak.

'You seemed okay a few days ago, but now . . .'

Christoph pushed the covers down a little. 'Has it been
that long?' His voice sounded a little stronger.

'Yes,' Julia said gently. 'I made the filets de maquereaux
à la flamande from the recipe book and the next day you
didn't get up.'

'I thought I'd been asleep. It was like a dream . . .'

Julia drew closer. 'You've slept a lot. Perhaps that's what
you needed.'

Christoph gripped her hand. 'But it was more than a dream,' he said.

'What do you mean? Did you dream about Sylvie?'

'It felt real. So did the feeling afterwards. A deep sadness: like cold seeping into my bones. I'm just so tired, Julia.'

'Tell me about the dream. It might help.'

Christoph told her fragments: the letter, Sylvie's death, marrying Hilde and then finding and losing Sylvie in Rome. His voice was heavy as he spoke, his words a confused jumble of recollections that he was unable to grasp.

'I found out she was alive, but there was nothing I could do. After ten years of marriage, Hilde was desperate to have children. When we got back from Rome, we spent another eight years trying. Hilde accused me of not being committed, but I was. It's just hard to love someone when you've already given your heart to someone else.'

'And then Daniel came along,' Julia said.

At the sound of his son's name, a smile lit up Christoph's face. 'A child, after all that time. He was a gift out of all the heartache. His birth was so special.' He glanced at Julia and smiled. 'Do you know, I've woken up with a yearning for fresh lemonade and lavender. It's strange, but I can almost taste it in my mouth.'

'Lavender?' Julia said.

'Look in Sylvie's book.'

'I'm not sure that's a good idea. Remember last time . . .'

'Please, Julia,' he said. 'Maybe Daniel will join us for some.'

Julia sighed. 'I'll go and see if there's a recipe.'

She took Sylvie's book down from the shelf. There *was*

a recipe for lemonade and lavender. It must be a good sign that Christoph had remembered it. Julia read the ingredients. It looked straightforward enough to make.

Julia took a pair of scissors from the drawer and went to cut some lavender from the garden. She rounded the hedge and there, digging up the old vegetable patch, was Daniel.

Since returning from Paris, her dreams had been laced with memories of that day in the apartment. His touch, his kisses, the delicious ache that had spread through her. Yet, here in Bonn, they were both more hesitant.

He glanced over at her. His eyes were green like the leaves, a smudge of mud on his cheek.

Julia nodded towards the flowerbed. 'I just need a few sprigs of lavender.'

He stuck the spade in the ground. 'How come?'

'Some more of Christoph's memories have started to come back,' she said. 'He told me about getting the letter from the private investigator, the one your mother told you about. He only married Hilde once he'd heard that Sylvie was dead and had every intention of making things work. But then, on their tenth wedding anniversary in Rome, he stumbled across Sylvie, completely out of the blue.'

'But that would have been in the early 1960s,' Daniel said, frowning. 'That means the affair started even before I was born.'

'No, that's just it,' Julia said, before he could jump to the wrong conclusion. 'Nothing happened. He stayed with Hilde, he had no idea of Sylvie's whereabouts after that chance encounter, and then you were born. He described it as a gift.'

Daniel's mouth tightened. 'Did he? Then why did he ruin my childhood by meeting her again later and having an affair?'

Julia shook her head; it was time to give Daniel a firm sense of perspective. He needed to either forgive Christoph and work it out or accept what might have happened. The childish hurt that he seemed unable to shake off needed to be out in the open and resolved.

'Daniel, you're so hasty to judge him. You haven't got any proof of an affair,' she said. 'You've only seen one side to this story – your mother's – and I am sorry for what happened to her, but you need to hear Christoph's side too. You can't keep judging him blindly.'

The air between them quivered with her words. For a moment, she thought he was going to argue back, but his shoulders dropped and he sat down on the bench, lost in thought.

'Maybe you're right,' Daniel said at last, looking up at Julia. 'I need to stop looking for reasons *not* to mend my relationship with Papa, because, deep down, that's what I really want to happen.'

Julia sat next to him, taking his hand. 'I know you do.'

'I guess talking to my father is the only way to accept things. If only he was able to remember it all and tell me.'

Julia sighed. 'He may not ever remember it all. But one thing is clear, his abiding love for you. That's what you must focus on.'

Daniel nodded. 'I'll try.'

Julia squeezed his hand. 'You need to do more than try,' she said. 'These past few weeks I've seen in you the man I remember from the train station, when I had no idea who you were. Kind, enthusiastic, understanding, thoughtful. That's the man I want to see more of. It's time to put the man who ruined the recital behind you. The one who gets angry and hurt and runs away from sorting things out. You're not him any more.'

Daniel clasped her hand. 'I'm not. Thank you for reminding me,' he said, his eyes clear as he gazed at Julia. 'I hope I can find a way to prove it to you both.'

49

Christoph

September, 1972 – Paris

Christoph hated coming back to Paris. His work as a pianist brought him here a few weeks every year when he
taught at the conservatory on the rue de Madrid. Everywhere he looked he saw Sylvie. In the streets. In the crowd.
Crossing the road. He remembered that terrible morning
when he found the apartment empty and was hauled off to
fight in Russia. Paris reminded him of everything he'd lost.

But there were only two more days to go and, tonight,
he was giving a concert. He felt buoyed by the thought
that soon he'd be home, Daniel's face lighting up when he
walked through the door.

He glanced from the wings out on to the stage. The
piano lid was open; a stool set back from the keys. The
lights were so bright he couldn't see the audience. It was
time. He walked on. Applause thundered. He sat down,
hands poised, waiting for silence, which came like a gift
falling into his lap.

He loved this moment, just before he played. It held
such promise. For twenty years now, he'd made the piano
his life. He'd learned to live with losing Sylvie a second
time. He hadn't thought it would be possible, but Daniel's
arrival had made it so.

Christoph began to play 'Gymnopédie No. 1' by Erik Satie. He'd chosen this first piece because it reminded him of his son. It made him think of the first faltering steps Daniel had begun to take in the garden, of how he found every leaf and flower enchanting. Watching his son living so contentedly in each present moment inspired Christoph to do the same.

After the performance, he went to the bar, mingling with his students. Anything to put off returning to the hotel and being alone with his thoughts.

The room was full of people, sparkling and chatting. Christoph drifted outside to the courtyard. He heard footsteps behind him. The rustle of a long skirt. Then a voice spoke.

'Christoph, is it really you?'

He wondered if the power of his memories had conjured her voice. He turned round expecting nothing to be there. But it was her. Older, greyer, more beautiful, a dress that fitted like a glove.

'Sylvie,' was all he could say. More an exhalation than a word.

She put her hand to her lips. 'I've had the whole concert to get used to seeing you, but being in front of you now . . .'

'You were there? In the concert hall?'

'Yes.' Her eyes shimmered with tears.

'I kept looking for you in Rome, but there was no trace. I never expected to see you again.'

'I saw the concert advertised and came on the spur of the moment. Perhaps I should have thought how you would feel . . .'

'Seeing you is all I ever wanted,' Christoph said.

Sylvie glanced round. More people had joined them in the courtyard.

'There's so much to talk to you about,' she said. 'I'm staying at the apartment. Would you come there with me? If you're not doing anything later.'

Christoph thought of Hilde. She'd be expecting the usual evening phone call and a bedtime story for Daniel. He didn't want to miss that.

'I'd love to,' he said, glancing at his watch. 'Would you mind waiting here for me? Just half an hour. There's something I need to do.'

'I've waited ten years to see you again,' Sylvie said. 'Of course I don't mind.'

The apartment building hadn't changed. When visiting Paris, Christoph always made a point of walking past it, touching the key in his pocket, which he'd managed to keep hold of all these years, gazing at the dragons over the doorway. He could have stepped inside a hundred times, but being outside was painful enough.

Now he followed Sylvie into the courtyard and up the stairs, assailed by a thousand recollections.

Sylvie looked for the key in her bag. Her bracelets jangled on her wrist. She opened the door, but Christoph hovered on the threshold.

'The last time I was here,' he said, 'the apartment was empty. I expected to find you, to start our new life together, but you'd gone. I don't know if I can walk in there and not be overwhelmed by it all.'

'Please, Christoph, I'm here now.'

Christoph shook his head. 'It's not just that. This is where I was seized and sent off to Russia. It was almost as if they knew I'd be here. I heard a noise at the door and thought it was you, but instead it was soldiers.'

Sylvie took him in her arms. Her hair brushed against his cheek; he inhaled her scent. 'I'm so sorry,' she murmured. 'I thought I was doing the best thing, that you'd be safer without Jacques and me to save.'

Christoph held her close. There were no words for this. She was with him again. Surely he could overcome the trauma with her at his side.

'Please, come in,' she said. 'I hope I can make you understand I never meant to hurt you.'

He followed her down the hallway; it still smelled the same. His memory flashed back to that morning, his voice echoing in the empty rooms, and later the soldiers dragging him out. He caught hold of Sylvie's hand, reassuring himself of her presence, and squeezed it tight.

He tried to push the past from his mind, entering the little kitchen and observing the differences that time had made to the apartment. She'd pushed the table up against the wall. A new kettle stood on the counter. The oven and fridge had been replaced, but apart from that it looked much the same. Lisette opened the fridge and took out a jug of lemonade. She sprinkled some lavender on top.

'I went to the Tuileries today and picked some when no one was looking.'

Her voice was soothing. She was here, right in front of him. She fetched some ice and poured the lemonade, the ice cubes clinking against the sides of the glass. That's when he noticed the gold ring on her finger. It caught the light, and his heart stilled.

'You're married,' he said.

She twisted the ring. 'Yes. Ten years now.'

'So much time has passed,' Christoph said. 'I was angry with myself for years for not staying with you and Jacques in the apartment that night.'

Sylvie moved her glass aside and took his hand. 'You bought us time by going back to the hotel. Jacques and I made it to the border because of you. I left because I wanted to protect you. I wanted you to survive.'

'What happened?'

'We managed for several weeks, but then I got caught. Soldiers searched the village where we hid, rounding people up. I created a diversion and Jacques managed to slip away. But I wasn't quick enough. I was sent to a camp with Jews and political prisoners, all awaiting transport to Drancy.'

Christoph gripped her hand. 'That's why your name was on the list of those who were murdered.'

'Yes,' Sylvie said. 'But Jacques came back to rescue me. He'd met up with the rest of his family who were preparing to cross the border to Swizerland. His grandmother was very ill with a fever. When she heard what I'd done to help Jacques, she insisted on paying the French guards and taking my place. She was the Sylvie Dubois who got taken to Drancy and died of typhoid, while I escaped with Jacques and his family. I owe her my life.'

'What a brave woman,' Christoph said. He stared at Sylvie. It was incredible how close she'd come to death.

'And you? How did you survive?'

'The thought of you kept me going in Russia. But when I found out that Lotte had been murdered, and later that you had died, I didn't know how to carry on. Your words inspired me and I went back to study the piano. I have a son, Daniel, who came like a miracle to us after years of trying. I travel, teach, give concerts, I go home, see my wife and child. I live. But I haven't felt alive. There was always a void where you should have been. Your absence seemed cruel and wasteful.'

'I never stopped loving you,' Sylvie said, her eyes shining with tears. 'Even when I got married, there was always the shadow of you in the background.'

'Who did you marry?'

'Can't you guess?'

Christoph thought for a moment. Of course, it made sense, but it still pained his heart. 'Jacques,' he said.

'We'd been through so much together,' Sylvie said. 'He kept asking me to marry him. That day I saw you in Rome and found out you were married, I ran out of reasons to say no.'

'I'm glad you found someone to love you.'

'I think he did once,' she said. 'We'd been through so much; it formed a bond that Jacques mistook for love. For me, marrying him was a chance at happiness with a man I cared for deeply.' She twisted the ring on her finger. 'We opened a restaurant together in Nice, but we never had children. I didn't want to. I couldn't bear the thought of bringing life into the world in case there was ever a war again. Our relationship buckled under the strain. Jacques realized he wasn't really in love with me. Apart from running the restaurant, we live separate lives now. We still care for one another, but we know that there is nothing but friendship between us now.'

After that, there was nothing more to say. Christoph met Sylvie's eyes and found that nothing had changed. Or rather, if it had, it was only to make her less hesitant, more certain of her feelings for him.

'Sylvie . . .' he whispered.

He moved towards her, closer and closer until his lips found hers. The years melted away. Desire came back, stronger, raw and more intense. The life he'd lived without her disappeared until there was only this: Christoph and Sylvie.

'Where are you staying?' Sylvie asked.

He lay in bed with her, her head resting on his shoulder, both of them spent after making love. The touch of her body against his was a pleasure he'd never expected to feel again.

'Just a small hotel,' Christoph said, running his hand along her shoulder blade.

'When do you have to leave?'

'The day after tomorrow. And you?'

'Next week. I'm here doing research for our restaurant. Jacques prefers to stay in Nice with his mistress. I come every year.'

Christoph propped himself up to look at her. 'Why did you come and find me now, after all this time?'

'I haven't been well,' Sylvie said, taking a moment before continuing. 'I had breast cancer last year. It's all right, I'm fine now, but when I was in the hospital I decided that if I got well, I had to find you.'

'I'm glad you did.' He caught sight of a black-and-white photograph tucked under the mirror. 'My goodness, is that you?'

Sylvie glanced over and blushed. 'Yes.'

Christoph got out of bed and fetched the photo. '*Sylvie, 1942.* That's when we met. You look beautiful. Who took it?'

Sylvie frowned. 'Oh, someone from Maxim's, I think. You can have it if you like.'

Christoph snuggled back under the covers, marvelling at the photograph. 'I'll keep it here. That way no-one will find it. Because I'll be coming back, won't I, Sylvie?'

Sylvie smiled. 'Who knows? Do you want to come back?'

Christoph nodded and took her in his arms. 'You know I do.' She was here. His. He didn't want to let her go.

The next day, Paris belonged to Christoph and Sylvie. They were free to go anywhere, sit anywhere, kiss anywhere. He walked arm in arm with her, past Le Meurice, half expecting to see faces full of scorn. But he wasn't a soldier in uniform any more; he was just the same as everyone else. They reached the corner of the street and both turned to each other at the same moment, a burst of laughter at the craziness of it all. Then he pulled her close, in a deep, never-ending kiss.

Later, they sat in a café near the Sacré-Cœur.

'Can I ask you something?' Christoph said. 'That night you left, a man came and arrested me in the apartment. He was there at the dinner too.'

Sylvie sipped her wine. 'What man?'

'He looked like that friend of your fiancé's, the one I

407

was so jealous about. He seemed to know who you were.'

Sylvie smiled briefly and fiddled with the scarf around her neck. 'Impossible. It can't have been the same person.'

Christoph nodded. 'I suppose not, it'd make no sense.' He took a sip of coffee. 'So, you left France with Jacques,' he continued. 'And then what?'

Sylvie stirred her coffee. 'I worked all over Europe until Jacques and I got married. We opened the restaurant in 1962.'

'Tell me more,' Christoph said, taking her hand. 'I want to picture your life. There are twenty years between the night I last saw you and that time in Rome.'

Sylvie frowned. 'All those years. I can't bear to think about them.' She pulled her cardigan tight around her chest.

'Then tell me about the restaurant. Is it successful? Do you like living in the south of France?'

'The restaurant's doing well. I like being by the sea.' She frowned. 'I'm sorry, Christoph. The gap of time between us is too big to fill. Can we just pretend it doesn't exist?'

Christoph nodded. Perhaps it was best to leave those years unspoken.

They finished their coffee and went into the street. The wind blew and lifted Sylvie's scarf into the air. Christoph caught it and wound it back around her shoulders.

'I can't let you go again,' he said. 'I meant what I said about coming back to Paris.'

'But we're married to other people.'

'I know.' He didn't want to think about that. Not yet.

Sylvie linked arms with him as they took the steep steps down the hill.

'Would it be so wrong to meet once in a while?' he said.

'Maybe not. Can't we just savour this moment and see what happens?'

Christoph nodded. She was here. Her body against his, the day only half over and a night still to come. For now, that would have to be enough.

Madeleines au Citron

4 eggs, separated
250g granulated sugar
125g unsalted butter
125g plain flour
Grated rind of 1 lemon

1. Preheat the oven to 200°C.
2. Butter and flour a madeleine tin.
3. Beat together the sugar, butter and egg yolks.
4. In a different bowl, beat the whites until they form soft peaks.
5. Add the butter, sugar, lemon rind and egg yolk mixture to the egg whites a little at a time, alternating with 1 tablespoon of flour and the lemon zest.
6. Place a teaspoonful of the mixture into each mould.
7. Bake for ten to fifteen minutes, until risen and golden.

50

Lisette

May, 1978 – Paris

Paris was bathed in sunshine when Lisette arrived. She'd got to the apartment early. The piano had been delivered and stood in the living room as a surprise for Christoph. She'd bought eggs, flour, butter, sugar and lemons and a special madeleine tin. She consulted the recipe book and mixed the ingredients.

She put the madeleines in the oven, glancing at the clock. He should have been here half an hour ago. Today, she planned to tell him the truth about her past: that she'd been a spy during the war. The secret had troubled her for too long. Up to now, she hadn't had the nerve. Since 1972, they'd managed to meet for a few days every year. There'd never been an opportunity to tell him. But this time, they were spending a whole week together.

Lisette took the madeleines out of the oven. She sat down and watched them cool, steam rising. The sun had gone behind the building opposite. When was he coming? How foolish they'd been not to make contingency arrangements. He could be ill or injured or anything and she'd never know.

At last, the telephone rang. It was Christoph.

'Where are you?' Lisette said.

'I'm here in Paris.'

'In Paris? What do you mean?'

'I'm with Daniel. We're staying near the Louvre.'

His voice was neutral. Lisette sensed him holding the truth down, clamping his lips over each word. Daniel. He must be eight years old now.

'Why has Daniel come with you? I don't understand.'

'Hilde thought it would be a good idea if I showed him Paris now that he's a bit older. My annual teaching job at the conservatory is finishing. I'm just here to tie up loose ends. I won't be coming back again.'

He sounded close to breaking. Lisette breathed fast. *She* was the loose end. He was here to tie up their relationship. Hilde must know about them.

'But Christoph, you can't just –'

'I have to,' he said, 'or it will be difficult to see Daniel.'

That's when it hit her. Hilde must have found out. His wife had made him choose. Daniel or her. She let out a deep breath.

'Is he with you now?' she said.

'He's asleep. I insisted on seeing you to end things properly. Hilde agreed, but only if I brought Daniel with me. To remind me of what I'd be losing if I didn't go through with it.'

Lisette sat down. 'Oh, the poor boy. It's not fair on him. How can she do this?'

'She has a knack for surviving,' Christoph said. 'She knows that no matter how much I love you, I can't desert my son. Sylvie, I hope you understand.'

'Yes,' Lisette said, because she did understand. 'It's still the worst news nonetheless.'

'Meet me tomorrow, please. I have to see you one last

time. I'll tell Daniel you're a friend from the conservatory, we'll go to the zoo. He won't ask questions.'

'No, Christoph, I can't do that. I can't spend the entire day with you pretending we're just friends and hiding the fact that my heart is breaking. But I will meet you, on the corner by Le Meurice. To say goodbye.'

'You're not going to talk me out of it then?' Christoph said, his voice barely a whisper.

'Do you think I could? Even if I did, I'd hate myself. He's just a child. He doesn't deserve to lose you.'

'No,' Christoph said. 'I'll never leave him.'

The line went quiet. There was nothing more to say. 'By the corner at eleven then,' Christoph said.

Lisette put the phone down and steadied herself against the table. So, this was it. The end had finally come. He'd never play the piano she'd bought for him. She'd never tell him what she did during the war. They'd barely spent any time together, not in the grand scheme of things. But each moment had had its own exquisite taste that she would never forget.

She glanced at the madeleines. Grief filled her heart and mixed with anger. Not with him – she knew he had no choice – but with fate and the circumstances that kept forcing them apart. She tipped the madeleines into the bin. He would never taste them now.

But she couldn't say goodbye without giving him something to remember her by.

The recipe book stood propped up by the fruit bowl. The story of their love was written in its pages: each recipe contained a memory. If anything could lead him back to her one day, it was this book.

*

The next day, Lisette walked to Le Meurice. She saw them waiting – Christoph pensive, a small boy wearing a duffel coat holding his hand – and nearly turned around. How could she say goodbye to him, here on the street corner?

But Christoph caught sight of her and waved. The little boy glanced over. He was so like Christoph it took her breath away.

'How are you?' Christoph asked in French, as if this was a normal meeting. His white, stricken face told a different story.

Lisette's heart splintered. The incalculable loss she was about to suffer began to sink in.

'I'm fine,' Lisette said, forcing a smile. She reached into her bag. 'I can't stay, but I wanted to give you this. To remember me by.'

Christoph felt the package and guessed what it was.

'I can't take it,' he said. 'It's yours. It means too much.'

'Please,' Lisette said.

'Thank you,' he said, thrusting the recipe book deep into his pocket. He pulled her close.

'I love you. I will always love you. Please don't ever forget that,' he whispered.

'I love you too,' she whispered back. Then, conscious of Daniel's puzzled stare, she broke away.

'*Au revoir*,' she said, smiling at Daniel. 'Have a lovely afternoon at the zoo.'

Then she went, tears streaming down her face, plunging back into the crowd, not looking back, not ever looking back, running away from the man who loved her and whom she loved. The man she could never have.

51

Julia

September, 2002 — Bonn

Julia lit the fire in the music room, as Christoph was feeling cold despite the autumn weather, and settled him on the sofa. The lemonade was long since finished. Christoph stared at the fire, watching flames wreath the coal.

'So, in the end, it was me who let her go,' he said. 'I remember gripping Daniel's hand, the recipe book weighing down my pocket, and walking back to the hotel. If it hadn't been for him, I wouldn't have had the strength to continue. I packed our things, hid the apartment key in the lining of the suitcase, and somehow made it back to Bonn.'

'You mentioned Sylvie had opened a restaurant in Nice with Jacques,' Julia said. She glanced at her notes. The pages were thick with memories. 'Were you ever tempted to look for her again?'

Christoph shook his head. 'Hilde would never have allowed it. I broke her trust and, if I didn't want to lose Daniel, I had to make sure that Sylvie stayed firmly out of my life.'

'How did Hilde discover about your affair?'

Christoph sighed. 'I told her.'

'Why?'

'I hated feeling guilty. We hadn't been close for a long

time. I thought she felt the same, that the marriage had run its course and we could part amicably. But it wasn't like that. Her mental health was too unstable, and I self-ishly hadn't realized how bad she'd become. She was distraught, almost on the brink of a breakdown. She told me I'd never see Daniel again if I left her for Sylvie. That's when I understood how serious things had got, and how disturbed she'd become. I gave up being a concert pianist and concentrated on teaching. I wanted to be around for them more, but Hilde pushed me further away.'

'It must have been hard to give up performing,' Julia said.

Christoph shrugged. 'In some ways it was simple. Daniel came first. I loved Sylvie with all my heart and soul, but the prospect of losing my son . . .' He shook his head. 'I never contemplated it for a minute.'

Christoph's face looked wan in the firelight. Julia laid another blanket over him and left a lamp on by the piano. His eyes were already closing.

She tiptoed out.

'Julia.' Daniel was sitting on the stairs.

'How long have you been there?'

'Long enough,' he said. 'I would have come in, but I didn't want to disturb his flow.'

'So, you heard about that day in Paris, what he did for you?'

Daniel nodded. 'I heard it all. Is it true, Julia? Did he really give up Sylvie because of me?'

'Yes.'

Daniel covered his eyes. His shoulders trembled.

'Mama told me he always put us second, but it wasn't true, was it? I heard him say it. *Daniel came first.*' He wiped his eyes. 'I just accepted what she said. He never lost his patience, no matter how much she insulted him.'

Julia had only ever had one proper conversation with Hilde, after the recital. It had been like walking across quicksand.

'Your mum was troubled,' she said, 'but I've no doubt she loved you. Perhaps if she'd got professional help or found her own independence, things might have been different.'

'Looking back, I think she was partly to blame for why I was so angry about your devotion to the piano. She'd taught me that pianists couldn't be in a relationship. She warned me to steer clear of you when she found out there was something between us.'

'And she spent a lifetime influencing your relationship with your father.'

Daniel breathed in deeply. 'I wish I'd known how much he loved me. To give up the woman you love . . . that's big, Julia.'

Julia squeezed his arm. 'You're his child, Daniel. That eclipses everything.'

Daniel smiled. 'I see that now. God, if it wasn't for you and your cooking, I'd never have found how how much he loved me, or how much he sacrificed for me.' He glanced at her. 'Do you think it's too late?'

'Too late for what?'

'To make it up to him.'

Julia sat by the coffee table in Daniel's room, holding her notebook. Two candles flickered. Six years ago, she'd sat in this very place. But how different things were now. *She*

417

was different. As she glanced at Daniel, she realized that while the piano would always be important to her, it was no substitute for people, for those deeper connections she hadn't known she needed.

Daniel was different too. His eyes were alert, his voice energized. Since he'd discovered what Christoph had given up for him, he seemed like a new person: lighter, freer, happier. He wanted to hear everything about Christoph and Sylvie, starting with that first meeting in Maxim's. Julia leafed through the pages, telling him about the dinner at La Tour d'Argent, how Christoph had played the 'Moonlight Sonata' on the rooftop, his visit to Normandy with Sylvie.

'So that's why the farm meant so much to him,' he said. 'His swim with Sylvie reminds me of the time we went night swimming.' His eyes lingered on her for a moment, and she knew he was thinking of how close they'd been.

'Yes.' Julia blushed.

'What happened next?'

'Back in Paris, Christoph thought she was seeing another man, and the Kommandant took an interest in her too. But she told him there was no one else, and that's when they started using the apartment as a place to be together.'

When Julia told him about Jacques, Daniel was astonished.

'I can't believe Papa helped Jacques escape. He could have been shot. All this time, I thought Papa had something shameful to hide. It turns out he did an extraordinary thing.'

Daniel reached for the notebook.

'But you found no trace of Sylvie Dubois,' he said. 'Except the listing of her death, which we now know to be false. It was Jacques' grandmother who died in her place.'

'Nothing,' Julia said. 'Nor when I searched for Lisette Munier, the name Seraphin's daughter knew Sylvie by.'

Daniel tapped the page and smiled. 'Your handwriting is terrible, you know.'

'I didn't know you'd be reading it.'

'No, I bet you didn't.' His smile deepened into something else, something that made Julia catch her breath. 'If you hadn't persisted with this search, I'd never have known. And to think I tried to stop you.'

'Maybe it took an outsider like me to piece it together.'

'You're hardly an outsider.'

The air vibrated with unsaid words. Moments such as this, like Christoph and Sylvie had experienced, were too fleeting and too precious to ignore.

'This will sound crazy,' Daniel said, 'but I'm going to say it anyway. When I saw you in that station, everything changed. I knew from the moment we locked eyes that you were someone special, that I could love you. Then everything got in the way.'

Julia held her breath. 'What did you just say?'

'That I love you,' he said softly. 'Your courage, your determination, the way you challenge me, your extraordinary talent. I've always loved you.'

He touched her cheek. Julia's skin tingled. She couldn't take in what he was saying. *He'd always loved her.* Her heart stammered in her chest.

'Daniel, I didn't know,' she said. 'I never dreamed you felt that strongly. I mean, I hoped, but . . .'

'I've been dreaming of you since that day in the apartment – hell, I've dreamed of you since the day in the station,' Daniel said, his voice husky. 'I thought all the years between would stop me wanting you, but they didn't.'

His words lit a fuse in her body. She tugged on his T-shirt playfully, pulling him closer.

'How much did you want me?' she said, her lips just inches away.

He groaned. 'God, Julia, you have no idea.'

Their lips collided in a kiss, deep and urgent. Desire switched up a gear in Julia's body. She pulled off his T-shirt, hands moving over his chest. He delicately unbuttoned her shirt, kissing her all the while, sliding his hands around to undo the clasp.

The sensation of his naked skin against hers was electrifying. She kneaded his shoulders, feeling the muscles ripple under her touch. She ached to hold him closer.

Skin to skin, heart to heart, she straddled him, guiding him inside, tightening herself around him. The sense of urgency, to be as close as they could be, was overwhelming.

'Oh, Julia . . .' he whispered.

His words tailed off in a moan. He held her firmly, eyes drinking her in, his pupils dilating as she brought him deeper and deeper. They moved as one. Faster and harder with each thrust. It was like a scale, climbing higher and higher, each note sweeter than the last, until the climax when waves of ecstasy broke over them both.

'That was incredible,' Julia said, at last. He gathered her up in his arms, aftershocks reverberating around her body. They lay entwined and spent. After a few minutes, Daniel pushed Julia's hair back from her face and stared deep into her eyes. '*You* are incredible,' he said. 'I don't deserve you.'

Julia snuggled up close to him. 'What do you mean?'

Daniel pressed his thumb against his temple. 'Maybe I caused the problem with your hands. What if you can't play because of some trauma connected with me kissing Kat and ruining your recital? What if . . .'

Julia shook her head, pressing herself against his chest. 'That night *was* awful, but I played a thousand times afterwards, for years, with no problems at all. Your actions didn't damage them.'

'Then what did?'

'I was thinking how Hilde's words affected your relationship with Christoph,' Julia said. 'It was the same for me. Mum's words affected my relationship with the piano. Looking back, the problem with my hands started after she died last year. I wasn't playing to impress her any more, so I lost all sense of why I was playing in the first place.'

Daniel nodded and ran his fingers along her arm. 'I see what you mean. But I didn't help, demanding that you choose between the piano or me. I'm sorry I did that.'

Julia moved closer. His face was so familiar: his green eyes, the line of his jaw, his full lips – yet it was like seeing him anew. Is this what it felt like to forgive, at last?

'You gave me that sheet music paper in the apartment,' she said. 'I haven't used it yet, but it's like a promise. You've encouraged that spark in me.'

'I'm relieved to hear it.' Daniel twisted a tendril of her hair around his finger. 'And you've made me realize that we have to help Papa find Sylvie.'

52

Julia

September, 2002 – Bonn

The next morning, Julia went downstairs to check on Christoph. She left Daniel poring over her notebooks. She opened the music-room door. Christoph lay on the sofa, his eyes open.

'How are you feeling?'

Christoph winced as he tried to sit up. 'I've had better days.'

'You look warm.' She touched his forehead. It was hot. 'I might need to call the doctor.'

'Fuss and nonsense,' he said, waving away her concern.

Footsteps thundered down the stairs. Daniel came in, holding the recipe book and Julia's notes in his hand. He looked elated.

'I've got it,' he said. 'Sylvie became Lisette Munier, and then, in 1962, she married Jacques and opened the restaurant in Nice? So, if we can't find Sylvie, at least we might be able to locate Jacques.'

Christoph stared at him. 'What do you mean?'

Daniel kneeled next to Christoph. 'I want to find her for you. I know what you did for me, Papa. I'm sorry I never understood.'

Christoph cupped Daniel's face. 'Oh, Daniel, I should

have told you more often how much I loved you. You and your mother were like a team, both of you against me. I retreated. Words were never my strong point and I just didn't know what to say because I felt so ashamed. I shouldn't have done that. I should have been more open with you, especially as you got older.'

'I think I understand things better now, that's why I want to help . . .' Daniel pointed to the notebook.

'But I've given up hope of finding her.'

'I don't think you should,' Daniel said. 'You let her go for me, all those years ago, and now, if there's a chance we can find her, I want to try.'

Tears welled in Christoph's eyes. Julia knew how much Daniel's words meant to him.

'You'd really do that for me?' he said, clasping Daniel's hand. 'But what about your plans for the farm?'

'They're not important. Finding Sylvie is. I've been puzzling it out all morning. Can you remember Jacques' surname?'

'It's such a jumble. I remember the attic storerooms . . .' Christoph closed his eyes. His breathing slowed. 'Jacques was crouched in a corner. I asked him his name, but he wouldn't tell me, not at first, and then later . . .'

'What?' Daniel whispered.

Christoph's eyes flashed open. 'Of course. The morning star. It seemed so incongruous up there in the blackness. Morgenstern. Jacques Morgenstern.'

Daniel clutched Julia's hand. 'That's it. Come on. Let's try and find him, and hopefully Sylvie too.'

*

Julia sat with Daniel on the stairs, the phone cradled in his hand. The search for Jacques had only taken a few clicks on the PC in Daniel's room. It was a distinctive name. The list narrowed further to just one name when they searched for the restaurant in Nice.

'You ring,' Julia said.

'No, it has to be you. You started this by finding the recipe book. Besides, you can speak French better than I can.'

Before Julia could reply, Daniel dialled the number and handed her the phone. While it was ringing, Julia recalled the pictures on the website. Restaurant L'Étoile du Matin, overlooking the white-capped Mediterranean Sea.

Someone picked up.

'*Bonjour*,' a gruff male voice said. 'Jacques speaking.'

It was him, the man from the attic, the man Sylvie had married.

'*Bonjour*, my name is Julia,' she said, her stomach in knots at the thought of how close they might be to finding Sylvie. 'I wondered if you could help me. I'm looking for someone called Lisette, or perhaps Sylvie.'

The line went silent. 'I haven't heard those names for a while,' the man said.

'I'm ringing on behalf of someone called Christoph Baumann. I believe you met him in Paris, a long time ago.'

Daniel bent near the receiver to listen.

'Is Christoph still alive?' Jacques said.

'He's very old. And I'm afraid that he's very unwell. He doesn't have much time left. He'd like to contact Lisette, or Sylvie as he knew her, before it's too late to say goodbye.'

'I have no idea where she is,' Jacques said. 'I'm sorry.

I haven't seen her since 1989, when we got divorced. I wanted to give her half of everything we owned, but she wouldn't accept a thing. Just took her bag, a few clothes and left.'

'Do you know where she went?'

'England, I think, but I can't be sure.'

'Do you have an address, a contact number?' Surely he had to know something.

'*Non,*' Jacques said, his voice tinged with sadness. 'You'll never find her. I tried to, but it was impossible. I think she changed her name again.'

Julia clutched the receiver. 'But we must find her. We're desperate. Time's running out.'

Jacques sighed. 'Before she left, she told me she wanted to become the person she'd been before the war. As you know, Sylvie was her cover name. Lisette was her code name. She said that her birth name, her real name, had been buried the moment she set foot on French soil. She said that maybe our divorce was a chance to go back to being that person.'

'And did she tell you her real name?'

'No, she didn't,' he said sadly. 'She disappeared. Became her old self, maybe. At any rate, I'm afraid I never heard from her again.'

'I see.' Julia said. Her heart sank.

'I'm sorry I can't help you more,' Jacques said. 'Please give my love to Christoph. He saved my life. I've never forgotten it.'

'Of course,' Julia said. 'And thank you.'

Daniel sighed as she replaced the receiver. 'So, she's eluded us again,' he said.

Julia nodded. 'It's like we're chasing someone who's always just out of reach.'

'We could go to England, search the SOE records if they're available. Maybe we could find her that way.'

'We could,' Julia said, glancing at the door of the music room, 'but we can't leave Christoph. He doesn't have long. We might have to accept that we've done all we can.'

Julia went upstairs with Daniel to tell Christoph the news from Jacques. His fever had grown worse. He was delirious, slipping in and out of consciousness, his head burning up. Thoughts of Jacques and Sylvie were forgotten. There was no question of leaving him now. The search for Sylvie really had come to an end.

The next day, Julia sat by Christoph's bedside. He muttered under his breath, his eyes closed. Julia mopped his brow with a wet flannel. His temperature had been caused by a urine infection, the doctor said, and his body, weakened by cancer, was struggling to fight it. Daniel had gone to get some medication from the pharmacy.

Julia picked up the recipe book from the bedside table. How could a love like that simply have vanished? Sylvie's false identities made it impossible to trace her. Julia sighed. It all hinged on a name.

She looked back over each recipe. Sylvie's food had been more than something to fill the belly. Each dish had conjured a memory for Christoph.

The last recipe was for madeleines. Julia took a closer look at the title. That was strange. The 's' in Madeleines had been underlined in pencil. She flicked back over the other recipes. In every title, one of the letters had been underlined. Some of the underlining had faded, but now that she looked carefully, she could see an indent where the line had been.

Could it be that the letters stood for something?

Julia copied out the recipes in order, with the underlined letters.

Fischkotlett
Crème Brûlée
Sauerbraten
Schweinsohren
Potage Fontanges
Canard à la Rouennaise
Brathahnchen
Fonds d'Artichauts Farcis
Muscheln
Eintopf mit Bohnen und Kartoffeln
Filets de Maquereaux à la Flamande
Citron Pressé avec Lavande
Madeleines au Citron

Her hand moved frantically across the page. It was like a game of Hangman. Letter by letter, recipe by recipe, appearing like a ghost from the past as she wrote down the underlined letters in order, a name emerged. Julia sat back and stared.

Clara Saunders.

Could this be her? The real woman behind the recipes. Had the answer been here all the time, hidden in the recipe book? Julia glanced at the dedication. *For Christoph, our recipes. I hope one day they lead you back to me.* It had to be her.

Julia glanced at Christoph. He'd slipped into a fitful sleep. She didn't want to get his hopes up. Nor Daniel's. She'd do this last part alone. That way, no one would know if it failed. If Clara Saunders was still alive, Julia had to find her.

53

Christoph

September, 2002 – Bonn

Christoph sat at the piano and watched Daniel and Julia walk down the path and into the street. Daniel stopped to hold the gate open for her. The look that flashed between them was like sunlight glinting on water. It made Christoph feel old, but also very happy.

It had been two weeks since his fever started. Time had passed in fits and starts, full of terrible dreams. Thankfully, Daniel had been there. Soothing words, a soft touch of his hand, and once, on the worst and most disturbing night, when Christoph had dreamed of Stalingrad, Daniel had climbed into the bed and held him tight.

Christoph still felt tired. His cancer was making him more exhausted by the day. Today, however, he wanted to play the piano. He'd persuaded Julia and Daniel that he'd be fine left alone for an hour whilst they went shopping for paint. Daniel had decided to redecorate his room now that he was staying. They'd spent the morning taking down all of Daniel's old photos and stowing them in albums.

Christoph played the opening bars of the 'Moonlight Sonata'. The memories in his mind were like a book he could read over and over. True, the ending was inconclusive, but he'd come to accept that it was better to have known and loved and lost Sylvie than never to have met her at all. She'd affirmed his humanity at the very moment when it had seemed most in doubt.

A movement caught his eye. Somebody was opening the gate and coming down the path. For a moment, with the sun shining in his eyes, he thought it was Julia. It reminded him of that day a few months ago when she'd arrived.

But it wasn't Julia walking up the path. This woman was older. Her hair was tied back in a neat silver bun. She glanced towards the window, unable to see him because of the sun's reflection, but he could see her. His heart stopped beating. The note he was playing died away. The woman looked just like Sylvie.

The doorbell rang and jolted him to his senses. *Silly old fool, you're seeing things. It'll be a neighbour or someone selling something.* But his heart stammered as he reached for his stick.

'I'm coming,' he called, out of breath at the sudden movement. He wrenched open the door.

It was a dream. But no, she was laughing and crying, and coming towards him. His Sylvie, after all this time, after all these years. His stick clattered to the ground and he pulled her close, gathering her in his arms. Her touch ignited the secret chambers of his heart that time had buried. Thank God she'd come.

A gentle breeze blew across the garden. The lavender swayed, bees losing their anchor on the flowers. Clara had made tea. He sat next to her on the bench by the vegetable patch, his arm around her. She fitted next to him like the other half of his being.

'Clara.' Christoph tried the name on his lips. It felt right somehow.

'It's strange to hear you say it,' she said.

Christoph smiled. 'Sylvie is the woman I met in the war. Lisette the woman who eluded me. But you, Clara, are all of them in one.'

Clara cupped his cheek, tears moistening her eyes. 'I've missed you,' she said.

'I've missed you too.' Christoph blinked back tears and smiled. 'It's funny. I've waited all this time, and now the past is catching up with me. I even spoke to Jacques a few days ago.'

Clara frowned. 'Poor Jacques. It wasn't fair of me to leave him like that, but I was going through something, a kind of crisis of identity. I had to go right back to the beginning and become Clara to escape it all.'

'Did it work?'

'I wanted a fresh start without being dragged down by memories of the war and you. But no, it didn't work. Instead, I collapsed. A wonderful psychotherapist helped put me back together again.'

Christoph drew her close and kissed her lips. It was hard to think of all the years wasted. He drank in her delicate scent, touched her hair. Then a thought occurred to him.

'How did you know I was looking for you?'

Clara smiled, the wrinkles around her eyes adding depth to her face.

'Someone discovered my real name. I'd left it hidden in the recipe book, in case you ever needed to find me.'

'That book was lost to me for years,' Christoph said. 'Julia found it. She's been cooking the recipes and helping to revive my memories.'

431

'Julia. That's who it was. She put an advert in all the English newspapers. Of course, I never saw it – I hate the news. But one of my employees read the classifieds, saw the name Clara Saunders and brought me the cutting.'

'Goodness, I had no idea Julia had done that.'

Clara clasped his hands. 'I've always felt guilty I never told you what I did in the war. I was afraid you'd see it as a betrayal.'

'I did at first,' Christoph said, smoothing his thumb over her palm.

'I was going to tell you that last time in Paris,' she said, 'but I never got the chance.'

'I never forgot you,' Christoph said. He reached into his pocket and took out his wallet. There, preserved in the folds of his driving licence, was a sprig of dried lavender.

'Is that mine?' Clara exclaimed. 'From all those years ago?'

'I told you I'd look after it. I posted it home to my mother, along with the key, just before they shipped me out to Russia.'

Clara opened her purse and took out a piece of folded card. 'Look, I kept this too.'

It was the postcard from La Tour d'Argent, the first time they'd had dinner.

'Keepsakes from another lifetime,' Christoph said, touching the creases.

'Oh, Christoph, I'm so thankful to be with you again. If it's not too late, I'd like to stay,' Clara said. 'I want to spend every minute here and make the most of the time we have left.'

'There won't be many minutes,' Christoph said, 'but they are all yours.'

54

Clara

September, 2002 – Bonn

As they sat talking in the garden, Clara heard the back door click open. Curious and wide-eyed, a young woman came out. She wore a long white skirt, a fitted black T-shirt and white pumps.

'You see it too,' Christoph said, noticing her gaze. 'Back when I met her, I'd sworn that I wouldn't teach any more students, I had practically retired, but I had to take her on. She had a look of you. I'm so glad I did.'

'Is this who I think it is?' Julia said, coming over. 'Clara Saunders?'

'Yes, it most certainly is.' Clara looked over at Christoph and smiled. 'He's been telling me how you cooked my recipes for him.'

'I'd never cooked in my life,' Julia said. 'It's been trial and error, mostly error.' She stared at the two of them. 'I just can't believe it. I'm so relieved you're here.'

'And I'm so grateful you discovered my real name.'

'Why didn't you tell me?' Christoph asked Julia.

'I didn't want to raise your hopes if it came to nothing. I didn't tell Daniel either, only Anna, she helped me out.'

Clara glanced back towards the house. She'd often thought about that little boy on the street corner. During the flight here, she'd wondered what sort of man he'd become.

'Daniel's here?' she said.

'He's unloading the car. I'll go and get him.'

'Oh . . .' Clara said, but Julia was gone, sprinting over the grass. Clara glanced at Christoph.

'Don't worry,' he said. 'He'll be fine. He knows that I gave you up for him.'

Julia returned with Daniel. He looked as nervous as Clara was. She took a deep breath and stood up.

'Daniel,' she said.

He stretched out his arm to shake her hand.

'It's so nice to meet you,' he said, but there was something guarded in his expression.

'This calls for a celebration,' Julia said. 'There's champagne in the fridge. I bought some last week, just in case.'

The awkwardness abated a little as the cork popped and the champagne fizzed in the glasses. It was like looking at the scene from afar. Christoph, weak and frail, but still recognizable by his shining eyes. Daniel, older, no longer a child but still wary. And Julia, almost a younger version of herself but with a grace and confidence that Clara had lacked.

Suddenly it was too much. Clara hid her head in her hands, sobs rising from the long-buried part of herself that had always loved Christoph.

'I'm so sorry,' she said, tears streaming down her cheeks. It was mortifying to break down in front of them all. 'It's been so hard, all these years. I've just realized how lonely I've been.'

434

Christoph's arms gathered around her, holding her tight.

'Oh, my dear,' he said. 'It's all right. You're here now. We're together again at last.'

It seemed she had come just in time. Or rather, there was no time at all. The doctor visited every day, although Christoph fussed and said it wasn't necessary. A nurse was employed to administer pain relief and make him comfortable. Clara couldn't believe that Christoph, her Christoph, was slipping away.

One day, Clara ventured up to Daniel's room. There were ladders propped against the wall and roller trays full of grey paint.

'Julia is evasive and polite when I ask her, and Christoph brushes off my questions, so I wondered if you could tell me the truth, please. How long does he have?'

Daniel put down the brush he was using to paint the edges and rubbed his hands on his overalls.

'A week or two at the most,' he said.

'I see.'

'Are you going to stay?'

'I would like to – that is, if you don't mind,' she said. 'This is your time with him too, Daniel. I don't want to get in the way of that.'

Daniel stirred the paint. 'Christoph was desperate to find you. Julia did everything she could. I'm afraid I was reluctant – well, more than that, if I'm honest. I thought it was a wild-goose chase, one that risked harming more than helping.'

'And now?'

'It's good to see him happy and at peace. But the bond you share is something I was never part of. Perhaps you even resent me for the fact that he chose me that time.' Daniel glanced at her. 'It's just a bit awkward, that's all.'

'Oh Daniel, you were only a child. I felt pity for you that day. You'd been dragged into something that was probably confusing and distressing for you.'

'But he left you for me.'

Daniel was so much taller than her, young and strong, yet vulnerable.

'He did leave me,' she said. 'But for a good reason. It made complete sense that the kind, loyal Christoph I knew and loved would never want to give you up.'

'Is that what you really thought?' Daniel said.

'It's what I still think,' Clara replied. 'I never had children of my own, but if I did and I was faced with the same dilemma I'd have done the same thing.'

She wanted to hug him, but she wasn't sure how he'd respond. Instead, she patted his arm.

'I'll let you get on with your painting,' she said. 'It's going to look really nice.' She smiled and went to the door

'Clara,' Daniel said.

She turned to face him.

'Thank you for being here,' Daniel said, and she knew that he meant it.

The next day, Clara found Julia in the kitchen. The place was a mess. Pots and pans covered the countertop. The sink was full of dirty dishes. Julia's face was red and flustered.

'Damn it,' Julia said. 'I can't get this mixture to be

smooth. I've tried it twice now and both times it's been lumpy.'

'What are you making?' Clara asked.

'The last recipe in the book. He's not eating much. The doctor said that's inevitable and not to worry. But if he's not eating, he'll keep getting weaker, and then . . .' Julia's voice cracked. 'I'm sorry.'

'Oh, my dear, you've worked so hard these last few months,' Clara said. She poured Julia a glass of wine and sat her down at the table.

'I want to make the madeleines au citron,' Julia said, 'but I keep getting it wrong.'

'It's fiddly with the egg whites,' Clara said. 'Let me help you.'

'But you'd much rather be with Christoph. Every moment is precious.'

'Every moment *is* precious. But he's sleeping now, and spending time with the young woman who reunited us is precious too.' Clara glanced around the kitchen. 'I can't work in this mess. One of the first rules in my kitchen is that a tidy workspace means a splendid dish.'

'I'll sort it out.'

'You stay where you are.'

Clara cleaned the dishes in the sink and put the ingredients in order. Underneath the madeleine tin, she found the recipe book.

'Goodness,' she said. She stroked the cover. A relic from long ago. 'I never expected to see it again. It looks so old and battered.'

'I found it under the stairs,' Julia said. 'Later, I found the key to the apartment in Christoph's suitcase. It's been

437

quite a journey, following his memories. I never thought a love like yours really existed.'

'And now?' Clara asked.

'Well . . .'

'You're thinking of Daniel,' Clara said, smiling.

Julia glanced up. 'Maybe, but I'm afraid. When I'm no longer needed here, what will happen? My career will start up again. Daniel will get on with his farming. We'll be apart and I'm not good at balancing everything.'

'It's hard,' Clara said. 'I'm not sure I ever managed it either. But does it have to be so intense? You're a good pianist – extraordinary, Christoph says. It shouldn't be a choice between doing the thing you love and keeping the man you love.'

'I suppose not,' Julia said. 'I'd love to do more composing.'

Clara took a fresh batch of eggs from the fridge and a bowl from the cupboard. 'The best way to separate the whites from the yolk is to crack the shell gently in the middle. Then shift the egg yolk back and forth between the eggshell halves, letting the whites spill over into the bowl. Here, you try . . .'

Clara watched Julia as she set to work. She had it all ahead of her – a life perhaps with Daniel, a career. Clara hoped that no war or catastrophe would interrupt Julia and Daniel's relationship, as it had hers and Christoph's. Yet if it hadn't been for the war they would never have met. Life was strange that way. Clara had given up trying to fathom it out.

That evening Clara carried the madeleines up to Christoph's room. Daniel and Julia came too. It was clear that he was very weak. But despite being so near death his eyes retained their old sparkle.

Christoph took a bite of the madeleine and looked over at Clara, puzzled.

'It tastes delicious,' he said, 'but I have no recollection of eating these with you. Perhaps the link between my tastebuds and my memory is waning.'

Clara stroked his arm.

'We never ate them together. I made a batch the day we were supposed to meet in Paris. After you called me to tell me it was over I threw them all away. This is the first time I've made them since.'

'You've had so little time together over the years,' Daniel said.

'I don't measure it in years,' Christoph replied. 'I measure it in moments. These last few weeks with you all have been more precious than anything.'

Clara wiped her eyes. His voice was so faint, but he was unmistakeably Christoph. Daniel got up and hugged him, Julia at his side. It was clear how much they loved him. Despite Christoph's words, time was slipping through his fingers.

Daniel and Julia went downstairs to wash up. Clara lay down next to Christoph. She tucked herself against his body, her hand resting on his chest. His breathing was almost imperceptible, his eyes closed.

'I love you,' he said.

'I love you too. I never stopped.'

He put his arm around her. 'Look after them, won't you?'

Clara nodded. She took one last look at him in the

soft light of the bedside lamp. His grey hair and etched face still bore the traces of the man who'd offered to bandage her hands at Maxim's all those years ago. The man who'd overcome her hatred by simply being himself. He'd never changed his name or been anyone else, and she loved him for it.

'Good night, Christoph,' she said. Then she turned out the light, closed her eyes and settled down to sleep in his arms.

55

Julia

October, 2003 – London and Effelsberg

Julia took the beef out of the fridge and heated up the frying pan. It was her last night in London before going to visit Daniel tomorrow. She'd come over to Anna's to cook a new beef recipe that Clara had taught her. Only, this time, she hoped she wouldn't make a mess of the kitchen.

Anna perched on a stool and watched her work. 'You really are getting the hang of this, aren't you?'

Julia dropped the beef into the oil and nudged it around with a wooden spoon. 'I know it's hard to believe, but I actually like cooking now.'

Anna glanced at Julia over the rim of her glass. 'I bet Daniel is looking forward to some home-cooked meals when you visit.'

Daniel had used the money from the sale of the house to buy the old farm. He'd been hard at work all year, tending to the cows and fruit trees.

Julia left the beef sizzling and took a sip of wine. 'Yes, I've promised to make Muscheln. It's one of his favourites.'

She thought back to the apartment in Paris. They'd made that dish many times since, cooking side by side in the farm house kitchen in Effelsberg.

'You must be looking forward to seeing him again,' Anna said. 'I must say, it was nice to meet him properly when he came to London. He was a real hit with Daisy.'

Julia smiled. He'd helped Daisy plant seeds from the garden centre, and she'd watered them every day, remembering his advice. It hadn't been easy maintaining a long-distance relationship, but they tried to see each other every few months. It was the best they could manage at the moment, with his work on the farm and Julia's work in London, but it never seemed enough.

'It's been a year now, hasn't it, since Christoph's passing and the two of you finally getting together,' Anna said, a look of concern in her eyes. 'Do you have any sense of what the next steps are?'

Julia turned towards the sink, scrubbing dirt off the mushrooms. 'We haven't talked about it. He's just had his first harvest. I've been busy composing and teaching. It's amazing when we're together, but we don't really discuss the future.'

'Well, that's understandable.' Anna sipped her wine. 'Are you sure you made the right decision, pulling out of the Queen Elisabeth competition? I thought being a concert pianist was all you've ever wanted.'

Julia turned down the gas and let the sauce simmer.

'It was a long-held dream,' she said. 'But after Christoph died, something changed. I picked up that blank sheet music Daniel gave me and the music just poured out of me. I suppose it was a way of coping with his death.'

Anna nodded. 'Christoph meant so much to you. I'm glad you could channel your grief into something so positive. I was worried how things might be for you, especially after you'd felt so guilty for not being there when Mum died.'

'That was the difference, I suppose,' Julia said, stirring the sauce. 'I *was* there for Christoph, almost right up to the last moment.'

'Well, I think you've been very brave, writing your own compositions and teaching at the school. I think Sebastian realized it was the right thing to do as well.'

'Well, it took some explaining, but perhaps he saw it coming.' Julia smiled. 'I had a postcard from him the other day. He's in Majorca, on holiday with Tanja, celebrating their engagement. So something good did come out of me not being able to play those concerts.'

'It certainly did,' Anna said, patting her hand. 'I'm so proud of you for forging your own path at last.'

Julia smiled. 'What would Mum have said?'

'God only knows.' Anna laughed. 'It doesn't matter any more. But I know Clara is immensely proud of you. She told me so when we came to see you play the other night. Dedicating your compositions to her and Christoph was a lovely thought.'

Julia tipped in some cream and stirred the sauce. 'If it hadn't been for Sylvie and Christoph's story, I don't think Daniel and I would have found each other again.' She sighed. The anticipation of seeing him was always tempered by the knowledge that, after a week, she'd have to leave again. Flying back and forth was the only solution for now.

Julia stepped off the train at the little station in Bad Münstereifel, the nearest town to Effelsberg. Daniel stood

443

waiting at the end of the platform. He strode towards her, smiling broadly, and lifted her up into a bear hug.

'This is some welcome,' she said, smiling.

'God, I've missed you,' Daniel said, standing back to look at her. 'It feels so long since we last saw each other.'

'I know, the months seemed to drag. But I'm here now.' She touched his cheek. 'I'm so glad to see you too.'

He moved closer, his arm around her waist, pressing the small of her back, until their lips touched. The taste of him, his woody scent, the brush of his stubble against her skin. It all felt like coming home. The thought of leaving in a few days clouded her heart. But she pushed it from her mind, determined to make the most of every minute they had together.

The farm was a twenty-minute drive, up the hill and along the road that led through the forest. The leaves glowed in the October sunshine, an endless shimmer of reds and yellows. Julia felt her London life ebbing away in this magical landscape.

Daniel glanced over at her. 'I love that look you get on your face when we head up the hill. It's like you're letting yourself relax at last.'

Julia smiled. 'I like to think of Christoph growing up here, and you visiting as a child, and now this place is your home.' She reached over and squeezed his knee. 'That's what you hoped for, isn't it? Somewhere that means something.'

That's what he'd said in the market in Paris. And she'd felt a pang of sorrow that she didn't have somewhere like that. Even now, she still hadn't found a place to call home.

Daniel nodded. 'I love it here.' He turned into the

444

village, driving past the cluster of houses and out towards the fields where the farm lay. 'But still, there's something missing.'

He pulled into the driveway and Julia unfastened her seatbelt.

'What's missing?' she said, taking in the view over the meadows, where cows were grazing, and the orchard. 'You have everything you need. It looks perfect to me.'

Daniel was looking at her, a curious smile on his face. 'Come on,' he said, picking up her suitcase. 'Let me show you what I've done since you last came.'

She followed him up the steps into the thick-walled farmhouse with its shuttered windows and stone floor. It was like stepping back in time. Of course, things weren't the same as when Christoph and Lotte had lived here. But the essence of the house conjured images of him coming in from the yard to see his little sister.

Julia smiled, imagining them here, Christoph at the piano and Lotte dancing, their mother watching them both. The furniture and piano were long gone, sold when Christoph had decided not to buy the farm when his mother died, but still she could picture it in her head from what Christoph had told her.

'So, I've knocked through to make this a kitchen/dining room,' Daniel said, breaking into her reverie. He pointed to the ragged gap in the wall. 'It looks a bit of a mess at the moment, but I've got the plasterers coming back next week.'

Julia glanced at the dustsheets. 'I thought this would all be finished by now.'

'Yes, well, so did I, but then I had an idea, and I asked

the builders to work on that first.' His eyes were shining as he took her hand. 'You see, I wanted it to be ready for when you came.'

Julia followed him down the corridor, towards the dilapidated old sunroom that lay at the side of the house. The last time she'd seen it, Daniel was using it to store the builders' equipment, and it had been filled with planks of wood, paint pots and ladders.

Daniel opened the door and gestured for Julia to go in.

She walked into the room and gasped. Gone were the boards at the window. The broken glass had been replaced and sunlight streamed in. The old carpet had been taken up and a new wooden floor laid down. But most startling of all was the object that stood in the centre of the room.

'Daniel,' Julia said, turning to him with tears in her eyes. 'It's Christoph's grand piano.'

She ran her hand along the top of the Schimmel piano. She thought it had been sold, as she had no room for it in London. 'You kept it.'

'I put it in storage until I could work out where there was space for it. Then I had the idea that this would make a perfect music room. It's south-facing, so there's sun all through the day, but the trees in the garden keep it dappled in shade.'

Julia glanced at the fireplace. There was a photo of Christoph playing fervently at one of his earlier concerts. He looked young and full of energy and passion. Next to it, in a small silver frame, stood the photo of Sylvie in 1942 among the roses, the one that they'd found in the apartment.

Julia gazed at Daniel. 'But I don't understand. What's all this for? You don't play, and I'm only here every few months. It seems a waste to dedicate a whole room to the piano when you haven't even got your kitchen finished yet.'

Daniel took her hand and led her round to the keyboard. There on the stand was a piece of paper, folded in half.

'Why not take a look at that?' he said. 'I think you'll find the answer to your question.'

Julia frowned, intrigued. She opened the paper out. There was nothing on it except for some markings:

_ _ _ _ / _ _/ _ _ _ _/ _ _

Hangman. She gazed at him, confused.

Daniel smiled and took a pen out of his pocket. 'Let me fill it in for you.'

He wrote the letters down behind his hand, then folded the paper again.

'Before you read it, I need to tell you something,' he said. 'This year's been manic, but every time we meet, however briefly, things are always better when we are together. That's what I want, Julia: you always with me.'

Julia looked up at him. He reached out for her. The touch of his hand made waves across her skin. Daniel bent down and kissed her, the warmth of his mouth sending a charge around her body.

'*Ich liebe dich*,' Daniel whispered, and pressed the paper into her hand.

She opened the paper and tears came to her eyes. There, in his slanted handwriting, he'd written:

M-O-V-E/I-N/W-I-T-H/M-E

Julia's heart soared. She wanted to laugh and cry at the same time. 'Are you serious?'

'I've never been more serious about anything in my life,' Daniel said, holding her close. 'You can use this space for composing, and for teaching the local kids, if that's what you want to do. And if you decide to tour with your new compositions, I'll support that too, and this will all be here waiting for you. I'd love you to live here with me, to make this your home. Because, without you, nowhere will ever truly be home for me.' He glanced at the photos on the mantelpiece. 'And Christoph and Sylvie will be here in spirit to inspire you.'

Julia remembered what Christoph had told her: *Music flows from the heart to the head and through the body on to the keyboard.* Daniel loved her. They were going to be together at last.

'I love you too,' she said, holding him tightly. 'I just want to be with you.'

'Come and try the piano,' Daniel said, with a smile, lifting the piano lid. He sat down on the stool. 'I had it retuned and everything. This farm is ours now, Julia, and this room is especially for you.'

He took her hand. Julia sat down on his knee, laughing, feeling his arms around her, a sense of belonging filling her heart at last. She glanced back at Daniel and kissed him, knowing this moment was everything she'd hoped for, that this day was just the beginning. Then, turning back to the piano, she took a deep breath and began to play.

Recipe Sources

Fischkotlett	*Schneider/Rupperath Family Recipe Book*, 1916
Crème Brulée	*Monet's Cookery Notebooks* by Claire Joyes
Sauerbraten	*Schneider/Rupperath Family Recipe Book*, 1916
Schweinsohren	*Backbuch* by Roland Goocks
Potage Fontanges	*Monet's Cookery Notebooks* by Claire Joyes
Canard à la Rouennaise	*Monet's Cookery Notebooks* by Claire Joyes
Brathähnchen	*Schneider/Rupperath Family Recipe Book*, 1916
Fonds d'Artichauts Farcis	*Monet's Cookery Notebooks* by Claire Joyes
Muscheln	*Schneider/Rupperath Family Recipe Book*, 1916
Eintopf mit Bohnen und Kartoffeln	*Schneider/Rupperath Family Recipe Book*, 1916
Filets de Maquereaux à la Flamande	*Monet's Cookery Notebooks* by Claire Joyes
Citron Pressé avec Lavande	Various sources
Madeleines au citron	*Monet's Cookery Notebooks* by Claire Joyes

Acknowledgements

Thank you so much to you, the reader, for choosing *The Paris Affair*. I hope you get as much pleasure out of reading the story as I did writing it. If you'd like to get in touch and discover more about my love of books, the past and writing, you can find me on Twitter (@_fionaschneider), Instagram (@_fionaschneider), Facebook (www.facebook. com/FionaSchneiderWriter) and on my website (www. fionaschneider.net). I would love to hear your thoughts about *The Paris Affair*, if you have time to leave a review, and if you've tried cooking any of the recipes, please let me know.

The source of the German recipes, and the inspiration for writing *The Paris Affair*, is an old recipe book dated 1916, which was found in the attic of my husband's family's old house in Germany. The book contains handwritten recipes that span three generations, including some that were added by my husband's mother, Katharina. It's been a special journey to retrace the recipes and taste the food that's connected with the past.

Exploring the events of the last century has also been a fascinating experience. I'm grateful to all the authors whose books helped me to research and write *The Paris Affair*, particularly on the subject of the Second World War and occupied Paris. Throughout the writing process, I was conscious of the sensitivities and complexities of trying to depict such a difficult and tragic period in history, and I hope I have succeeded in holding everything together.

I'd like to thank the whole team at Penguin Michael Joseph for publishing *The Paris Affair* and championing the novel far and wide. I'm grateful to everyone in editorial, rights and permissions, marketing, sales and distribution, and all of the other teams for working so hard to produce this book and bring it out into the world.

I am especially indebted to Hannah Smith, my editor, whose insight, encouragement, and editorial expertise have shaped *The Paris Affair* into the book it is today. I have learned so much from her perceptive comments and suggestions, which have added new layers and dimensions to the story and helped bring the ideas in my head on to the page. I would also like to thank Bea McIntyre, Sarah Day and Fiona Brown for their vital input with copy-editing and proofreading the book.

I am also very grateful for the continued support of my agent, Becky Ritchie at A. M. Heath. She has been with me every step of the way, right from our first meeting several years ago, and I trust her advice and insights implicitly. Thank you for listening to my outline for the novel, making incisive suggestions, reading drafts as it progressed and encouraging me along the way. Thank you to the whole team at A.M. Heath, particularly Florence Rees and Harmony Leung, whose support has been invaluable.

I'd like to thank all the friends and family who've kept asking, 'How is the writing going?' over the years. It's been a long journey and your support and positivity have meant a great deal. In particular, I'd like to thank Caroline and Dave Lamb, Susan Hall, Mike Shackleton, Caroline and Adrian

Meadows, Claire Smith, Alison and Paul Branston, Johannes and Helga Schneider, Georg and Martina Schneider, Michael Kaes and Annika Franck, Gurdeep Kaur, Sara Cole, Sarah Aldred, Rachel Francis, Becky Scott and Caroline Khoury. I'd also like to thank my supportive colleagues at OWN Trust, which includes Orton Wistow Primary School, Nene Valley Primary School and Woodston Primary School. In addition, I'd like to give a special mention to Joy Schaverien, who helped me to believe that I was truly a writer at heart.

And finally, the biggest thank you of all goes to my children Max, Karla and Lukas, and to my husband, Michael. You've come with me on research trips around Europe, been enthusiastic and supportive, given me time and space to write when deadlines loomed, and inspired and encouraged me at every stage. I love you all more than words can say, and I could never have done it without you.

He just wanted a decent book to read ...

Not too much to ask, is it? It was in 1935 when Allen Lane, Managing Director of Bodley Head Publishers, stood on a platform at Exeter railway station looking for something good to read on his journey back to London. His choice was limited to popular magazines and poor-quality paperbacks – the same choice faced every day by the vast majority of readers, few of whom could afford hardbacks. Lane's disappointment and subsequent anger at the range of books generally available led him to found a company – and change the world.

'We believed in the existence in this country of a vast reading public for intelligent books at a low price, and staked everything on it'
Sir Allen Lane, 1902–1970, founder of Penguin Books

The quality paperback had arrived – and not just in bookshops. Lane was adamant that his Penguins should appear in chain stores and tobacconists, and should cost no more than a packet of cigarettes.

Reading habits (and cigarette prices) have changed since 1935, but Penguin still believes in publishing the best books for everybody to enjoy. We still believe that good design costs no more than bad design, and we still believe that quality books published passionately and responsibly make the world a better place.

So wherever you see the little bird – whether it's on a piece of prize-winning literary fiction or a celebrity autobiography, political tour de force or historical masterpiece, a serial-killer thriller, reference book, world classic or a piece of pure escapism – you can bet that it represents the very best that the genre has to offer.

Whatever you like to read – trust Penguin.